Queen of
the Jews

QUEEN OF THE JEWS

A NOVEL

NL Herzenberg

ISBN: 0692675620
ISBN 13: 9780692675625

Published by Philistine Press

Cover image: from a stained glass window in Metz Cathedral by Marc Chagall

Philistine Press

ALEJANDRO

NOW THAT IT'S ALL OVER—NOT only the hitting but everything else too—I wonder what would have happened if I had simply walked away that evening and left her to her fate. Whatever her fate would be, it would be none of my business. But I made it my business, and here I am. Was it worth it? The answer is always the same: no. Not worth my time. And by "time" I don't mean something short and flippant. I mean time spent in the detention facility, which is just another word for prison... without sunlight, without freedom to walk wherever you want at whatever time of day or night.

Freedom. It's not just a word. The detention facility is walls, guards, being told when to sit, to stand, to move. The only difference between walls and executioners is that here the walls have eyes and ears while executioners have none. The executioners are not human; the walls are human in the worst way. Yet I'm learning to love my walls. I have four of them in my room. I have a desk, a chair, a bed. I sit on the chair. I stare at a wall. I've become quite a Zen master: I can look at my wall all day. When a guard calls out "Dinner!" and unlocks my door, I see poor wretches file past on their way to the feeding room, yet I don't move. I can go without dinner. One meal a day is enough. I will use my time here to understand what brought me here.

My wall seems to have all the answers. The longer I stare at it, the more I understand something that wasn't given to me to understand earlier, when I obeyed the Professor, when I lived for revenge. Now I have only one friend, who is more than a friend, and I will lose this more-than-a-friend when I'm deported. I know it, yet I long to be deported because the sky is better than the wall. I stare at my wall all day and tell myself that I don't need anything else, because I have nothing better to stare at here, nothing better to love. I haven't been given the date of my deportation yet, but my lawyer says I don't have long to wait. I tell him it doesn't matter what country they deport me to as long as I get the sky. To be able to see the sky, this is my only goal in life, my only mission, my only task. My lawyer nods, smiles, shakes his head in disbelief. "Just give me the date," I say quietly. "I need nothing else." He smiles again. He is only a lawyer. You can't expect him to understand.

TWO YEARS EARLIER

GALIA

Everything was broken in the house where I used to live. I understood, of course, that when there's construction, there has to be some destruction first—at least that's what the architect guy told me so I knew what to expect. So I had expected some destruction, but I didn't know they were going to total the place. They said if I didn't like it, maybe I shouldn't come over so often, but how could I stop coming over? And even if I stopped, I'd see what they'd done anyway, because during the construction I lived two doors down, in an apartment I was renting from a neighbor who had moved with her two boys to Philly just in time for me to rent her place, because even though at first I wanted to stick it out in the basement for the six months of construction—a person can survive without hot water and electricity, I said, we've become too coddled in this civilization—I couldn't imagine what the so-called interior walls would look like when they were all broken down so you'd have to step over piles of debris on your way to the bathroom, where the construction guys had taken away the toilet and left only a hole in the floor.

So every day I'd pass this horrible place that used to be my home— I'd pass it in the morning on my way to work and in the afternoon on my way back home, and on the weekends I was always there, hanging around. Even if I didn't actually enter the construction site, I was totally aware of the situation, as were all of our neighbors, who didn't exactly mince words in telling me I was destroying not just my house, which was after all my own business, but their lives, which wasn't my business at all...and because it was their business, they demanded to know how much I was paying the contractor and if the contract included a clause about not disrupting the peace and quiet the neighbors had enjoyed before this effing construction began, and if it didn't, then who knows, maybe the only thing they could do was file an official complaint, and if they were successful, they said, I might just end up living forever in the apartment of the woman who had left for Philly with her two boys, my house still a pile of debris and I'd be paying for both the rest of my life, the rented apartment and the broken house. Poor girl, they said. What will happen to her if we win? They pitied me but never filed an official complaint. The talk of filing it gave them so much satisfaction that they didn't need to bother with the real thing.

I went away for two weeks to re-energize my writing, and when I returned, I visited the site that had once been my home. It had new interior walls. It even had a new bathroom. This new bathroom, located in a completely new spot, had to be tiled, and Tom, the contractor, said it was my job to choose the tiles so I wouldn't spoil his blood later with complaints about things that could not be changed. He took me to a tile store, and I pointed at tiles I liked—dark blue, like in the bathroom of my hotel room in Mexico. He said, "Didn't you look at the price? The contract allocates a certain price for tiles, and this is ten times as high, so choose something else."

But there were too many tiles to choose from and I was too inexperienced and Tom too impatient, so he pointed at an unevenly colored, light-brown tile. "This is what everybody wants," he said.

"I'm not everybody," I said.

But he made the decision, and I had failed to make one, so I had no right to spoil the man's blood anymore. The next morning, when I entered the construction site, I saw stacks of tiles on the floor near the bathroom. A disheveled man emerged from a corner, a palette knife in one hand and a brush in another, and said, "You choose these tiles?"

"No," I said, "Tom chose them. "Me, I don't like them at all."

"So why you let Tom get them? Whose house is it, yours or Tom's?"

He spoke with a ferocity that I found unusual and appealing. Russians speak with this kind of ferocity when they're drunk, but even they tend to lose it when they embark on their Americanization process. And here was this Mexican speaking like this—or at least that's what I thought he was, given that most of Tom's crew was either Mexican or Polish, and this guy certainly didn't look Polish, and it's not like I thought all Poles were blond and blue-eyed, it's just that I could tell an Eastern European a mile away, and this guy, not only was he somewhat dark, which can happen even to an occasional Pole, but he was definitely not a European, not even an Eastern one. Yet he had something, I could tell right away.

Maybe it was this emotional ferocity coming out of a huge man with the face of a little boy—and it wasn't a Mexican thing or a Polish thing, it was all his own. I fell for it instantly, like a fly falls for honey. I didn't know that I was stuck, not until some weeks later, when we were standing in front of an unpainted wall with rollers and brushes in our hands, and trying to ignore something that shimmered and emanated from him, I said I didn't want the wall to be all one color. I wanted it to be many colors, like a painting. I was grateful to him for being willing to try different colors, one beside the other, one on top of the other, with unusual finish techniques like color wash, rag painting, stippling, graining, and streaking. Cans of Benjamin Moore paint stood all around us on the unfinished floor. Alejandro—that was his name—crumpled up a plastic bag, dipped it into paint called Tiger Dawn, and left it on the wall for thirty seconds or so. Then he removed the plastic.

"This is beautiful," I said.

He crumpled up another piece of plastic, repeating the procedure with a different shade of yellow.

I was glad he was willing to stay after work hours and show me things that could be done with simple wall paint. I asked him, "Were you a painter in Mexico?"

"What?"

"What did you do in Mexico? Did you make pictures? Were you an artist?"

I meant it as a compliment. But he reacted as though I stepped on his dignity. He struggled to make a sentence in English, and what finally came out was a furious, "No!"

"No!" he said with tremendous force. "Miss! In Mexico I...doctor!"

"You were a doctor? What kind of a doctor?"

"Doctor...fish!" he said with the same force.

He used to be a veterinarian, I figured, the kind I'd never heard of because his patients were not dogs and cats, nor cows and goats, but fishes. I had never heard of that, but that's alright, I liked things I had never heard of.

I asked him, "You were a veterinarian?"

"No!" he roared in despair at his inability to express himself. He made sea waves with his hands. "No miss! No veterinarian! Doctor! Mare! Water! Sea! Doctor...fish!"

"Doctorate of sea?"

"Yes!"

"You mean...marine biology? You have a doctorate in marine biology?"

"Yes!"

I wanted to say: "So you worked in Mexico as a marine biologist, and you came to America to paint walls?"

5

But I didn't say it. The realization that the disheveled man hired to paint our walls had been a scientist in Mexico, a marine biologist of all things, would sink in gradually, over days and weeks, and in the end, I would find myself so totally in love that by the time I discovered the truth about him, it no longer mattered.

The next time I saw Tom, I asked, "Did you know that one of your guys has a PhD in marine biology?"

Tom said, "What?"

"PhD…it's a…doctorate. A degree, you know."

"Who?"

"Your wall painter, Alejandro."

Tom remembered Alejandro saying that he used to work on a boat and that it was like a giant factory.

"What kind of factory?" I asked. Tom said he had asked Alejandro the same thing and that Alejandro's answer was "catching fish, cutting fish," but I no longer veered between belief and disbelief. I firmly decided in favor of belief, and I said, "Of course he worked on a boat. Where do you think a marine biologist conducts his research?"

I didn't know that by telling Tom about Alejandro's distinguished past, I was giving him away. Tom's "guys" were not supposed to talk to clients. The fact that I knew something about Alejandro's past meant that one of Tom's ironclad rules had been broken. He paid his guys for working not for talking, and every minute lost on talk was money gone from Tom's pocket. If he'd hear any more stories of Alejandro's glorious past as a scientist, he'd be fired. That's that…no more talking on the job.

One day, when my writing about life in the second century B.C. wasn't going anywhere, I hung around the construction site, making up excuses to spend a few minutes with Alejandro while he was painting walls on the second floor. Every half hour I brought him coffee or a glass of grapefruit juice or a sandwich with salad from a Russian store. He accepted my offerings as though he was doing me a favor by not rejecting them outright. I'd place them on the unfinished floor and stand there, holding forth on my particular way of brewing coffee or the wonderful health benefits of grapefruit juice. I'd list the varieties of salads available at the Russian store—Olivier, mushroom, beet, eggplant—and I'd say that the one with the French name was the one that everyone thinks of as *the* Russian salad, while it's actually not so different from the American potato salad. You like potato salad, Alejandro?

"Yes, Galia, I like potato salad."

He continued to paint the wall silently.

"Your coffee is getting cold. You should drink it."

"Ah, yes," he said carelessly, as though he was thinking about something else. But he stopped painting for a second, picked up the cup from the floor, and emptied it in one gulp.

"Good?" I said hopefully.

He grunted noncommittally, as though praising my coffee would send me a wrong message. A phone rang somewhere, and he said could I bring it to him; his gloved hands were covered with paint. I ran and found a flip phone on an unpainted windowsill and as I opened the lid, the name of the owner, Ammar Agbaria, flashed by, making me think that it couldn't be his. I quickly closed the lid and handed it to Alejandro. He took off one glove and, as he reached for the phone, his naked left hand accidentally brushed mine, and I sprinted down the stairs like a child, my hand on fire.

ALEJANDRO

She keeps coming over and talking to me and showing me the bathroom door she did and wanting to hear what I think of it. It's Venetian stucco, and Tom likes it. I can hear him say "Gorgeous!" and "Great!" and "How did you do it?" It's just Tom's PR, which is another word for bullshit, this is how he talks to customers, praising them, flattering them, so they'll spread the word about him being the best contractor and, oh, such a charming man, so contracts will start falling into his lap, which is something we must all want. And we do, because we are his guys; without his contracts, we don't get paid. I go on with my work, hearing everything and saying nothing, because that's what Tom wants me to be: a silent laborer.

But he takes his PR a little too far this time because the next thing I hear him say to her is, I'll hire you as my wall painter instead of Alejandro! This is when my blood begins to boil and I can't help myself; I run downstairs and see Tom admiring the door so much, he has his hands all over it, like it's a desirable woman. I put my hands on the edges where the Venetian stucco is rough and say, "Shitty job!" Tom glares at me like I spoiled everything for him, all his flattery work on this female customer gone and done with, and it's all because of me, his dumb painter who can't keep his big mouth shut, and just wait till we're alone, he's going to show me who is boss! But the lady just stands there and smiles and looks happier than ever, as if my telling her she did a shitty job was some kind of compliment. Tom doesn't glare at me anymore, because the customer is happy, so whatever I say about her shitty job on this door must be okay. He goes to the basement to check on the other guys and leaves us standing there. Still smiling like a fool, she asks me why I think it's a shitty job and what can she do to make it better.

I say, "The edges."

I touch the edges of the door to show her where they could stand some improvement.

"You mean the edges are a little rough?" she says.

She promises to work on the edges. I can see that she is trying to please me, to make me feel like I'm a master painter and she's an apprentice, learning from me, asking for my advice. She's paying entirely too much attention to me. It's my workplace, not my home, like it is for her, and the other guys are beginning to notice. They nudge me at lunchtime and want to know when I'm going to take advantage of all the attention she showers on me. These are not the words they use, but this is their drift.

Next day she asks me to take a look at the door, I say, "I'm busy, can't you see? I'm working."

She says okay and comes back during my break with a cup of coffee for me, like usual, asking me to go look at the effing door again. I can say, It's my break time, I'm supposed to rest, instead of looking at your door, but something restrains me. She is a lady, after all, and a client, and Tom tells us all the time that we must keep the client happy.

She says, "What do you think?"

I look at the door this way and that. I let my fingers roam over it as though a touch can tell me more than a look, like I'm a real Venetian stucco expert—and of course, I am, compared to her, that is.

"Better," I say at last. "But still...here, see?" I point at a couple of spots on the top.

She nods. She is trying to show that she agrees with my criticism. Learning to act like one of our women: always agreeing with a man.

Then she does something only a Western woman would do: use her female weakness to provoke a man.

"But it's too high for me," she says. "I couldn't reach up there. I'm not that tall."

What can I say to that? I'd like to be nice and helpful, but this is too much. She wants to do a man's job but she can't do it because she's not a man. She is hoping for compassion: small woman, big man. Big man help small woman. I'd like to tell her that our women don't stick their noses in a man's business. Construction is a man's job. You need to have the strength and you need to have the height. You're a small woman; don't try to do man's work; do woman's work in the house. But she is one of those Western women who think they are a man's equal in everything, even in construction, and I know I'm supposed to be polite, I can't say this sort of thing to her. So I'm silent for a moment, thinking, controlling myself. "Stand on a chair," I say coldly and walk away.

———◆———

She stands on the chair and the chair is wobbly. It's wobbly only a bit, just enough for me to see that its wobbliness can be increased. I'm not really thinking this. I'm just reacting to what I see: a young woman on a wobbly chair. A young woman who doesn't take precautions. A young woman who doesn't realize that someone—anyone—with a wish to make that wobbly chair a bit wobblier can put her in mortal danger. I'm not saying I'm that man or that I have a wish to endanger the life of this woman. But I have been entrusted with a task, and it's the task I think about when I see the woman on the wobbly chair. It's the task that makes me realize that the wobbly chair can bring me closer to fulfilling my task. The woman can fall off the chair as if by accident. An accident that doesn't need help from me. It's no one's fault if the woman falls off the wobbly chair. There will be no witnesses except for the chair and the walls. The walls don't talk. If it happens at the very end of my workday, I can be far from here when they come. If a person decides to do Venetian stucco on a door that shouldn't have any Venetian stucco to begin with, and if that person is a woman without any experience in such things, a small woman who has to stand on a chair to reach the top of the door, what can you expect? Just as no one heard me say, "Stand on a chair," so no one would see me put my hands on the back of the chair to make it a little wobblier, or to make sure that when she falls, she falls hard, or to approach the woman lying on the floor and touch her neck with the tips of my fingers. She will not be found until the next morning, unless one of her neighbors comes over to complain about the noise of the construction or about our trucks taking up all the parking spaces on the street.

ALEJANDRO

After work I go to my friend the Professor's house. I call him my friend because that's what he calls himself: I'm your friend, he says; I'm a friend of your people. It's true, he is helpful and generous, all of which makes him a benefactor more than a friend, because even though a friend can be generous, the Professor is generous in a specific way, as everything he promises me, such as legal protection, is done for a specific purpose, which is the Professor's purpose, not mine, notwithstanding the fact that he likes to present it as mine or my people's more than his. He is fighting for me, he says. He, an American college professor who could have been thinking about usual trifles of academic life, is fighting for me, a disowned Palestinian. He can have everything he wants, he says, but he cares more about my people's rights to our stolen homeland than he does about his own tenure. So brave and thoughtful of you, I say, and thank you very much for all you do, but sometimes I think thoughts that I don't express because I know that they run contrary to what he expects of me, his domesticated terrorist, as he calls me, even though I'm no such thing. One time I said to him, don't call me that word, it's not what I am or was, and he smiled and said, okay, then I'll call you my brave militant, you like it better? No? What about my freedom fighter? Not that either, I wanted to say, but I could see he was so intent on his idea of me as a fighter for my people's freedom, something that existed in his imagination more than in the truth of my life, that I was silent and only moved my head ever so slightly in a kind of half nod. I don't want to offend my friend the Professor even though, as I've already said, friend is not the right word for what he is to me; maybe a benefactor, but not even that; he-who-would-be-my-benefactor-if-I-do-as-he-says, at this point.

When he talks about my residency permit, he says he has his channels, and I stop short of asking him what channels, because he says it in a meaningful way which shows he is an important person who knows exactly what he is doing and who shouldn't be questioned about what channels and how long it's going to take. The very fact that he's willing to help is to be respected and admired for its own sake. I nod, because I need a green card more than anything, more than money, more than my wall painting job, more even getting than off the hook with the guys we both know, which is another favor I want to ask him. And as for his channels, sometimes I wonder why he calls them that and why they are taking so long. He tells me not to worry; I can rely on him and his network. I open my mouth to ask what network he's talking about, when he says look here, my domesticated terrorist, although I asked him enough times not to call me that.

Look here, he says again.

He lets me sit on a couch in the living room while he putters in his kitchen, filling his kettle with water, opening and closing cabinets, taking things out or putting them away. When I hear the kettle's soft whistle, I cross the living room and watch my friend and benefactor pour hot water into a glass with mint leaves on the bottom.

"This is how they drink it in Morocco," he says, offering me a glass of mint tea.

"Okay," I say to my benefactor, who knows all about how they drink mint tea in Morocco because he gets his summers off and has plenty of money he can spend on travel.

"You've been entrusted with a mission," he says solemnly, carefully pouring water into another glass.

He brings his mouth close to my ear and whispers that he allows me to grant my target two months—a gift of life, he calls it, and adds, "The gift is temporary, but so is all life."

The Professor wears silk shirts and navy-blue dress pants and his cheeks are as smooth as a baby's, and he has a winning manner, a mixture of Eastern hospitality which he says he learned from my people, and Western worldliness, which is his own, because he is, after all, a Western man, a professor in an American college, and a die-hard liberal, a radical, as he calls himself as though confiding a secret that everyone already knows but longs to hear anyway. I don't tell him that I think his so called radicalism is a kind of affectation; that what he really cares about is his tenure and all the perks that go with it. I don't want him to see me as what I really am: someone who cares about getting a green card more than about being a rebel against the Zionist colonialism. If he wants to see me as a freedom fighter, a kind of rebel with a cause, I let him, because he's the only one who cares enough to do something about my immigration issue through his so called channels and also because he gets me jobs, like the wall painting job with Ted's crew in Galia's house. As long as he wants to help me, I'm his man.

The Professor presents himself at parties as someone who wears many hats. Although at first I didn't understand the expression and actually expected to see a hat on his balding pate, I know its meaning now, and I can see that the hat he's wearing today is different from all the ones he wore before. Today the Professor wears a hat of a Mastermind, and no matter that at first I wasn't sure what exactly he was a mastermind of, he makes it clear to me soon enough.

He mentions my green card and his channels as he usually does, then he coughs significantly and adds, "But only after the Galia job is done."

I know from experience that there's no taking his mind off his new role, so I play along and nod, until the nodding is no longer enough and I have to say something, even if it's just one short question.

"Why you want to eliminate her of all people," I say.

He thinks for a while and says he's willing to give her two more months, which, together with the first two months he granted earlier, makes four months total. The poor woman has no idea that a man she has never met has just extended her life from two months to four. The Professor gives me a glass of mint tea, and we sit on soft chairs in his spacious living room and we stir mint leaves in our glasses and we feel very good about ourselves, until I say that I still don't have a clue what Galia has to do with any of this.

"You've been entrusted with a mission," he says solemnly, carefully putting down his glass.

He brings his mouth close to my ear and whispers that he allows me to grant my target two months—a gift of life, he calls it, and adds, "The gift is temporary, but so is all life."

He is so pleased with my consent to do the job that he says I could ask him for anything, and again I remind him of his promise to use his connections in the Naturalization Department to get me a green card, and he says, yes, of course, but only after the Galia job is done.

He wants to make it clear that he's making an exception in my case, because all I have to know is how to do the job right, not why and what for and what did the poor woman do to deserve this fate and certainly not all the history that went into his decision. If he lets me in on the history, I should see it as a kind of bonus, a little something on top of helping me get me a green card through his channels, which is how he refers to his connections in the Immigration and Naturalization Department.

"So where was I?" says the Professor. He goes on and on about my people, "your people," he says, about how we had our land from the ancient times until the middle of the twentieth century when the Jews stole it from us, and he says there's no need for him to speak of my people's sufferings, their struggle and the goal of their struggle, that I know it as well as he does.

"Yes," I say. "I know it very well."

"And how do you prove, how do you achieve your goal?" he says. "If there are people in our time claiming to be descendants of the Hasmonean dynasty of Jewish kings?"

I still have no idea what he is talking about. He asks me if I remember what he told me a while ago. I understand that he is giving me a hint, but a hint of what? Which one of the many things he told me a while ago is the one he is talking about now? I see hesitation in the movements of his hands and in the way he folds and unfolds his legs, even in the way his nostrils puff the air in and out. I wait. It's up to him to decide to disclose more or to keep it to himself.

"You remember that time when I was trying to find out the identity of a person who was posting chapters of the so-called *Hasmonean Chronicle* online? The first chapter about Judah Maccabee was posted six months ago, in one of so-called writers' forums. The chapters turned up in different websites, and whoever was posting them was very good at hiding their identity."

I say yes, I remember him telling me about spending hours at his computer, trying to discover the identity of the author. "Well, I found it," he says without a trace of the hesitation I saw a few seconds ago in his arms and legs and nostrils. "Or rather, I found *her*."

I follow him with my eyes as he walks over to his desk at the far end of the room, turns on his laptop, waits, clicks a few times and makes an inviting gesture with his right hand.

"Once you read this you will know why."

I join him at his desk. With obvious sarcasm, he says that I will surely enjoy Galia's writing style, and he will let me read it in solitude so I can enjoy it even more. I hear him putter around the room, taking away our dirty glasses and rinsing them in the sink. When I look up from the screen, he says that the fate of my people--your people, he says with emphasis--is in my hands, and surely I don't want to fail my people. I say nothing to that, both because I heard him say such things before and because I'm busy reading. When I'm about halfway through the first section, he says,

"Now you know what a glorious task has been laid on your shoulders, my fine wall painter."

Without looking up at him, I point at the screen, then, just as silently, at my forehead: I have to concentrate. I have to figure it out. Let me read this in solitude. Please.

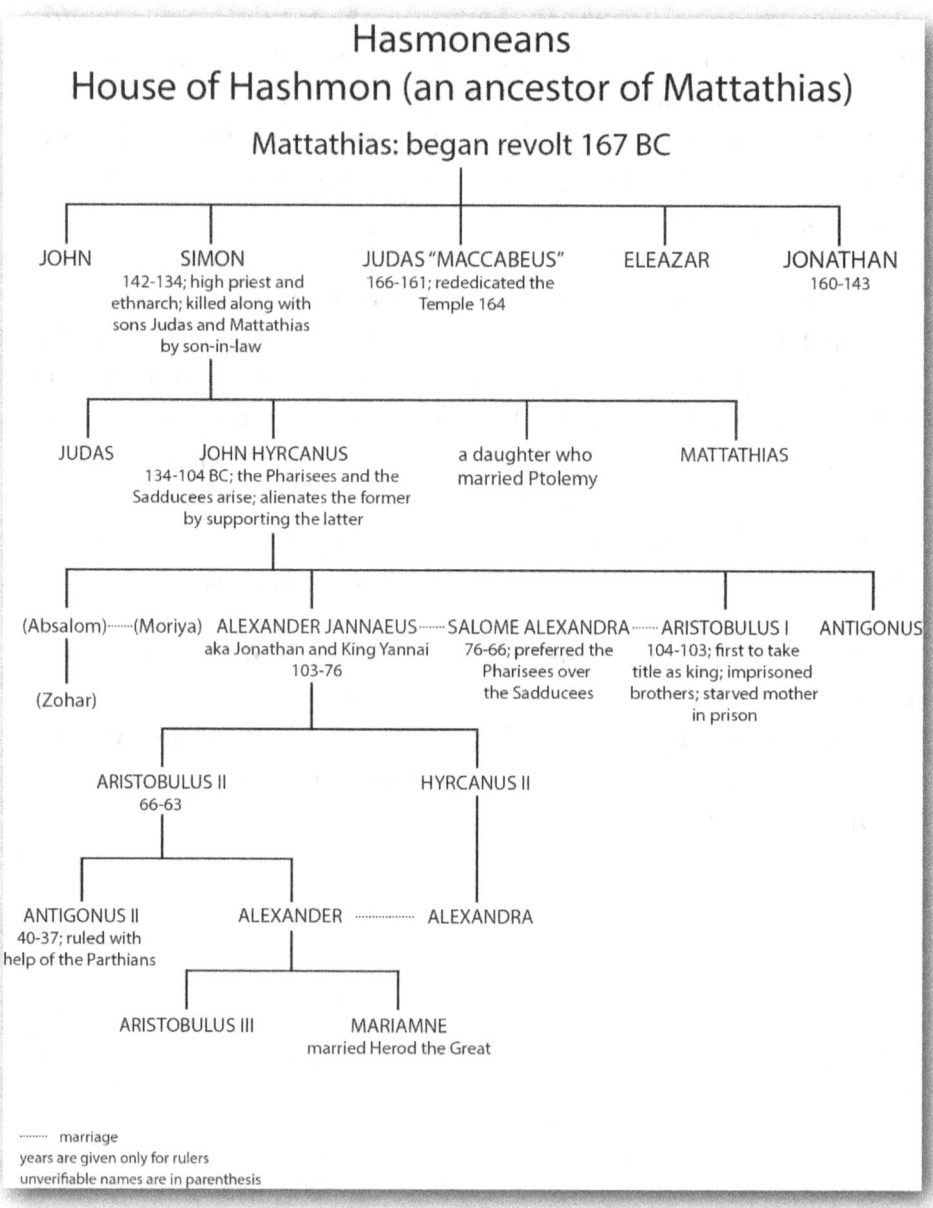

Hasmoneans
House of Hashmon (an ancestor of Mattathias)
Mattathias: began revolt 167 BC

JOHN

SIMON
142-134; high priest and
ethnarch; killed along with
sons Judas and Mattathias
by son-in-law

JUDAS "MACCABEUS"
166-161; rededicated the
Temple 164

ELEAZAR

JONATHAN
160-143

JUDAS

JOHN HYRCANUS
134-104 BC; the Pharisees and the
Sadducees arise; alienates the former
by supporting the latter

**a daughter who
married Ptolemy**

MATTATHIAS

(Absalom)······**(Moriya)**

ALEXANDER JANNAEUS······**SALOME ALEXANDRA**······**ARISTOBULUS I**
aka Jonathan and King Yannai   76-66; preferred the   104-103; first to take
103-76   Pharisees over   title as king; imprisoned
                                 the Sadducees   brothers; starved mother
                                                           in prison

ANTIGONUS

(Zohar)

ARISTOBULUS II
66-63

HYRCANUS II

ANTIGONUS II
40-37; ruled with
help of the Parthians

ALEXANDER ················ **ALEXANDRA**

ARISTOBULUS III

MARIAMNE
married Herod the Great

······ marriage
years are given only for rulers
unverifiable names are in parenthesis

THE HASMONEAN CHRONICLE

JUDAH, SON OF MATTATHIAS, ENTERED Jerusalem limping. He didn't think a severed toe was a big sacrifice, considering the might of the Seleucid army and all those finely sharpened swords that outnumbered both swords and men in his own army. There was the further disadvantage of his men refusing to fight on the Sabbath, while it was precisely on the Sabbath that Antiochus IV had ordered his army to attack the Jews. He was smart, that Antiochus. He knew the piety of the Jews was an impregnable fortress that would bury them. A thousand of them were slaughtered that day: men, women, children, all letting themselves be pierced by Greek swords. Better death with God than life without Him, they reasoned, and burned like candles in the night.

It was known well beyond the boundaries of their land that the Sabbath of the Jews was untouchable and that made them all the more touchable themselves. On another Sabbath, when the Greeks expected another easy victory, they thought a band of disheveled, poorly armed men was a vision sent to them by Dionysus, the god who gifted them with much drink and merriment the night before. It's a vision, Antiochus's men cried as they fled, while Judah, son of Mattathias, son of Hasmon, was more of a vision than others, walking in front of his men, a sword in one hand, a stick in another, and a toe cut in half, leaving a bloody trail. He stopped only when they reached a village where his family temporarily stayed. He signed to the one who walked directly in his bloody footsteps and with words, "Nehora will do it!" dispatched the man to bring his wife.

When Nehora appeared, her black hair cascading down her shoulders and her white robe delineating her charming form, he offered her his foot as a greeting. He knew her so well that he was certain of her response. She took his foot with its hanging toe and surveyed the haggard troops with their swords and sticks and stones.

"Whoever has the biggest stone, step forward!"

Twelve shaggy men, one for each month of the Jewish year, stepped forward, and she selected the one with the biggest stone. She pointed to the ground, silently ordering him to put the stone in front of her. He obeyed and retreated into the rows of men, whereupon she lowered her husband's foot onto the stone, took a knife that was rumored to have been King Solomon's out of an ornamented cloth bag, raised her hand and let the knife fall on Judah's toe, severing it completely from the foot.

She said, "Whatever is half-severed must be severed completely, for a half-severed part is the enemy of health." We know this because her many disciples wrote down her teachings in a book called *Wisdom of Nehora*—but as an apocryphal book, it was banned by later rulers.

"We are back to basics here," said Nehora, perhaps envisioning medical instruments of a more advanced time. She wrapped her husband's foot in a leaf of a tree famous for stopping bleeding. This tree was not to be found in Judea or anywhere else after the healing of Judah's foot, which is a great pity indeed, both for people as well as for the tree.

Judah considered the matter of the toe finished, *finis*, done with. It was noted that not a single cry of pain had escaped his lips during the procedure known in future centuries as the Severing of the Great Toe. Indeed, he had set new standards, or rather new heights, for tolerance of pain in manly silence, not a single facial muscle betraying him by a sudden shaking or jerking or twitching. It was said that he had triumphed over pain just as he had triumphed over the Greeks with their effeminate habits and that he had fulfilled an ancient prophecy about a man with a missing toe who was to win the desecrated Temple back from the enemy. His deformed foot became something of a sacred object itself, and wherever in the Temple he stepped, sacredness reestablished itself as if it had always dwelled there, as indeed it had but with some unpleasant interruptions, the most recent of which had been engineered by Antiochus IV and his minions, who had installed a painted Zeus at the altar.

As soon as Judah stepped inside, he saw pigs' heads lying everywhere and pigs' tails sticking out from cracks in stone slabs. He couldn't breathe. He felt as though his breaths were trying to escape through cracks in his ribs but instead were getting stuck like pigs' tails on the floor. He turned his head toward the entrance and saw his men waiting for a signal from him. "But it is defiled!" he cried. He shook his fist at the painted Zeus statue, and they understood at once. They jumped at Zeus, pulling him, pushing him, breaking his head with mallets, treating him the way no Olympian god had been treated in his homeland. But this was not Zeus's homeland. This wasn't Greece, nor was this the Seleucid Empire, with its pagan worship of the very same Olympians in Antioch, nor was this Rome, with the very same painted gods renamed to sound as though they were born and bred there: Jupiter instead of Zeus; Juno instead of Hera; Venus instead of Aphrodite; Bacchus instead of Dionysus. "How could they even think that people would believe in them?" said Zephirious, one of Judah's commanders. His Hebrew name, Yemin, was an exact reflection of his position in life: Judah's right hand. That's what he was, and Judah trusted his Yemin like his own self.

He also trusted Nehora, but no matter how great a medic she was, a man could trust a woman only so much.

Three years before, when he was still married to Miriam, he went on foot from village to village, looking at the young men lined up just in time for his arrival. His orderlies went ahead of him to prepare the locals, so he wouldn't have to linger and wait for them. In every village he'd say a short speech in front of a crowd of well-formed men who listened with their ears and eyes wide open, catching every word—and the words were to everyone's liking, for who among them didn't want to teach a lesson to the Greeks?

"Who?" asked Judah rhetorically.

"We all do!" roared the men. Whereupon he watched them wrestle, paired off on a dusty village road, and he invariably chose the winners, while the losers rolled away, covered with the same dirt and dust as the winners.

In one village he saw a young woman ministering to the losers, and as she poured water from an earthen jug onto bruised bodies, he saw that her face was the moon and the sun, her eyes the stars and her mouth a river of honey, and he wanted nothing so much as to go on watching her care for those poor wretches who would never win the honor of pushing the Seleucid army into a hell of their own making where they belonged as surely as their Zeus belonged on the Olympus, which, Judah had never failed to add, was a mountain in Greece...a mountain, you understand, in Greece, you understand, not in our Judea, where hills we have, yes, but mountains—no! He approached her with his arms out-stretched—wash mine, too, woman! But she silently showed him the empty jug: not a drop left, and as she put it down on the ground, he continued to stand like a beggar in front of her, his hands outstretched, as something better than water was pouring onto them.

"The force!" he exclaimed inside his own head, for although he had power over men, he had none over women. Or at least he thought so, which is why he made that exclamation about the force inside his own head, instead of letting it out of his mouth and into her ears, which surely were as well-formed as the rest of her. But beauty was not the point; the force was the point. What he said out loud surprised Yemin, his right-hand man: "I'd rather you were a hag." Judah dwelled on this for a second, and then added, as an afterthought, "'Tis true, be a hag."

A few more moments passed while she stared at the ground, not daring to meet his eyes. After standing there for as long as he could bear, he finally turned to Yemin with the words, "Let us proceed," and without so much as a look or any kind of farewell, he left her standing next to her empty jug.

He collected the winners, and with an all-inclusive gesture ordered them to walk beside the winners from previously visited villages. And so they walked on to the next village, where they watched another wrestling match, and again winners were added to the growing army, and losers were left with women who poured water onto them and ministered to their pitiable scratches. But none of the women had a face like the moon, and certainly none like the moon and the sun combined, and anyway it was not the face that mattered, he said to himself in the darkness of his own mind. He could no longer remember the face, only her force that still encircled him like a shimmering cloud. He could not escape from that cloud even at home when he made love to his wife of many years, his faithful

Miriam, daughter of Miriam the Senior, herself once a woman of beauty, now only a rag of bones and skin and disjointed mumbling.

His wife, Miriam Junior, could sense something unusual, as though the shimmering cloud in which the other woman enwrapped him was her own doing, and he too wanted to believe that this amorous shimmering was for the love of her, his wife and the mother of his sons, but he felt the shimmering go out of his body precisely when he touched her. He didn't like this new feeling, and he repeated to himself that he loved his wife, he loved his wife.

He went to the village a few weeks later, alone, and demanded to see the woman of the jug. When she was fetched by an old hunchback, half-male, half-female, and stood before him with her face like the moon and the sun, he said loudly, as though to convince himself: "I cannot love you, for I love my wife."

She said nothing at all; she only sent forth more shimmerings. The cloud that had enwrapped him in her absence became so dense that he found it impossible to breathe. It was beginning to get into his nostrils and his lungs, the shimmering that emanated from this woman of the jug. She had no jug. She had nothing at all. She stood defenseless in front of him, except for the shimmerings that must surely be the work of Satan himself. Or else of God. "Yes, why not God?" he asked her, and as she made no answer, he commanded her: "Speak!" She remained silent.

"I shall tolerate your silence no more," he roared. "For I am certain of one thing, if ever I was certain of anything, it is that I have been bewitched. But I must know on whose orders I have been bewitched. God's? Or Satan's? And speak you shall, because you are the tool he used, and doubtless you are familiar with the perpetrator."

She continued her silence, so he tempered his impatience and changed his roar into a sweet voice no woman could resist and again asked her to name the perpetrator, as he called the force that had outdone him. The sweetness of his voice was more powerful than his roar, and she said simply, "It was neither God, nor Satan. His name is Eros. He is the son of Aphrodite, the goddess of love."

Ah, how he cursed upon hearing that it was the Greeks again! The Greeks had bewitched him, even as he was walking on his own two feet from village to dusty village, gathering the strongest Jews to defeat them, there they were, the

Greeks, preemptive as ever, defeating him in the guise of their child-god, Eros, and this woman who had been sent by Eros to unman him.

"A battle is looming between the Jews and the Greeks," he said to her quietly. "By siding with the Greeks, you turn yourself into a traitor."

After a brief pause that he himself could barely tolerate because the shimmerings were becoming too powerful for him to remain standing, he said, "And you know what happens to traitors. It is not a pretty picture at all." He had to summon all his legendary willpower to resist the shimmerings as they were pushing him down, onto the ground, with her in his arms. If she had said it was God who had made them pass through her into him, he would have succumbed, because obeying God's will, no matter how incomprehensible, was a man's duty, a badge of honor. But he would not succumb to a Greek child-god with a quiver of toy arrows that he shoots at random.

"Are you sure it was him?" he asked. "Describe him."

"He was a boy," she said. "He was laughing as he played with his arrows." And she added, "He had wings. Like a butterfly's, only bigger."

"Perhaps you made a mistake? How did you recognize him if you had never seen him before?"

"I'm certain it was him," she replied. "And I'm certain he meant no harm. But what is done is done. The shimmerings we both feel are nothing but the result of his shooting us with his arrows. You don't have to turn your life upside down because of them."

"What else can we do?"

"Leave it alone," she said.

"Leave it alone!" he roared again, this time with laughter so powerful it hurt his insides because the shimmerings had already reached his lungs.

"I shall go home," he said, "I shall go home to my wife, and I shall love her as she deserves to be loved. No Greek boy-gods with their arrows are going to stop a pious Jew from loving his lawful wife."

And away he went, leaving her with half of the shimmerings, which she wrapped around her body like a shawl, for the sky was growing darker and the air colder.

GALIA

I want to do more writing but I can't concentrate, so instead I proof the first chapter of my Chronicle and stop where Judah is walking away from Nehora hoping to rid himself of his obsession with her. Proofing bores me. I have to do something creative--if not writing, then painting, my first and almost forgotten love. In the evening, the construction site is darker than the street, and the debris on the floor looks monstrous. I make my way with a flashlight, stumble and almost fall a couple of times before I reach the wall where Alejandro experimented with crumpled plastic bags and other unusual painting techniques. I open a bag and take out cans of dark red, orange, and yellow wall paint, two small brushes, and a couple of rags. I used these brushes years ago for oil painting, and I think they'll do just as well with wall paint, since I'm going to use the same technique as I did with oil. I shine the flashlight on the wall: the patterns Alejandro made during the day look more interesting at night. I set to work.

I finish at 5 a.m., get to bed at six, sleep late, and dream of his reaction at seeing the results of my night work. He jabs at the shapes on the wall with his finger, saying, "Why? Why?" I wake up in a panic at the thought of his anger. I expect to find him the way he was in my dream, accusing me of having done something terrible, but when I see him in the basement, he is stirring some mixture in a bucket, and when I say hello, he barely turns his head in greeting.

I ask him if he has seen the wall, and he says, "What wall?"

"Come. I'll show you."

He grumbles. He has to finish his mixing first. When he finally follows me to the first floor, he walks so slowly that I run ahead of him and wait for him by the wall.

"It looks different in daylight," I say. "It was much better at night."

"What's this?" He points at a shape in the center: a boy shooting arrows into the upper right-hand corner of the wall where two shapes, male and female, stand at some distance from one another. "So you artist, Galia? Why you do this?"

"I thought you'd like it."

"But it's wall," he says. "It's wall, Galia! Not painting!"

"I know it's a wall and not a painting, but I want it to look like a painting. If you're worried about what Tom will say when he sees this wall, don't worry, I'll tell him the truth. I'll say I did it, so he's not going to blame you."

"I don't worry about Tom, I worry about you."

"Thank you, Alejandro, you don't have to worry about me."

"This man," he points at the wall. "You paint this man?"

"The man is looking at the woman…you see the woman there? And the woman is looking at the man because—you see these arrows? The boy shot them with his love arrows."

"Not true!" he says with ferocity. "Not with arrows!"

I don't know why he reacts so strongly. These are just pictures, images made of paint. Perhaps he thinks I'm trying to tell him that he is the male figure, I'm the female one, and the love arrows shot by Eros are the future I have in mind for us. I wasn't thinking of this at all last night, and now I'm embarrassed because he thinks this is the reason I painted it. I must convince him that he's wrong, that it has nothing to do with him and me, that this is just my technique, the way I've been painting for years. I can show him my canvasses as proof.

"It's a myth, Alejandro. Not real life. And anyway, I painted them just because this is what I saw in the patterns of paint after all that color wash and rag painting and stippling you did for me on this wall. You did that for me, and I wanted to do this for you."

"Thank you," he says sarcastically. "What pleasant surprise!"

"You sound like you think I spoiled your work."

He steps away from the wall, folds his arms on his chest, smiles with his eyes.

"You hate it, Alejandro, admit it."

He continues to stand there, totally composed, as though folded into himself. I watch him from my spot at the other end of the wall, and I want to tell him that it's the first time in years that I have seen a man smiling this eyes-only smile, and that the smiles I see everywhere, lips pulled apart and eyes reflecting nothing, are worse than no smiles at all, in my opinion.

"I have work," he says forcefully, with emphasis on "work," making it clear that I'm nothing but an idle little woman who wiles away her time painting silly pictures on walls that a man has *worked* on and who doesn't understand that Tom pays him by the hour, and that every hour and every minute is *work* for a man like him.

CHAPTER 1 (CONT.)

THE HASMONEAN
CHRONICLE

———◆———

WHEN JUDAH ENTERED HIS BEDCHAMBER with a hope of squashing the shimmerings by loving his wife as well as he could, he did not find her there. Nor did
he find her in the kitchen, where the cook told him that the wife had said she
wasn't feeling well and that a walk might do her good. He went out and walked
the ancestral field, from end to end, without seeing a sign of his wife. At the edge
of the field he saw a ewe, and he wondered if it was a new addition. He briskly
guided the animal toward the barn. The ewe followed him unwillingly, and at
the entrance to the barn it stopped and looked at him with the eyes that seemed
to remind him of something, but filled with the shimmerings of the woman of
the jug, he couldn't remember what.

"I'm looking for my wife," he confided to the ewe, and as the animal continued to stare at him, he added, "I love my wife; she is the only one for me." The
ewe came so close to him that he could breathe its smell, which again reminded
him of something. He fondled the animal's snout, a quick disinterested touch,
to which the animal responded by standing up on its hind legs and bleating,
and in its bleating he thought he could distinguish sounds that were almost
words: "Your wife! Your wife!" But he had seen men go insane for the love of a
woman, and he had no intention of following in their footsteps, especially now
that all signs pointed to those rascals again, the pagan gods, because who else
would play such an idiotic joke on him. This was their way of being preemptive,
because they knew that when it came to a real battle, once they lost one, they
lost them all.

Back home, he questioned every family member and every servant separately, and they all said the same thing: she said she wasn't feeling well and went out into the field for some fresh air. Which is what she was wont to do, he had to admit. But now that, instead of the faithful wife, he had an extra ewe that stood on its hind legs and bleated human-like words when he petted it, he had to figure out two things. First he had to figure out which enemy god had perpetrated this evil deed, and second he had to figure out what do with the shimmerings and with the woman who had sent them forth, even though he was aware this wasn't the right way of putting it, as she wasn't the one who had sent them forth: she was simply the one through whom he experienced them.

The Olympians were having a bit of fun with him; he had to give it to them. Yet wasn't the very fact of their paying him so much attention itself a sign that they were unsure of their victory? The Greeks must be very weak indeed, if their gods resorted to low tricks like this one, turning his wife into a ewe just so he could bring home another woman. Now he could see it all. It was all so clear to him. The pagan gods had tried their hands at military strategy, and all they could come up with was this new woman and the disturbance she would create in his family as well as in his inner self—for if there ever was a one-woman man, it was Judah, son of Mattathias, nicknamed Maccabeus, the progenitor of the Hasmonean dynasty that would extend the Jewish rule over the Galilee and Iturea and Perea and Idumea and Samaria and that could boast of great advances in every field.

But one thing it could not boast of was having a man of Judah's purity and resolve at the helm. He remembered a small, shifty man he met in Tyre who had introduced himself as Hermes, and at first Judah thought it was just a name: Greeks loved naming their kids after their gods, and who could blame them, since they had so many of both.

Yet there was something especially odd about this man—so odd, in fact, that Judah had to ask him for three extra days to weigh the pros and the cons of a deal that at first had seemed a deal of the century but turned out to be a total failure. Hermes, the god of merchants and thieves and of all kinds of trickery...the ewe was his job, no doubt about it. If he could meet him now, Judah would break his jaw, he would indeed, said Judah to himself, because being a peaceful family man and a pious Jew was no longer enough: a man had to be able to avenge himself. Especially when one of the enemy's lesser gods decided to turn one's wife of fourteen years into a ewe, and another god, a mere child in brawn and brain, shot his love arrows simultaneously into him and a woman who was a complete stranger to him. And all of it just to take his mind off the looming battle that he was sure to win, because why else would they be trying so hard to distract him?

He did not go to Nehora's village again. He sent Yemin, for they would remember him no less than they remembered Judah himself, with a written order to bring the woman who had ministered to the losers. The woman with the jug. He omitted the comparisons of her face to the heavenly bodies, as he knew that such things were subjective, and that no matter how objectively beautiful the woman was, no one else might see her resemblance to the moon and the sun and the stars, and the fact that he had the little Greek god Eros to thank for this—he couldn't name it, whatever it was, still concealed in the shimmering cloud; it was more than lust, and even more than love. Whether it was Hermes or Eros who had brought it about, he didn't care. He had his God. And even if she of the shimmering cloud had been sent forth by the enemy gods with the single purpose of creating a commotion in his life and weakening him before the next battle, they had failed, because when the cloud finally receded, he saw that he had a new wife and that she was faithful of heart and mind. She adored his children. After the initial period of pain in which they couldn't help but miss their mother, the children grew to love Nehora too. And she feared his God, the one and only, and him, Judah, she loved fiercely and fully, the way she loved winners and ministered to wrecks.

"Hey, Hermes!" he shouted. "Where's that commotion you so hoped for? And to you, Eros, I'd give you thanks, I'd bow low to you, forehead to the ground, thank you, thank you, thank you, if only I could be sure it's the last time you play with your arrows in my land."

He wanted to say, "In my head," and in fact almost said it, but it came out as "in my land." And this slip of his tongue was better than what he wanted to say, because this *was* his land. And it wasn't in his head. His land was real.

His dirt-rich, black-soil and sandstone land in which his father, Mattathias, lay and his father's father, Yohannan, son of Simeon, son of Asmon, a Levite and fifth grandson of Idaiah, son of Joarib and grandson of Jachin, a descendant of Phinehas, third High Priest of Israel, they all lay in it, and their wives and mothers and their sons' wives and their sons' wives' mothers, lay in it too.

GALIA

By the time I move back into my half-finished house, I can no longer think of my writing because all I do is listen to the footsteps of the laborers upstairs, never failing to tell which ones are his. Wall painting, tile setting, and other surface jobs are part of the last stage of construction, and this stage is all his. Although other workers scamper about doing this and that, only Alejandro comes every morning at eight sharp while I'm still in bed, rubbing my sleepy eyes, and leaves at five, unless I stand in his way, babbling away about Mexico because I can think of nothing else that might interest this silent man. Mexico, after all, is where I think he is from.

He is putting away his tools in the basement and not looking at me at all while I stand there holding forth on the films of Alejandro Jodorowsky: *El Tope, The Holy Mountain, The Rainbow Thief.* I'm so sure that the intellectual inside this simple laborer not only has seen these rare films but can enlighten me with a critique of the Mexican director's vision that when he grumbles about not having seen the films and not having the slightest interest in seeing them, I brush it off, thinking, *He is so modest! He puts so much effort into seeming like a simple laborer!* My mind creates illusions about a man, and it persists when they're proven wrong.

"I don't watch those kinds of movies," he says.

"What kind of movies do you watch?"

"I don't go to theatres. I watch TV."

I ought to be disappointed, but I'm not. On the contrary, I think: *Ah! It's his masquerade again. He doesn't stop pretending to be a laborer, a lowly TV watcher, a lesser-than-himself.* But I know better. I know he is not a simple worker who likes watching TV. I've caught a glimpse of his real self, the intellectual with his head in the clouds, or rather, deep in the sea, *mare*, doctor fish, an oceanographer in a laborer's garb.

"I'm not even from Mexico," he says. "I just lived there for a year."

"Where are you from then?"

I expect him to name another Latin American country, Ecuador or Colombia perhaps, but he reverts to his usual silence. He gathers up his tools, cleans his hands with paint thinner—an unhealthy practice, I want to tell him—and I know that in a moment the door will shut behind him and I will feel like running after him. He must tell me where he's really from and why he let me think he was from Mexico.

The door shuts behind him. I know better than to run after a man.

Next morning I wake up to the sound of his footsteps. It must be eight: he's walking upstairs. I know his routine better than my own. He will spend five or ten minutes on the second floor, thinking or just staring into space. Then he will go down to the basement to get his paint rollers or scrape knives or whatever tools he needs for the day. I dress quickly and run into the basement, so I'm there to greet him when he shows up for his tools.

"Good morning," I say brightly, and he grumbles back in a mixture of languages.

I'm not discouraged by his grumbling; I have a plan. When he is putting his brushes in an empty bucket, I ask if he would be willing to do odd jobs for me after the construction is over.

"What jobs?" he asks.

"Jobs not covered by Tom's contract," I say. "Like putting up a new shed, or maybe a fence in the backyard, I don't know yet. Things will come up. I just want to make sure I have someone who can fix things when they do come up."

He turns away from me so I can't see his face and pretends to examine the left basement wall where a water meter was installed last week. After three or four long minutes he finally says, "You can call me any day, Galia. You have my number."

"Yes, Alejandro, I have your number."

He goes upstairs to work, and I decide to paint my furniture in bright colors, for no reason other than I'm in love with the man who paints walls. It's not enough for me to be his customer. It's not enough for me to be a writer inspired by him, even though I know he will never read my "Hasmonean Chronicle". I want more. I want to be part of his world. I put on old pants and an old shirt that I won't mind getting splattered with paint, along with painter's gloves that I bought in the Benjamin Moore store where they all know my name, not just because I'm there every other day but because I'm the customer who can't decide, the one who compares samples of color and asks, "How is this shade different from that one?" and, "What's the difference between gloss and eggshell?" and, "Can you make this color a little darker? A tad lighter?" I paint furniture like Alejandro paints walls. I pour some primer into a tray, dip my paint roller in it, and apply it to every side of an old dresser. When the primer dries, I paint the drawers Utah Sky and the body of the dresser Mystical Grape. I get much more joy from painting furniture than I do from my day job (teaching) or from my real job (writing), and I cheerfully announce this to anyone who will listen.

I'm so involved in putting a second coat of green paint on a headboard that when someone hands me a paper cup of coffee, I flinch. It's Alejandro, and he's smiling, holding out the cup. I can't believe that our roles have reversed: usually I'm the one who brings him coffee and he is the one who reluctantly accepts it, but today he is the one who brings it to me.

I say, "Oh, Alejandro, you shouldn't have. I can make my own coffee here at home."

He sits down on the floor, sipping coffee from his paper cup and talking to me. Very unusual: he is talking to me!

I don't want to think less of him. I don't want to think that he is talking to me just because I offered him repair jobs in my house, post-construction.

I'm so happy just to see him sitting there on the floor. I don't have to pull words out of his mouth as usual—he speaks without being prompted, as though he really wants to be heard by me.

He says he remembers that I had a question for him yesterday. Right before he left. When he said that he wasn't really from Mexico, that he was from some-place else.

"Yes," I say.

"So," he says. "You still want to know the answer?"

"Yes. But why do you talk about it like it's some state secret? Are you a spy? Are you on the run from the CIA or something?"

He says, "You heard of Palestine? Okay. So I'm from Palestine."

I'm thinking what to say. Maybe, "How interesting, and you know, when I was twelve, a refugee from the Soviet Union, I lived in Israel, in a town near Lebanon, and I went to school in Netanya, so maybe we were neighbors, you and I, isn't that interesting?" I decide against saying it because I don't want him to think me the kind of ignoramus who doesn't know that being neighbors in that particular part of the world is more like being enemies than friends. And I so want to be his friend. I don't care where he is from. I just want to be his friend, that's all I want.

He was born near Hebron, he says. Most of their neighbors fled in 1948, but his parents decided to stay. After graduating from high school, he studied biology, then oceanography at the university, and then—

"Which university?" I interrupt him.

"Al Quds University of Jerusalem," he says quickly.

And then things happened, this and that, no job in his field, so he worked on a boat, but not as a simple sailor. "You understand: first, it's a captain, and then I, a chain of orders—"

"A chain of command," I say.

"Yes, command. And then what? Then wife, marriage, child, two childs."

"Children."

"Children," he repeats like a good pupil. Wife said no more sailing, help with children. So he stayed. Again, no work. So he came here. This and that. Got construction jobs, met Tom. Tom said, "You're a good guy, educated guy. I need guy like you to make us look good to customer."

I want to ask him about a strange name I saw on his phone. I don't even remember the name itself; I only remember my surprise at seeing it. Whose name was it?

"My real name. Ammar."

"What about Alejandro…isn't it also your real name? And what about Mexico?"

"Ah, Mexico, yes. Was a sailor, second-in-command, went to Mexico. Two times went to Mexico!"

"But you know some Spanish," I say. "I heard you speak it with the other guys."

"Ah, yes, learned."

"And your wife and children…I thought they were in Mexico. You said so, didn't you?"

"Ah, no, family in Hebron. All family there. Mother, wife, childs. Mexico, that's different story."

"So you have another wife in Mexico?"

Suddenly he gets up from the floor, throws the paper cup away, and with large, decisive steps walks out of the basement.

"Alejandro," I shout after him. "I was just kidding! I didn't mean it seriously about you having two wives!"

———◆———

He's a married man, so I have to hide my feelings and talk about other things. Things that matter to him. Like painting walls, for example. When I can't choose the color for my living room walls, he gives me a CD about different faux finish techniques. I watch it on my laptop, and it gives me ideas for things I can talk to him about. One idea is to buy this special sand that you dump into a can of paint and mix it really well, then you paint with this mixture, and the result is a beautiful grainy surface. Beautiful, that is, if you get it right. I tell him that's what I want for my bedroom walls, and I buy the sand, and we mix it together. I tell him I want different shades of light purple for that room, so that every wall is almost the same but not quite, and you'd have to be really attentive to see the difference between Benjamin Moore's Sugar Plum, Heather Plum, and Grape Ice.

If I was asked, Why him? I would have had nothing to say. Was it his boyish face, his broken English, the fierceness with which he said "I doctor…fish," or the fact that I could see through him the way I could not see through others? In New York there is no dearth of men who speak broken English, men with boyish faces, men with degrees or no degrees. But the fierceness in his voice and the energy I felt when I was near him, these were no one else's. They were uniquely his. His running away from me was also uniquely his, but that was not what made me fall for him; it was what made me suffer. I've known intelligent men whom I could not love back; I've known writers and artists. Yet I fell for a man who would never read my writing and who cares more about some rough spots of Venetian stucco on a bathroom door than for being a gentleman. What does my falling for this man say about me? Perhaps nothing. Perhaps it says something about Eros's arrows, the way they are aimed at random and fall at random. That is, if in the second decade of the twenty-first century we can speak of Eros and his arrows with a straight face. If I said that once they fall, they feel like fate, I'd be told that it's an obsession, common enough, and harmful enough not to be left untouched. Work through it. Go into therapy. Don't live out your myth—your Greek one or your Jewish one; they are nothing but fairy tales, and you know how fairy tales end.

What do I say in response? That his voice moves me to tears, that for all the intellect of my articulate male friends I never heard anything as charming as Alejandro's "Doctor Fish." That no matter how many times he runs away from me, he is the one. No matter whether he really has a doctorate in marine biology or doesn't have any degree at all, not even a bachelor's; no matter whether his English is funny, as it usually is, or strangely normal, as it seems sometimes; no matter that he will never care to understand what's most important to me--my writing--why I do it or what it means. He is not yet aware of an arrow sticking out of his chest as I'm aware of mine, and it doesn't matter that the arrow is only a metaphor. Helping him to become aware of the arrow...this is my task. I have no other tasks but this.

CHAPTER 2

THE HASMONEAN
CHRONICLE

———◆———

IT WAS NOT JUDAH BUT his father Mattathias who had started the rebellion. On
a certain morning of a certain day, a very important day in the history of the
Jews—which was not yet history as it was not yet in the past—Mattathias awoke
with a bad feeling in his heart. It was a hard and unforgiving feeling, and it was
not because of the Greeks that he had this feeling...or rather, it was not only
because of the Greeks, as the Greeks were an abstract mass to him, too abstract
to be bothered with. It was his own flesh and blood who gave him this lump in
the throat of his heart. His own son Eleazar, who unlike his brothers with their
abundant beards, could not grow anything but meager wisps on his chin...three
hairs, is what his father called it. "Three hairs you got, son. If you can't grow a
full beard, there must be other ways you can render homage to the ways of your
elders. Go and seek those other ways."

"Yes, beloved abba, I shall seek those other ways," said Eleazar and added, too
quietly for Mattathias to hear, "I'm not sure you shall approve of those ways, but
nevertheless I shall seek them, as you yourself have advised me, and I'm a faithful
son." He concluded this little speech with a giggle.

"Disgusting mockery!" cried Mattathias as the unmanly sound issued from
his fourth son's mouth.

Eleazar vanished, knowing full well the punishment that awaited him if he
stayed—and he was no fool, even if he did appear to be foolishly in love with
ways not his own. He came home hours later with a fully shaved chin.

"Are you Greek?" Mattathias shouted in disgust, "Or are you my son?" He raised his right hand to slap the smooth cheek, but someone caught his hand in midair. It was Nehora, the woman sent by Eros, who held his hand as it was about to fall on Eleazar's face, the same Eleazar who had laughed at her, calling her the woman of the jug, and even worse, the whore of Eros, and who added these two insults together and came up with "the whore of the jug of the Greek boy-god Eros," while she, being a woman, could not hit him on his foul mouth to put a stop to this stream of abuse.

Now that she had stopped his father's hand from falling on his cheek, she had certain expectations of Eleazar, and she was sorry to see that once again she was wrong. She expected Eleazar to be grateful, or at least not as against her as he had been in the recent past, but when another giggle issued from Eleazar's naked mouth, she knew she had utterly underappreciated his *chutzpa*, because not only did he fail to thank her, he actually mocked her. She couldn't believe it; she refused to admit that such lack of family devotion could exist. His was the only naked mouth in this family of five men: the mouths of his brothers and his father were as finely hidden in the curly forests of beards as Eleazar's was open to everybody's eyes.

Mattathias went out, muttering under his breath, "Flesh of my flesh, blood of my blood, my very own son, as smooth shaven as a pagan Greek! What to expect of other people's sons if my own offspring forfeits the ways of his ancestors?"

Judah, the most accomplished of the brothers, ran to catch up with his father. Nehora saw the two men walking in the field long after the cool of the early morning gave way to a heat wave, and she thought they too should give way and forgive, but they were still walking and talking, and whatever their discussion was about, forgiveness did not figure in it. She was sure of that.

Later, Mattathias had Eleazar brought to his chamber by an old servant, Yariha the Idumean, who was so called despite having been born in the household of Mattathias's father, Yohannan, of parents of possible Idumean stock who worshipped the same one God and not, as it was sometimes rumored, the pagan deities of the old Levant, El or Baal or Asherah. Eleazar stopped by the entrance, not going in, even though his father commanded him to stand near so he could see him better.

"Why do you wish to see me, Father?"

"I want to see whether you have remained a Jew in the most intimate part of your body," replied Mattathias.

"It is called intimate for a reason, abba."

"It is rumored that you participate in games in the gymnasium and anyone there can see it."

"Those games are sports, and as such they are not part of daily life. What is done and seen during sports, or athletic exercises, as we call them, in the gymnasium cannot be seen in the house of one's parents."

"It was your father and not your athletic companions who saw you when you emerged from your mother's womb," Mattathias said pointedly.

"Indeed, abba, but that was a long time ago. I'm an adult now."

"But what kind of an adult? A Greek kind? Engaged in fatuous efforts to restore your foreskin? Isn't that what they do there, in that gymnasium built on the orders of Jason? Jason, who had as little right to be named high priest as any traitor of our faith? And like you, he had a worthy brother."

"I have four of them," Eleazar remarked glumly.

"Yes, you're four times lucky."

"Four times more burdened, abba."

"Virtue is not a burden. Your brothers have the faith. You're the one who shames them. In and out of that gymnasium, where you try to pass for a Greek, throwing disks and darts and who knows what else. Everything you do there, you do naked, with your lack of foreskin identifying you as a Jew…and you don't want to be a Jew anymore, do you? You're one of those young people who wants to blend in, assimilate, look like a Hellene, talk like a Hellene, worship their gods, and only when you come into your father's house you take off your Greek mask. Now take off your clothes too."

"Abba!" cried Eleazar. "It is one thing to show one's face, but the body is something completely different!"

"Take them off!"

"No, abba, I can't."

"Off!"

"Abba!"

"Son!"

"I swear by the Name that I did not engage in the abominable practice of what some call...ugh...how can I even pronounce it? Allow me to take a breath before saying it: foreskin restoration. Excuse the unpalatable words, abba. I speak the truth. And thus I do not have to parade naked in front of my abba just to prove that I'm still a Jew."

But Mattathias's heart was filled with darkness, and this darkness would not be driven away by his fourth son's antics. He'd heard it all: he was a father of sons. He wasn't going to sit and listen to this most unworthy son using the Name in vain in the blabbering speeches he had learned from the Greeks.

"You're quite an orator, son. But oration is a Greek thing, a thing of words and ornaments, not a thing of faith. Faith has no need of words, son. Faith has only need of faith."

Eleazar said nothing to that. Saying more would only prove to his abba that he had indeed turned into a Greek, and for his abba there was no abomination worse than this. One of his sons had become a Hellenized Jew. A Hellenized nothing. Eleazar was smart, after all. He had no desire to be disowned: for where would he go, where would he live? He liked this house. He had known no other. His abba's house was his. He was born here. He grew into a boy here. He was an awkward adolescent here, and now he was an elegant young man. Too elegant, in fact, for his abba's taste.

The father observed the son. He felt not unlike a king observing a hapless young subject, only he was a priest, which was better than a king, he thought, considering that all the kings who had ruled over Jews in the last four hundred years had been pagans, foreigners. It was much better to be a priest, to be powerful in the spirit that was in daily touch with God. And this daily touch was not nothing in earthly terms either: look at all the understanding of secret things it conferred on him. No wonder then that the silent thoughts flowing through his son's immature mind were as clear to Mattathias as though they had been said out loud.

And then a memory came. Mattathias stood with his own father, Yohannan, watching the parade of Greek Syrians in the streets of Jerusalem: first the soldiers, then the chariot with the king, then more soldiers, and then the king, Antiochus the Third, father of the current tyrant, standing up in his chariot and shouting something to the crowd in Greek, with the crowd of Jews shouting back. What did they shout? Mattathias was as fluent in Greek as he was in Hebrew, but he did not know what they shouted, because the part of him that knew Greek refused to translate the hateful words to the part of him that knew Hebrew and Aramaic, so he stood next to his father and listened without understanding, and when a man standing close to the two of them had shouted words in Greek that seemed more than a requisite welcome, he threw himself at the man, and the crowd fell silent. It would have ended very badly—and not for the man who shouted in Greek but for Mattathias, who would have ended up speared by Seleucid soldiers if his father hadn't pulled him away from the scuffle and shoved Mattathias behind him.

The same force that many years ago had made him throw himself at that man in the crowd made him now throw himself at his own son, his Eleazar. It made him claw at his son's garments, forcing him to disrobe so that, he, the father, could sleep with certainty that his son had remained a Jew. Although Eleazar was stronger and quicker than his aging abba, he couldn't kick or push or hold him to the ground because his body remembered the love he had felt for his abba in the days of his infanthood, when his abba rocked him on his knee or gleefully lifted him up and swayed him in his arms right-left, right-left, and then counted one-two-three before tossing him on a bed.

Now that his abba was tossing him on the bare floor instead of a soft bed, Eleazar's respect for his abba made him unable to resist, and so he let himself be pushed and disrobed and inspected with harshness that brought tears to his eyes.

His abba beheld his son's fully circumcised organ, and shame overcame him and he hung his head low as though only now he realized what he had done. He had attacked his own son, and for what? For nothing. This was a good son. As good as the other four, or at least no worse. Flesh of his flesh, and so forth. Mattathias left the room, his heart too heavy for words.

Later that day, during the annual celebration of top-tier Olympians, Mattathias stood a little away from the crowd of celebrants, knowing full well that as a priest he would be expected to act. He purposely shied away from his duties, for they were duties only in the eyes of the Greeks or of those Jews who, out of desire to survive, had convinced themselves that there was not much difference between the multitude of painted pagan gods and the one invisible God of the Jews. So convenient for them to pretend there was no difference.

The crowd approached the garlanded statues of Zeus, Poseidon, Athena, Demeter, and Hera. The people stood still, as though waiting for the gods to start speaking, and in the hush that descended upon them, a voice spoke in Greek, and the few women in the crowd were on the verge of giving themselves over to the hysteria of the miracle, their hands flying up to their hair to tear it out by the roots and to present it to the gods, who must surely value the offer. Only it was not the voice of any of the garlanded gods but of a bald representative of the Seleucid government: a strident voice asking Mattathias to step forward and perform his duties as a priest. Two attendants of the gods were goading a balking pig forward, and the squeals of the animal blended with the noise of the crowd, wildly clapping and roaring. Only one group stood still. The silence of this little group was all the more striking considering the punishment that was known to befall anyone who dared not join in the celebration.

People in the crowd, familiar with the Greek lore more than with the faith of their own fathers, swore later that Mattathias and his sons were concealed in the same cloud with which Artemis had hid Iphigenia from the eyes of the waiting crowd and from Agamemnon, who held a sacrificial knife at the hollow of his daughter's neck. One more time the voice of the Greek Syrian official rang out, ordering Priest Mattathias to step forward and perform the required sacrifice. The legs of the animal had been tied and its squeals muffled with a cloth pushed into its mouth. Mattathias didn't move. When the order rang out the third time, a man stepped forward and said, "I shall perform the sacrifice, your honor."

The crowd turned its eyes on the man. Mattathias was still standing a little apart, silent. The crowd held its breath because it feared the display of one of the two angers: the anger of Mattathias or that of the official. The crowd was hoping that, no matter whose temper was displayed, this remained a harmless incident that didn't get reported to King Antiochus IV. It was hoping for a spectacle; it got a war.

"You are a Jew," roared Mattathias. "Not a Greek. A Jew."

He stepped close to the man, the sun shining on a sword in his raised hand. He lowered the hand with the sword, the man fell down, and a dark puddle formed quickly under the man's neck.

"A more precious sacrifice than a sheep," said Mattathias quietly. "Isn't this what they hunger for, your painted idols?" The silence was palpable, gathering like a crowd, urging him to say more. After searching his soul for words, all he could add was "Your honor," with sarcasm so cutting it seemed unnecessary as he had already cut so much.

The man lying in a widening lake of his own blood was only the beginning. He was not the evil itself, only a traitor—and now the evil had to be struck, and there were no excuses to be made for its many gods.

Mattathias approached the official. "You called on me to step forward and perform my duty," he said, giving the official more than enough time to get away, as if the slowness of his rising hand and its equally slow descent were both part of the punishment.

Mattathias watched his hand as if it was carrying someone else's will, as indeed it was, for he believed that it was not he but God who struck down the official and who now went after his gods. The gods were falling, one by one, painted noses and cheeks breaking off from painted heads, and painted arms from painted torsos, lying in a heap on the ground, and there was no telling anymore which piece had been part of Athena and which of Zeus or Hera. The body of the official was lying in the same heap as the gods.

"Wasn't he faithful to you till his last breath?" Mattathias asked, kicking a painted head. "If you failed one of your own, perhaps you're trying to tell us that you are done with, vanquished, gone."

It was then that the famous words, recorded in the First Book of Maccabees, came out of his mouth without a will of his own. Even though they were ascribed to him, and even though generations upon generations over the next millennia would think of those words as his, Mattathias himself knew with absolute certainty that he had no choice but to obey the One who had created those words, just as the One had created him. And even those who had been willing to worship the painted statues of the Greeks, even they had a change of heart when they heard him shout, "Let everyone who has zeal for the law and who stands by the covenant follow me!"

When the warrant for his arrest was issued, and he and his five sons sought safety in the wilderness, their refuge seemed less like a family hiding place than a military camp. Every day the camp was filling up with men, young and old, yet it was an army without weapons, a great concern for Mattathias and his sons, who knew that sheer courage could not defeat the Seleucids, that only courage supported by numbers and weapons stood a chance.

And that was when Judah, Mattathias's most capable son, had an idea. It came to him one morning upon waking, but he insisted that it didn't come to him in a dream.

"There are better ways at getting at the truth, and finding weapons to defeat the oppressor is one of the truths," he said to his father and his four brothers.

Five days later, piles of arms and armor lay on campgrounds as though donated by an army that had renounced war. What army could it be that no longer needed its weapons or its armor? Perhaps, people said, an army that had its victories as well as its defeats behind it was no longer an army of fighters but of peace-seekers.

One day Jews too would be peace-seekers, but that time hadn't come yet; peace was the luxury of strong nations. That was why the huge pile of arms donated by the unknown army was a boon…indeed, a promise of victory. Wives and children were so adept at spreading the news of the arms that had come from nowhere that suddenly so many joined their army the camp seemed more populous than Jerusalem itself, and even if, strictly speaking, it was not as populous as that most ancient of cities, there certainly was more hope in it than in the streets of their capital, which had been taken over by the Hellenizing Jews, the ones who worshipped Zeus and competed naked in the gymnasium and argued the subtlest points of Greek philosophers in the language of those philosophers. Their Greek was so fine, their Hebrew so poor, they were more Greek than the real Greeks.

Eleazar was now at the heart of Mattathias's camp, and he brought with him many of his friends. One of them said that it was Mattathias's hand that had brought them when, after the killing of the Greek official, it struck down the pagan gods. Mattathias objected: it was not my hand; it was the hand of You Know Who.

Another man said, "Remember that when God gave this land to us, he expected from us something in return, and we all know what was required from us above all else…that we express God's light unto nations. And this means that even if they do terrible things that originate from their low level of development, we should not fall to their level and do terrible things in return. We must hold ourselves to a higher standard if we wish to hold on to this land; for if we are to express God's light unto nations we must learn to defend ourselves without taking the lives of those who wish to take ours. We must do better than them; we must leave 'an eye for an eye' behind us and find new ways that do not end in blood, ours or theirs. We must remain a light unto other nations, no matter what they do to us."

The man had hardly finished speaking when Mattathias the Hasmonean responded forcefully: "Should we go beyond the eye-for-an-eye stage? What choice does a man have when an executioner's axe is raised over his head? His first choice is to submit, and his second is to fight the executioner with whatever means are available. If we choose the latter, it's only because we tried the former, and the results were nothing to be proud of. And pride matters. Yes, sir. It matters as much to a people as to a single man; in fact, much more to a people than to a man. And we have been deprived of it long enough, haven't we? Four hundred years is a long time, and now for the first time instead of submitting like usual, we're getting ready to fight, organizing ourselves, living on courage alone, on courage and prayer. These two are one, for to pray to the God forbidden by conquerors takes courage.

"So come and stand before me and tell me I'm not serving my God as righteously as He was meant to be served. What can I tell you other than that I follow His will as it is revealed to me. Little by little, every day, every hour a small insight is given, not enough to call a revelation, but added together they create a pattern that gives meaning to everything I do. And you tell me that we were not meant to fight back, only to submit, and that even though they do not hesitate to spill our blood, we must not fall to their level, we must be better than them and not spill theirs in return. If the world allows the Jew to stay alive only with his back bent, his eyes cast down, his light can go nowhere other than into the ground…a light unto the nations indeed: dead nations only."

The man who had provoked this rant did not stay to hear it to the end, as Mattathias's eyes were shining too brightly, and the words flying out of his mouth were accompanied by growling, and it was not hard to imagine that something untoward might have happened to the man if he had stayed.

The nation that, according to the peace-seeker, was forfeiting its God-given obligation to serve as light unto other nations had amassed enough courage to fight the enemy, but no one could fight well on an empty stomach. There was now not just one peace-seeker but many, and they were getting organized into something called the True Word of God group and also a Light Unto Other Nations group, and the two groups became one large group advocating nonviolent opposition against the Greeks, as well as against the Jews led by the Maccabees. Despite having won many battles against the Greeks, the Maccabees were starving for the simple reason that the nonviolent camp had found a way to dispossess them of their provisions. The peace camp felt that, as it did not possess arms, it had to possess something, and what else was there other than arms and food? So they chose food.

Weapons were made by men, and therefore were evil; fruits, vegetables, and wheat were made by earth, and were therefore good. And if there was not enough food for all, somehow it seemed permissible to the peace-seekers to steal the food of the Maccabees. What they called the "warmongering" of the Maccabees' camp was, they believed, so contrary to the spirit of God and of what He expected of His people that they were sure He would forgive, if not actually applaud, their secret raids of the Maccabees' provisions. As a lot of tactical thinking went into organizing these raids; they were hugely successful and remained unknown to the other side, which kept on winning battles against the Greeks despite living on air rather than food, despite beginning to look like skeletons—or, as their sympathizers said, angels.

"Our nonviolent opposition theory," said the peace-seekers' leader, the man who had introduced his Light Unto Other Nations idea to Mattathias before the first battle with the Greeks had been fought and won, "allows us to use unconventional methods."

So it was that the unconventional methods of the peace camp led to the Maccabees' fighters being seen as "angels," because their thinness gave them the air of immateriality that, combined with their absolute belief in their cause, produced a kind of halo. It was rumored among villagers and city folk alike that it was not so much the Maccabees' skill in battle that set the Greeks running as the halos around their emaciated heads.

"To defeat them we must feed them!" cried out the chief peace-seeker's wife during a particularly tumultuous love-making with her husband, who made their marital encounter tumultuous on purpose, as he was well aware of his wife's tendency to come up with solutions to any crisis during a climax that she called, afterward, her "time of ascent up high and seeing the world from the peak of Wisdom Mountain."

"Feed them! Feed them!" she repeated, a little calmer but with her eyes still closed. "For only when they are fed will their halos-of-hunger vanish. Only when the Maccabees' stomachs are full will the Greeks stop running from them on the battlefield, and the cause of just Jews who follow God and who don't forget that He holds His people to a higher standard than others will prevail."

"You're right as always," said the chief peace-seeker, rolling off his wife's body.

"We can do so much better than an eye for an eye, in spite of what the enemy is doing to us. But if we behave like they do, then we do deserve their fate," the wife continued as one possessed.

"Whose fate?" chief peace-seeker asked cautiously.

"The Greeks," said the wife. "Who else?"

"But they're not our enemy. The Maccabees are our enemy."

"The Maccabees are our misguided brothers," said the wife with her eyes shut, a signal that a higher power was still speaking through her.

The chief peace-seeker followed the advice of the Voice to the letter, as if it was indeed He manifesting Himself through the aftershocks of their marital love. The chief peace-seeker was aware that the more passionately he made love to his wife, the more powerfully the Voice spoke through her. This was the reason he had evolved into a consummate lover, even though this was alien to his earlier nature as a docile follower of the Law, and it was only his marriage to this particular woman who spoke in voices when she climaxed that led him to become a furiously passionate lover, instead of what he used to be: a listener who couldn't hear, a soul without direction, a spirit blown about by the wind.

"Yes, our misguided brothers," the wife repeated, and by the slight tremor of her eyelids, he could tell that the time of revelations was drawing to a close. If he wanted to find out anything else, he would have to hurry.

"Should we let the Maccabees lose?" he asked God, and God, who had never failed him before, spoke to him through his wife's lips in a husky voice, like a drunk getting over a hangover, "Lose…"

After this the chief peace-seeker lay on his back for so long that, when his wife spoke to him in her usual wifely voice, standing over him with a vat full of water, "Wash your hands, husband, before you sit down to your morning meal," he stared at her and said nothing and didn't make any attempt to sit up. When she repeated her request out of a sense of wifely duty, he lunged at her like a wild beast, the water from the vat splashing all over the bed, and he pulled her down and lay on top of her and said, "I want to hear more God!" And even though his request was made in as passionate a form as any woman had ever heard from her husband, the wife refused him.

"You cannot get God from me if it is only God you want!" she cried. "Only if you want me, and only me, and what only I can give you, will God come speaking through my lips!"

"Then I want you!" he cried, passionate for God.

"No, you want Him!" she said. "You still want Him! He knows when to speak and when to remain silent. Only when you truly seek me, He comes."

"Then I seek you!" He squeezed her face between his hands with so much force that she cried out, "You'll crush my bones!"

He let his head fall onto his pillow and said helplessly, "If the Maccabees are our misguided brothers, then why must we let the Greeks defeat them? One doesn't abandon a brother to the enemy who will readily cut him up."

"I don't remember what He said," the wife said with an apologetic smile.

"That's why I need to hear more," said the peace-seeker, moving her white legs apart with a brisk movement she was too slow to resist and inching his fingers closer to the furry wetness. "I want to know how…I want to know why." He didn't have time to finish specifying what he wanted to know, because she was already trembling under his fingers, and her eyes were closed, and her mouth opened slightly to let out the words, "Nourish them, and you shall see." There was a pause during which his fingers furiously massaged the small roundness that made her shudder with particular abandon, and her upper mouth opened again, "Nourish them and you shall see! No more shall be said to you until their provisions are returned!"

The chief peace-seeker ordered sacks of provisions brought to the Maccabees' camp.

At first the rebels viewed the sacks with suspicion as though there could be poison in them or the meat of a pig or something equally nasty that could hasten their departure from this world, without all the victories they expected to win. The peace-seekers, seeing the indecision of the Maccabees, did the turnaround that no one, themselves included, expected of them: they repossessed a few of the sacks and, to prove their utter harmlessness, prepared a feast to which they invited all five Maccabee brothers with their wives and offspring. Mattathias was also invited, but he couldn't come, as he was too weak and on the verge of meeting his Creator to whom he unceasingly addressed questions about upcoming battles. He had both the inner fury to form the questions and the patience to wait for answers, and when finally an answer came to his question about the outcome of the battle of Nahal el-Haramiah, he called his son Judah to him.

"Remove the sword from the body of Apollonius," he whispered. Apollonius, governor of Samaria, was the first to fall in the battle that hadn't taken place yet, but the answer Mattathias received from his Creator had foretold his end. "Possess his sword until your own death comes for you," he said, adding, "Use it fairly, and you shall succeed."

"Yes, Father," said Judah, bringing to his lips the hem of Mattathias's robe. These were the last words heard by Mattathias the Hasmonean. Although his body was still alive when the battle was fought, his spirit had left him.

ALEJANDRO

He is the Professor, therefore he knows things I can't know with my small mind of a domesticated terrorist. I'm not a terrorist! I want to say, but I keep my mouth shut because I don't want the Professor to think that my mind is as small as he says it is, and I don't want to let go of the green-card dream, even though I don't know how exactly he can get it for me through what he calls his *channels*. What channels? I want to ask him, but it is forbidden to ask, because asking may sound as though I doubt him, and doubting is forbidden too. The Professor is not just any professor, the common variety you find at any American college. Officially he specializes in political science but in reality he is a professor of what he calls Adjoining Ideas, because everything is together, he says, literature, art, politics, and everything points at one thing. What thing? I want to ask, but I don't dare interrupt the thought processes of the Professor, not only because I know what he's going to say, the usual words about a small person like myself unable to judge his intellectual prowess, as he calls it, but mostly because I fear his anger which can be much more than a simple outburst without consequences for the poor wretch who caused it, and which, according to him, only proves that he's much more than an academic. Indeed, he says, he's one of those movers and shakers, who stay behind the scenes and look unassuming enough yet no world event of any significance takes place without their knowledge or direct involvement in the decision making that goes into every event big enough to be known by a man in the street. Here it is. That word again. A man in the street. A domesticated terrorist. A poor alien longing for a piece of paper commonly called a green card. He has many names for me, and he calls me now one thing, now another, and even though none of the names are right for what I know of myself, I let him think that he knows me better than anyone. Better than I know myself. I don't want to irritate the Professor. I don't want him to suspect that I'm not entirely happy being called a domesticated terrorist or a brave militant or a man in the street, and not only because my green card depends on his so called channels but because there are times when I truly respect the man. Sometimes he talks about other faculty members in a way that makes me think he's just an envious little man. He calls them department rats, tenure mice, academic nonentities, and other words I don't remember. They steal his ideas, he says, and they're not going to give him his tenure because they know, deep down in their small hearts and minds, that he is the real thing, the man for whom ideas are actions, not just the usual academic blah-blah-blah. That is why they fear me so, he says with a look that I myself would fear if I didn't know that he needs me almost as much as I need him.

"Now that you've read parts of her Hasmonean Chronicle, you understand why you must not fail your people?"

"But what does it have to do with my people? This story is not about us. It's all about *them*."

The Professor rubs his smooth cheeks and answers that it only appears to be about *them*.

He says that even though a casual reader might think this so-called chronicle is simply a story of a line of Jewish kings, you'd have to be very simpleminded indeed to believe this is all there is to it. He says that almost everything in this so-called historical writing is code for major milestones of the conflict between us and the Jews, and that the fact that this *Hasmonean Chronicle* already exists is a boon for my enemies, while for me and all those who sympathize with my people's plight…what is it for us? To us it is a call to action.

"What action?"

"You, of all people, shouldn't be asking this question. I do my part, which is deciphering the code. And you do your part, which is—"

The Professor is still wearing his mastermind hat. He is getting so used to it that he forgets that it is only a hat, that he is not what he pretends to be, a mastermind of actions against Zionist colonialism, and there's no telling him that most of his actions originate in his head and stay there, a sort of a game he plays with himself, with me and his other guys as willing participants. When he plays his mastermind role, there's nothing I can do, nothing I can say that doesn't go with the part he has assigned me. I'm his Domesticated Terrorist, and if I become stubborn and say no, I'm no terrorist, I never killed anyone, and I don't want to play this ridiculous and dangerous role, he'll find someone to replace me, and then bye-bye green card. I quickly think what a seasoned terrorist would say, how a man with blood on his hands would finish the good professor's open-ended sentence, and I say the word I think he wants to hear:

"Killing."

He nods. I got it right. I just hope that this play-acting won't go any further than the talk.

"I spared no effort in positioning you in the target's house. You are in daily contact with her. You're more experienced than any of our guys in New York, which is why you will not be under suspicion when the body is found."

Target. Body. Our guys. Suspicion. These are words I wanted to escape by coming to this country.

The Professor says that he knows very well what I'm thinking.

"You think that I'm only *imagining* it to be a code for what they're doing to your people. How I wish you were right. My fine wall painter," he says gravely, "to convince you that it is not simply my imagination, I will give you proof." He opens a new file called "Hasmonean Chronicle Decoded," and I see a list of points, each two or three lines long. I read the first point. It says: "Nehora cutting off Judah's toe. 'Cutting off' = separating the toe from the foot. Whether we are the 'toe' and they are the 'foot,' or the other way around, it means the same thing: as the toe is cut from the foot, so we are crushed under the enemy's heel/foot/toe."

I'm unpleasantly struck by the word "we". How is he one of us, I would like to ask, and how far does he expect me to take this play-acting, and why does he need to drag Galia into this?

I don't have time to read the rest of the points because he quickly minimizes the file.

"Well?" he says, peering into my eyes in search of admiration for his code-cracking skills.

"I don't know," I say, "maybe you're right, but as for me, I didn't quite—"

"Of course you didn't see it!" His voice rings with pity for my lack of talent as a literary detective. "It takes a mind well-versed in literary tricks to be able to find and interpret them correctly." He asks me if I think it was for nothing that he worked for years as a literary editor for a major New York publisher, and when I remain silent, he asks if I want to see more. He enlarges the file for me before I have time to say yes or no. I have no choice but to read point two.

"Hasmonean Chronicle, Chapter Two. Mattathias's son Eleazar and the Peace Seekers ('Hellenizing Jews'). This is a code for the Israeli peace camp pretending to agree to cede us land; their 'peace lovingness' and their professed standing up for the rights of our side are not to be taken at face value. Their real intentions are yet to be deciphered. The *Hasmonean Chronicle* should be read as a key to their intentions."

He says, "Well?" and again I sense that he wants me to compliment his decoding skills, and this makes me still more uncomfortable, because again I have nothing to say. I don't want to tell him that I, too, was able to detect some parallels to the conflict—for example, in the chief peace lover's speech to Mattathias and in Mattathias's reply to him—but this parallel was an obvious one, and the idea that it might have been meant as a code had not occurred to me.

He waits for me to read another point, about Judah's first wife. "The *Hasmonean Chronicle*, Chapters One and Three. Judah's sheep wife is a symbol of us and our flocks. Our sheep grazed the land where the settlements stand."

He is watching me as I read. I don't know what he wants, but again I think he expects me to admire him, so I say "M-mmm." But it's not enough for him. He expects more than "m-mmm"; he expects praise, and I realize that by withholding it, I fail him almost as deeply as I do by delaying the fulfillment of the task.

"I'm not a literary critic, so I can't judge your cracking this code as well as someone trained in this field."

"I'm not asking you to praise me, my fine wall painter. My intellectual prowess is not in need of your untrained compliments. The only thing I want from you is to realize the significance of your task. If you wait any longer, the construction will be over, your work in her house will be finished. The task will remain unfulfilled."

I'm ready to go, and when I put on my jacket, he says, "Be equal to your task, my proud freedom fighter." I'm glad he didn't call me his domesticated terrorist. The door shuts behind me but I still hear his parting words, "Remember, it is not a task—it is a mission."

GALIA

When he says, "Galia, why you writing this story and posting it online?", at first I have no idea what he is talking about.

"What story?"

"This story about your ancestors, how they lived in Palestine long ago."

"I don't write about Palestine, Alejandro. I write about Judea. Palestine was the name the Romans gave to that area after they conquered it in the first century AD. The story I'm working on takes place before that time."

"It shows your intentions."

"What?"

"Your writing. It shows your intentions."

"What are you talking about?"

"Your intentions."

"Whose intentions? Mine? Really, Alejandro, I have no idea what you're talking about."

"You should know. You're who wrote it. About that woman cutting off Judah's toe. Cutting…separating toe from foot. Our people are 'toe' and your people are 'foot,' or we are foot and you toe? Meaning is the same—"

"Where did you get this? It sounds like nonsense."

"So it's right? That's meaning of toe."

"This is just silly, Alejandro. I didn't know you could be this silly, to tell you the truth."

"But why you write about this?"

"I write about this just because thinking about it fertilizes my imagination, you know what I mean?"

"No," he says firmly, and the honesty with which he admits it makes something perfectly clear to me: this is what I love him for. I want to put my arms around him and plant a loud kiss on his cheek.

"Okay, I'll try to explain. It's something that I don't know how to tell you, Alejandro. It's as though someone is dictating these words to me, and I'm just writing them down. Like automatic writing. It's not something I decided, or planned, to write—it was decided for me. Every word is a surprise and a revelation."

"You have revelations, so you prophet? Prophet Galia?"

"Of course not. I'm just trying to tell you…I hear it like listening to a dictation. A little bit at a time. Whatever is dictated to me, I record. I'll give you an example. Suppose I were writing this…this piece about the dynasty of ancient kings that makes you come up with those crazy theories. Suppose the dictation stopped for a minute, or maybe I just stopped listening. So as a result I'd be left without a name for Judah's younger brother who ruled after Judah died. I'd wait patiently and suddenly the name Jonathan would be dictated. Then I would do some research—I would do it only after the dictation, not before. And the research would confirm that the name of the king who ruled after Judah was really Jonathan. So tell me—how could I know it before I looked it up? Who is doing the dictation?"

"This is nonsense to me. Nonsense." He repeats this word forcefully, stressing both syllables—"Non-sense"—then adds significantly, "I know something you don't know."

I want to say that he sounds like a little boy when he says this, but I keep it to myself, because I know that a man who doesn't want to be thought of as a little boy wants one thing: respect. That is, not counting the usual thing that men want from women.

"I know something," he repeats darkly. "I'm trying to protect you from it."

I'm not asking him what he is trying to protect me from. Boys who want to be men love creating mysteries in which they assign to themselves the part of a hero who rescues a damsel in distress. But whatever dangers await me in Alejandro's imagination, I'd rather let them stay there, because to dissuade him from his role as my savior might result in his losing interest in me altogether. His interest is so recent, so new, and so tenuous that I fear a wrong word might blow it away.

"If you stop writing about your ancestors and posting it online, then maybe I help you stay alive," he says glumly.

"This sounds so ominous, Alejandro. You know this word—'ominous'?"

"No, Galia, I don't know this word 'ominous.' You think life is words? You think death is words? Life can change to death without any words. And you won't even know that I was man who did it."

"Did what?"

"Person who changed life to death."

"If you want to frighten me, Alejandro, you should try something more direct. And anyway, I'm not writing about my ancestors. I told you, what I write. It's fiction."

"Fiction," he says scornfully. He thinks for a moment, then repeats, "Fiction!" with a loud snort.

———◆———

He says no to my sandwiches and to my other unappetizing donations. He sits on a stepladder with his coffee, cradling the paper cup with both hands as if to warm them.

"Are you cold?" I ask.

"No."

"The way you're holding your cup. Like you're warming your fingers."

He says, "It's September," as if telling me how dumb it is to suggest that he might want to warm himself in this weather. I'm so used to reading between the lines with him that when he says "September," I think what else can his naming the month point to. I become so enmeshed in the silence between us that if I don't say something in the next thirty seconds, it might suck me in.

"What did you used to do in September when you were young?" Nothing else comes to my mind but this boring question.

"I took care of Maryam," he says after a long pause.

I thought he would say "spend time with friends" or "play ball" or something equally innocent. I don't like the sound of this "Maryam"; she must have been a wife—early marriage is common in the part of the world he is from.

"Who is Maryam?" I ask suspiciously.

"My sheep."

What a relief. Not a wife…just a ewe. I was a fool for being jealous of a sheep. I don't want to ask him any more questions, but he breaks his silence himself.

"My father had a farm," he says. "Many sheeps. My brothers spent all day with sheeps."

"Sheep," I correct him gently. "Irregular plural."

"Sheep. At first I was little, then I grew and I had my own…how you say?"

"Flock?"

"Yes. Flock. Ten sheeps—"

"Sheep."

"Ten sheep, and I cared for them. One year, two years, everything good, every sheep healthy. Then one girl sheep was sick."

"A female sheep is a ewe."

"You sheep?" he smiles. "You, that's right. My favorite you, Maryam. I gave her food from my hands. When I was in school and my brothers put food in front of her like to all sheep, the others see food in front of them, they eat, but Maryam, no, she turn away. She didn't want to eat like all sheep. She wait for me. I come from school, I run to Maryam, she run to me, I give her food from my hands." He is silent for a moment. "Even when she was sick, she run to me. It was hard for her, but she run. One day I came from school and my mother says Maryam disappeared, and I go to Maryam, and she is not there. We look everywhere, every grass, every field. No Maryam. And then we hear that neighbor's son take our sheep and cut up and sold the meat and wool to make money for smoke and other things…The neighbor says to me, 'If you want, I kill him for you.' I say no, that won't bring my Maryam back."

"That's nice that you told him to spare his son," I say.

Alejandro says, "Ugh," and I'm afraid that he might think my comment ironic. I must quickly correct this impression to show him that making fun of him was not at all what I had in mind.

"You really loved that sheep," I say, and even before I finish saying it, I realize how lame this sounds.

He throws away his paper cup, and I ask him why all the workers throw their cups into our living room. He says it doesn't matter, it'll be cleaned up when they do the floor. "Now it's all garbage," he says firmly with a resolute wave of both arms as he turns away and walks upstairs to work on second-floor bathroom walls.

———•———

I bought the wrong kind of grout, and he's helping me carry three bags of it back to my car so I can exchange them in the tile store for the right kind. I tell him I had no idea that floor grout was any different from wall grout. He smiles knowingly at my innocence, and again I'm charmed by his pride, the childlike way he has of showing that he knows more about construction than I do. I also think that the reason he is acting like a gentleman today, carrying these heavy bags for me, must have something to do with his wanting to acknowledge that he likes me. I'm so touched by this rare sign of attention that when I come back from the tile store and he helps me carry the new bags out of the car, I bravely ask him to look at a dresser I've been painting and tell me if the top looks right to him. I show him the dresser and wait for his reaction.

"You had to sand it first," he says, "because you see this?" He slides his finger along the painted surface so I can see how rough it is. I also see little hairs from the brush that got stuck in the paint.

"Cheap brush," he says with a disdainful look at my collection of brushes. "I give you my. Okay? I wash for you." He runs to the backyard to wash his good brush in a vat full of rainwater. I sit on my haunches next to him and dip my cheap brushes in the water. He shakes his brush in the water and comments on the whitish circles it makes: "Acrylic paint, water based. No thinner."

I make similar whitish circles.

"It's like making scrambled eggs," I say lightly, hoping he'll smile at this, but he continues to stir with a thoughtful air.

I decide to try again. "Tina de lavar," I say a Spanish word I remember from college. Again no reaction. "It's Spanish for 'a wash tub,'" I inform this man who, according to his story, lived in Mexico long enough to know every word I struggle to remember from my studies.

"Yes, Galia. Tina de lavar." A few more minutes of this dreamy stirring of paint-filled water and I'll be so fused with him that I won't be able to stand up.

"What are you thinking about, Alejandro?"

I catch a quick look of surprise, as if no one had ever expressed any interest in his thoughts, as if the very fact of my question is beyond what he considers proper. He stands up, shakes the brush so vigorously that droplets of water fly in every direction. Like a good pupil, I do the same with my cheap brushes.

"I told you about neighbor. You know that I was, how you say…kidding?"

I don't know what neighbor he is talking about. Is he talking about my neighbor Brad, who is so bored at home that he feels he has a right to come over any time and stay here for hours, criticizing every step of the construction and ordering workers around? When I asked Brad to leave, Tom said, "Galia, rule number one when doing construction on a street like yours is keeping neighbors happy. Having your neighbor here acting like he's boss is better than having him threaten us with filing violations, you understand?"

I ask Alejandro if he is talking about Brad, but he reacts as though I have offended him, and I apologize for not realizing he is talking about his childhood neighbor, the one whose son killed Maryam, the sheep that used to eat from Alejandro's hands. But he isn't interested in my apology. He wants to make sure that I know he was just kidding about the neighbor. He repeats, "Just kidding about Ahmed!"

"So who is Ahmed?"

"I said it to see if you believe, how you say, stereotype? That you people have about us? Like we are all just shepherds and olive farmers, that we don't know about things like science and self-discipline, and that a father can want to kill his son just for nothing."

"So you never had the ewe called Maryam? And your neighbor's son didn't kill it? That whole story you told me, it was just to see if I believed the stereotype?"

"Maryam was real." He frowns as if thinking of the ewe still gives him pain. "But my neighbor Ahmed didn't say he kill his son for it."

I want to say, "So how did I do? Did I pass? You wanted to see if I have a stereotype that 'you people' have of 'us,' and did I fail your expectations?" But standing next to him in my backyard, watching white swirls of paint and dirt in the tina de lavar, I become tongue-tied. I want to tell him about this too, about how I become tongue-tied around him and how I can feel the flow of his thoughts in my own body and how distressing it is because even though I can feel them, I don't know what they are.

"Alejandro," I say quietly, "why did you look me up online?"

He stands still, the brush in his half-raised hand, a look on his face as though I have caught him in a crime. Now I realize that all the little things I said to him in the last few days were leading up to this question.

"I didn't," he says at last.

"Then how did you know I was writing about those ancient Jewish kings?"

He stands still again. He shrugs. He lowers his hand with the brush. He opens his mouth to say something and decides against it. He runs toward the house and down the steps to the basement. I want to shout after him, "Only someone who is interested in me would bother looking me up online!" But he is already inside. If I follow him, it might look like I'm pestering him. I will myself to stop. I'll wait for another chance to ask him about this, and if he runs away again, I'll have to conclude that Alejandro the wall painter has more surprises up his sleeve than a doctorate in marine biology, a childhood as a Palestinian shepherd boy, and an indefinite number of wives spread over several continents. I would have to think that this man who ignores me, runs away from my questions, begrudges me my success with the Venetian stucco door, and doesn't observe elementary rules of politeness when I bring him coffee or sandwiches has developed a morbid interest in me. It's this interest that makes him think of me when he is finally home, after a day of ignoring me at work, and it's this interest that makes him do more than simply look me up online: he actually reads the many pages I post on the writers' forum. The fact that he misunderstands the nature and the purpose of my writing is far less important than the fact of his interest.

ALEJANDRO

She shows me her brushes and I say these are shitty brushes, the cheapest kind, and she laughs when I say "shitty," as if the way I say it is so funny that she just can't help it. Just like that time when I said it about the Venetian stucco she put on the bathroom door, and she went around telling everyone how I said "Shitty job." Today I was trying to be nice to her. I said, "I let you borrow my brush." Tom gets high-quality brushes, not the kind she buys because she doesn't know any better. She agreed to try my brush for painting her furniture, which is another silly thing she does. I don't tell her that no one paints furniture with red or purple wall paint. It's the kind of thing people just don't do, and I won't even talk about it, period. I point at the uneven surface and say, you should've sanded it first. She's a woman, what does she know about sanding? I would have to do it for her, but I work for Tom, and he is not going to pay me extra for sanding her silly dresser. I point at brush hairs under the coat of paint and say, "Here's my high quality brush for you," and then I give it another thought and decide to be even more generous: "Okay, I'll wash it for you."

She follows me to the backyard with her cheap brushes and sits next to me. When I dip my brush in the water, she dips hers, and we sit there, and I think my own thoughts, about how she always follows me and how this stands in the way of my carrying out the task, because even though I don't have the feelings for her that the Professor accuses me of having, I do feel something, and whatever it is, it makes it hard for me to accomplish my task. But I must do it. She says something in Spanish, and when I don't react, she acts surprised as though she expected me to know everything in Spanish because in the beginning she thought I was Mexican, and now she is confused about me. She doesn't know that I lived in Mexico long enough to learn some Spanish, which doesn't mean I have to know every single word. Like how to say "wash tub" in Spanish. "Tina de lavar," she says proudly, as though she knows something I don't know. Her Spanish pronunciation is the worst I've heard in years.

When she sits on her haunches next to me near the wash tub, I think how easy it would be to push her head into the water. So quick, she won't even suffer. I can hear the Professor saying, "Don't let go of this chance." But then I hear Tom's voice saying, "Why was my client found dead in the backyard of her own house and who pushed her head in the water when there was no one there but you?" So I let it go. The Professor is my boss and Tom is my boss, and they pull me in opposite directions.

And then there's Galia. She stands up when I stand up, she shakes her brush when I shake mine, she's like a trusting puppy that follows its master's every movement. This trust makes it even harder for me. I'm now like one of those tender-hearted Western men who spend all their time examining their feelings this way and that way, and when it's time to act, they are so entangled in their feelings they can't do a thing. Never thought it could happen to me. Now I begin to regret having told her about my childhood and how I loved Maryam. I don't even know how she managed to pull this out of me, how she made me tell her everything. One thing I didn't tell her though was how this thing with Maryam changed me. It hardened me, because only years later I understood that it was after what Ahmed's son did to Maryam and I saw her wool in his hands that I stopped being the boy I used to be and became what I am today.

On the other hand, sitting next to Galia, standing next to her, missing chance after chance to carry out my task and fulfill my responsibility to the Professor, I may no longer be the man I am—or was. I've changed so much that I don't even know if I can accomplish this mission. And just at the moment when this thought dawns on me, she demands to know why I looked her up online. "I didn't," I say, because it's true. It was the Professor who showed me her *Chronicle*. Should I tell her that I don't have time for looking up anyone online? That I'm too busy for such nonsense? When I come home after a twelve-hour workday and an hour-long train ride, all I want is to take a quick shower and collapse in bed.

CHAPTER 3

THE HASMONEAN CHRONICLE

———◆———

A FEW DAYS AFTER THE feast with the peace seekers—who proved to the Maccabees the high quality of the grain and other provisions they had gifted them following God's edicts—the Maccabees defeated the small Assyrian force at Nahal el-Haramiah. It was as though the prophesied victory couldn't wait, as though it was hiding right around the corner. It came almost as soon as the battle began and with hardly any loss of Maccabean blood.

By then the Maccabean meant not only the five brothers—Judah, Jonathan, Eleazar, Simon, and John Gaddi—but the whole army of traditionalist Jews who defied Antiochus's edict to worship the Olympian idols and who couldn't forget the loss of a thousand women, children, infants, and old men; hundreds had been massacred in the space of three days and hundreds more sold into slavery on the orders of the same Antiochus who had sacked Jerusalem and whose protégé Apollonius was among the first to fall in this most propitious battle.

Judah removed the sword from the hand of the corpse that had ruled Samaria, and later, at night, when everyone slept exhausted by the day's battle, he cleaned and shined the blade until it gave off a light of its own. In the morning he announced to the citizens of Samaria their freedom from the pagan yoke. As he spoke to the crowd of Samaritans, he held the sword in his raised hand. The crowd did not need to be told who it had belonged to—they all knew that the man who ruled them so ruthlessly lay dead. In Judah's hands, the sword became more than a mere weapon, because by fulfilling one prophecy—Mattathias's last words to Judah were now common knowledge—it became a promise of more prophecies similarly fulfilled, although not as easily as the victory at Nahal el-Haramiah.

The people remembered Judah's first entrance into the Temple, when he had laid his eyes on the defilement inflicted by Antiochus's lackeys. Now, at his return to it, they gathered to celebrate. Pigs' heads and tails had been removed from the Temple and carried far out of Jerusalem in order not to contaminate anyone inside the city walls.

The guests poured in, looking for empty seats on the long benches that lined the walls of the reception hall. This was a very special occasion indeed: the return to Jerusalem and the rededication of the Temple.

"How many millennia does one have to live to witness a miracle?" Judah asked the guests.

He spoke to the guests, the Sadducees and the Pharisees and the Essenes, and to those simple souls who did not belong to any faction but had helped him win battle after battle. He said it was the fervor of these simple souls that he valued most in battle, because it was not just the fighting of Greeks or Jews that mattered, as it was not simply mortal men fighting each other but the gods of the Greeks with the God of the Jews—and this is where faith mattered, he said. In his speech, as at a start of battle, Judah was carried along by a force. The force knew what he had to say, so he didn't have to make any decisions because the words came naturally to him and at the right time, like fruit falls from a tree: all he had to do was adjust his energy to the flow of the force, and the force took over. Now the force was saying, "Behold the visitors!"

Later, when he had time to think, he began to doubt it was really the force that had said those words or any of the words that followed. He noticed that Yemin, his right-hand man, was no longer by his side, and strange as it was not to have Yemin near, it was even stranger to see a man of Yemin's stature standing in the back of the hall, behind the benches, in the dark corner near a back wall. Judah heard the clamor of the guests change abruptly from a roar into a stunned silence, as if indeed there was a miracle being performed. He felt it with his whole being, down to the small hairs on the back of his neck, which were rising as though magnetized. He turned around slowly, so as not to appear undignified in case whatever it was behind him had the power not only to surprise him but to awe him as well. When he turned and saw the three visitors, he no longer cared about appearing dignified.

"You spoiled the vision," he rebuked Yemin later, when the hall was being cleaned by Idumean servant girls who had been instructed not to utter a word of what they had heard, under the penalty of death.

"You, Yemin, with your face to that back wall, either imagined or dreamed it in your half-sleep, and with the grain of doubt growing and overshadowing the vision, you transmitted it to me. Everything I saw and heard was marred by your doubt, and I no longer know whether it was real or not. What can I do now, my Yemin?"

Yemin said, "You are simply upset that they appeared to me and not to you. No one denies that you, Judah Maccabeus, are a great hero and that you shall live in legend far longer than in the flesh, while I, your comrade-in-arms who followed you into every battle, shall die nameless and forgotten by my descendants. If our forefathers had appeared to you, you would have been held responsible by future generations for any flaw in the retelling of the vision. Any other man as unremarkable as me could have been our forefathers' choice. But I'm close to you in mind and spirit; that is why they chose me over other unremarkable men. It was my devotion that saw them in the shimmering, similar to the kind you experienced upon meeting your second wife, a simple village girl and not anyone's wife yet."

"Your words are disrespectful on the surface, my Yemin, but I sense the truth of them. You know me quite well, and I must admit that what you say about my feelings upon meeting my wife is true, and although the shimmering between us has dimmed, there are still moments when it attains its full power like in the early days when the Greek boy-god, whose name I prefer to forget, made Nehora and myself targets of his arrow practice."

Yemin said, as softly as before: "I heard voices in the silence, and I knew it was the three visitors speaking to each other loudly enough to be overheard, yet quietly enough for anyone listening to realize that this was a very private conversation, the kind that happens in a dream with the soul of a dear departed, and the fact that I was allowed to eavesdrop on it had to do with a wish of these visitors to make the private public, a custom that has much to recommend itself, certainly more than keeping the private private, a practice that would have deprived the people of His Word.

"I saw a house being built. Some of the builders, who had already finished the foundation and most of the first floor, were now working on divisions between rooms on the second floor. That was when one of the visitors, who until that moment was standing with the other two to the left of the construction site, went up to the master builder and asked if the floor they were working on was intended for him, and when the master builder said no, his was actually the foundation, the patriarch exclaimed, 'What? You're putting me in the pit?', whereupon the master builder explained that the pit was not quite the right word for the lovely quarters they had built for him, and as the foundation had been completed, he offered to give Abraham a tour, to which Abraham grudgingly acquiesced.

"'This would be your own room,' said the master builder, after they went down a few newly built steps, 'And this,' he said with a circular gesture, inviting Abraham to make himself comfortable, 'is the room of your miracle. Since it was the first major one, it has become the foundation of our faith, which explains why we placed you in the foundation of the house.'

"'Which miracle was that?' Abraham grumbled like the old man he was, and the master builder hurriedly reminded him, 'The one where your own beloved son, lying tied on top of a mountain like a sacrificial lamb, was spared death by his father, the one in which your own hand with a knife raised over his shivering form had let go of the weapon. The one in which your faith had been tested, don't you see it reenacted again and again?'

"The master builder pointed at the center of the room, which was round and elevated to look like the top of the famous mountain, but Abraham shrugged and said that it was a pity he had misunderstood His command and had been ready to sacrifice his own son, which had scarred poor Isaac for the rest of his life.

"'The misunderstanding was a lesser miracle,' the master builder said quickly, 'We moved it into a corner, as you can see.'

"He pointed to what would have been a corner if the room hadn't been completely round. At this point the distinguished visitor expressed a wish to go outside, for the lack of air in the foundation was hard to tolerate. The builder obliged, supporting the old man as he climbed up the stairs, while Abraham moaned and complained of pain in his knees and back. When he rejoined the little group and told the other two visitors what he had seen, they too expressed a wish to see their quarters.

"It was the turn of Moses to look at the first floor with its large parlor, the far side of which was divided evenly into ten spaces, one for each of the plagues, the builder explained. When Moses gave his guide a look of utter incomprehension, the man hurriedly listed the plagues, pointing at each of the stalls:

"'Blood in rivers. Frogs. Lice. Wild animals. Pestilence. Boils. Hail. Locusts. Darkness. Deaths of the first-born.'

"'But you're housing miracles like livestock in a barn!' Moses said with indignation so terrible it made the man tremble with fear that the old one's next miracle might well be directed at the poor builder himself. In his defense he said that, indeed, this was to be a house of miracles, and it was being built according to specific instructions they received from you-know-who, as each miracle was to be preserved for future generations 'intact,' the instructions said, and as the space was limited, and as there were so many miracles to be housed on the first floor, they were forced to…as you can see, we have them all here.

"'Is that my burning bush?' Moses said in a voice that the master builder would hear in his sleep every night to the end of his days. They were both looking at the center of the room.

"'This is not for me to say,' the master builder said diffidently. 'We're building to exact specifications…We invent nothing…'

"'Very well,' said Moses, 'I shall speak with the one who's behind it all.'

"He went outside and told the other two what he had seen, whereupon the third one, known for his wisdom, said he would pass on the tour of the second floor, and not only that, he said firmly to the disappointed builder, he also wanted to offer his own part of the house to the Maccabees, because their miracle was the kind that would light up the hearts, while his was merely wisdom.

"You remember, Judah," said Yemin, "After I mentally transmitted these words to you and you said them out loud to the public, the people began to stir. The people have done plenty of listening; they demanded to see the shimmering patriarchs and the house of miracles with their own eyes. The benches were creaking as the men were stretching their arms and legs, an exercise you taught them to perform before battle as it helped them to restrain themselves from un-controllable movements, such as lunging at an enemy just when that enemy was ready to chop off their heads or pierce them with a sword, and the restraint had worked wonders as it allowed our men to prevail not merely by staying alive or eliminating the enemy but by taking the enemy alive in order to make him talk. Sometimes making them talk was more important than silencing them forever, you used to say."

"True," said Judah.

"But this time," Yemin continued, "the creaking benches and the stretching of limbs had nothing to do with conducting themselves a certain way in battle. It only signified their desire to see the house of miracles and to walk where the forefathers had walked—the foundation, the first floor, the second, and all the adjoining wings—and when they were told that the Shimmering Ones appeared only to one man, of all the ones gathered here, they appeared only to Yemin—not even to great Judah himself!—the people were offended. They felt especially hurt that on a day like today, a day like no other, they had been treated to a scam, a fraud, a swindle. What little shimmering they were able to see for themselves was quite formless to them, and as they could see neither the house under con-struction nor the patriarchs themselves, they became quite agitated. Someone shouted, 'Impostors!' More voices joined in, and soon a loud outcry shook the hall: 'Impostors! All three of them! Bring water, pour it on them! That'll teach them how to fool us with their shining!'"

"And then you, Judah, rushed to the center of the hall where the Shimmering Ones stood still, as though they couldn't believe that this blaspheming crowd had descended from the same people they had led out of captivity and protected and ruled with patience and wisdom. No, these must be some other people, if they couldn't recognize their own forefathers, shimmering and translucent though they were. You held your arms wide apart as though to protect them from the crowd, but your outstretched arms must have seemed more of a menace than a comfort to them as their shimmering grew duller and soon dimmed altogether.

"'No!' you cried, "We are still your people! Your great-great, and so forth, sons! But we're tired of old stories and thirsty for new miracles. I wish to ask you...'

you lowered yourself on your knees, 'to address the assembly, one of you, or all three of you…if you could give meaning to us, something to raise our spirits and give us hope, a true speech, words that come directly from God. Inspired words are what we need, because we are a people that cannot live without inspiration.'

"'What inspiration do you want other than the miracle of the oil, which will shortly take place in the Temple?' said Abraham.

"'No,' said Moses decisively. 'Words are not the way to impress a new miracle onto the weary consciousness of our people. We must create a symbol strong enough to be reenacted every year, for millennia. It shall be called Hanukkah, and it shall be born thus. First, we must make them see the small cruse of oil, the only one that is still sealed. Then we must impress upon them that there is no oil left anywhere else. They must see it with their own eyes: not a drop, anywhere.'

"'We don't have to try very hard since they've seen empty jars lying among the refuse that littered the Temple. The Greeks had opened them and poured the oil out just to spite us,' you said.

"'Still, it would be nice to impress it upon their consciousness how little there is, or was. How it can't last longer than a day,' said Solomon.

"'And when it does…' said Moses.

"'There's your miracle,' said Abraham.

"'You don't mean,' you said to them, "you don't mean to say that all miracles…are made like this?'

"In the beginning you thought you knew exactly which one was which, but now, watching as one passed a small cruse of oil to another, and that one passed it to the third with a huge white beard, you realized that what you were witnessing was more than just a vision, more even than a miracle—it was a coming together of three distinct eras of history, and these layers, these eras needed you to do something for them: only you could do it, but you didn't know it yet.

"'Take this, Judah,' said one of the three, handing you the small cruse.

"'That one is Abraham,' I told you mentally.

"'No, no, he's Abraham,' said the forefather. 'Me, I'm Moses of the burning bush and the ten plagues. I hope you can remember all of them.'

"'I know the stories,' you said sullenly, like a child scolded by a teacher.

"'Not stories!' said Solomon strictly. 'Not stories!'

"'I didn't mean it the way you think I did. There are stories that give birth to a nation. There's no nation without its stories. And these are ours.'

"'That's right,' said the one who had earlier identified himself as Moses. 'You wouldn't be a nation without these...how you say it...these not-stories. They are—'

"'Truth-messages? God words?' you suggested.

"'In your case, they shall be all of it, and history too,' said Abraham weightily. 'Now, take this cruse from me. Make sure every man in the crowd gets a chance to see how little oil you have here. When you turn back to look at us, we shall be gone. Now, go on, face them.'"

When Judah turned to face the people, he saw that their eyes were measuring the oil in the jar and he saw them thinking: "It will last a day; nay, not even a day," none of them foreseeing what was about to happen, that for the next two thousand years the eight days of the oil would be reenacted annually, and that a candlestick or a lamp of every possible shape would be lit, one candle per day, every year for the millennia and another millennia—and how many years does it come to? How many menorahs? How many presents, if we count one per day, per child?

Judah walked over to the door of the hall with the jar in his careful hands, and the men followed him silently, obeying the mute call of oil that was yet to transform itself into a miracle, and just as he was stepping outside and thinking that soon he would be in the Temple, pouring the contents of the small jar into the first lamp, there was a loud bleating and he saw three of his men chase an animal outside.

"A stubborn one," commented one of the men as he helped the others push the ewe out the door.

Exactly at that moment his wife, Nehora of the merciful water jug, ran in and almost collided with the ewe. "'Tis she!" cried Nehora.

But Judah was in no mood for a family scene, not even one involving his current wife and his old one, who was not so old to tell the truth, and if her slightly frayed coat could be overlooked, not so ugly either.

He opened his mouth to shout, "Let her go!" but instead of words, something like a bleating came out, and while his men looked at him with horror, the sheep gaily ambled toward him and rubbed against his side. He transferred the jar into his left hand and buried the fingers of his right one in his first wife's fleece. The occasion was not the most suitable one for a public display of affection for a number of reasons, one of them being the sheer importance of today's proceedings, history-in-the-making or history-in-reverse, the past as seen through the prism of the future, very unusual indeed. But what could he do if he was living in the beginning and not at the end of things, and when so much that was meant to happen hadn't happened yet, and somehow it depended on him, Judah, to make it all happen? Every small gesture counted, every movement he made was to be seen in the light of history, and who was he to say, living as he was in the relative beginning of things, whether the delay due to his burying his fingers in his ex-wife's fleece could affect the future of his people?

Hadn't he searched far and wide for this wife? Whether or not she was a sheep now, what mattered was that she was, finally, beside her husband, and he had no right to hurry her, nor to nudge her away, no matter what symbols of faith were waiting to be created by him, symbols that would keep his people together, despite their imminent dispersal to the four corners of the world. Yet wasn't it just this that the Shimmering Ones impressed upon him, and what his faithful Yemin told him? And wasn't this the reason behind their coming here and their giving him this oil, which was more than oil, and even more than a miracle, because miracles have a tendency to lose potency after a number of years, his wife's fleece being one such miracle? But a promise to keep his people together as a nation throughout centuries of dispersal—no, this was no old wife's fleece. His hand was still in it, and he was cooing sweet words to her as she continued to rub her sheep face on his thighs. History would wait. Nationhood, faith…all that would wait. This was the mother of his sons, and in whatever shape she chose to come, and no matter what her reasons were for coming to him at this moment instead of any other during the years he searched for her, she had a right to his time and affection. Nehora stood aside and gazed at her husband caressing the sheep with tenderness he gave her during the day but without the passion she knew so well at night, and she too felt tenderness for this poor wife. She came close to the two of them and murmured softly in the animal's ear, "Let's step outside. You'll come back to us again. We want you with us. We love you." And the sheep followed the woman.

Judah stood by the altar, and as he was about to pour a few drops of oil into each of the seven lamps, the jar in his hand reflected the light that wasn't coming yet from the menorah because it was still unlit. But the light was there, the light was of the future, and as he looked at the men around him, he saw their faces lit by the glow of this future light, and he saw everything that would come from this moment, all the prayers for all the Hannukahs for millennia to come, and all the humiliations, all the expulsions, and all the massacres, but he couldn't remember the details because they flashed by so quickly, and the men behind the menorah were still saying the words of a prayer when the vision evaporated and his hand dropped the first drop of oil into the first lamp.

It was much later, after five years of war, as Judah was getting his men ready for the battle at Elasa—against twenty thousand infantry and two thousand cavalry led by Bacchides, and not by Nicanor, the Seleucid army general he had defeated at the Battle of Adasa—that the miracle of the oil came to haunt him.

He was convinced that the miracle would be repeated, but this time with men. The numbers of Bacchides's men and their ammunition and horses exceeded his by such a wide margin that only a miracle could bring victory. Judah was summoning the Shimmering Ones, and as they were not coming, he tried to lure them with new promises. They still did not appear, and he thought that perhaps he had become too much of a doer, a quality important in a commander but superfluous in a visionary. He told himself that just for these few days before the battle he should again become the man he was when the Shimmering Ones spoke to him, first through Yemin, his right-hand man, then without an intermediary of any kind.

Since Yemin had been killed in battle two months after the rededication of the temple, he had only himself to rely on now. He called them by name; he reiterated old prayers and made up new ones. He begged them for a sign, anything to get if not a hope of victory, at least guidance as to the next step he should take. Yet there was absolutely nothing in response to his pleas. Were they tired of him? Were his pleas expressed in a tone that repelled them? If so, what tone was right? What had he been then that he wasn't now? How could he improve his ties to the Shimmering Ones so they would not only hear him but be willing to respond and offer their help if he asked? And what if thinking of them as the Shimmering Ones was the problem; when and why did he begin calling them that? He remembered: it was simply the experience of seeing them as transmitted through Yemin, his comrade and bodyguard. They shimmered in the banquet hall; therefore to call them the Shimmering Ones was a statement of fact.

Yet how much of a fact was it, his seeing them through Yemin? Some in the crowd said that they, too, saw a certain glow, but for them it was not bright enough, and not continuous enough, to form any recognizable shapes. A little glow, that's all they saw. There was no need for him to remind himself that not only had he seen them fully outlined, but that they actually spoke to him, and if he referred to them as the Shimmering Ones, it was out of a kind of modesty, if you will, out of respect that didn't permit him to call them by names that were so well-known that they could make the whole thing a travesty. "I saw Abraham, Moses, and Solomon! The forefathers spoke to me! Abraham said this, and Moses said that, and Solomon tried to reconcile the two of them in his famous Solomonic way, and one of them, the one whom I mistook for Abraham, gave me the small jar of oil, and seeing my mistake, identified himself as Moses of the ten plagues." Imagine saying: "Moses gave me the jar!" It would have sounded immature, almost boyish. Calling them the Shimmering Ones was not only a mark of respect; it camouflaged their identities, too well known in his circle.

Seeing his men asleep on the ground and in makeshift tents, he smiled at the word "circle." Is that what they were for him, these ragged, disheveled men, embracing their primitive weapons in their sleep? His circle. He remembered his childhood, playing with his brothers outside their father's house. Mattathias was gone now. His brothers, all four of them, were among these sleeping men, hugging their weapons instead of wives. As for the wives, it was better not to think of them, not to start on that slippery slope of longing, because this was the kind of thinking that weakened a man, and he must not let himself weaken on the night of a battle.

The Shimmering Ones heard him after all, because even though they did not appear to him in person, they sent their emissaries. There was a rustling, a hushed voice and then another, and footsteps and another kind of sound he couldn't place, and then they appeared, his two women, or more correctly: his two wives, the woman and the ewe. They came to wish him luck in the coming battle and to say good-bye, without knowing whether this good-bye might actually be the last one. They lay down on both sides of him, and as he caressed the fleece of one and the hair of the other, he thought he saw the shimmering, far off in the distance, and it moved, or seemed to move, with the unevenness of a dreamed-up glow— yet he knew that he wasn't dreaming. His wives knew that too, and Nehora's fingers ran through his hair and then just as gently through the sheep wife's fleece, mixing the two together, entangling them, as though unable to tell where his hair ended and her fleece began. He must have closed his eyes for a moment, because the shimmering was suddenly so close that it appeared to hang right above him, and despite the darkness he had no trouble recognizing Solomon.

"Wrong again," the shape said. "Not Solomon. Moses. He of the Ten Plagues and the Ten Commandments."

"Ah! Forgive my mistake…You are alone, so I thought…I do hope the other two are fine."

"They are fine, but a little under the weather. Old age, you know. Even with us, it counts for something."

"I thought that at this stage of development it no longer mattered. I'm so happy that you have come. I begged and begged…waited and waited. I need your advice very urgently."

"And my advice you shall certainly have," said the enterprising prophet, shimmering above the man, the ewe, and the woman, but visible only to the man. "To be honest, I had no desire to come here today, but the others sent me to you because they are worried. We all are. So I have come, despite my usual aches and pains, and now I command you to rouse your men and leave, before the battle begins tomorrow morning."

"Oh no, I can't," said Judah, automatically reverting to his old belief that the ignominy of a cowardly escape was more frightening that the possibility of defeat.

Moses must have read his thoughts because he said, "Not just a possibility, Judah. Not even a probability. A definite end."

"Thank you for coming," said Judah slowly. "And thank you for the advice. But I shall not follow it, not because I wish to disobey you, but because I cannot obey. I cannot run. Running is not part of my destiny."

"You shall do as I say, Judah. Or you shall perish."

"Fine," Judah said, with his eyes half-closed. "So I shall perish. This will be my last sleep then."

"No, not sleep," said Nehora quietly, and he was awed once again by the generosity of her love. The sheep guarded them, standing a little apart, facing away from the couple, and when the man and the woman rested from love, the ewe caressed the man's face with its tongue, and this mute caress made him smile as he lay on the ground with Nehora.

When he awoke in the morning, the shimmering was gone. The wives, both the woman and the sheep, lay next to him. He went to rouse his men, going from one to the other, with a call to battle that was no less sure of victory than any of his previous calls to battles that had been won, again and again. None of the men knew what he knew, either because he had buried the knowledge too deep inside himself or because he simply denied the defeat foretold at night by Moses. His army was ready to take off, when something stopped the men in the front row, and then in the next, and so forth, until the whole host stood still. He looked where they looked but saw nothing.

"What are you looking at?" he asked Jonathan, his brother and his second commander-in-chief. "If you get transfixed by clouds, how shall we be able to fight?"

"Those are not clouds, Judah, and we shall not fight today. We are told to turn around and walk away, and no matter how profoundly we respect your orders, we shall obey this command as it comes from an authority higher than yours."

"Whatever it is you see there," Judah said, "you shall stay and we shall have yet another victory."

"Not only shall we not win, but our defeat is going to be so total, it'll set us back for years to come. Leave with us, Judah."

"I shan't," he said firmly. "If you want to go, go. I stay."

They left, guided by a shimmering invisible to Judah, because the miracle of the light comes only to those who are willing to see it, and as he was set against their advice, the Shimmering Ones had abandoned him. So it is perfectly understandable that his chest was pierced by the enemy sword in the very beginning of the battle, which ended almost as soon as it began, a defeat as prophesied.

GALIA

One day I see Alejandro working inside a wooden enclosure the crew built in front of my house to keep onlookers out. I walk into it and stand near him. I try to resist a wave of attraction, which makes me so dizzy that I almost fall. I'm searching for something to say and not finding anything, because the happiness I feel in his presence is so extreme it shuts down the thinking.

"Galia," he says in a voice that vibrates with deep feeling. With bated breath, I wait for him to say the words that will let me say that I, too, yes, I too…

He works in silence, visibly struggling with himself. I want him to say it. I want to hear it. It's the only thing I'm conscious of.

It comes at last, the confession of love. "How…" he says, stops, and then plunges forth, "How…long it take you to do that door?"

"Umm," I say. "A day? A day and a half?"

"Because," he speaks more calmly now, "I have evening job. You know."

"Yes, I know. You have these evening jobs. You work ten hours a day at this job, then you go to work somewhere else. I think it's too much work. You should rest once in a while."

"No. Rest, no. I like work! We do Venetian stucco in a big apartment too long. Already four weeks."

"Oh," I say quickly. "I could help! I can do it fast! Can I come and help?"

He takes so long to think this over, and with so much seriousness, it's as though I've just proposed marriage or some other indecent act that might break his loyalty to his wife, or wives, back home, wherever that home is.

"It's only men," he says darkly.

"So what?" I say.

"You are woman."

"It doesn't matter. I can do Venetian stucco. You saw my door. I can do it."

"Yes. Door. It had edges." He gestures to show the roughness of the edges.

"But I fixed it. You saw that I'd fixed the edges! Didn't you see it? And anyway, it was my first time. My second time will be perfect."

"We can't have woman there working with men."

"Please," I beg him. "Please…I'll help. I won't get in anyone's way."

I'm ready to do anything, hold up cans of paint, stand around with cups of coffee or beer or vodka, you name it, any subservient role a woman can play with a group of men working on Venetian stucco, just so I could go on feeling this energy that makes me so deliriously happy. I had never felt it in such an extreme way; it's like a drug. It's as though my brain was hit by a lightning rod and every pore of my body has been lit up.

But he has made a decision. "No," he says firmly. No woman belongs in the men's world of construction, wall painting, and Venetian stucco. Even if she did do her own Venetian stucco door. Even if she fixed those rough edges. The edges were too high up for her, so she stood on a chair and fixed them anyway. But that's the point—they were too high for her. She is a woman; she must remember that.

———•———

Next day I go down to the basement, expecting him to be there with his paint buckets and brushes. I don't see him at first in the semi-dark, so I walk around piles of sheetrock, beams, and pipes until I find him half-lying, half-sitting on the stripped floor. He is barefoot, his right leg extended and bleeding around the toes, and one toe seems to be hanging loose, and when I ask what happened, he says, "Nothing."

"That's very macho of you, Alejandro, but I can see you're hurt. Should I call an ambulance to take you to an emergency room?"

"No! No ambulance!" he roars with the ferocity that endeared him to me when we first met.

"But your toe is hanging. It's probably broken. They can do an X-ray and put it in a cast."

"Sticky strip," he mutters. "You have?"

"What sticky strip? You mean Band-Aid?"

"Yes. Band-Aid. And water. And towel. Paper towel."

"That's not going to be enough, Alejandro. You really need to have a doctor look at it.

"No insurance...no doctor!"

"If you go to the emergency room without medical insurance, they'll treat you anyway. For free. And if they won't, I'll pay for you. Just this once!"

"No! Woman no pay for man! " he roars. I notice that his English tends to deteriorate when he is under stress. "No emergency room! Strong man don't go to hospital! Band-Aid and paper towel!"

"Sure, just a second," I say meekly and run upstairs.

When I'm back, I rinse his foot carefully with water and pat it dry with a paper towel and tell him that when the bleeding stops, which it is bound to sooner or later, I'll try to make a splint for him. I'm afraid he'll reject this like he rejected the hospital and the doctor, but he accepts it readily and even says we'll make the splint together; he's good at this kind of thing. He tells me to bring more paper towels, a whole roll, maybe two, and a bucket of plaster from the storage place, which is what he calls the debris-free area in the basement where Tom has accumulated so many cans and buckets with various compounds that it takes me a long time to check labels on all of them. When I finally find the one I need and tell him it's too heavy for me to lift and carry over to him, he says if I just open it and spoon some into a bowl, that'll be enough. I bring him a bowl of plaster, and he dips paper towels into the bowl of plaster and fashions something that looks like a small bow. He puts his toe on it and molds it until it's the right shape and size.

"Look here, Galia, we made a splint."

I say, "It's more like a cast." What I really want to say is that I admire his skill and that he could work in the emergency room making casts for patients instead of painting walls for Tom's clients, but the fear of his reaction to the words "emergency room" stops me and I say nothing.

———————

I don't even need to listen for his footsteps or look out the window to know he's coming out of the house or going in or doing work in the smaller bedroom of the third floor. I always know where he is. I don't need to look at a watch to know it's five o'clock and he's leaving my house because my house is his work. It happens every day, and I can't let this happen anymore. He's halfway to the subway stop already, and I won't catch him if I walk or run. So I get into my car and drive until I see him walking in front of me. He is talking on his cell phone. I slow down. I shout, Alejandro! He sees me, puts away his phone, and comes over to the car.

"I was going to a store," I lie to save face. "And then I saw you. Walking there. Talking on your phone. So I thought I could give you a ride to the subway."

He gets into the car. "I not go to Manhattan today," he says. "I go home."

"No Venetian stucco today?" I'm making it sound light, as though I don't have hard feelings about him not taking me with him to his Venetian stucco job, but I'm not very good at making things light, so it comes out heavy and ironic, as though I really do have hard feelings about him not letting me help him with Venetian stucco.

He asks where am I going now, and I say, "I'm giving you a ride home, I have some time on my hands, might as well give you a ride, to save you the price of a subway ride." I'm so nervous that my driving is even worse than usual. The car makes unexpected jerks as though it's about to throw up, and I hope it's not us that it'll throw up when the time comes. To make him feel like a macho man rather than just a passenger in a jerking car, I tell him that I'm a new driver and would he please help me by telling me which lane I should be moving into. So he says, "Right line...Left line," and my fingers tremble on the wheel, because seconds before jumping into the car, I had gulped down a glass of red wine for courage to chase this man who runs away from me every day promptly at five o'clock.

His directions are so devoid of any expression, they could have been coming out of a GPS. I want to make him talk to me. I try to think of a topic that could interest him, but all I can think of is construction, and what do I know about construction other than what I see in my house—and what was it that I saw today, what is it called?

"What is it called...what you were doing today, with Marek and Ernesto?"

"What?" he says.

"When you were putting up walls, that greenish material, looks like a light-green board, I forgot the name for it, what's it called?"

"Shitrock?"

"That's right. Sheetrock," I say, "It has a long e, like in 'sea.' The way you said it, with a short i, makes it sound like something else."

"Ah!" he says.

"Yes."

The conversation ends. I rack my brain for another topic. I'm not hoping for any help from him, but the silence has become so oppressive that even he feels the need to break it.

"You stayed home today," he says.

"Yes," I say. "It's Columbus Day."

"Columbus Day," he repeats thoughtfully.

"Yes," I say. "An American holiday."

"You celebrate Columbus Day?" he says doubtfully.

"Me, no. But schools are closed. So I stay home. That's my way of celebrating. A day of rest. Rest and writing."

He doesn't respond. There hasn't been a "right line/left line" instruction coming from him for some time, and the silence is oppressive again. I need to think of something else to say, but nothing but good old Columbus Day comes to mind.

"I wonder what American Indians feel about this day," I say. "I doubt it's a happy occasion for them."

There is another long pause, but this time he breaks the silence just as I begin to search for another topic.

"Maybe their schools closed too, and they celebrate like you. Their day of rest."

I say, "Maybe. Only I meant it as a joke, you know. Just because this is how I am doesn't mean that's how other people are. Got to account for individual differences, you know. You, for example." I make a significant pause, hoping to arouse his interest.

But either he sees through my trick or he has a much thicker skin than I thought. A few minutes pass in silence. When I think that he has completely forgotten what I said, he asks, "Me?"

"Yes, you like to go to work. You said so yourself. That's why, instead of going home to rest after a ten-hour day, you go to your evening jobs. You want to work fifteen, sixteen hours a day."

"Evening jobs finished. Recession, people don't have money, people don't give me jobs," he says pitifully.

"Oh, Alejandro," I say, moved by something like motherly love. "I'll give you jobs!"

Throughout all this, something else is going on, and I'm acutely aware of this deeper level where every trivial word we say acquires significance, and where my belief in his feelings for me is so unshakeable, it refutes all evidence to the contrary. I want to tell him that what we feel for each other is more than simple attraction; that we have known each other in lifetime after lifetime. If he is a Palestinian, is it too much to suppose that his ancestors and my ancestors were one people at some point? What if this love is a call from our ancestors, and even though it seems that I'm the only one who hears their call, I'm sure that at some level he does too.

When he says, "Make a turn on Steinway," I think how his indifferent voice can mislead anyone, even me, into thinking that he feels nothing for me.

I imagine how, when it's time for him to get out of the car, his shadow will fall over me, his face will move close to mine, and I think how much meaning this will open up, in ourselves and in the world at large.

I stop the car. He sits still for a moment, then he opens the passenger door, gets out of the car, and walks away without a word.

How hard he tries to hide his feelings, but it's useless. He can't hide anything from me.

ALEJANDRO

"You haven't fulfilled your obligations," the Professor says. "The glorious task that had been laid on your shoulders—what happened to it?"

It has become a burden, I want to say, but I control myself because I still have some hopes for a green card and also because when the Professor wears his mastermind hat, he has no need of my words; he wants my obedience.

"Not only is she still walking around, healthy and in one piece, not only is she still posting more chapters of her ancestors' story online and networking with her Hasmonean relatives on how to repossess the throne of the Jews with best consequences for the Jews and worst consequences for your people...not only is she still alive. She is in love—with you!"

I would like to defend myself either by denying that she is in love me or by saying that I have nothing to do with her falling for me. Some women are like that: they choose a man they like no matter whether he returns their affections or not. In this case, not. Definitely not. I was painting her walls and she fell for me.

"Why did she choose *you*? Of all the men working in her house during the construction...why you?"

"How can I know? A woman's heart..." I know there's a saying about it, but I don't remember the exact words.

"Maybe she can sense why you are there. That your painting walls is just a cover and that your real goal is something else. She doesn't know what it is, but she feels that it has to do with her. She is confused. She mistook death for love. She is one of those confused Western women. You don't find them in your culture. You protect your women not only for their own benefit, which is what the West erroneously thinks you do, but for the sake of their own inner peace. If I didn't know about her plans for global domination through her Hasmonean heritage, I might have pitied her. She is so confused that sometimes I feel I want to protect her by making her one of our own. But things being as they are, the only way she can find peace is through you. You know the saying, Cut off the head of the snake...How does it go, about the snake with the cut-off head, how does it end? It ends well for those who don't want to be bitten, my friend. Which is exactly what she is confused about: death, love. Read this. We intercepted this last week."

I briefly wonder who "we" are. I don't like the sound of it. It makes me think of the guys I separated myself from: I thought I had left them for good, but it looks like I didn't. Maybe there's no getting away from the guys--once in, always in, there's no out. That's another favor I want to ask him, to get me off the hook with the guys he and I both know; it's as important to me as the green card, but he hands me a printout, and I don't have a chance to decline it.

Just because a woman in love with me wrote this doesn't mean that I want to read it. It has words I don't understand, like "misconstruing" and "GULAG" and "Treblinka," but I can't ask the Professor for a dictionary or ask him to explain these words for me. This time he's taking this play-acting business so far that I no longer know what he wants to see me as. It seems that I'm not only a wall painter and an illegal in need of a green card. I'm now someone who has failed to fulfill my responsibilities as a killer and therefore besmirched myself in the Professor's eyes. I besmirched myself even more by making the target fall in love with me. The fact that I've become her love interest against my own will is not something that the Professor, in his role as the mastermind, is willing to consider; the fact that I did not take advantage of her affections is not sufficient proof of my innocence in his eyes. Because I'm an object of her affections, I must be able to read anything she writes. To reveal a small weakness he's known all along, that my English reading skills are poor, would be to fail yet again in his eyes.

I read:

"I get so preoccupied with my feelings for Alejandro that I forget to post completed chapters of my Chronicle on the writers' forum, and only when I get a particularly disturbing feedback from someone, do I remember that other people are reading and perhaps misconstruing it, like Alejandro with his theory that my writing is a code for Israel's intentions regarding the Palestinians and that my goal is to repossess the throne of Judea for which I have not only natural rights but also concrete proof—all of this completely undiminished by my telling him that this is crazy, that I never thought of claiming the throne, such as it is, and that I write *The Hasmonean Chronicle* just because this voice in my head is dictating it to me, so I'm not really writing it—it is writing itself. This feedback is from someone whose online name is "Pen+", and I'm sure it's a man, even though gender doesn't show in the user name, unless you're one of those people who tend to see the plus sign as a sign of masculinity. "I don't know why a cut-off toe has to appear in every generation," writes Pen+. "Why a toe? Is it a relic or just a vision? If you need a symbol to show continuity from generation to generation, from century to century, choose something that is not so gross. Something more meaningful. A manuscript, for example. A scroll in which a chosen member of each successive generation records key events of his or her life and then passes it on to the next generation and the next, from antiquity to our time. I can't see how you'll bring off 'the toe' appearing to a twentieth-century Hasmonean descendant dying of cold and hunger in the GULAG or from a KGB bullet in the Lubianka basement, or from a Nazi bullet in Babi Yar, or in a Treblinka gas chamber.'

I write "Thanks for the feedback" and never hear from Pen+ again.

"Are you done?" the Professor says impatiently. I return the printout to him. I want to say, "So what?" He waves the printout in the air, puts it on the table, and pokes it with his thumb.

"She admits it herself," he says. "She is so sure of her success that she doesn't care to hide her intentions. Look: 'My writing is code for Israel's intentions regarding the Palestinians. My goal is to repossess the throne of Judea for which I have not only natural rights but also concrete proof.' She says it in plain words: her goal is to repossess the throne of Judea. She has not only natural rights but also concrete proof. And then she's talking about the voice in her head that dictates her writing to her, and you know what it means when a person hears voices—you can expect anything from her. While you were wasting precious time on making her fall in love with you, she's been busy plotting the takeover of Jerusalem. You mustn't wait any longer, my friend. Yes, you're still my friend, even though you have not fulfilled your obligations to your people and to me. Remember that by getting entangled with this woman you deny yourself a chance to eliminate her. You're letting her proceed with her plans, and we cannot allow this happen."

I'm not entangled with her, I want to say. I've been successfully resisting her charms, which are considerable. I've been planning to carry out my assignment, but the duty to the Professor conflicts with my duty to my boss. I don't think Tom will be happy to find out that I killed the client who's been faithfully writing him checks for every step of the construction, and that instead of painting her walls in eggshell white or haystack yellow I splattered those walls with her blood.

But I know what the Professor is like in his Mastermind hat, and I know what I can say to him and what I must keep to myself.

He wants me to speak. He wants me to give him the date and time of the deed.

I must come up with a solution quickly. "In the beginning of our conversation you said something that interested me. You said, 'I feel I want to protect her by making her one of our own.' What did you mean by that? One of our own? Do you mean that if she gave up her Hasmonean ambitions and converted to Islam, you'd accept her?"

"It would never happen," he says firmly.

"You wouldn't accept her?"

"It would never happen because a descendant of Jewish kings will never consider converting to Islam. So this is nothing but idle speculation, empty talk, while I expect deeds from you."

"But what if she did…if she agreed to convert…to become one of us…if she said the Shahada…Would you release me from this task? Would you remove her from the list of the targets?"

"This is nothing but idle speculation, as I've already said. The target will not agree to convert, not in a thousand years. Not the queen of Israel. "

"But if she does? What if she does?"

"Then she'll be forgiven," says the Professor graciously. "I shall remove her from the list of targets and release you from your task."

CHAPTER 4

THE HASMONEAN CHRONICLE

———◆———

THE FOLLOWING CAME TO PASS after Judah's death, when Bacchides, the Seleucid Greek general who had defeated Judah's forces at Elasa, was himself defeated by Jonathan, brother of Judah, after the siege of Bethbasi, a town fortified by the Maccabees with everything contemporary warfare had known, which was why the siege proved fruitless for the Greeks and another victory for the Jews. Not only did Bacchides take an oath of never again making war upon the Maccabees, and not only did he promise to withdraw his troops from Israel, he actually fulfilled his promise, and with that "the sword ceased in Israel," as First Book of Maccabees tells us.

Jonathan was not, by nature, a warrior. He wanted peace, not only with General Bacchides, who had readily accepted Jonathan's offer, but with his own beloved wife who, contrary to all expectations and to her anti-Hellenic upbringing, decided to give herself to a Greek god. And not just to any Greek god. It had to be Apollo. Jonathan knew his wife well, and he knew about the one thing she wanted more than anything. She was a poetess, and the thing was inspiration. She could only get it through a man who loved her, but she claimed that Jonathan couldn't give it to her because he didn't have it. Apollo had it, and he promised it to her in return for her favors. Now that she was inspired all the time, writing verses she dreamed up at night, it could mean only one thing—she had given him her favors.

Jonathan refused to think of it. His whole being resisted a half-conscious attempt to imagine his Yedida in the arms of the Greek. He called him "the Greek," even though he was a god, because emphasizing his rival's ethnicity was a way of making him small, while calling him god would have been to admit that Apollo had powers that Jonathan lacked. No, he couldn't call him a god. There was only one God, the God of Abraham, Isaac, and Moses. Where were the Shimmering Ones who had appeared to his brother Judah? If they had come to Judah, shouldn't they come to him too? Didn't he deserve their help? Or perhaps woman trouble didn't count as trouble enough for them?

Meanwhile, Yedida, his wife, wasn't exactly inventing anything new. She was merely following a path on which others had trod, and among those others was Nehora, Judah's widow, the woman of the jug, the woman whom Judah, who could have had any girl he desired, chose as his second wife, because his first one—we know what happened to her, and we do not need to speak any more of misfortune.

It was at Judah's burial that Nehora strayed. When the remaining Maccabees were gathered around the family tomb in Mod'in, watching silently as Judah's body was being placed in an assigned niche and his covering adjusted by Jonathan's careful hands, Nehora turned her head to the left. No one noticed this slight movement. No one saw that her eyes were no longer on Judah's body, that they were following a shape in the distance that didn't look human at all. A shape that looked like an animal. She made a step in the direction of the shifting shape, then another step, and another, and still no one noticed. They were all so intent on what was going on with Judah that she wondered if she was the only one who knew that nothing was going on. Judah was dead, and their love, however great, was in the past, finished, done with, while the shape that moved in the distance was alive. It kept on moving, further and further away, and Nehora moved too, with it, toward it, away from the people, closer to the donkey shape. At one point Yedida, her sister-in-law, Jonathan's wife and Nehora's friend, turned her head sharply in the direction of the receding figure, but she couldn't believe that Nehora could actually do this, walk away in the middle of her husband's burial ceremony, so she blinked at the fading figure, thinking it to be some other person, not even a woman, perhaps a man, perhaps one of Judah's soldiers, as there was nothing especially feminine in that far-away silhouette.

When Nehora was far enough, the shape stopped. Nehora saw what it was: a donkey. But not just any donkey. There was something extremely graceful about this one. The way it walked. The way it turned its head, nostrils widening and then flattening again. The way it stood there not like an animal, someone's run-away cattle, spiritless flesh. It stood there like a prince. That's the word she was searching for: a prince. Now that she found it, she wouldn't let go of it. A prince. A youth. A future king. The most graceful male she had ever beheld, even if just a donkey. She was bewitched. She was stupefied, dazzled, under a spell. When the donkey stopped, so did she. When the donkey moved on, she followed. Finally the animal stopped for a feeding, and from her experience with animals, she knew how long it would take. A while. Longer than a while. The donkey lowered its neck, took a mouthful of grass, chewed, looked up, bent down, chewed again. She stood there, watching. Barely breathing. More than fascinated: transfixed. The donkey made a few steps in her direction, and she made the kind of sweet sounds she used to make for any domestic animal. Easily understandable by animals, they meant: come closer, don't be afraid, I like you, I won't harm you, all I want is to pet you.

By the time she actually managed to lay her hands on the animal, she was no longer on solid ground: she was riding the donkey, and it was speeding away with her, and the longer she sat on its back, the more comfortable and happier she became, as though it was not the spine of a farm animal she sat on but a luxurious armchair, its lower legs shaped like an animal's hoofs, the kind that Judah, her late husband, used to lounge in after his victories over the Greeks at Beth-Horon and Emmaus as a way of rewarding himself for the hard work of fighting.

The donkey stopped. She continued to sit on its back. She didn't know what the donkey wanted her to do. Stay? Get off? She felt that the animal had not only a mind of its own but also a will. And it was its will, more than its mind, that she felt in her innermost being where not even Judah, in their many nights together, managed to penetrate—and it was not a donkey anymore, it was a god, and he whispered his name in her ear, ever so softly, as he ravished her on the grass next to where he had stood just a moment ago in the shape of the animal with her on top of him. Now he was on top of her, and it felt right. Wasn't it this that she felt from the first moment, when she spied his donkey shape in the distance, and when she made that one fateful step away from Judah's burial?

She felt this without being aware that it was this: this lying on the grass with a man—a god, he said, but she still thought him a man—with her legs spread open, and the very center of her so open for him, so receptive, as it never was for Judah, and yet she had loved Judah, and she didn't think she loved this man. When she wanted to find a word to define her feeling for him, she could think only, "His will, I'm so open to his will," and she couldn't think any further because he proceeded to ravish her in ways that were so beyond the furthest reach of her imaginings that she became temporarily mute.

When it was over and she regained her speech, she remembered stories in which Zeus had had his way with mortal women. She remembered one in particular, about a young woman and a bull, how the girl found herself crossing the sea on the back of the animal…and then the same thing as now, his godhead moving between her legs, and of course this story, like all other stories about the pleasure-loving gods, was unmentionable in her family, which rejected everything Greek. A pity, she thought, because if she had been more familiar with these tales, she might have developed a resistance in herself; she might have recognized Zeus in the donkey shape and found in herself the strength not to follow him…Now he lay next to her, looking at her from under his matted hair, or fur.

It was time to go back, yet she couldn't make herself stand up. It was time to hear Jonathan and the rest of the family proclaim her a traitor or even worse, a whore, and if that was not enough, a temple prostitute—because wasn't that what they called those unmentionable women who copulated with pagan gods? Not that she did anything like that. He copulated with her, not she with him. Or maybe that's just what they meant by those terrible words, "a temple prostitute," and maybe she *was* that, even though there was no temple in sight, nothing but grass and an occasional shrub and flowers. And then another thought occurred to her, even stranger than all the ones so far, and by that she meant both thoughts and events of the last half hour: what if *this* was his temple? "This" was the field, the grass, an occasional shrub and flowers; "his" meant they were the possession of the donkey. Not a donkey but Zeus. What an abominable thought. More abominable than all the others, and God knows, the others were bad enough. Not the thought of the donkey turning out to be Zeus, but that all of this—the field, etcetera—was his temple, no less than the whole creation was a temple of God, who was the real God, not some donkey that could change himself into a man for the sole purpose of rape.

There was a certain distinction in belonging to a coterie of women ravaged by this king of pagan gods who in his spare moments was said to reside on top of Olympus or Olympos—she couldn't remember the exact name of that mountain in Greece.

He was reclining next to her, a man in his prime, close to forty-five, she couldn't tell exactly, although she had been famous for guessing the age of many a middle-aged man—famous for embarrassing those who wanted to look younger and were jolted back into their true age by her uncompromising intuition, so much so, in fact, that guests in Judah's house would announce their true age right at the threshold: so-and-so, forty-two years of age!, for the fear that, were they to hide it, she would denounce them as liars. Yet it was not her intention at all, because despite everyone thinking of age-guessing as her specialty, she knew of course that she did it simply because she was right every time.

"Your husband," said Zeus as he made himself comfortable on the grass next to her, "will go down in history as the one who threw off the yoke of the Seleucids, and for this accomplishment children born two thousand years from now will learn his name and his deeds, which means that you were married to a very great man indeed."

"Were you speaking of my husband Judah?" she asked.

"Why, have you other husbands?"

She said no, she didn't have other husbands. One was enough. One, one. This word, "one," was not just a sound. It had meaning. He was the one. In that case, what was she doing here, dallying on the grass with another man, whatever he really was, man, donkey, god? At this moment, he looked like a half-naked man. Judah was being buried at this very moment, and she was here with this man...what did he say he was? Zeus, king of the Hellenic religion because of which all this started. By "all this" she meant both the war and the resistance, because the war *was* their resistance.

"He'll kill me," Nehora said.

"Who? The man who is being put into a tomb or the one rising from it?"

"Which one is rising?"

"Never mind," said Zeus. "I'm mixing up the future and the present. Afflictions of memory, just like a mortal man's, with the difference that my memory encompasses both what was and what will be."

"What will be?" she echoed.

"Nothing you're not already feeling. Guilt. Remorse. The inner voice ordering you to expiate for the sin of fornication."

"Is that what it's called?"

"It's also called adultery. Don't tell me you never heard the word."

"I heard the word—"

"Now you've done the deed," he said smugly.

"But it was you...you who...made me come here. You lured me!" she cried.

"You saw a donkey and you decided to follow. How can a dumb animal be blamed for the deadly sin you've committed—lying with another man as your husband is being lowered into the ground?"

"You...another man?" she said.

"What else am I going to call myself?"

"Anything but a man," she said stubbornly.

"That definitely sounds like an insult. None of them ever complained of my manhood. And there were many of them. I make every woman happy."

"Huh!" she laughed. "I make every woman happy! Ha ha!"

"Don't you dare laugh at my manly powers," said Zeus. "My prowess is such that no mortal woman, ever—"

"I'd like to talk to some of those women, in private, woman-to-woman, just to compare notes," she mocked. "Pray tell me what shape you assumed to lure them?"

"They were mortal. You can't talk to dead women."

"Ah, how well you loved them! They're all dead."

"There were centuries between each one. I'm not as profligate as they portray me."

"One in a few hundred years isn't much," she agreed. "To what do I owe the honor?"

"You're one of the vehicles," he said gruffly. "Every couple hundred years there is one."

"And what does it mean, a vehicle?"

"A vehicle is a woman who carries forward the seed of immortality bequeathed to her by a god in a moment of passion—not random passion, but chosen and planned and carried out with the specific purpose of creating a line of future kings."

"And queens?" she interrupted.

"Kings," he continued, unperturbed, "who will be capable enough to shoot the arrow of the original faith further into the gene pool of the future."

"Gene pool?"

"Creating history, in other words."

"I don't know what you're talking about," she said.

"I could tell you names but you wouldn't retain them. The Essenes, John the Baptist, Herod, Joshua aka Jesus, Saul aka Paul, Vespasian, Caesar, Hadrian… No need to waste my breath naming them all. The future doesn't stay in the minds of mortals."

"You're saying you lured me from my husband's burial so you could start a line of little Zeuses by planting your seed here?" she pointed at her stomach, her finger freezing in midair as if accusing the stomach, not the man, of bad behavior.

"It is the destiny of your line," he said dryly, "to grow into a royal line of Hellenized Jews, with names like Alexander and Aristobulus and Hyrcanus in the next two generations, and thus the destiny of your sons and grandsons and great-great-grandsons is to bear Greek names while remaining Jews, just as the masses they rule over. Yours is the last line of Jewish kings. It will all crumble when the Herods come. That is why you are special, you see."

Nehora said she didn't see anything and would he please repeat himself so that people like her, people with normal habits of living, not like those used to fancy and quaint things, could understand what he was talking about.

"I'm talking about the future!" he shouted with so much irritation that she cringed in fear of a blow, and among the thoughts flitting through her mind, one was particularly loud: "My Judah would have never...ever—"

But Zeus would have never raised a hand at her either. He was, after all, a gentleman. His point being a difficult one, he did not expect her to understand it right away, but if there was one thing he expected from a woman it was patience and respect for the ideas and words of the male. Patience and respect, if not outright interest and comprehension...was it too much to ask?

She said she understood the female-respect-of-the-male rule well enough. It was his words about the future, the part about folding it into the present, like you fold a sheet, two times, four times, so the ends meet, that had seemed like ramblings.

He said he was talking about assimilation.

"What's assimilation?" she asked.

"It's when a Jew tries to be not like a Jew."

She said, "Oh." And then, after some thought, she added that she didn't believe it was possible for a Jew to not be like a Jew because this was something one couldn't help; one could never stop being a Jew. Once a Jew, always a Jew, and what's inside is outside, the inner relates to the outer in unmistakable ways, and no matter how you try to hide the essence, it'll come out no matter what.

"No matter what!" she repeated passionately, and at this moment again she was Nehora, the wife of Judah Maccabeus, defending his stance with a ferociousness he would have been proud of. She knew that silent appreciative look of his, just as she knew that what had happened here with this donkey-turned-man-turned-god should, for obvious reasons, be kept from her famous spouse, or now that he was dead, from the legend of him that would last and last.

"Your line will end with a whimper instead of a bang," said the donkey man, "the result of petty quarreling among your descendants. They will tire papa Pompey with their complaints and quarrels so much that he will kick the Hasmonean kingdom with his iron boot."

She wanted to know how could anyone kick a kingdom with a boot, and the donkey man said that he was speaking metaphorically, didn't she understand, and when he saw a certain expression on her face, he added that "metaphor" was another one of many Greek contributions to culture. She ought to know, he said, that his people contributed and would continue to contribute more than any other to culture, and that for centuries to come it would be the Greeks whose ideals of beauty would live on in sculpture, poetry, drama, philosophy, and ways of governing, while the Jews, the only people whose contributions rivaled the Greeks', would be so soaked in the warm bath of Hellenism that they would look Greek and talk Greek. But no matter how much they try to resemble the Greeks, no matter how much they assimilated and went out of their way to speak Greek and adopt Hellenic culture, they would never be taken for real Greeks.

"This is what I was saying," she said, "when I was talking about the inner and the outer Jew...the essence will come out no matter what."

"Not the essence, lady!" he shouted impatiently. "Even in their essence, some of them will want to be like us: they will take our essence and try to assimilate it, but we will still not accept them as Greeks. We will still continue to call them Jews, and it will not be just us, it will also be the Romans, and all the European nations that will be come later, they will all say to the Jews: assimilate! And no matter how much some of you will do your utmost to fulfill the request, you will still be called Jews and seen as Jews. And you will pay for it with your lives!"

"So what's your point?" she said. "You're losing me."

He explained that she shouldn't be ashamed of what she did with him here. On the contrary, she should be proud and happy, for he chose her, of all women, and by performing the act with her that can only be performed in the shape of a man, he had added a little drop of his own to the mixture in her womb...as a way of protecting the Jews of the future from the host countries' accusations of being "Jews" and therefore different from everyone else. From then on, they could honestly say that being a Jew and a Greek was almost the same thing.

"You inseminated a woman who will not live past this hour," interrupted a familiar voice, "and therefore we Jews shall remain Jews in essence as well as appearance, and we will fight against assimilation with every fiber of our body and spirit for thousands of years to come, which we shall survive, while you shall be gone. We shall survive without a gift of your semen in my sister-in-law's belly, thank you very much!"

It was Judah's brother Simon who said these words and who raised his sword over Nehora, and she raised her right hand to it as if to greet it, and she said words that made Simon think—but unfortunately not for very long. She reminded him that she was his brother's wife, and she asked didn't the Sixth Commandment command us not to murder, and didn't the Tenth Commandment say something important about thy brother's wife?

Simon replied that the Tenth happened to be not about a brother's wife but about a neighbor, and it was not about killing, which was what he was about to do to her, but about coveting his wife. And he, said Simon about himself, certainly did not covet her. It must be plain as day even to her. He had to eliminate her, he said, not because of any personal motivations such as coveting or not coveting—the coveting part he was willing to leave to his fellow Greeks, he said with a nod at the donkey god. Yes, Simon said with a heavy sigh, like a man burdened with carrying out God's will. He had to do it; yes, he was forced to, in order to cleanse the line of the future kings of Judea—to cleanse it, he said loudly, of the Greek seed. And anyway, he said, even though the Sixth Commandment does say Thou shalt not murder, does it apply to murder in a battle? It doesn't, and who said this wasn't a battle...of a different kind, but a battle nevertheless?

"Let me be, Simon," said Nehora. "I don't want him to throw a thunderbolt at you. Or do something even worse," she added. At that moment they heard what no mortal man or woman had heard before: a god muttering to himself.

Nehora and Simon distinguished the following words in the mutterings of Zeus: "I had the idea first. I could have given the Commandments to my people. So what that they didn't cross the desert...Olympus is no worse than Sinai as a scene for revelation of our will...I said 'our' because it's yours and mine...I didn't say we were brothers, Jeh. It was a royal we, not a brotherly one...So now you want to be brothers? No thanks, I have enough brothers. I grant you that the Commandments were your idea. Fine. They were. So what? I had other things. Such as the right to fornicate with your mortal women. Ah, you know what I mean, not your women, you old prude. You long since banned for yourself the pleasure of female company. But even for you there will come a time to form a family—because even you will tire of being alone. And when you get yourself your little family, you will shun the female, you will not let her in, just the son and the Holy Ghost and you, all three of you either male or of indeterminate gender, if I may remark. Mary will be neither seen nor heard—not until after some twenty centuries you'll allow her in: Father, Son, Holy Spirit, and She. When it comes to family matters, you can't beat mine for its size, the colorful characters, in pictures and statues. That's where I shall get you. You forbid people to make images of you, while I gladly allow it. Gladly, I repeat, and proudly."

"Ramblings of a madman," said Simon.

"You fool," Nehora said. "He's not a madman at all. Just because you don't understand –"

"There's nothing to understand," Simon said, raising his sword again, but there was nothing for the sword to do but hang limply from his hand, because Nehora fell on the ground like an apple falls from an apple tree or a grape from a grape vine, and it was not the sword's doing but the donkey god muttering, "She's not the right one for my seed," while making a dismissive gesture in her direction.

Simon opened his mouth to defend his sister-in-law's rightness but closed it just in time to realize that to be right in this context meant something he did not wish for her, for who would wish to defend the dishonor of a dearly loved older brother's wife? And he did love her, because she was Judah's love, and Simon venerated his older brother and loved everything that Judah had loved. But she lay white and still on the ground, and Simon understood that Zeus's gesture was not simply dismissive. This was a god, after all, and look at him strutting away in his donkey shape. He could have changed into something better in her honor, something more presentable than a donkey, but then what can you expect of a pagan god?

He had a hard time explaining to his family why he returned without Nehora. First he had to explain why he went in that particular direction, and as he couldn't explain it, then explaining why he found her alive and saw her die shortly afterward made as little sense as saying that he had met a god in whom he did not believe, and it was the pagan, whom he wouldn't call god, it was he who did it, with that gesture of his. No, it was not a rude one. If anything, it was dismissive. Why? How would anyone know why? Maybe it was to prove he knew how to do some of the things expected of a god. Like kill, maim, ravish. No, our God does not ravish. But he was not our God. He was theirs. And he did ravish.

Not her, no. She died untouched by him; she would never let a thing like that happen to her, certainly not with some pagan idol worshipper calling himself Zeus. She willed herself to die because she didn't want to go on living without her husband, and a love like this deserves to be recorded in the book of our history, because even a few years from now, no one will believe it or even think about it, and when we say history, we're not talking about a few years from now, we're talking about millennia. Do not ask me where to bury her: hasn't she earned the right to repose next to Judah, in the Maccabean tomb? What more could she have done to prove herself worthy of this grave? Hadn't she earned this right by leaving her body just as his was being lowered in the ancestral tomb?

Leaving the body. He shouldn't have said it. But it was too late. It flew out of his mouth like a bird out of a nest: try and catch it. This slip of the tongue tormented him for days, because he imagined everyone shocked by it, while in fact no one even noticed it. The only one who did notice was Tzadikah the wife of Simon, and she talked about it to Yedida, the wife of Jonathan, who said that she also noticed, and the two of them discussed the slip at length when they were alone.

Yedida told Tzadikah that in one of her inspirations—and let's not forget this was the lady who willingly and in full presence of mind gave herself to another pagan god in exchange for inspirations—in one of them, she said, she heard a voice, don't ask whose, things were bad enough as they were, but here's what the voice said: "Listen," it said. "Listen again to what Simon said: 'leaving' and 'the body.' How can anyone ascribe words like these to chance?" The voice told Yedida that "leaving the body" was a code that gods used to communicate with men. Yedida thought that the voice said "gods" but it might also have been "god," the plural ending being one of those things she wasn't very sure about.

"Try to remember," said Tzadikah.

"It doesn't matter."

"It does," said Tzadikah.

"But why?"

"Because if it's one God, then it's ours. And it's good. If it's many, it's theirs. And it's not good."

"We're simply talking about the plural ending! We're not talking about which religion is better," said Yedida.

"One God or many?"

"Tzadikah, listen, I tell you, a grammar point does not make for a religious revelation."

"God is not grammar, Yedida. God is more than grammar. Small ending, small god. No ending, God without end."

"Why are you taking us away from the real understanding that the voice has given me? What's your interest in this? Why are you so concerned with the plural or singular ending and not concerned at all with the meaning of 'leaving the body'?"

Tzadikah told Yedida that she didn't want to hear any more silly nonsense about Yedida's voices or her famous inspirations. Yes, famous enough for everyone to know who gave them to her and at what price. Yedida said, "Wait, you didn't hear the most important part, the one that came after 'leaving the body,' the one about you."

Tzadikah found this so funny that she almost fell on the ground laughing. "The one about me?" she said between attacks of laughter. "I'm not the one who allowed a pagan god inside my body!"

"But you will!" Yedida shouted. "All three of us Maccabean wives must go through it: me for my inspiration, Nehora for her dying, and you…you, my dear, for what really counts…for the progeny to create a dynasty of Jewish kings. It will be called a Hasmonean dynasty, and it will have a special mission in our people's history, for with the end of the dynasty will come the end of our sovereignty, and with the end of our sovereignty sooner or later will come the end of Judea, and with the end of Judea will come the beginning of Diaspora. We don't know this word yet, but the voices do, and it is the drop of foreign gods' blood that our line has to carry in order to fulfill the prophecy and bring about the dissolution of the state. This is our destiny—do you understand? This weakness will be used by another empire, not the Greeks. It'll be the Romans, the treacherous ones with whom our Judah signed the treaty. They will burn Jerusalem and destroy the Temple, forcing our people to flee to every corner of the Roman world. We will be enslaved and we will rebel and we will wage three wars, which will go down in history as the Jewish Wars, and despite our bravery we will lose, and we will suffer in the Diaspora for two thousand years, living out our Jewishness, a stigma for which we will burn, time and again, until the largest conflagration will engulf six million of us, and we shall come back here. Here!" Yedida pointed down.

"I didn't get that," said Tzadikah. "All that will happen because of…what?"

"Because you, like me and like Nehora, you will—"

"No, I won't," Tzadikah said flatly.

"The voice said that you will."

"I'm tired of your voices! They lie!"

"The voices never lie," said Yedida.

"You were the one to whom the voices told this, so, Yedida, it must be you, not me, that they were talking about. A drop of Greek blood! You already got it from one of their gods. Plural ending, pagan ending…Do not drag me into this, sister."

"I conceived from my god only inspiration," said Yedida. "You shall conceive kings."

"If Simon could hear you now, he'd have you punished. I'd rather not imagine how."

"It's not going to be Simon who rules for the next ten years, Tzadika. It's going to be my Jonathan."

"Well, then Jonathan should punish you!" Tzadika cried. "A man must punish his wife for saying these kinds of things. If he is man enough!"

"He is man enough!"

"Then, Yedida, tell him what you're telling me!"

"I'll tell him not to make an alliance with the Romans against the Greeks! It will hit us in the back!"

"How can it hit us and what back are you talking about?"

"I'm talking about the end of Judea."

"Why are you worried about things that might never come to pass?"

"They came to pass before. They will again."

And so the sisters-in-law continued their bickering while the other Maccabees slept.

GALIA

He's hitting my poor metal fence with a tool to remove old chipped paint before he applies fresh coats of primer and paint. I don't know the name of the tool in his hand, but I know it's metal because the sound of metal on metal has the kind of fury that only metal can evince from a man, by making him fuse with the metal of the tool the way he would with the metal of a weapon.

I stand behind him for a long time before he turns his head and acknowledges me with a nod and a half smile. He turns back to the fence, raises his hand with the tool, and extracts another cry of defeat from the railing.

I want to say something to start us talking, but nothing comes to my mind that could be of interest to him and that is not about construction. I'm sick of construction.

"So you have four brothers," I say finally. "Tell me something about them."

"Nothing to tell," he says without turning.

"Are they like you? Working in different countries? Or do they stay in the village with your parents?"

"In the village. All. Except my young one. Shame of family! Shame, shame," he says with disgust while the hand with the tool attacks the fence with more fury.

"Why? What did he do?"

"He went over to the other side." He stops assaulting the fence, wipes his forehead, shakes his head. "Too much pain to talk about it."

"What other side?"

"What...what other side? You don't understand? I told you I from Palestine. So if I from Palestine what the other side?"

"I'm just not used to thinking in terms of 'sides.' But you mean...your brother went over to the Israelis and by doing so he brought shame on your family?" He nods in satisfaction—I finally understood him.

"So what does your brother do in Israel? Did he join the Israeli army, or did he become some kind of spy by telling them everything he knows about who goes in and out of your village?"

"No. He loves them so much, he thinks they have—" He stops his hand in midair, trying to think of a word. When he finds it, he hits the fence harder.

"Progress. They have progress, and all we have is old ways. Old ways not interesting to my brother."

"So what does he do in Israel?"

"You know kibbutz?"

"I know about kibbutz."

"That's where lives. On kibbutz."

"So he hates farming yet he lives on a kibbutz? Isn't that what they do in a kibbutz? They work the land, just like in your village?"

"They have machines that do the work. My brother, no, he thinks it not like our village at all. He thinks we have to learn from them. Instead of resisting them, we have to learn!" He finds the idea so preposterous that he throws up his hands and issues a little moan of disbelief.

"So what exactly does he do in the kibbutz? Does he operate a tractor?"

"No tractor for my brother. He went to university there, now he engineer, he works on…how they say it." He looks at the fence as though the word he is looking for is written there, and after some moments of patient staring, it comes to him. "Bioimaging systems!"

"I think that's great. You should be proud of your brother instead of being ashamed of him. I didn't know that's what they did nowadays in a kibbutz, but it sounds great. And also that they let him in, that they trust him."

"They trust him too much." He says this almost helplessly, like an old woman grumbling and sighing to herself because she is unable to change the new generation.

"Why, is he going to betray their trust?"

"Betray their trust?" He laughs. The idea of betraying the trust of kibbutzniks is too ridiculous to be a serious proposition; he throws his metal tool on the ground to better enjoy his laugh.

"What's so funny, Alejandro?"

"I wish he betray their trust. I wish." He tries to calm down, wipes tears around his eyes. "But my brother not like that. He so happy that they accept him. That their kids have bikes—he thinks bikes are great. And computers. And violins."

"Why violins?"

"He plays violin in their music school. Tzlile Harim. They play all kinds of instruments there. First he learned there, now he teaches. Sometimes he plays in…quartet. He sent us CD of his playing—"

"You have it? Could I listen to it?" I'm hoping that I'll have something other than construction to discuss with him: interesting things like violins, his unusual brother, music school at the kibbutz.

"No, I not have it. Our mother threw it away. We ashamed of him, you understand? Ashamed of my brother living in kibbutz Kiryat Anavim and playing Pa-ga-ni-ni!" He grimaces in a most terrible way when he says "Paganini," as though the name gives him toothache.

"What's his name?"

He doesn't react. Talking about his brother who went over to the Israelis to play Paganini is just too painful.

"He had a good name. Now he has his new name Eleazar. It's a Hebrew name. Like Lazarus who came from the dead. So who is the dead, I ask…we, our village, you came from us? You came from our family, yes?"

"So what does he say to that? When you ask him why he took the Hebrew name?"

"He says stupid things. I don't want to repeat."

"Please, Alejandro! Tell me!"

"Why you want to know?" He turns to me, gives me a look as though figuring something out about me that he didn't know before. "Okay." He hits the fence one more time, throws the tool on the ground and lets his fingers run along the surface of the fence to check for remaining paint chips. "He says he Jew because if our people lived on this land for thousands years, then our ancestors were Jews who converted to Islam after Palestine was conquered by Muslims. And if our people did not live here for thousands years, he says, where is our argument? So this what he says. My brother Eleazar." Alejandro spits to show his contempt for his brother's views.

"Alejandro," I say quietly. "I meant to ask you something. Why did you tell me that lie about having a degree in marine biology? It was a lie, wasn't it?"

He stands up and walks away in decisive steps. I've seen him walk away like this before, but I still don't know what it means—extreme anger or something else equally extreme. I would rather it were this something else, because I love him and I don't care whether or not he has a degree in marine biology. I just want him to tell me the truth. His lies are the only thing that puts me off. I want him to tell me the truth about everything, even if it's the kind of thing that shows him in a bad light. Even if, say, he were plotting to kill me—I'd want him to tell me that too.

ALEJANDRO

She brings me coffee and juice and sandwiches, which she says she buys at a Russian store, and I'd like to ask if this Russian store is Jewish, because when I hear people say Russian and Jewish here in New York, it sounds like it's the same thing.

She stands there, watching me eat, like a mother making sure her child cleans his plate, and she praises her coffee or talks about one of those salads from the Russian store. It's called Olivier, and it's a simple potato salad with a fancy French name but, she says, the world thinks of it as the Russian salad. And the world, she says, likes it and thinks of it as something very refined because of its French name, while it pours scorn on the simple potato salad. She wants to know if I like "salat Olivier," and I say, yes, Galia, I like your Russian potato salat.

I think maybe now I can work in silence. But she doesn't let up. She says that she saw this salad on a menu in a restaurant in Guadalajara, and she wants to know if I've been to Guadalajara. I don't say anything, and not only because Tom wants me not to talk on the job but for reasons of my own, which I'm not free to divulge to her. She gushes about her love for Mexican colonial towns: Puebla, Oaxaca, Atlixco, San Cristobal de las Casas. She keeps dropping these names as though she expects me to love her for knowing them, as though her travels to Mexico brought her close to some secret point in my life, a kind of crossroads where she can meet me and see me the way I really am, or was. She even says it—"the way you were in your youth."

Babble on, woman, I think as I work in silence, you will never know a thing about my life, just like you'll never know what I really am, as I myself no longer know whether my job in your house is about painting walls or about purging the world of you and all the remaining members of your Hasmonean network. Cutting off the head of the snake, as the Professor, aka the Mastermind, said. His voice in my head is so strong that I forget who I really am, an illegal hoping for a little help with a green card through his secret channels, or an expert assassin that he likes to think I am, and because the first identity fades, the second one becomes stronger, and I tell myself that I can do it and I can do it well. You may be in love with me, lady, but that doesn't mean I'm here to take the blame for liquidating you. I want to walk out of here clean, you understand? I watch you out of the corner of my eye, lady. Every movement you make, every step you take, I watch it. I think: Maybe now?

She talks about a white hotel in Atlixco, and how she was the only tourist in that colonial town, the only person staying in a hotel built just for foreigners, and how she wasn't afraid at all to be the only foreigner in the city even though she had practically no Spanish. She would learn some simple phrases before going there, but in the rest had to rely on her ability to pick stuff out of thin air. That's how she puts it—my ability, out of thin air—and she goes on about an outdoor swimming pool in the hotel's inner courtyard and how it was surrounded by wild blooms, all kinds of tropical plants, and how breathtaking it was, all of it, swimming in that pool where she was all alone, and the red, green, yellow, and purple of the plants and the white stucco walls of the hotel against the bright blue sky. I could tell her a thing or two myself, but in my tale there would be no seventeenth-century cathedrals adorning a zocalo in a Mexican colonial town, or quaint restaurants serving fancy food from around the world, or hotels built with the express goal of extracting money from American tourists.

———◆———

I walk home, talking to Tom on the phone, telling him how much I have done today, when I see Galia's green Ford. She stops and waves for me to get in. When I'm in, she says she was going to a store to buy groceries, and I know it's a lie, because she's been running after me all day. I try not to show her that I'm glad, that I was aware of her all day, that at any point during the day I knew exactly where she was in the house, even if I was working on the second floor and she was in the basement, I always knew. When I tell her I'm not going to Manhattan, she says, No Venetian stucco jobs today? The way she says it reminds me of her asking me to let her come along to my evening job, and again it makes me think about Western women not understanding that there are things that only men can do and places where a woman's presence is inappropriate.

She tells me that she's been driving less than six months, but her driving makes me think this is worse than six months. This is one month and a week, or maybe no more than a week, because the car jerks and jumps, and it makes me want to go down on the floor and pray to get home in one piece. She asks me to help her by telling her when it's time to switch lanes, and I say, Right line, Left line, and she smiles when I say "line" as though I'm not saying it right but it's okay with her anyway. I don't think women should be allowed to have this effect on men, and I don't want to help her with her hopeless driving anymore. Then she starts talking about the work I was doing today, and she wants to know what the stuff is called, and I don't know what stuff she is talking about. She says, the stuff you and Marek and Ernesto were putting on walls today, and when I say shitrock, she smiles again and says shitrock is incorrect. I want to say, You were the one asking me what it's called and now you tell me it's incorrect. We don't talk after that, and I can see she is uncomfortable with not talking. Western women don't understand silence and how nourishing it can be. If there's too much silence, they begin to fidget and fill the air with empty words. I take pity on her and say the first thing that comes to my mind, something about her staying home today, and she says it's a holiday, Columbus Day, schools are closed. I ask if she celebrates it, and she says this is how she celebrates, by staying home. I think to myself that if this were my holiday, I'd celebrate it in a real way, and I could tell her a thing or two about how American Indians feel on this day, because that's how we feel on Yom Ha'atzmaut: for them it's their celebration, for us it's Nakba; they celebrate, we cry. But instead I say small words, "Maybe their schools are closed too."

I don't know how we switched to talking about my evening jobs, maybe because she said she liked to rest and she knows that I like to work long hours, ten at my day job and more in the evening if I'm lucky. I like to keep myself busy, I say. I like to tire my body so masculine urges don't torment me, but I don't say this to her. I don't discuss masculine urges with a woman. The other reason I like to work thirteen hours a day is money, but this too I don't want to tell her. She might ask what do I need so much money for, do I send it all to my family, or do I save it, so I say some empty words about not having enough evening jobs, and she says, "Don't worry, Alejandro, I'll get you jobs, you'll have money."

I get tears in my eyes when she says it, but then I tell myself, don't get soft, she's just a target, a job, an object to eliminate, not someone to trust. I tell her to make a right turn, and she makes it and waits for me to tell her where to stop. The street is empty. Now is a good moment to do it. My hand is deep in my pocket, on top of a knife. I remind myself about my duty to the Mastermind. I can hear his voice in my head, "No one would see it. You can walk away and no one will know. The street is empty; you won't get another chance like this. She is nothing but a target, nothing but a job." Without turning her head toward me, she can see my slight nod. She can see every tiny movement I make, and she knows the nod means stop. She brakes. She turns toward me, her eyes glisten, and I can't help myself. I get out of the car and walk away. I don't know why I didn't do it. I don't know how I'll explain this to the Professor. She should be happy now. She is alive.

GALIA

It's Friday, end of work day, and he doesn't just leave as usual. He looks for me in the backyard where I'm putting Venetian stucco on the back of my headboard. He doesn't say, "What are you doing that for?" or, "Nobody puts Venetian stucco on furniture," because he said that before. He has something else on his mind now. I can see it. Maybe he is finally ready to tell me that he loves me, that he wants us to meet after work, or on a weekend, or some other day or time. I hope this is what's on his mind, but I won't keep my fingers crossed, because I expected this confession from him earlier and got something else instead.

"I will not come here next week," he says. I note that his English has improved since the time I first met him.

I put down my scrape knife and take off my sunglasses. The way he says it, it sounds like he's not coming back at all. I can't imagine not seeing him here.

"Why?"

"Tom sending me to another job. Apartment in Rego Park. Must finish in five days."

"But you are coming back here after those five days, aren't you?"

"Maybe. If Tom says come, I come. Tom is boss. You know."

"Yes," I say. "Tom is boss. I know."

"So," he says firmly. "Good-bye."

I can't just say good-bye. I can't let him go just like that, because I already miss him, and the fear of missing him for a whole week makes me say the first thing that comes to my mind: "How do you say 'good-bye' in Arabic?"

"Arabic?" he says in a changed voice. "Why you want to know?"

"I just wanted to say it in your language," I say, feeling as though I made an unpardonable mistake.

"Arabic is for Arab people only," he says coldly. "You can't know a language you not born to know."

"You weren't born into English, but you speak it." I could have added "not very well," but I was already walking on a minefield.

"English is for everyone. Like America. But Arabic is not for everyone. You not born into Arabic, you can't speak it. Don't try."

"Okay, I won't try. But I think I know how to say it anyway. Salam aleikum."

He turns and leaves without a word. I can almost see his anger like a small cloud over his head. I want to run after him, to say I'm sorry, I won't do it anymore, whatever it is—saying those two Arabic words that the whole world knows without being born into them. But his anger is too hot; he won't even stop to hear me out. I must wait until it cools. I say to myself, it's a good thing that I've seen his anger in action. I know him better now, and I know about anger. Mine always cools.

—————◆—————

It's only the beginning of the week of his working away from my house, but it feels too long already. I can't do anything. I can't think of my Judean kings and queens; I can't think of anything but him. I have to meet him, if only for a moment. But how and where will I look for him? An apartment in Rego Park, he said. I imagine him toiling in the apartment, setting tiles in a bathroom, painting walls, finishing the floor, and so forth. I know Rego Park well, and I'm aware that even though it's not what you'd call a large neighborhood, it's large enough for me not to be able to find him.

It's the second day without him in the house. I just got home from work, tired, hungry and longing for a nap, but I can't stay here. I know I won't find him, but I have to try. I remember Alejandro saying he likes women in feminine clothes, like skirts, for example, or dresses, and he does not at all like the kinds of pants or tights American women strut around in, as though they don't know the meaning of modesty.

I change my clothes, so that in the 1 percent chance I have of finding him, I look modest enough to be his type of woman. A long skirt, black leggings, a shirt, a jacket. I look at myself in a mirror and it dawns on me why he runs away from me. It's this simple: I'm just not attractive enough. I put on a long black coat instead of the short jacket and tell myself it'll do, good-bye, mirror on the wall. I walk out of the house in what looks like a Hasid's long coat, a dark skirt, and a pair of black boots. I did my best to make myself look modest for an over-educated Mexican house painter who turned out to be a Palestinian second-in-command-on-a-fishing-boat, and if I find out that the only way he likes his women in public is with covered head, face, body, I'll make it clear that this is as far I'm willing to go, even for him. But I tell myself that my love itself is proof that he has no set rules about what should or should not be covered.

I drive on Queens Boulevard. It's so crowded on both sides of this wide street that it's impossible to see each person's face. I tell myself that I shouldn't even try to search for him here. He might just as well be walking on one of the many side streets, Sixty-Third Road, say, or Sixty-Fourth Drive, and since there is a drive, road, and avenue for each number, the task of finding him seems more hopeless than ever. I must think of something quickly, because I must see him today or I won't be able to go on. Suddenly it dawns on me that I could call him and simply ask him where he is. Why haven't I thought of it before? I must sound casual, as though I just happened to be in the neighborhood and suddenly remembered that he was working here this week.

I take out the phone and wait for my fingers to stop trembling so I can scroll down to his name. When I finally get to his name, I stare at it for a long time, because I don't have the courage to press the call button. All it takes is one slight push of a finger. Now it's ringing. Why isn't he picking up? He doesn't want to speak to me...or he remembers my saying those two words in Arabic...or the sight of my name on his caller ID repels him. My mind is full of absurd fears when it comes to this man.

Finally, he picks up and says hello in a dull voice.

"Hi, Alejandro." I try to sound as though there's nothing odd about my calling him at his other job.

The way he mumbles hello makes me regret that I've had the courage to push the call button. I tell him that I'm in Rego Park, and if he's leaving work now, I could meet him in the lobby of the building where he works and give him a ride back home, or if he has one of his evening jobs in Manhattan, I'll give him a ride to the subway...

"I not working in Rego Park today," he says. "I have day off today, I home."

Maybe I don't understand him because of his broken English, the way he skips forms of the verb "to be." Or maybe I just don't want to take it in, that he isn't here, when I came all the way to Rego Park, and I even got dressed in a special way to look both modest and attractive, even though it's not my way to dress up for a man. I was expecting to see him in five minutes, maximum ten, and if I don't see him today, how will I live the rest of the week? How will I survive? How will I go home?

My mouth is doing something, saying things, without asking my brain. My mouth says, "I wanted to talk to you about something."

"We talk another time, Galia."

My mouth says, "But I'm here in Rego Park, and I won't be here another time."

"I not in Rego Park, Galia."

He tries to sound patient, and I don't like it. I'm not someone who needs to have simple things such as "I'm not there" repeated or explained—it's just that my mouth got separated from the rest of me when the rest of me was trying to absorb the pain of his not being there, and it was my mouth, not me, that was producing helpless noises and making me sound like a fool.

I don't ask him why he took a day off, even though it's so unlike him to sacrifice a day's pay.

He says he's in a hurry, he wants to get to a mosque before the Asr prayer begins, and we can talk another time, okay?

Okay.

Driving back, I feel nothing. No feelings. No thoughts. When I'm home I barely have the strength to take off my silly clothes. I change into my old pants and stay on the couch the rest of the day and night, without moving a muscle. My thoughts repeat themselves like a broken record. So he's going to a mosque. Why should it concern me where someone is going on his day off? And since when have I started running after construction workers anyway? I have two master's degrees, I've read tons of books, and now I suffer because a construction worker is in a hurry to get to a mosque and won't speak to me when I come all the way to Rego Park to spend a few minutes with him? He can go to his Asr prayer if that's what he wants, his religion doesn't concern me, live and let live, as they say, and I can only hope he's not running away from me just because his religion is different from mine. If that's the reason he is running away from me, we must talk this out, even though I don't like talking about "my" religion and "your" religion; it's silly. Yet this pain I feel must be proof of something real about him. I wouldn't suffer like this because of a narrow-minded man. Construction worker or marine biologist, Arab or Mexican, he must stop making me suffer.

I realize that all this time I've been staring at a spot on the ceiling that looks like a stain. I briefly wonder whether it was caused by a leak from upstairs or whether it's the result of Alejandro's painting it a different shade of white, and if it was Alejandro then what was he thinking and why did he make this mistake? The longer I look at it, the blurrier it becomes, and I'm no longer looking at the spot on the ceiling but at something between the ceiling and my couch. The thing I'm looking at wasn't there before, and its outlines seem the same as those of the stain. At first I can see through it, then it solidifies and acquires the shape of a toe. It circles above my couch, and its orbits are so recklessly wide that I fear it might bump into a wall. Yet somehow, despite its wild circling, the toe manages to avoid the wall, like a pendulum swung by a drunk who is aware of limits. The circles become smaller, as though the toe has made its point; it is satisfied with the impression it has made on me and doesn't need to call attention to itself anymore. It appears to shrink, from adult-size to child-size to almost nothing. My unhappiness is lifted. I can move my arms and legs for the first time in the eighteen hours of lying here. I jump up from the couch and look for something to write with: I don't want to miss a single sentence from the dictation that has already begun.

CHAPTER 5

THE HASMONEAN CHRONICLE

———————

THE GOD WHO HAD HIS way with Tzadikah had no statues erected in his honor in Judea, yet he was quite a powerful little god in his own unusual way. His name was Janus, and he was not a Greek but a Roman deity. He presided over thresholds and thus had a way of seeing the past and the future simultaneously, as any god would or should, but for him it was more a job than a pastime. He was that seam between what was and what will be, and it was on the borderline between past and future that he had his way with Tzadikah, for she, like him, was a kind of seam. It was her offspring, and her offspring's offspring, whose actions would pave the way to a sequence of predicted events that would eventually result in her people's loss of their homeland, and their homelessness would last for two thousand years during which countries would appear and perish and everything in the world would change, except for her people's longing to return. When they would finally do so, some of them would find themselves standing at the very place where Tzadikah stumbled at a loose plank in a doorway.

She fell at a threshold of her new house, and a cry of pain issuing from her mouth was so loud that her husband had her brought into their bedroom, which was second in magnificence only to the banquet hall. Jonathan was high priest and strategist of Judea, and Simon, as the high priest's brother, had the power to summon the best physicians to care for his wife. Tzadikah's pain continued unabated as the physicians consulted with each other and administered every possible salve for her body and soul. Once the pain subsided they left her alone.

It was then that Janus came to her bed.

She half-saw his face, which had a good side and a bad side, but as she was unconscious, she had no reaction, and he possessed her with the incredible ease he had always dreamed of. Incredible, because she was Tzadikah, always right, and because she was the most virtuous of the Maccabee wives, the most stubborn in her virtue, and neither Zeus nor Apollo, well-versed in seduction of mortal women, had managed to get anywhere with her, while this little god of the future made himself not only comfortable in her bed but was also unquestionably accepted.

Yet it was not the body of the two-faced deity, rising and falling in rhythm to his unshared delight, that she felt in her innermost being, but the rise and fall of her children's children's fortunes—and when Janus thought that she cried out from the euphoria induced by his energetic love-making, it was a spasm of a different kind that made her tears flow. She was still only half-conscious, therefore she couldn't tell him that she was seeing the future to which the offspring she was to bear from this union would eventually lead her people, and that this terrible future could not be avoided, for the seed that both Zeus and Apollo had unsuccessfully tried to sow in the other Maccabee women had finally been implanted. She gave out another cry, even louder than before, and again the deluded two-faced god mistook it for proof of his prowess, and this flattered his boyish ego. As he was about to rest at her side with his possessive hands on her belly, he heard a commotion outside, and just before the door opened, he fled.

Tzadikah was so relieved to see Simon with a bevy of priests and physicians burst into the bedroom that she sat up in bed and lifted her arms to Simon and begged him to catch the fleeing god, but because of the fear and pain and who knows what else, the words came out of her mouth garbled, and the ones that reached her husband sounded more like "Oh my god" than a request to catch the god guilty of raping her. Behind Simon stood Nehemiah, the royal physician, appointed to this post by Judah, whose various wounds he had treated with salves made of herbs prepared to Nehora's specifications. Behind Nehemiah stood one of the priests from the Temple; Tzadikah couldn't remember his name, but he looked vaguely familiar and definitely Sadducean. Behind him was a retinue of five or six priests, all summoned here by Simon to offer prayers for his wife's recovery. Behind the priests stood Tzadikah's children, two boys, Mattathias and Judah, and a girl, Shifrah. The boys, twelve and thirteen, were just about to enter their adolescence, while Shifrah, who was fifteen and in full bloom, had already been promised in advantageous marriage to Ptolemy, son of Abubus.

Shifrah was the only one who was not congratulating Simon on Tzadikah's recovery or loudly wondering how a healthy woman of thirty-three could have fallen at the smooth threshold she had crossed so many times without any mishap. The boys jumped and hugged their father and mother, and the fact that in their hugging they seemed to favor their father noticeably more than their mother led Tzadikah to remark that they loved Simon more than her, who was, after all, the cause of this little celebration. The older boy said that their father's round belly made it easy for them to hug him, that it was like a handle they could hold onto, and his brother added that it was like a pillow they could put their heads on and relax, or like a ball they could squeeze, and that the belly was easier for them to reach than his head or his shoulders. The boys would have gone on enumerating the advantages of hugging their father if Tzadikah hadn't put a stop to it with an imperious "Enough!" Simon, seeing how affected Tzadikah was by the boys' neglect of her, said that love was not a matter of roundness of certain parts of one's body but the ability to tell right from wrong that a parent conveys to the child, and that this love is like a chain that binds the child to the tradition of his elders.

It was quite a little speech, and Simon would have continued it if his eyes hadn't met his daughter's. Shifrah was standing alone, as far from the family scene as she could manage. Her gaze was full of dark watchfulness, and Simon felt unpleasantly reminded of something, but as he did not wish to search his heart for what it reminded him of, he took his eyes off his beloved Shifrah and moved them back onto his beloved Tzadikah, or not so much Tzadikah herself as her right knee, which was being treated by Nehemiah, their royal physician and trusted friend. Nehemiah was touching the knee with finger-length instruments of his own making, for which he was duly famous far beyond the borders of Judea. Even physicians from Antioch or far-away Athens and Rome came to learn from him and desired to possess his instruments, which cured a patient as though by magic.

As Tzadikah held up her leg very straight, Simon realized the impropriety implicit in this scene: his wife holding up her naked leg for the physician, while the room was becoming more crowded by the minute, and not only with immediate family members or close family friends. He gave the order for everyone to leave the room, and it was obeyed reluctantly as though the sight of the Maccabean woman's knee was indeed something to behold and to brag about later in the far and near corners of Jerusalem. Even Nehemiah left after a few more minutes of kindly deliberation. The knee was fine, he said, as fine as could be expected of a knee that just a short while ago had more suppurating wounds than he was able to count, and just as Tzadikah's fall that brought forth those wounds had no explanation so did the sudden disappearance of the wounds, he said, gathering his famous instruments into an elegant silver kit. Simon urged the boys to leave too, and they finally obeyed, pouting and patting their own bellies instead of their father's for a change, which Simon thought a good sign, considering their age and their overall silliness.

Now that there were only three of them in the room—husband, wife, and daughter—the girl's sullen demeanor dominated the room, and no matter how little the parents wished to acknowledge her sullenness, no matter how they tried to avert their eyes from the wall on which she leaned and with which she blended, they had to admit to themselves that their Shifrah was obviously unhappy.

"Why?" Simon asked.

No answer was forthcoming from Shifrah, but her sullenness grew, as if his question made the sullenness aware of itself, and instead of disappearing, it increased and focused on his face and chest and even his belly, whose roundness had elicited squeals of delight from his immature sons.

"You've been spending your days at the well, Shifrah," said Tzadikah. She wanted to say more, but her female intuition told her not to, yet as it was the same intuition that had failed to warn her of Janus showing up in her bed, she doubted that stopping now was the right course. Nevertheless, she stopped.

Then Simon spoke again, and listening to him, Tzadikah thought about how fortunate she was to be married to this man who was as loyal to his wife as he was to his people. Years later, when he became the successor to his legendary brothers, some of his detractors claimed that he gave more attention to his family than to the state, yet Tzadikah knew this was a lie, because Simon did not need to steal time from the state to give to his family: he gave equally to each.

Tzadikah had a brief glimpse of something, but she didn't know that it was a glimpse of the future. She saw a great assembly of priests and elders in Jerusalem; she saw them voting unanimously for her husband to be their leader and high priest forever, or until "there should arise a faithful prophet," and she saw a man with the whitest beard and a hidden hole for a mouth through which words came like an echo from a cave, the only man who didn't vote for Simon. He explained his decision not by his distrust of Simon's qualities as a leader of the Jews but by the repugnance he felt for the voting process, which, he said, was Greek and therefore suspect—but other than this tremendous repugnance that, he said, deprived him of his nightly sleep, Simon was the man...He certainly was the man for her, notwithstanding today's little episode with Janus, which was already gone from her mind as though it had never happened at all.

Now Simon was speaking to their daughter, trying to dispel her gloom by praising smoothed-cheeked Ptolemy as a wonderful match. Seeing that he was not succeeding, he switched to praising Ptolemy's great house whose mistress she would be, and whose famous baths she could spend all day luxuriating in, and whose multitude of servants would be at her total command, competing with each other in carrying out her every whim. Not that he, as a father, approved of his children's whims, but now that Shifrah was about to stop being a child and become a woman—a wife—a limited number of whims were allowed, he said.

The sullen look on Shifrah's face spread around the room, and Tzadikah noticed that a walls looked darker, fresh-cut flowers in a vase drooped, and even Simon, the great speaker and leader of the Jews, could not go on with his cheerful lies about his daughter's marriage in the face of so much sullenness. He closed his mouth, and the sullenness spread its tentacles over his face like a hungry vine taking possession of its victim.

Her parents didn't know that in her room Shifrah was plotting the end of the marriage that hadn't yet begun; that meals brought to her three times a day on a silver platter were eaten by her in bed; that she was becoming fat and sluggish from lying all day, and that she knew she was becoming fat and was satisfied with that, because Ptolemy, son of Abubus, would reject a fat bride, and she would be happy again, and she wouldn't have the dream that came every three nights in which her bridegroom was instructing someone to murder her father and another voice was disagreeing with Ptolemy by proposing a more effective way of killing. There was no use telling Simon about it. She had tried telling him once, after the dream came the fifth time, and not only had he brushed her off without paying her any attention, but when she persisted in asking him not to give her away to the man who contemplated his murder, Simon sent his Essene to talk it over with her, visionary to visionary. The Essene, who spent his life in contemplation and therefore was an authority on spiritual matters, listened to her with barely concealed boredom and, when she finished, sighed and said that pubescent girls were known to have hysterical premonitions that revealed less about the future than about their own fears, and that Shifrah's recurrent dream was no more than a reflection of her own uncertainty, which, understandable though it was, was not at all unusual. This uncertainty was something she had to deal with by telling herself that she was not the first girl to marry a man chosen by her father in the interests of the state, and that belonging to a ruling family had its drawbacks as well as its benefits, and as the benefits surely outweighed the drawbacks and her dream was the only drawback she could complain about, she was a lucky girl indeed.

On the day of the wedding, they broke down her door and forced her into a wedding gown that ripped at the seams because the tailor who had made it knew only her old dimensions, as did everyone, including her parents, whose surprise at seeing her flesh bulge out of the gown was matched only by dismay on the face of the groom. Yet his look was not a simple dismay: it was mixed with satisfaction, as though this was just what he expected, a fat wife, a girl who was rumored to have been pretty but who became ugly just for him, which was her way of saying "don't touch me"—and he was only too glad to comply, because he did not consent to this marriage in the hope of finding a solution to his natural urges. He had enough concubines waiting for him at home. The thing he wanted was not the girl but power, and his mild disgust for the bride's flesh suited him just fine because an attraction would have made it harder to carry out his plan.

When it was time for Ptolemy to depart with his new wife and his retinue of slaves and soldiers, Shifrah ran to her father and clasped her hands behind his neck, clinging to him with all her strength. She wouldn't let go of him, even as Simon gently tried to push her away. She cried so bitterly and clung so desperately that the guards sobbed as they tore her away from him and half-carried, half-dragged her to the carriage and lowered her onto a seat next to Ptolemy. When the horses began to move, she shrieked like a madwoman, "Remember the dream, abba! Blood in the dish, abba! Blood in the dish!"

Years later, Simon and his two older sons, Mattathias and Judas, were inspecting the cities of Judea, talking to both rich and poor, questioning them on their needs and having a clerk record everything, a service he performed for his descendants who could learn from the fairness with which Simon treated his people, as well as a service for the immediate needs of the citizens. The clerk's notes would be copied the same day and taken to Jerusalem, where helpers appointed by Simon would go over the list and gather the needed provisions to be sent to the parties in question.

When Simon and his sons went down to Jericho, Ptolemy sent his minions to show them the way to Dok, a little stronghold he had built on a cliff northwest of Jericho. Once there, they were given seats of honor in a banquet hall decorated with as much gold and silver as Simon's own banquet hall, and this led his son Mattathias to remark that Ptolemy had aped his father's style of home decoration, while Judas, his other son, piped in that he hoped Ptolemy aped not only the splendor of their father's walls but also the brilliance of his ideas and the glory of his fair rule.

They expected Shifrah to come out and greet them but were told that she was unwell. Simon hadn't seen his daughter since the day of the wedding when she was torn away from him and carried to Ptolemy's carriage by guards who could still remember the grief her body left on their hands like paint that wouldn't come off. Mattathias quietly told Simon that he didn't believe Shifrah could be so unwell that she wouldn't come out to greet them.

"I know my sister," he said with conviction. "I know her."

Simon stopped a servant who was carrying a dish with so much meat it resembled a mountain topped with a tower of olives and grapes. He asked whether Ptolemy was going to join them and was told that the master was busy but that he would come for the dessert.

"The most extraordinary dessert known to man," the servant assured them as he set the huge dish between the father and the two sons.

The famous wine of Jericho was served in the shapeliest goblets Simon had ever seen outside his own palace, and he praised the wine as goblet after goblet was refilled for him from a large barrel decorated with two emeralds, one in the front, another in the back, which, young Judas noted, suggested a lack of taste, while his brother, too drunk for words, nodded his agreement as he fell asleep with his head on a plate.

Ptolemy kept his promise and showed up for the dessert, the most extraordinary dessert indeed, bloody and vicious and quick, as twelve armed men sprang up on the unsuspecting guests and cut their throats like piglets. Their blood poured into plates and jars and goblets and the open barrel, where it mixed with the famous Jericho wine.

Thus Shifrah was proven right, but no one told her that her dream had come to pass, nor did she need to be told, as she never doubted its reality. She whiled away her days as one of her husband's concubines, and nothing mattered to her, except one thing: Ptolemy's own head on a plate. She saw it everywhere. The floating head dessert, she called the image, and added a caption: "He repaid my father's good with evil, and this is how he ended up."

ALEJANDRO

The Professor tells me to pay more attention to her writing. He says that my inability to accomplish my task comes from my not realizing that all I have to do is follow her story as closely as I can.

"Your weakness," he says, "comes from your not taking her writing the way it should be taken, which is seriously." He says that her story is a map, and that she herself has no idea that she is writing a map, a kind of guidelines for us. He repeats again and again that if I could only see that the solution to the problem between us and them lies in her story, I would know how to accomplish my task.

"Follow her book to the letter," he says. "To kill for the sake of an idea, you must have a complete understanding of the enemy's thinking. For example, who is that Ptolemy, son of Abubus, that she portrays as such a monster? When you have a deeper understanding of her ideas, if you can call them that, you realize that he was one of us because he did the right thing." When he sees that I don't understand, he suggests that I reread the chapter in which Ptolemy invites Simon and his sons to a feast in his fortress, and a servant promises "the most extraordinary dessert known to man" which, as we find out a few paragraphs later, is the Jewish king's own head on a plate—his and his two sons.

I want to say, "So you think that her writing is telling me to cut off her head and let her blood pour out and mix with wine?" But all I say is, "She doesn't drink."

"Of course she drinks," he says good-naturedly. He slaps my back and says that I'm a fool to think that anyone could write that kind of story without consuming alcohol. All writers drink, he says, he worked in publishing, he knows. All of them, he says with conviction, but especially the ones who don't understand the significance of their own writing. And it's obvious that she doesn't understand the significance of her story, because if she did, would she be...?

"Would she be what?" I ask.

"You're not a fool. You should know."

I tell him no, I don't know. He says, "She's helping us, you understand? She's giving away things they kept secret, things what make them strong, and I don't mean weapons, I mean their other kind of strength, the kind that you can know only by belonging to them. And she doesn't realize that she's giving us all these ways to defeat them, because the secret history of their kings was meant to remain secret for a reason. By telling it to the whole world she's not simply weakening them but giving us step-by-step instructions what to do about the situation we find ourselves in."

"The situation?" I repeat after him like the fool that he just told me I was not.

He tells me he was wrong when he said I wasn't a fool if I don't understand what he's talking about. Even a baby would understand what situation he's talking about, but only a mature man would be able to actually do something about it. He thought that I was such a man. He squeezes my upper arm and says that my biceps are strong but they are not enough, a man has to have something in the top compartment too. He points at his head and says it's unfortunate that the man he chose for this vital mission is sadly lacking in the top compartment.

I don't like his calling my mind the top compartment. I don't know where he got this expression. Speaking of heads, I would like to tell him that his suggestion to follow the example of Ptolemy, the smooth-cheeked crazy from Galia's manuscript who had his guests' heads cut off at a dinner table, is not exactly the way things are done in our time, no matter what he says about her book being a manual that we must follow to achieve our aims.

"Even if she doesn't drink," he says after a prolonged silence, "you can do it. You can find a way. The main thing is ... use your," he taps his head again. "The main thing is you make her trust you."

I would like to tell him that trust is not a problem. She trusts me more than I want her to; she follows me around like a puppy. When I was away from her house for a week, she came to Rego Park just to talk to me. I said we could talk another time, and wasn't I going back to work in her house in just a few days? But she couldn't wait, she had to talk to me right then. What happened? I asked politely. Nothing, she said. Then why so urgent? I'm just a construction worker employed in your house, why should you go to another part of town just to talk to me? I thought by telling her I was going to the Asr prayer I would make her understand that she couldn't follow me there. But even this didn't stop her; she wanted to go with me. I could say: You're a woman, you can't go to the mosque with me. Or, I could say, You're a Jew, you can't go to the mosque with me. Or, I could say, a mosque is not a bar or a disco; it is not a place to go out for a lady and a man. It's where you go to meet God, not man. But I kept these words inside my mind, and with my mouth I said: "I must hurry. The Asr prayer. Very sorry. We'll talk another time," and I hung up.

The Professor tells me that I've made him wait too long, just because my target looks nice and sounds nice. He says she tricked me into making me feel something for her. "You must fight these feelings, my friend, not only because they are forbidden by your religion, but because your task is waiting for you; your people are waiting for you. They waited long enough, while you've been wallowing in forbidden attraction, like any weak man in the presence of a nice-looking woman." As the Mastermind speaks, he rubs his smooth cheeks, and every word he says becomes etched into my heart. I forget that I wanted to ask him to get me off the hook with the guys; I forget that he hasn't delivered on his promise to get me a green card; I even forget something strange I figured out just before coming here, that the guys and those channels he always mentioned, which could help procure a green card for me, might be one and the same.

He says, "You're strong, solitary, and your duty to your people comes before any personal needs. Do not look at her, do not listen to her, cut her down and be on your way."

THE HASMONEAN CHRONICLE

———◆———

PTOLEMY, SON OF ABUBUS, WROTE a letter to Antiochus, son of Demetrius, requesting a large army to help him wrest the country from the Jews, now that he had gotten rid of their king and two of their king's heirs, an accomplishment he was certain Antiochus would appreciate.

Antiochus was coming out of his new bathhouse when he was handed Ptolemy's letter. While two of his female servants were drying him and pampering his skin with fragrant oils, he read the missive and thought the wording not sycophantic enough. Nevertheless, he gave an order to send some troops to Ptolemy, son of Abubus, governor of Jericho, because wresting Judea from the Maccabee brothers had been his intent for some time, and in Ptolemy he had a perfect figurehead, the tone of his letter notwithstanding.

"Judea shall be mine," said Antiochus, saluting himself.

He was so used to being saluted to by others that he was surprised it occurred to him only now that he could be his own most fervent admirer, and that the admiration of a man like himself would feel better than the admiration of lesser mortals, who feigned admiration out of fear or because they wanted something from him, like this Ptolemy, son of Abubus, governor of Jericho. Let him have the troops. Simon's youngest son, John, the last Hasmonean offspring, must be dealt with swiftly and decisively, before he learned of his father's and brothers' murder and before he set himself up as a strategist and commander of the Jews' army, something every Maccabean had in his blood.

"Cut down the third son before he has time to think up a single stratagem," he said in the privacy of his thinking room, the only room in the palace his ubiquitous first wife had no access to. Later, when he stood in front of his generals, his arm outstretched in the salute to himself he had devised in the privacy of his thinking room, he uttered the same words, in a voice imbued with royal intransigence.

"Cut down the last Maccabean before he has time to think up a single stratagem."

Yet, although Antiochus's words were obeyed to the letter, John, known as son of Simon but really son of Janus, engendered on the day when Tzadikah stumbled on a loose plank in the doorway, was not cut down.

The men sent to Gazara by smooth-cheeked Ptolemy with the intent to kill John were late, for one of Ptolemy's men, who nursed sympathy for John and hatred for Ptolemy, had notified John of the welcome his father and brothers had received in Ptolemy's fortress. Astounded as he was, John had the presence of mind to arrest the men, and in exchange for promised mercy, they gave him a detailed account of Ptolemy's plan to assassinate him and to see Judea squashed under his heel like a bug—a bug, repeated one of Ptolemy's men, while the others nodded.

John considered pardoning them, for in his mind they were not so much traitors as mere tools in the hands of an enemy, but his wife, seeing the softening in his eyes, was quick to remind him that these were the very same men whose hands had wielded weapons that turned his beloved father and two older brothers into bloody pulp and that even a slave could refuse to become a tool of a murderer.

"How can he, if he is a slave?"

"If his faith is strong," she said, "he can."

"A slave exists to carry out his master's orders."

Ramah was tired of her husband's leniency. Being a Hasmonean and a son of high priest did not automatically make him a man of high ambition, and she was determined to change him into the kind of man she deemed herself worthy of. Her man would become a man of deeds, a man who would make history. She spoke so passionately of the need to be firm with enemies and of his place in history that, to please her, John had his would-be assassins put to death and their bodies thrown into a ravine on the outskirts of Gazara where birds and rodents had their way with them. A new resolve filled young John. Now he knew what to do with the army sent by Antiochus, son of Demetrius, in support of Ptolemy's attack. He silently rode in front of his troops, his silence and the silence of his men more lethal than weapons that Antiochus's soldiers had in abundance but which they had no use for. Armed with the silence, John watched as the men who had been sent to turn him into bloody pulp threw away their weapons and ran, seeking refuge from their own shadows.

Back to Ptolemy, whose defeat was so total and whose existence so devoid of glory that the only way he could feel even slightly alive was by making Simon's daughter dance naked in front of him. His enjoyment of Shifrah's humiliation was even more complete when he ordered her to lie like a corpse on the stone floor and to keep this pose for as long as it took him to tire of the spectacle. It always ended with his stepping hard on her toes or fingers and then squeamishly wiping his feet with a cloth he kept for this purpose and muttering "Simon's offspring!" when she squealed in pain. With time, however, she learned to repress the cry of pain and lay there like a real corpse, which, she knew, was not as enjoyable for this killer of her father and brothers, who would not hesitate to use still harsher methods to elicit her cry—but because she practiced self-control and was helped by an image of her father lifting her up and saying, "Be strong, Shifrah," no moans came out of her mouth. Ptolemy's methods grew in cruelty until, fed up with her silence and her stubbornness, he pulled open her eyelids and realized that she was indeed a corpse. I'm done with the Jews, he said as he left the room.

But he wasn't done with them, because there was Tzadikah, Simon's wife, a woman so quiet and self-effacing you'd think she had never lived in a palace, had never tasted power, had not been accustomed to having her every wish carried out, because now she had no wishes at all, not even a small one, not even to see her daughter, which was the reason she had followed Simon and their two sons to Jericho. She had come here to delight in Shifrah's happiness. She wanted to touch it, to hold it, to pat it lovingly, as if it were a belly with a baby inside. And even if there was no baby, she wanted to see her daughter happy with her woman's lot, if only to relieve herself of the pangs of guilt that troubled her at the memory of Shifrah's cries of "Blood in the dish! Blood in the dish!" as she was torn away from her father and carried into her bridegroom's carriage.

Ptolemy had Tzadikah taken into the women's quarters, which in reality were nothing but cells the size of a closet. He had chosen the women's quarters for a reason—only one wall separated it from the banquet hall, and he was sure that this nearness would allow her to hear the moans of her dying husband and her two boys. She recognized the voices of each and was not surprised that Mattathias's cries were louder than Judah's or Simon's. He was always a wild boy, Mattathias, always "expressing himself," as he called it. She called it "throwing caution to the wind." "Talking out of his heart," he called it. Even at important occasions, such as meetings with foreign emissaries, he failed to restrain himself and considered this failure an achievement, despite his parents' disapproval. The self-control of others was a sign of cowardice, he claimed, and he didn't hesitate to say so in front of a Roman envoy, which was why Simon forbade him to appear at state banquets. Maybe in these last moments of his life, Simon wished he had forbidden him to come to this one too, not only because it would have kept this son alive but also because with his cries and whimpers he was an embarrassment to Simon's Maccabean dignity and strength. The other son, Judah, barely uttered a cry as he was overpowered by two large men in Ptolemy's employ, but that single cry was so painfully recognized by Tzadikah in her little room that she immediately lost her consciousness. She regained it days later. She did not know how many, because no one cared to inform her of the passage of time, nor did she wish to know, dragged as she was through various rooms of Ptolemy's fortress, her head hitting the cold stone floor, room after room, all of them the same, unrecognizable, alien, except for gold and silver decorations she recognized as wedding gifts from Simon. They brought her out onto the turrets of the castle. She saw the sky and took a gulp of fresh air for the first time in days, and that gulp helped her regain her consciousness. She felt something smooth touch her neck but didn't know what it was. A second later, when it touched her neck again, deeper, she realized that it was sharp, a knife, perhaps a spear, she wasn't sure, they were all the same to her, men's tools for killing and maiming. She was only a woman, and an old woman at that. Surely Ptolemy wouldn't do this to his mother-in-law? What "this" was she couldn't imagine until the sharpness penetrated still deeper and her cry of pain was echoed by a man's cry from down below. She couldn't see who it was, but the voice was so familiar, so dear, that it could only be that of her one remaining son, John. Now that she was certain it was him, she wondered why he was there; what was he doing in the place where his father and his two brothers had been murdered? Had he become infected with the longing for death? Was he here to give his life to smooth-cheeked Ptolemy in an odd solidarity with his father and brothers? This was so unlike his life-loving self that at first she suspected her youngest son had gone mad with grief and it was the madness that had summoned him here. In the moments that followed his first cry, she heard other sounds, and they filled her with hope, because they were voices of Simon's men, and they were shouting her name and demanding her freedom, and just as she began feeling joy in the realization that they had come to take her away from here, the sharpness that had tormented her neck migrated south, under her left breast, and the louder they shouted down below for her freedom, the deeper it went in, and she tried to restrain herself from crying out but couldn't.

She heard John's cry of compassion echoing hers of pain, and she understood everything: that she was brought out onto the turrets with the sole purpose of stopping her son and his soldiers from storming the fortress, and she also understood that smooth-cheeked Ptolemy was smarter than any of the villains the Hasmonean family had encountered in the past. The thought that she had given her poor Shifrah to this villain penetrated her deeper than the torturer's spear. Now the physical pain inflicted by the spear became a refuge from the pain of her soul. Instead of crying out in pain, she called out to John and in disjointed words ordered him to go on with his pursuit of Ptolemy instead of standing there like a victim paralyzed by the sight of her pain.

"In the name of your father Simon, your brother Judah, your brother Mattathias, and your sister Shifrah, I command you to ignore my pain and to go on with your righteous conquest."

John made an earnest attempt to surround the castle, but every time he heard his mother's cry of pain, a look of madness appeared on his face, so disorienting to his troops that they could not muster the courage to confront Ptolemy's soldiers, who scattered them like crows simply by making a few steps forward and waving their weapons. John realized that if he didn't stop feeling his mother's pain like his own, the castle would be lost and his father and brother left un-avenged—therefore he numbed himself to his mother's cries and rallied his men.

The attack was so sudden that Ptolemy's men retreated, and John pursued them until he was within the castle walls, at which point Ptolemy, who had been watching the battle from his hiding place, resorted to the trick he'd been saving until the end and had the torturer drive the spear into Tzadikah's heart. As his mother breathed her last on the castle's turrets, John fell on the ground, uncon-scious, and had to be carried away by two of his men. The battle was lost, John's contingent retreated to Jerusalem, and smooth-cheeked Ptolemy, son of Abubus, governor of Jericho, went on as before.

ALEJANDRO

When the Professor ends his speech, his eyes are shining and his smooth cheeks are red from all the rubbing, which I think he does in order to help himself put more power into his words. I would like to tell him that he doesn't have to rub his cheeks for his words to have power over me. I would like it not to be so, but there's nothing I can do. The next time I find myself standing next to Galia, I'm ready to turn them into action. Here she is, showing me one of those silly pieces of furniture she painted, and wanting to know what I think.

"You want to know what I think?" I repeat after her, and instead of saying something I would usually say, like "It needs sanding," or "Why you use cheap brushes?", I move my right hand ever so slightly, but she obeys me beyond my wildest expectations, and there she is, standing with her back to the wall, ready for something that she has no understanding of. It's the same wall she painted those silly figures on, a boy shooting arrows at two adult figures, male and fe-male; I don't remember what she said about it, what deep significance it has for her, but whatever it is to her, to me it means nothing. Nothing, I repeat. She thinks I made that slight gesture with my hand because I want to kiss her and she stands on tiptoes to bring her lips closer to mine, and she looks me in the eyes with the look women have when they're ready to give themselves to a man, and I tell myself, in the Mastermind's voice, "Lady, you're the central point of the Hasmonean conspiracy; you're a danger to us; you're the job. You have no idea what you are for me: not a woman but the target." She closes her eyes and looks like she is ready to swoon from being so near me, and I say to myself: "The task is above attraction; desire is as irrelevant as pity; mercy is a weakness to overcome."

She takes my hand and puts it on her shoulder in such a way that my thumb can easily reach her throat. The Professor's words echo through my mind: "With a sharp knife cut the rope of attraction that binds you to her eyes and face and voice." I have no need of a knife. A little pressure in the right spot will do the job. I must find the spot and press it with my thumb. I can hear his voice again, "You must shake off this feeling, this strong feeling you have when she seeks you out, speaks to you, and looks at you as though her life depends on you."

"Your life depends on me." I think rather than say it, so I'm surprised when she nods eagerly to show that she agrees. She doesn't know that my thumb is almost on her throat and that she can be dead in the next few minutes. Her lips open, she stands on her toes, as though she wants to reach my lips with hers. Her misunderstanding of my intentions is so total that I pity her. I whisper the Professor's instructions, "I'm strong, solitary, and my duty to my people comes before any personal needs." She hears only the first two words and says, "Yes, you're strong, Alejandro." Her voice breaks through the Professor's voice in my head, making it sound ridiculous, and my thumb slips from her throat. I turn away from her. She's not the target but a woman, and I can't cut the rope of attraction that binds me to her eyes and face and voice. She puts her hand on my shoulder and says softly, "What is it, Alejandro?"

I turn to go, without a good-bye.

CHAPTER 6

THE HASMONEAN CHRONICLE

———

JOHN OBSERVED THE LAW WITH piety his grandfather Mattathias would have been proud of, and on those occasions when his talent for statecraft was dwarfed by contradictions embedded in the dual office of king and high priest, he sought Mattathias's advice.

When John was deciding whether to assume the Greek regnal name Hyrcanus, Mattathias's spirit was categorically against it, since the name stood for everything he had struggled against in his physical life—abomination of desolation, as it came to be called. After many furious debates, during which the young man was as patient with the old one as he could only hope one day to be with men of flesh-and-blood, Mattathias relented and even put a shimmery hand on his grandson's shoulder during the official ceremony as a sign of his good will.

John Hyrcanus summoned Mattathias's spirit again when the army of Antiochus Sidetes surrounded the walls of Jerusalem. John knew he was outnumbered. He asked his grandfather for permission to open King David's sepulcher to pay off his enemy, but Mattathias's spirit did not even let him finish his question.

"You shall not disturb the dust on King David's sepulcher!" he said, and there was so much fury in his half-whisper that his grandson decided not to pursue the subject.

Antiochus VII was the same enemy for John as his namesake, Antiochus IV, had been for the first generation of the Maccabees, but unlike his predecessors, this new Antiochus thirsted for silver more than for actual subjugation of the Jews. Although Antiochus's debts were not as tremendous as his army, they were large enough to make him uncomfortable when he lay with one of his many concubines, and as his male potency was more important to him than the size of his army, his insistence on not freeing Jerusalem until he was paid off had to be taken seriously.

John Hyrcanus, as he was now called, had to decide between paying Antiochus the outrageous sum he demanded or refusing him and thus precipitating the repeat of abomination of the desolation: Zeus installed in the Holy of Holies; mothers of circumcised babies thrown off city walls. He chose the first, not because he was a coward, as Mattathias accused him, but because he was a good man. The spirit of his grandfather had to be placated with an argument of freedom over subjugation, peace over war, even if the peace was to be bought with the sacrilege of opening King David's sepulcher and removing from its sacred depths the three thousand talents stipulated in Antiochus's ultimatum.

"The sepulcher shall be opened, for I cannot get this sum anywhere else. Grandfather," he said, "sometimes compromise takes as much courage as revolt."

But Mattathias's spirit refused to materialize for this treasonous talk, and John found that he was speaking to himself, putting his hand on empty air and mistaking it for his grandfather's arm. Tired of gesticulating like a madman with no audience to convince, he went to consult his wife. Unlike Mattathias, she lived in the real world, and her reality mattered to him more than loyalty to a ghost.

Ramah, named after the place where Samuel had lived and died, was a proud woman. None of her ancestors had relinquished their traditional names in the era of compulsory Hellenization, and she bore hers bravely, although courage to bear a purely Jewish name was no longer required, the victory of John's grandfather and his uncle Judah having made Jewish names acceptable again.

"I want you to tell me," she said, after John stopped talking, "the difference between two kinds of victories. One, a victory through compromise, and the other, a victory through war."

John was inclined to laugh off his wife's attempt to solve this problem with logical thinking, but seeing the seriousness in her eyes, he suppressed his initial reaction and said that a compromise does not necessary lead to a victory.

"No, it doesn't," she agreed. "It may lead to defeat."

"You think just like Mattathias!"

"I'm only saying that just as compromise and war can lead to victory, either one may just as well lead to defeat. If your aim is victory, why worry over which road takes you there?"

"But—"

"No buts," Ramah cut him off unceremoniously. "I wish to see the siege lifted as soon as possible. And without a single drop of blood shed by either side."

"Why should we care about their drops," said John, "if they didn't care about ours?"

"Because we're better, that's why. Because we abide by the Ten Commandments, it is incumbent upon us to care about not shedding blood, even of those who harm us. As the only Hasmonean wife who hasn't been tainted by a drop of Greek blood—or more precisely, a drop of an Olympian god's seed—I dare say I have some authority in the matter."

John said that he did not understand what she was implying with those words. This sounded like sheer madness to him—what Olympian god's seed was she talking about? Was she implying some impropriety on the part of his mother Tzadikah, the most virtuous of women, tortured to death in front of his own eyes by Ptolemy, or of dear auntie Yedidah, or of auntie Nehora, all of them paragons of womanly and every other kind of virtue?

"I was not trying to insult the women in your family," Ramah said. "I was only stating a little-known fact that, if looked at in a certain way, gives you the right, if not outright authority, to open King David's tomb, given that your aim is peaceful. Your Hasmonean predecessors reestablished the Law, but their wives broke the royal Davidic lineage required of Jewish kings, so your opening King David's sepulcher is an inherited right: by being the only one to come so close to King David's remains, you gain a chance to cleanse your line of all the impurities accrued since the first Hasmonean wives accepted an Olympian god's seed. I shall name no names. I have no wish to besmirch the reputations of our women. I'm simply providing you with reasons that can help you to see your opening of King David's sepulcher not as a terrible transgression but as a mitzvah. A good deed."

Untainted by an Olympian god's seed she may have been, but the fact that Ramah had a mind of a Greek logician could not be refuted by one not similarly trained. John Hyrcanus congratulated his spouse on being an exceptionally clever woman. That same day, he opened King David's sepulcher, without any help from craftsmen who had the tools and the skills necessary for opening tombs untouched for centuries. He lifted a slab of stone that served as a lid, and another one that served as an inner door, and yet another that served as the tomb's fake bottom but in reality was a cleverly disguised treasure chest. He dipped his hands into the chest and counted exactly three thousand talents. He left the rest intact, returned the slabs to the exact position where they had rested for centuries, all of this with the outmost care not to disturb the sacred remains, which he did not see because he ordered his eyes not to see and his hands not to touch, not even by chance, the dust-and-cobweb-covered king. He put the silver into a linen bag he had brought with him and walked back to the palace under the cover of darkness.

That same night he sent his envoy Shemer to Antiochus Sidetes with a message that the tribute money would be transferred into his possession as soon as a meeting, with an appropriate security for both sides, could be arranged. Remembering only too well the fate that befell his father Simon, as well as that of his uncle Jonathan, he sent a delegation of his best men instead of going to meet Antiochus in person, as he did not want to test his suspicion that the Seleucid king might be less forthright than he, John, had wanted to believe on the memorable day when his wife Ramah, the one who did not carry in her body a drop of Greek blood, convinced him to pry open King David's tomb in order to pay the price of freedom. Having delivered the tribute, his delegation returned intact, with greetings from Antiochus and eyewitness accounts of Seleucid commanders shouting orders to their soldiers to gather their belongings.

A day passed, then another, and on the third day, in response to John's constantly asking "Are they gone?", Shemer, who knew the enemy's every move, said, "Almost," and on the fourth day, the answer was, "As far as the eye can see."

Ramah had no shortage of opportunities to speak about her advice that had saved the nation. As the king's wife, she had plenty of captive audiences, all of them treated to successive versions of the story. As more colorful details were added, the story grew into a legend that everyone knew, even those who lived as far away from Jerusalem as Hebron and Beersheba and who had never set their eyes on Ramah. They told each other how John entered the secret chamber and laid his hands on King David's sepulcher, which, as soon as John uttered the words of a psalm of David, "Hear the voice of my supplications, when I cry unto thee, when I lift up my hands towards thy holy miracle," opened by itself. They said: "So great is the power of God, that when we act righteously and in the right moment, He helps us open every door."

"Every door, children," Ramah repeated to her sons, Aristobulus, Antigonus, and Absalom. The older boys' Greek names were due to the same Hellenizing influence that made even John take on a Greek name, but just as she called her husband only Yohanan, never "Hyrcanus," so she called her sons by their Hebrew names. Her repetition of the story of her husband's opening of King David's sepulcher became fused, over the years, with the story of the period of stability that followed the retreat of Antiochus's forces from Jerusalem. Later, when the benefits of stability were exhausted, she would use it to explain why that period of calm was followed by a period of brash military conquests.

"King David's power," she would tell her captive audiences, "inspired my husband to the victories David himself would have been proud of. Trans-Jordan, Samaria, Galilee, Idumea: aren't these conquests worthy of David himself?"

Those who were guests of the Hasmoneans for the first time were regaled with the whole story, instead of a summary. The longer version usually began with, "If you want to understand how these conquests came about, with a peaceful man like my husband Yohanan at the helm, all you have to do is remember the miracle of the Opened Sepulcher."

Ramah needed fresh listeners. Her maternal instinct grew stronger as the boys grew bigger, and while she wanted to continue seeing them as small and in need of her care and storytelling warmth, they vehemently tore at the ties that bound them to her. When the boys' angry shouts became an everyday occurrence, John proposed that they have another child. Perhaps this time it would be a girl; after three boys, she surely wanted a girl, didn't she? She absolutely rejected the idea, saying that three pregnancies were more than enough for a fragile woman like herself—an intelligent woman, she called herself, not a breeder.

"But," said her husband, "I thought you were—everyone can see this, you're so maternal with our boys who no longer need to hold onto a mother. Boys grow up fast, while a girl can linger in her childhood. Besides, the docility that is a trait we all would like to take hold in our girls makes them good listeners. And a good listener is what you need."

Ramah didn't like to have her needs so clearly seen and catered to. She preferred to think of herself as taking care of others' needs—whether or not they wanted to, as her husband cleverly asserted, a little too cleverly for her taste. In the depths of her soul, she was a simple woman, she said. If her husband wanted a girl, there was no need for him to burden her womb. She heard of a little orphan girl brought from Samaria by a Pharisee priest famous for successfully converting locals through peaceful means: so great was his power of persuasion that people whose land had been conquered by the sword followed this man whose only weapons were faith and word. Could the little orphan girl be given to Ramah to raise as her own? This way she could have a daughter without taxing her womb yet again, she said.

Although he wielded the double power of high priest and king, John was powerless when his wife wanted something very much. It wasn't clear yet how much she wanted the little orphan girl, but if his wife persisted in asking for her, he would have to give in. The girl could be a servant in the eyes of the world, Ramah's little play-daughter at home. He thought of finding a way to have the two of them meet without drawing unnecessary attention, and he came to the conclusion that it was safer to have the girl brought to the palace than to have Ramah visit the girl.

When John Hyrcanus was alone with his thoughts, the humiliating terms of the truce with Antiochus VII Sidetes stood in front of him like arrows aiming at his heart. What did he pay those three hundred talents of silver for? For the countryside around Jerusalem, looted by Antiochus's men during their year-long siege? For refugees from the Judean defense effort who were not allowed to pass through Antiochus's lines and were trapped in the middle between the two armies? And if only the silver from the Tomb of David had been enough! The terms of the truce were very specific in their intent to humiliate him personally and Judea generally: break down the battlements on the walls of Jerusalem;

fight alongside Antiochus in the Seleucid war against the Parthians; recognize the Seleucid control over Judea. He agreed to all of it. There would have been no truce if he had rejected even one term.

Ramah's voice interrupted his thoughts.

"The priest's servant is waiting, Yohanan. He wants to know if you wish the girl brought here today."

"If you want her to be brought today, tell him so."

He didn't know how to say it, that her will was law inside the palace, and that the little girl was definitely an inside-the-palace matter, so it had to be what she wanted, not what he wanted, because in the inside-the-palace matters he was guided by the evasive sense of Ramah's pleasure. In moments of self-effacing honesty, he admitted to himself that it was Ramah's ambition, more than his own thoughtful inaction, that prompted him to put together a large mercenary army, something that had never been done in Judea, and with that army go out and conquer Samaria, Trans-Jordan, Galilee, and Idumea, crumbs that made Judea into a chunk instead of the small piece it had been upon his return from the Seleucid army. Now that the Idumeans had been subdued, their men-folk learning the essential words with which to address the God of the Jews, their women readying their hearths for the sacred inactivity of Sabbath, only now, finally, he had time to reflect.

Just as Ramah's ambition was responsible for his pushing the boundaries of Judea into the lands of the perennial enemies of the Jews, or, as she whispered to him every night before sleep overtook her, restoring Judea to its former size, so it was Ramah's ambition, or rather her need, that brought the foreign girl into the palace. With the foreign girl came domestic tumult, which robbed Hyrcanus of the time he had set aside for reflection. A month after they took her in, Ramah sensed rivalry between her three sons for the affections of the girl, who could not legally be a match to any of the three, for no matter how obediently Moriya observed the Law, her alien origin disqualified her from becoming anything other than what she was: a step-daughter loved by all, too much by some. Moriya was nine years of age when she was taken into the palace; she was fourteen when golden-haired Aristobulus, John's oldest son, informed his parents of his wish to marry her and to make her his queen.

"You may not contemplate your future kingship until I pass," his father said. But the son's passion for his step-sister was so great that it swept away his father's words, just as it had swept away the girl's resistance, as formidable as it was doomed, for he was stronger and a son of the king while she an alien, no matter how beloved.

Aristobulus was devious and spoiled and selfish, while she was a creature of dreams. Her favorite pastime was collecting small sticks and stones in the field outside city gates. The three brothers competed with each other in bringing unusual pieces of wood for her collection, and once Aristobulus even brought her a snake that could stay so still and straight it looked like an unusually beautiful stick, and only at his command would it move at all. Instead of inspiring her with awe for the hapless youth, the snake trick filled the girl with an even greater disgust for him, and she went straight to her step-parents' bedroom to report on their son's misdeeds. She knew he would be severely punished, just as all three brothers had been punished for hiding behind the bathhouse and peeping in a chink in the wall while she was removing her clothes and readying herself for a bath. The king and the queen were already in bed, and while they listened to her complaint with their usual patience, her stepfather's face made her think that something was amiss, and the queen, too, had a preoccupied look, and whatever it was that preoccupied her, it had little to do with snakes that could look like sticks.

She learned much later that a few weeks before a worthy bride had been found for Antigonus, but he had refused to come out to greet her and kept refusing to do so for days on end, and therefore this bride was offered to Aristobulus, who accepted her. Aristobulus had fewer hopes of winning Moriya's affections than Antigonus—not that the latter had reason to entertain any hopes, despite bragging to his brothers about winning much more than a casual glance or an equally casual touch, which was all that any of the brothers could hope for. On the very day Moriya entered her step-parents' bedchamber with the complaint about their oldest son's snake trick, a marriage between Aristobulus and Salome had been formally agreed upon by the parties involved, John Hyrcanus and Ramah representing the groom, and Simon ben Shetah, a revered sage and honorable citizen of Judea, representing the bride.

This was the explanation for the preoccupied look on her step-parents' faces, Moriya learned when none of it any longer mattered, because on the day she found out about the marriage agreement, a terrible thing happened to her, more terrible than Aristobulus's snake trick and even more terrible than the three brothers watching her through a secret chink in the bathhouse wall.

Moriya's temple was destroyed.

It was a miniature temple of sticks and stones built in an empty cabin in a lot behind the furthest wing of the palace. She told no one that the small knoll of stones on which she had built her temple was a replica of Mount Gerizim, because if she had said "Mount Gerizim" aloud, not only would she be confiding her innermost secret to the indifferent world, but her step-parents, who always protected her from every danger in the palace and beyond, might stop loving her and bar her from the palace forever, and where would she go, a girl alone in Jerusalem, a Samaritan girl, no matter how observant, a convert, a foreigner, alone in a strange land, an orphan? Her memory of her early years had become so hazy that she was afraid she might forget her parents completely, and to conquer her fear of forgetting them she created the replicas of their faces on the outside wall of her little temple. But deep inside she knew that it was only a trick of her mind, that her mother and father were either killed in the battle for Shechem or gone in some other, equally final way, and there was no chance of her ever seeing them again, except for in her mind's eye, where they gazed at her from the wall of her little temple.

"So the stones were for Mount Gerizim and the sticks were for the temple," she heard the brothers whisper at supper. She didn't look up to see which one it was, but it sounded like Aristobulus. He should be busy thinking about his bride, she thought. Maybe she should tell her stepmother Ramah, who always listened to her with love, patience, and pity. Moriya could put it in a way that showed she was concerned about Aristobulus's well-being: "It's a bad sign that instead of thinking about his bride Salome, Aristobulus follows me into my hideaway and destroys things that are dear to me."

This was only a thought, because no matter how much like a real mother Ramah was to her, it wouldn't be wise to test her love with a story of a miniature Samaritan temple Moriya had built in her hideaway. Everyone's patience had a limit, and besides, Ramah was the wife of the man on whose orders the real temple had been destroyed, so possibly her little toy temple amounted to treason, and if her stepmother told her stepfather, he might have no choice but give her over to the Sanhedrin to be judged. No, no, he wouldn't do it; he loved her like a father.

She was getting tired of these thoughts. She resumed collecting sticks and stones without any hope of building anything, just letting them pile up in the shed. She had just two piles, one of sticks and one of stones, without any suggestion of a temple, without any purpose. She couldn't help being what she had become: a collector of stones, a gatherer of sticks. They were a sickness that she couldn't cure in herself. Her arms and legs had become strong from carrying heavy loads, and her skin had become bronzed from spending so much time in the sun. She wanted to stop, yet she couldn't stop. She would sneak out of the palace every morning at dawn and come back late in the evening, tired, silent, and hungry. She had gotten used to being by herself, to not needing anyone, like a lone beast. Sometimes she talked to herself. Aristobulus, her oldest step-brother, came to her shed once, to talk. We have nothing to talk about, she said. He said yes, there was something to talk about. She didn't ask him what it was that he wanted to talk about, because she already knew. He wanted to talk about her. Her life. What was she doing with her life? Wasting it, she said, what else was there to do? He said that a girl her age was expected to marry and have children. She said, I wish you luck with whatever else you've come here to say, it shows you've no thinking of your own. Get out, she said after an uncomfortably long pause. I will not, he said. He added that he had come to guide her in matters personal and political. She said that she was not involved in political matters, and as for personal ones, she had none and she hoped to keep it that way. These are matters of grave importance, he said, reaching for her hand.

She did not make an attempt to withdraw it, as her attention was temporarily distracted by a sudden warmth throughout her body. She did not connect it to Aristobulus's hand holding hers. For a moment she thought that it might be some sickness, but the warmth was so pleasurable that she let go the worry about a disease. She made her hand into a fist, but Aristobulus's fingers gently unfolded it. She made her body into a fist, but his fingers unfolded it just as gently. The warmth was becoming almost unbearable, yet she resisted it without wanting to resist it, unfolded as she was to the utmost edge of her being, of which she had not been aware, pulsating to the rhythm of his flesh. "My queen," he said softly, and when she did not respond because the haze that had enveloped her temporarily robbed her of speech, he said gruffly, with a finality that startled even him, "My queen, I said. You shall be my queen." He covered her nakedness with the edge of her robe and stood up.

Aristobulus had much to think about: brothers who competed with him for Moriya's affections and a bride who had been foisted on him by his parents. The brother problem was easier to solve than that of the bride. He looked around the shed: sticks and stones, these were the interests of his future spouse, the one to be entrusted with the power of ruling Judea with him. Yet he could want no other woman. He knew this as surely as that his name was Aristobulus, or Judah—the Greek and the Hebrew of it. A Jewish king with a Greek name—this they will accept, both the people and the Sanhedrin. But a Jewish king with a Greek name and a Samaritan wife—this was asking for more than the Sanhedrin could allow, even now, with the limitations on its power imposed by his father.

In the following days and weeks, between visits to Moriya's shed and his solitary walks in the fields and orchards where he picked up interesting sticks and stones as presents for her, he devised a plan, simple and awesome at the same time. Simple, because it guaranteed him what he wanted most—marriage to Moriya; awesome, because the risk he would take upon himself by getting rid of Salome and then making the world think that his Moriya *was* Salome was awesome.

The world he had to convince that Moriya was Salome was huge: it included his father, his mother, and his brothers light-hearted Antigonus and gentle Absalom, who were as much in love with Moriya as he was and therefore eager to undermine his plan. It also included servants in his father's palace, all the functionaries in his court, all of his father's Sadducee friends, and all of his Pharisee enemies, the scholars and members of Sanhedrin who, incensed as they were at Hyrcanus's withdrawing all religious power from them, would not let the false identity of his son's bride slip through their fingers.

Aristobulus was pacing his room when his brothers Antigonus and Absalom came in without knocking. Absalom sat down quietly in a corner, as he usually did, without a word. Antigonus stood, his arms folded at chest level, and watched as his brother paced—but after watching him pace until dusk settled in the room, he decided to sit down and invited his brother to sit with him. "I'm here to help," said Antigonus, known as light-hearted.

"I'm not asking for your help," said Aristobulus, still pacing.

"How do you intend to get rid of her?" said Antigonus.

"I don't know what you're talking about, or for that matter, who," said Aristobulus.

"Her," said Antigonus, "her...you know who I'm talking about."

"No," said his brother.

"Princess Salome. How are you going to get rid of her?"

"She is not princess yet. And who told you that I want to get rid of her?"

"Anyone can see what's going on between you and Moriya. The way you two sit at supper not daring to lift your eyes at each other or, for that matter, at anyone else, because you're so terrified that we will read your secret in your eyes."

"Nonsense," golden-haired Aristobulus said. "Who is terrified? What eyes? What secret?"

"Over there in the cabin." Antigonus winked at him.

"I don't know what you're talking about."

They went on like this for some time, until Antigonus, tired of beating around the bush, said that he was willing to take the disappearance of Princess Salome upon himself, to dirty his hands with crime, so to speak, if Aristobulus could talk Moriya into sharing her favors with him—what are brothers for, after all?

"You persist in calling Salome princess," said Aristobulus. "Her being Simeon ben Shetah's sister doesn't make her princess, no matter that he is the Nasi of the Sanhedrin."

"You know very well that Salome's line can be traced back to the Davidic dynasty and some in the Sanhedrin believe that her brother has more right to the throne than any of us Hasmoneans. She doesn't need to be married to you or me to be a princess," Antigonus said.

"What are you proposing?" Golden-haired Aristobulus stopped pacing and was about to sit down next to Antigonus when Moriya came into the room. She walked like an unseeing shadow, her hair loose and so long and so abundant that it covered her like a black curtain, and even though one could suppose she wore clothes on her body, there was no need of any, for her hair was enough. She stopped by a far wall without turning around, weighing words to say to these brothers whose desire for her was clouding their judgment.

Aristobulus and Antigonus were so much alike, that even she, who knew one of them intimately, had trouble telling one from the other, and as she stood with her back to them, she felt that her unseeing back had as good a chance of identifying them as her eyes. She didn't tell them that she liked Salome; that, after the first time she had briefly met Salome at a reception in the palace, Salome sent her an invitation to visit her and a carriage to make her ride pleasant. Moriya accepted the invitation but refused the carriage, and when she knocked on the door of Salome's house and a servant let her in, it was Salome's brother Simeon ben Shetach, the first sage and the thinnest man she ever saw, who was the first to welcome her, and it was he who said, pronouncing words in a way she had never heard before, "Ah, so it is you!" And when he saw her uncomprehending look, he clarified,

"You, with whom the Hasmonean brothers are so madly in love that they don't want to look at my sister who is a perfect match for either one, being of Davidic origin and as beautiful as yourself."

He invited her to follow him, and they walked along a corridor with many doors on either side, and each door was closed, and Moriya wondered silently who could be living in all these rooms. Simeon ben Shetach turned to her and said, "No one. This house was built by my great-grandparents, who had a large family living here, but these days it's only me and Salome." After a few more steps he added, "Now I see why our royal brothers want you so much they can't think of any other woman but you: you send out thought signals."

When they came to the last room in the women's quarters, Moriya saw that the walls were hung with draperies the color of Salome's hair, and Salome herself was rising up from her seat to greet her, and when Moriya looked Salome in the eyes, she saw something that made her weep, and she did not restrain herself: she let her tears flow freely. When she felt that all the water that had been in her eyes was out, she bowed to Salome, turned, and tiptoed out of the room. Simeon ben Shetach, the first sage and the thinnest man she ever saw, was waiting for her, and he led her back along the same corridor with the closed doors, and as he opened the front door for her, he said gently, "You saw my sister, and you understand what they're planning to do to her. You must talk them out of it." She nodded and left.

Now she stood with her back to the Hasmonean brothers, who were plotting exactly what Simeon ben Shetach had warned her about, although Simeon ben Shetach had not told her just what it was they were plotting and neither did the brothers say anything, yet the threat implied in their silence mingled with the scents of wild flowers that grew in the open spaces where she liked to roam, and with the stench of horses housed in numerous barns of the palatial yard, and with the smell of precious oils and sweat from the princes' bodies.

"You should not even contemplate it," said Moriya quietly. "Besides, by killing her you shall be killing me, and I doubt that is your intention."

"If killing her would be the same as killing you, then it follows that marrying you would be the same as marrying her," golden-haired Aristobulus said.

"What do I hear?" Absalom, the brother known as gentle, said from his corner. This was the first time he had spoken that day, and his voice sounded rusty, like a gate opening for the first time. "Truly 'tis the blood of the Greeks and their gods, all those Zeuses who forced our mother and grandmother to lie with them, that is speaking through you," he said to his brother. "Truly 'tis their kind of thinking. Their logic." He pronounced "logic" with contempt he reserved for the Pharisees, whom he greatly disliked and whom an old Sadducee acquaintance of his called "those who explain clear things." He assumed it was simply because the Pharisees, whose name, *perusim*, meant "separatist," competed with the Sadducees for the status of the best interpreters of the Law, which was something he could relate to, having competed with his brothers for Moriya's affections.

"I shall not let you kill Salome," Moriya whispered.

"Even if he wanted to, sister," said Absalom, "he wouldn't be able to. There are too many people behind Salome and her brother. The Sanhedrin sages and all the Pharisees would point at us. Even our golden-haired Aristobulus, no matter how arrogant and uncaring he is, does not wish to go down in history as the one who started his reign by unleashing a civil war."

Moriya wondered why Absalom was talking about Aristobulus's reign while their father, John Hyrcanus, was still alive. But instead of saying this out loud, she retreated even further behind the veil of her hair, unaware that by becoming invisible she was even more desirable. The three brothers, looking at the black veil of her hair, experienced the kind of longing that was almost too much to bear, and when she left the room, they had to perform a series of calming breaths they had learned from Yohanaan the Essene to regain the ability to walk and talk as if nothing had happened.

Later, in his own quarters, Aristobulus was trying on his father's crown, turning and twisting his neck in an attempt to see the back of his head, and as his reflection in the looking glass was not as imposing as he wished it to be, he fluffed up his golden hair in the back and smoothed it in the front. He was about to turn the crown sideways when his Edomite servant knocked and said that his father was calling him. He knew what this visit to his father's bed would lead to. Hyrcanus was on his sick bed, dying, and the future reign of his eldest son was approaching. As he made his way through a crowd of family members and courtiers, he cast a quick look in search of Moriya and was satisfied to see her standing near the bed, next to his mother, holding Ramah's hand, not like a little girl she once was but like a woman conscious of the healing power of her touch.

John Hyrcanus saw Aristobulus through half-closed eyes. He tried to lift himself up on his elbow but fell back into the bed. He opened his mouth and asked for something, which only Ramah, bending toward him, her ear on the level of his mouth, was able to discern. She voiced his request: "Leave me alone with my eldest son."

Aristobulus, perched awkwardly at the foot of his father's bed, regretted leaving the crown in his room, because if his father asked for it, and its whereabouts became known, his dreams of the throne might seem too greedy to the dying man whose one word was enough to deprive him of kingship. After a long silence, the word finally came, and he strained to hear it: it was not a request to see the crown but a plea for the presence of Ramah his wife and for all three of his sons and the girl Moriya, for she was like a daughter to him.

Again the family members stood in mournful poses around the dying king's bed, and John motioned for his wife again and, like before, she bent toward his lips, and he whispered to her, and when she straightened, she voiced his will.

"None of my sons will wear my crown. Too greedy for power, they will not rule well. My wife Ramah will succeed me. Our people need a patient and fair ruler, and Ramah will be a fair and patient queen—"

What came out of John's mouth next were not words but sounds like bubbling water, and then they stopped, and then one lone bubbling breath came out, and John Hyrcanus was no more.

"Liar!"

Pointing his finger at his mother's chest, Aristobulus accused her of misrepresenting his father's words on purpose. Ramah's only motive was power, he screamed. Her desire to be queen at the expense of her oldest son was shameless, she was stealing the crown off his head, and she would pay for it...they would all pay for it, he screamed. He shook his finger at them. He drilled it into the chest of each of them. He might have continued screaming and shaking his finger, if Moriya, her hair now in a neat bun, hadn't stood between him and the family and hadn't said that his behavior was abominable, that she despised him for making a mockery of his father's will, and that she, too, had heard the dying man's words, which were exactly what his mother transmitted. She continued that it would certainly be better for Judea if Ramah wore the crown, because it would be a disaster if the power had been given to him: it would destroy his character, she said, if it hadn't already. When Aristobulus, green with rage, ordered her to be silent, she produced the crown.

"He left it lying on the floor of his chamber," she said, shrugging, and it was this shrug that, according to some authorities, determined the course of Jewish history for years to come.

GALIA

A week later he's back at my house, pasting ten-inch pieces of parquet to staircase steps. He starts on the top floor and works his way down, and when I stand at the front entrance looking up, I see him crouching with his back to me, a few steps above the door of the second floor apartment. He is wearing his usual black work pants, and because he crouches on the steps, his pants slid down an inch at the waste to reveal his underwear. It's the most macho-looking underwear I've ever seen—not that I've seen a lot of men's underwear sticking out from their pants, but this one, with its camouflage color, is certainly not the white Fruit of the Loom kind worn by most American men.

I walk up a few steps, sit on the second floor landing, and take a pack of cigarettes out of my pocket.

Without turning his head, he says, "You smoke?"

"Sometimes," I say. I bought the pack ten minutes ago, because coming here, uninvited, required the kind of courage I wasn't sure I had. I can't tell him that I need courage to be near him and that the cigarettes help.

"So the construction is almost finished," I say.

"A day, maybe two. Maybe three. Depends on Tom."

I take a drag on my cigarette. I exhale. Courage. I take another drag. I exhale. More courage.

"I'll miss you," I say.

There is a long pause while he is working, his bent back to me.

"Me too," he says quietly. This is as much a confession of love as I'm ever going to get from him, so I should remember this. I should remember the way he is kneeling on the steps, the way his back is bent over his work, and the top of his camouflage underwear sticking out at the waist, and the embarrassed voice in which he says, "Me too." I don't know why he sounds embarrassed. From what little I know of the culture he is from, it's unusual for a man to feel embarrassed in the presence of a woman who confesses her feelings to him. Perhaps a situation like this isn't even possible in his culture, and that's why he is embarrassed.

I exhale and aim the smoke away from him.

"You don't mind that I smoke?" I ask.

"I lo-ove smoke." He says "love" with so much feeling that it makes me jealous. I wish he had this much feeling for me.

"Why did you quit then? If you love it so much?" Talking about his relationship with smoking is a kind of preparation for asking about his feelings for me, but that kind of talk is hard and requires more drags on the cigarette, while talk about smoking is easy.

He moves his right hand as though pushing something away: this is how he quit smoking. He pushed it away like this.

I inhale again. I'm getting closer to saying what mustn't be left unsaid. I'm almost ready. I exhale. Now.

"I really missed you last week when you were working in Rego Park."

No response from him. A few minutes pass in silence while he works and I smoke.

Then he turns to me.

"I kill you," he says quietly.

I want to say, "You know, it does feel like you kill me every time you don't want to talk to me." But instead I say, "Even this...your sense of humor...I'll miss it when the construction ends."

I can't see his face, because he is looking down at the parquet piece.

"Not sense of humor."

He makes an attempt to push away air, like he did a few minutes ago when he showed me how he quit smoking, but this time the wave comes out weak and unconvincing, almost childlike. This childlike quality, coupled with odd ferocity, is what drew me to him in the beginning. I never saw an American-born man looking so obviously embarrassed.

"Then what do you mean by you 'kill' me?"

"I must, Galia. I must."

"Why?"

"It's my job."

"You mean construction? Construction is your job? My talking bothers you?"

He doesn't respond, so I fill the silence by chatting about my own job and about how I prefer painting to teaching and how I couldn't make a living as an artist, and that's why I had to get a teaching job. I want to do something I really like, and now that I've tried my hand at wall painting and Venetian plaster, I realize that I like doing this almost as much as painting pictures. Painting pictures doesn't pay while painting walls pays, so this is a good field for me. "What do you think, Alejandro?"

Alejandro says he is talking about something more than painting. He is talking about life, death, and writing. "You write, Galia, yes?"

"Yes," I say, not quite sure why he's going in that direction again.

"Why you write against my people?"

"I don't write against your people, Alejandro. I told you this before. I don't write for or against any people. I write from inspiration. You know about inspiration?"

He grumbles something unintelligible, while furiously covering a parquet piece with varnish.

"You know, Alejandro, I'm secular. You know this word 'secular'? I don't follow dogmas of any religion. But when inspiration comes, this is how I experience a kind of…divine will. I don't call it 'God,' just because I'm not a believer in the usual sense of the word. When inspiration lets me know the right time to write, I write. Whatever inspiration gives me, I take. Basically, I record what I'm given. Exactly what I hear. Sometimes I don't even know what it means. I become an instrument—of hearing and recording. Do you know where the word 'inspiration' comes from?"

There is no time for Alejandro to give me his thoughts on the etymology of "inspiration," because we see Tom walking toward the house.

"Here is your boss," I say to Alejandro. "Here's Tom."

I automatically switch to a light voice, so different from the one in which I just had the intense exchange with Alejandro. I feel like a different person. Light, shallow, quick, funny.

Alejandro works faster. So fast, in fact, that he is finishing one step after another in seconds. As each step is completed, he goes down a step, without turning around and without interrupting his work, and as he descends, I must descend, too, so as not to be in his way. At first I don't understand this change, but then I remember that Tom pays him by the hour, so the more work he does in an hour, the better for Tom, which is why Alejandro is trying to please his boss by working fast.

There is a flicker of surprise in Tom's eyes when he sees me sitting a few steps away from Alejandro, as if he can't believe that I may be interested in one of his lesser guys instead of in his own elegant, golden-haired, confident self.

"What's this? You smoke, Galia?" he says lightly. "And where do you throw ash? On the floor?"

"Actually, Tom," I say peacefully, "I have this plate I'm using as an ashtray."

I show him the plate, but I might as well be showing it to a wall, that's how little effect it has on him. Tom is on his kidding track, and nothing can stop him now, especially since he knows that I don't mind his kidding at my expense. He spreads his kidding like an unstoppable charm that has won him hearts and minds of all my neighbors and many contracts with people like me.

"And who will clean up after you? Alejandro? So I'll have to pay him for extra time to clean up after Galia's smoking? I'm not a millionaire yet, you understand, eh?"

"There's nothing to clean, Tom."

"Nothing, you say? And what's this? Eh? What's this? And that? I don't want to pay for this, you understand?" He points at cigarette butts lying around.

"Those aren't mine. They must be Simon's." Simon is an electrician who leaves cigarette butts on the floor. I pick up one butt and hold it out to Tom. "See? These are Marlboros. I don't smoke Marlboro. I smoke Indian Spirit. Look." I show him the pack. "I would never smoke Marlboro. That's why these aren't my butts."

Alejandro is laughing quietly, his eyes on his work. It's good to see him laugh at my banter with Tom. I wish I heard him laugh more often so our conversations with their black holes of silences would be slightly less intense, but I like Alejandro the way he is, intense and hard-to-communicate-with and secretive about his other "job."

"Alright, Tom, I'm cleaning away Simon's cigarette butts. Next time maybe you should tell him not to throw them on the floor or to pick them up himself."

This doesn't stop Tom. He will tease me until he drops or he'll have to switch to Alejandro, and teasing your worker isn't as much fun as teasing your customer. That's what I am for Tom: a customer. And a customer, as a rule, doesn't know anything about construction, so whenever Tom speaks to me, he peppers his speech with "you understand?" and I'm not sure that he can say a sentence that doesn't end in "You understand? You understand?"

"Tom, why do you always say 'You understand?' Do you think I'm stupid? Because I'm not, Tom. I'm not stupid."

"I didn't say you're stupid, Galia."

"Then why do you always say, 'You understand? You understand?'"

"It's a habit, Galia."

"It's a bad habit, Tom. You say it to everyone. You say it to all your guys. And why do you call them guys? They're people. People find it demeaning. You understand?"

Tom is taken aback by my mocking him. He says I'm mocking him too much, and he looks to Alejandro for support, and Alejandro agrees. Yes, I'm mocking Tom too much—don't I understand that a man has his pride, and it's something you can't touch, no one can touch a man's pride, but especially a woman, you understand?

Now it's Alejandro mocking Tom with "You understand?" but Tom is so carried away with his own charm, it's as though he has charmed himself into not noticing that a guy working under him, whose livelihood depends on Tom, could be mocking him. I get carried away, too, and I hear myself say that we don't have Sharia law here, and a woman can touch a man's pride if he deserves such a touch, and Tom laughs at my witticism, and Alejandro shrugs in disdain, and when I see it, I regret my words because I want Alejandro to like what I say and I should've known that he wouldn't like my words about Sharia law and about a woman touching a man's pride.

Feeling witty, important, and charming, Tom goes to the basement to check up on his other guy, Ken, who has been working on the water meter. I hear Tom say what I have heard him say many times before, that the water meter is not Tom's responsibility; it's the responsibility of Tom's subcontractor, a plumber whose name is Bob but whom everyone calls the Chinese. The water meter was supposed to work, and Tom had already applied for a certificate, but when the DEP inspector came, he said that the water meter was dead, and not only was it dead, it was the wrong kind, because the DEP had new regulations, and the inspector was in a hurry and Tom had no time to explain anything to him when the inspector said, "Take out this meter and install a correct one." Now just when we need the Chinese again, he's vanished, says Tom, maybe he went to China, even though he wasn't from mainland China—he never lived in China at all, he was from Madagascar, can you believe it, the Chinese are everywhere, even in some island off Africa, but wherever this Chinese is from, he's gone, and now Tom has his best guy, Ken, working on a new meter, and Ken is Tom's most expensive guy. Tom even pays for Ken's medical insurance, you understand?

I'm sitting in the living room, trying to read, when Tom enters without knocking or ringing. During the construction, Tom and his crew use my house as their own, which is why, when Tom walks past me to the bathroom, I remind myself not to be surprised. On his way out, no longer in a rush, he stops in the middle of the room and surveys the cardboard boxes stacked one upon another next to three empty bookcases.

"Ah, you shouldn't drink so much, Galia!" he says, and only now I notice the words "Sauvignon Blanc" on every box.

"Those are books, Tom. Not wine. Books. I brought empty boxes from a liquor store to pack up all my books when I had to empty the house before the construction."

"Ah, books. Sure. Tell me about it. Books. You got all that wine for yourself to drink at night when nobody's looking. You should share a bottle with someone."

Joke with a female customer and she'll forget she wanted you to tell her about water meter problems, which she is not going to understand or care about anyway.

"I don't mind giving you a drink," I say, on my way to the kitchen. "Only not from a bottle from one of these boxes, because honestly, Tom, they contain only books." I take a glass, a bottle of Armenian wine called Kagor and show the label to Tom. He nods okay. I pour until he says, "That's good."

"What about Ken? I could go downstairs and ask him if he wants one too."

"Don't ask. Just bring it to him," Tom says on his way out the door, the wine glass in his hand like a rare bird.

A minute later I'm in the basement, standing with my hand outstretched in front of the two men. Ken takes the glass from my hand with a soft movement big men reserve for contact with women. He drinks, and I look at the new water meter, and while I'm thinking what to ask Tom about the meter, I feel Tom's hand on the back of my neck, pressing it softly, the way a big man touches a woman's neck after he drinks a glass of sweet Armenian wine called Kagor. Suddenly I realize that I'm half naked, the left strap of my black tank top has slid off my shoulder, and I interpret the manly squeeze not as an acknowledgement of my feminine powers but as a tribute to Kagor and the heat in the basement and the long day of work.

That's fine, because I have no feelings for Tom, even though he's an elegant, golden-haired, and confident man, and Alejandro has none of these fine qualities, yet my feelings for him are an ocean in which I drown. Tom's hand stays on the back of my neck only a fraction of a second, while he's talking to Ken about aspects of the water meter installation that are too technical for me to follow. I'm only half listening to them, because I'm thinking of the Muslim man with a Spanish first name and a secret Arab name and with who knows how many wives, this wall painter with a degree in marine biology and another "job" that he doesn't want to talk to me about, and an interest in my writing that he can't explain, if I don't count his mutterings about it being somehow against his people as an explanation.

I'm on the porch, watching Tom jump into his car, slam the door, start the engine, and wave to me in a devil-may-care-way of a former Eastern European, and I want to shout "good-bye" to him in Polish. I know the word, but I can't remember it now, just when I need it.

I turn around and see Alejandro on the stairs with a rag in one hand and a brush in another. "You said it well to him," he says, and I think he is talking about my mocking Tom for his "You understand?" habit.

I want to tell him that Tom interrupted our conversation, and that it was a very important one, for which I had to smoke cigarettes, something I don't do very often, and while the smoking helped to say certain things, we still need to talk, because the construction is almost over, two or three days, and I might never see him again.

Perhaps it looks like I've lost all shame, the way I sit on the porch, waiting for Alejandro to finish his work, so I can offer him a ride home. I don't even pretend to be doing anything. Just sitting there, waiting, with a newspaper on my lap. I don't read the paper because concentration on foreign and national disasters is not something my mind is capable of now, my poor mind that is so preoccupied with Alejandro that the only thing it lets me be aware of is Alejandro's footsteps in the basement as he cleans his brushes and washes his hands with paint thinner—an unhealthy practice, I told him once, but he shrugged it off. When he finally comes out, he walks past the porch where I'm waiting for him with my paper spread open on my lap. I gather up the courage to call out to him, "Alejandro! I can give you a ride, if you don't mind!"

He doesn't mind. I open the passenger door for him, and he climbs in with surprising agility. I drive in silence for five minutes, but to me it seems longer, because I want to talk to him so much, yet the longer we sit in silence, the more tongue-tied I feel.

Finally, he opens his mouth. I'm so happy to hear him talk that at first the meaning of what he says doesn't quite register. He says it's good that I put something over that tank top, because it was embarrassing the way I was wearing almost nothing, and there were two men there, not counting him, not because he is not a man, but because he feels like he already knows me. Still, as a man he expects purity in a woman. A woman is like a tender rose that has to be protected from the wind.

"What do you mean? Protected?"

He mumbles something about modesty and about how women must not interfere in men's conversation.

"But, Alejandro, I thought you liked the way I let Tom have it about 'You understand' and all that."

"I like. Yes, but want you understand how I am. I love my religion, and the rules of my religion are my rules."

"So are you saying that if I don't accept the rules of your religion, I can't be your friend? Is that what you're saying, Alejandro?"

"That's right. I love my religion," he says contentedly. "And my country suffered so much from all people who don't like us. If you're like them, you can't like me. Bye." He puts his hand on the door handle.

"You're not going anywhere while we're driving in the middle of all this traffic."

"Bye," he says, like a child with pouting lips.

"Look. All I said when we were talking on the stairs today before Tom came and interrupted us, all I said was that I…missed you. And I'm afraid I'll miss you terribly when the construction ends and you stop coming here to work. I don't want to miss you. I missed you so badly those five days you didn't work in my house, I couldn't even do anything. I don't care about the rules of your religion or my religion or about Westerners who don't like Muslims or Muslims who don't like Westerners. And I apologize for that silly joke about Sharia law. I didn't mean anything by it."

"You talk about my people like we're not people, like we don't have feelings."

"I didn't say anything about your people not having feelings. Where did you get that from? I would never say a thing like that."

"You said you don't care about rules of my religion."

"I said it because religion has nothing to do with this. What does any religion have to do with my missing a particular person? That's all I meant. I do respect rules of other people's religion. Did I tell you that years ago I worked in a Muslim school? The big one on Queens Boulevard? I taught students from all over the Muslim world. Egypt, Iraq, Yemen, Syria, Iran, but most of them were from Egypt. And I obeyed the rules. I even wore a headscarf when I was there. I didn't have to, because I was employed by the city, not by the school. As a New York City employee I was under no obligation to cover my head. But I did anyway. Out of respect for the rules of the Muslim school."

"That's nice," he says after a minute of what seems like deep thinking. He fills his lungs with courage and asks, "And what religion in Russia?"

"There are many religions in Russia," I say evasively.

"Yes, many," he agrees quickly. "But which?"

"When I lived there, it was a Communist country. You know what Marx said about religion—that it is the opium of the people. I first heard it in kindergarten. So the way I was brought up, religion didn't matter to anyone. But now it's changed, there's the Russian Orthodox Church; that's the main one. And then there are Catholics, and Muslims, and Jews, but most Jews are gone now."

"That's good," he says with strong feeling.

"Why is it good?"

"Good that Jews gone. Good for Russia. But bad for my people."

I say, "Oh? How is it bad for your people?"

"They go to Israel and kill my people. And when my people resist, they call us terrorists."

"When your people resist," I say, "by flying rockets into Israel's homes. And when Israel defends itself, the world press screams of disproportionate response, anti-Israeli boycotts multiply, and commissions to investigate war crimes are set up, which happens with no other conflict in the world. So tell me, do you personally know any of those who are called terrorists because they resist?"

"Me?" he says with a look of someone coming out of a deep sleep.

"Yes, you? Have you met any of them?"

He shakes his head. "Me, no."

"And do you personally know any Jewish people who come from Russia to Israel and who, as you say, kill your people?"

"No," he says after some consideration. "I saw them from distance."

"You saw them from a distance! And now you see one of them close up."

"Who?"

He really doesn't get it. It's the first time in my life that I'm in love with a slow man, yet it doesn't make my love for him any smaller. How strange life is.

"Me," I say. "I'm Jewish."

"You, Galia? You Jew?"

"Yes, me Jew," I say warily.

"I thought you Russian!"

"I was born in Moscow. But you insisted on knowing my religion."

"Not your religion, Galia. I asked, what religion in Russia."

"Yes, that's what you asked, but what you really wanted to know was my religion. You wanted to ask me about my religion but you didn't know how."

"You go to synagogue, Galia?"

"No, I don't go to synagogue, Alejandro."

"You don't go to synagogue, then you not Jew!" He is so happy with his conclusion that he stamps his feet and slaps his knees.

"One of the reasons I don't go to a synagogue is because when I was growing up, as I told you, there was no religion. It was an atheist country. In kindergarten, in school, this was the message we got. I was an unaware Jew. A Jew who didn't know the meaning of 'Jew'. I swore my allegiance to the red flag like a good pioneer and a symbolic red flag was tied around my throat. I was very proud to be the first in my third-grade class to become a pioneer for having the best grades. That's the kind of Jew I was."

He says that Communism comes from Jews. He says that Jews don't believe in God, that's why they made Communism and capitalism, too. Jews sit in all banks, and Jews control the world's media. All the trouble in the West comes from Jews. And in the East too, all the trouble in the world, it's from Jews.

I tell him that I don't know any Jews who are bankers, even though I'm sure they exist—and what about Jewish scientists or musicians or doctors or scholars or authors? Why does he say Jews control the world's media and banks? Do I look like a banker to him?

"But, Galia," he says softly, "you not really Jew. I told you, you don't go to synagogue, so you not Jew. You okay."

I say yes, I am a Jew. I'm 100 percent Jew for two reasons: one, I'm a memorial Jew, which means I'm a Jew in memory of my grandparents who perished in the Holocaust, and two, because my birth certificate says, in Russian, "Father, natsional'nost: Jew. Mother, natsional'nost: Jew," even though my parents didn't go to a synagogue, and their parents were as secular as I am, maybe even more so. But in the land of my birth the word "natsional'nost"—ethnicity—was in a passport, and it didn't matter that most Russian Jews didn't know anything about the religion. The passport said "Ethnicity: Jew," and everyone knew that this person was a Jew, and he would not be allowed to forget it, no matter how hard he tried.

Alejandro says it's not true. Not true that we would be reminded of our Jewishness at every step in Russia. I say, "I didn't say that it was 'at every step,' and anyway, how can you know if you never lived there, not even one week or one day or one hour?"

He says that everyone knows that Jews invented the Holocaust to make themselves look like victims, but everyone knows they're the ones who control the world.

"If you don't believe the Holocaust happened, I can tell you about my grandmother and her sister and the sister's husband and their small son who were among the twenty-four thousand taken into a forest on the outskirts of Riga where they were ordered to lie in a freshly dug ditch and wait for their turn to be shot. There wasn't enough room in the ditch for everyone, so those who didn't fit the first time were made to lie on top of those who were already dead or still dying, the head of the top person lying on the feet of the bottom one. The inventor of this method called it sardine style. They didn't have enough bullets for so many people, therefore mothers were ordered to hold their babies very close so one bullet could be used for two…Do you want to hear more?" I say.

He tells me that he knows a Jewish guy who has so much money, you wouldn't believe it, and when I interrupt him to say that I'm sure there are also Italians who have a lot of money, and Chinese, and Greeks, he shouts no, this Jewish guy is richer than all Italians and Greeks, he can just walk into a bank and they give him whatever he wants, ten thousand, a hundred thousand, two hundred thousand, all he has to do is shake hands with bank people and they give him the money.

I say, "Sure, there's a magic handshake that only Jews know, and they pass the secret from generation to generation."

My friend doesn't hear the irony in my voice. He is telling me how the Jews control the world with their handshake, how they send huge sums of money to Israel with a special code, and how Israel uses that money to kill his people, and then America, Israel's best friend, starts wars with one Muslim country after another.

"And all that, the wars and so forth, because of a magic handshake that helps your Jewish guy get money in a bank?"

We're on Steinway, near Alejandro's house. We've been sitting in the parked car for some time now, arguing about Jews controlling the world, and I can see Alejandro is upset that I make fun of his ideas about Jews. I don't want him to be upset, so I take a deep breath for courage and I touch his arm and say, "Alejandro, it's just that I thought so highly of you, and when you say these things, it's harder for me to continue thinking highly of you, and I want to continue, but how can I, when you say things that are…repulsive to me?"

He withdraws his arm from me and says that his faith does not permit a touch between himself and a…woman. He doesn't say "a Jewish woman," but the effect is the same as if he did say it, and my hand hangs limply in the emptiness before going back to rest on the wheel. He opens the door and steps out of the car without a single word.

ALEJANDRO

She comes when I'm so busy with staircase steps, I can't even greet her with a look. Not that I want to look very much, because my religion forbids looking at half-naked women. She has no idea why I don't look, that it's something to do with her tank top and her shorts, the way they reveal more than they conceal, but if I point it out to her, she'll say that everyone dresses like this in the summer, and she'd be right—but it doesn't mean I have to approve of it. I thought I made it clear to her, but she goes on with her illusions. Nothing can stop a Western woman in what she likes to think of as "love."

I work with my back to her, and she sits quietly for a while, and then I hear her light a match, and I smell cigarette smoke. I'm surprised because I never saw her smoke before. "You smoke, Galia?"

"Sometimes," she says. I think she is doing it to impress me with how worldly she is, but she is wrong, because it does not impress me at all. Smoking is something one does because one can't do without it, like I couldn't, which was why I quit—and if she only smokes sometimes, it's just a game, not a deadly habit it was for me.

I can feel her gathering her words in her mind, and with every exhalation her words are getting closer to the surface. When she finally says them, I'm surprised at how tame they are. I don't know why I expected more, something more reckless, something wilder from this Western woman wearing a flimsy set of shorts and top and now even this, smoking. She says the house is almost finished, and we both know it means that I won't be coming here anymore. There's always another construction site for me, because when it comes to getting contracts, there's no one like Tom. He impresses ladies with his elegance and wit, and they in turn tell their husbands to pick Tom and forget about all other contractors. The world will be a better place if only guys like Tom sign contracts with customers, no matter if houses come out all similar-looking, as long as it keeps the ladies happy.

Galia takes another drag on her cigarette and says that she is going to miss me. I can't let her see that maybe there's a small chance that I'll miss her too, because if a man lets a woman know this sort of thing, he is giving her the power to turn him into mush. And isn't that the root of all evil, all the problems with this society, this so-called Western world, this freedom for all, letting their women walk all over them wearing nothing but halter tops and shorts, and men no longer being men, because they've lost the power they were meant to have, and what is a man without power? I won't let a woman turn me into mush, no matter if I too, yes, I too, will miss her a little. So I say to her, "Me too," hoping it'll suffice. If she starts acting like she wants a complete confession of feelings, she'll only embarrass herself, because I don't let a woman turn me into mush. But she doesn't understand this; she wants more, and when she takes another drag on her cigarette and says again how she missed me last week, she comes close to achieving her aim. It's what the whole culture teaches them to do, all those women's magazines and shows, it's all about teaching them ways to turn us into mush.

I tell her I have a wife waiting for me in my country, which is true enough, but the reason I say it is not to show that I'm taken but to restore my power. A man has to have power over a woman, and he can use whatever means he has at his disposal, but what means do I have here? I have nothing, not even the strength to accomplish the mission for the Professor. So I tell her about my wife. I say just a couple of words. A wife. Kids. I should be more careful because this is a woman who knows how to trick a man. She asks, "How many?" I say, "Two", because I'm talking about my two kids, a boy and a girl. But as always she twists my words and says, "Two wives?" I have nothing to say to that. She asked this when we first met, and now again. Maybe she thinks that I'm going to say, "Yes, two wives, two kids with one, and two with another." I would like to know how she manages to trick me into talking about myself. Just when I was thinking about restoring the correct balance of power, she said this to me, putting me in danger because polygamy is against the law in this country. She said it to my face, without any embarrassment. I'd like to tell her that a woman has no right to speak to a man like this. I'm a man, and she is a woman. She has to know her place, not babble about things she can't understand. I give her my pushing away gesture, not touching her at all, just pushing hard at the air, and I turn away from her so she won't see my face.

When Tom shows up, I start working faster, because I know that's what he wants to see, that's what he pays me for. Galia is here with her cigarette, and Tom does the trick I've seen him do many times with female clients. He reprimands Galia for littering the floor with her cigarette butts, and she laughs because she thinks he's flirting with her. He thinks that he can twist her around his little finger, like he does with his other clients, making them forget whatever complaints about construction they thought of bringing up to him. But this woman has an answer to everything, the way she twists his words around, like she does with the cigarette butts being not hers but Simon's. Can't he see they're Marlboros, and she doesn't smoke Marlboros, her brand is Indian Spirit. Then she tells him not to say "You understand" all the time, and he tries but he can't. It comes out of his mouth every second: "You understand? You understand?" He is my boss and she takes him down a peg, and I like it. But I also don't like it, because she is a woman, and a woman has no right to speak to a man without respect in her voice, as I was trying to tell her before Tom showed up.

At the end of the workday she sits on the porch, reading a newspaper, but I know that her newspaper is just a cover, and what she is really doing is waiting for me, and that as soon as I appear on the porch she is going to ask if I want a ride home, and I'm not going to refuse. I had a long day, I'm tired, and I would like a ride, yes.

In the car she wants to talk about unimportant things, "small talk" they call it here, but I tell her exactly what I think: the rules of my religion do not let me tolerate this kind of behavior in a woman, the way she talks to Tom and me without respect and the way she dresses. If she wants to go on this way, she can't be my friend, so she has to choose, I tell her, and she says she doesn't want to choose, why should she choose between being my friend and following the rules of my religion? I become angry, because I feel she is getting close to defacing my religion, like so many people in this country who say bad things about it, and I'm not going to take it from anyone, especially her. I put my hand on the door handle. She says that religion is not important. I try to open the door but she keeps it locked. I can't get out, I'm stuck here, having to listen to her

Western views on how religion doesn't matter, and then I decide not to waste any more time and to ask the question I wanted to ask her for a long time but didn't have the courage. But I can't ask her this question point blank. I have to go the roundabout way, so I ask her about religion in Russia, and she tells me there isn't just one religion. She sounds like she doesn't want to talk about it, but I insist, because that's how I hope to get around to the question about her religion. She names three or four religious groups in Russia, and one of them is Jews, but she says most of them left already, and I say, "That's good," and she wants to know why it's good, and I tell her what they do to our people, they kill us, and I can see she doesn't like this kind of talk. She wants to know if I personally met any Jews in real life, and when I say I'm glad I didn't, she says, you're seeing one of them now. And I know that I don't have to ask my question anymore, because I have the answer. All this time I was hoping that the Professor, aka the Mastermind, was mistaken about her. Even though I read her writings, there was still a bit of a doubt left in me. I had a slight hope that her writings were just imagination, and that the Mastermind was wrong about her wanting to proclaim herself a descendant of those ancient kings, because if I could convince him that it was all imagination and that he was wrong about her, the task would be cancelled. It would be a relief not to have the thought of how to kill her go through my head, while she's talking to me or bringing me one of her sandwiches with the Russian salad that tastes like a badly made potato salad or giving me a ride like she is doing now, just because she wants to be with me a little longer. There she sits, almost next to me, with not enough clothes on her body, and having no idea what her presence is doing to me. There is a certain type of woman who never thinks about sex but just wants to *be* with a man she likes and misses him when he is away, and if I told her what I would like to do with her, she would be shocked, because she is one of those women who is pure in their mind despite their bodies being so scantily clad that a man has to look away just to control himself. And if I told her what I must do to her—not want but must—she would be more than shocked. She would not even believe it. She is a woman in love, and I may be a fool for letting her give me rides and sandwiches with *salat Olivier* and letting her trick me into talking about my personal life, but all this time while she thinks she can see into my mind and read me like a book, she hasn't the slightest idea that the Professor demands her life, and that I have left all the deadlines behind, one after another.

———•———

The Professor was so set on this idea of her as a Jew that if I told him she is a person like any other and not so bad as a woman too, and how can a nice person be a Jew, he would say I was forgetting my duties. I had an obligation to avenge the honor of my people and the honor of my father, who himself had given his life to avenge the honor of *his* father. If I told him that I had never heard her talk about the Hasmonean network or about her plans to proclaim herself queen, he would say that a woman's naked face had gone to my head and turned me into a weakling. But more than anything else, and despite the proof of it on every page of her writing, I believed that he made a mistake about her being a Jew, because even if she did get on my nerves with her sandwiches and her Venetian stucco door, she was a nice person. Too nice to be a Jew. I would like to tell the Mastermind that things are not as they used to be, and that he can't expect me to carry out his orders after what happened last time. I'm sure he hasn't forgotten it.

Soon after I met him and became what he called his "right hand", he wanted me to connect with a sister cell. It would've been more appropriate to call it a brother cell because it was all men. On the other hand, it is also true that we were not brothers anymore; we all stopped being brothers after we had lived here long enough to find our bearings, because to find our bearings here meant we had to stop being part of a group and become individuals. Individuals don't fight for a cause; they fight for themselves. That's why the people in our group weren't brothers; that's why "sister cell" was the right name, even if it sounded wrong at first. That's why, too, the Professor was the best leader we could have hoped to have, even though he was not, technically speaking, one of us, and maybe precisely because he was a Westerner, a professor in an American college, as well versed in the ways of individualism as anyone, he was able to fill us with ideas and determination and made us into something more than would-be fighters and amateurs: he gave us a reason to go on, to survive in this Western world, where we would have been lost without his guidance, because what worked back in our homeland no longer worked here. There our loyalty to the cause created a sense of brotherhood: we were all one another; we had no identity outside our devotion to the cause. But here a different thing was in the air, and no one could escape it, because individualism swallowed you up as surely as tribalism did over there.

After a few months of living in New York, I started seeing how different we were from one another. We were not real fighters; we were not even true believers in our cause; we were amateurs, because fighters must be united and we were not. Our differences grew the longer we stayed here, and since the only thing that still united us was our allegiance to the cause, I kept the allegiance in my role as the Professor's right-hand man, but I cut the brotherly ties. Perhaps "cut" is a wrong word for what happened; perhaps "avoided" is best. I avoided the brotherly ties, but by becoming the Professor's right-hand man, I thought I could keep myself out of danger. In the old country the cutting of the brotherly ties would have spelled danger to myself and my family, but it was different here, or at least I hoped it was.

I knew that I risked being misunderstood by the mother cell, but the guys here had no qualms with my separation, since everyone felt separate already, even if they didn't admit it. Each one of them had stopped being a brother after living here for a while, because the emotional climate here was not the kind that encourages selfless bonds. Here you were supposed to work out an identity that was more of an individual preference than a group destiny. Here even beggars who slept in the subway were individuals. Group identity was a thing of the past here. When I broke off with the cell and began to worry about something happening to my family, the Professor assured me that no action would be taken against Fatima and the kids. My mother and my sisters, too, would be safe from any act of revenge, and dishonor would not taint their names. He said this to reassure me, because even though there were times when I thought he was just playing the role of a mastermind to spice up his academic life with a bit of real-life adventure, he did have real connections to "his guys", as he called them, and even though we were amateurs, he knew how to make us feel like real fighters; he knew how to whip us up into a frenzy about our ancestral land and the Jews who colonized it. Jews: there was nothing like the sound of this word to unite us, to make us feel like brothers again.

When I heard from the Mastermind again, I was surprised. It was a direct order to act quickly in the house I was working on in Queens. A house belonging to a Jew, he said. A Jew with connections to other Jews. A worldwide Hasmonean network, he said. The kind that makes the world go round, with Jews controlling everything: banks, commerce, press. This woman with her writings about an ancient Jewish dynasty is the dot that connects all the other dots. Erase the dot, he said. That's when I started wondering: is she a Jew? I got to know her, and I said to myself, No, she is not a Jew, and her writings are not proof that she plans to install herself as queen of the Jews, or that she believes herself to be a descendant of those kings. I couldn't conceal this thought from the Mastermind: I was transparent to him, he knew everything that was going on inside me. Even though he was a Westerner, I began to fear him precisely because a Westerner who adopts our ways is to be feared more than one of us. I began to avoid dark streets on my way home from my evening jobs; I was on my guard every time I stepped outside. I asked myself--was Galia worth the risk? I wanted to get out but I was trapped in the Mastermind's words like a fly in a cobweb.

We're still in her car, and she is still talking, trying to find out what we have in common—not a lot, I'm glad to say. I ask her the question I wanted to ask for a long time, and she says yes. She doesn't even feel the need to hide it. She has no idea what this admission may cost her. It wasn't easy for me to disagree with the Professor, but I defended her to him when I said that she was not a Jew, and that her writings about those Jewish kings meant nothing, that his information was incorrect. But now that she herself admitted it, she must change it, and fast. If there's one thing worse than a knife in my ribs it is the fury of the Professor, when he rubs his smooth cheeks and demands to know why the Queen of the Jews is still alive.

There is only one solution. It's only too clear how much she likes me. It's almost indecent, the way she runs from wherever she is as soon as she hears my footsteps. When the idea of conversion first dawned on me, I thought it would be hard to convince her, and that her initial reaction to my proposal would be repulsion. But if I tell her that she is not safe, if I explain that her life is in grave danger, and that the conversion will give her peace and protection, she might consent. She's not so different from our women; she is a woman in love. She will do anything I say.

CHAPTER 7

THE HASMONEAN CHRONICLE

———◄►———

YANNAI ALEXANDER WAS JOHN HYRCANUS'S son by a woman whose name history did not preserve. She might have been his mistress or his concubine, but whoever she was, her presence on the sidelines of Hyrcanus's life caused Ramah so much pain that not only did he banish the woman to please his wife, he also sent Yannai as far away from the Hasmonean palace as he could, within reason. The boy was taken to Galilee to be raised by Hyrcanus's old friend, owner of a wealthy estate, who gave him every freedom a young person could dream of.

Upon hearing the news of his father's illness, Yannai set out for Jerusalem in the company of a servant whose loyalty he did not doubt but whose horse sensed danger ahead more acutely than its master did, because not only did it refuse to move after a rest-stop but it threw off its rider with a tender viciousness that was clearly meant to teach him a lesson without actually harming him. Yannai and the servant abandoned the horse, and for the rest of the journey the two of them rode together on Yannai's mare. It was night when they saw what looked like twinkling stars in the distance. They weren't sure of the unreality of their vision until the twinkling materialized into a troop of soldiers with torches. It was only when an officer shouted, "By the order of King Aristobulus, son of John Hyrcanus, son of Simon Hasmonean, son of Mattathias, son of Yohannan," and had his soldiers surround them, pull them off their single horse, put them in fetters, and transfer them into a prisoners' cart that Yannai remembered the prophetic behavior of his servant's horse and regretted not giving it the attention it had clearly demanded.

"You are dealing with a person of royal blood," he cried, "I'm Prince Yannai, John Hyrcanus's son. This man is my servant. Whoever you intended to capture, you have made a mistake—"

A soldier's fingers forced him to open his mouth so wide that his jaws seemed to break, and then the same rude, smelly fingers pushed a dirty cloth deep into his mouth. His servant was similarly gagged. After several hours of bobbing up and down in the cart, they heard the officer bark another order, and the same hands that had earlier gagged them now blindfolded them. They were not to see the approach to the fortress. They were not to see the grove of cypress trees on both sides of the road, the moat under the high wall, the gate slowly opening and shutting after them. When the shackles, the gag, and the blindfold had been removed, they felt they were delivered into a paradise rather than a dank fortress, so great was their relief at being able to see and to move their limbs and to open and close their mouths.

After the joy at being unshackled passed, Yannai realized he was looking at the wall of a cell. "I shall die here," he thought, "from loneliness or hunger or disease." After days and nights when death did not visit him and instead, solitude became a friend, his cell was opened and he was ordered to come out. He made step after step in the dark corridor, behind a shaggy man who had brought him his daily meals. He thought of how his time here, after the free-roaming youth in the Galilee, had taught him patience for small steps, like now, when he was apparently being taken into another cell, hopefully a better one, with more light—a small step forward—or perhaps with no light at all, a small step back.

He was taken into a large hall, empty except for a table on which a female corpse was laid out. Yannai recognized his stepmother, despite the years that had passed since he saw her as a boy on one of his rare visits to the Hasmonean palace in Jerusalem. An unshaven young man was sitting in a mourner's pose on a bench in front of Ramah. Absalom must have recognized his half-brother without raising his eyes, because he whispered, "Yannai!" to the woman lying before him, as though making her aware of Yannai's presence or asking her advice on the best course of action to take with this stranger, for despite Absalom's instant recognition of his half-brother, Yannai had been nothing but a rumor that had turned into a legend in Absalom's impressionable mind, and although he knew all sorts of ancient stories by heart, dealing with a legend in real life was something this youngest legal son of John Hyrcanus had absolutely no experience with.

"Yannai!" Gentle Absalom said again, this time looking up at him from his low seat. Adoration lit up his face. He had heard of Yannai's adventures in the Galilee, and he had constructed an image of his half-brother that was everything he himself was not: Absalom was shy, Yannai was daring; Absalom was bookish, Yannai a man of action; Absalom was soft-hearted and given to silent crying, Yannai was as hard as flint. He would have cried now too, but he perceived in the appearance of his mythical half-brother a sign from the above. Rising from his seat, he vaguely gestured at the space around him, perhaps thinking it the only proper way he should treat this man who was both a legend and a brother.

Yannai sat next to Absalom on the bench and looked at the dead queen with an expression that reflected a loss he could not possibly be feeling. He was unaware, until now, that Ramah and Absalom were being held in the fortress, fellow prisoners like himself, and it took him a few long moments to take in the truth that Ramah had starved herself to death as protest against their imprisonment. Only in fairy tales, he said, does a son jail his own mother. Yet this is no fairy tale, he mused aloud. This is as real as these walls. Gentle Absalom confirmed that this was real, but added that he found his imprisonment beneficial in some aspects, and when Yannai wanted to know more, he said that he found a way to meditate on God that made the Word come alive in ways he had never thought possible.

"I speak to God, and he responds," Absalom said modestly. "There are moments when my silent prayer becomes so full of joy that I can see signs of His presence in everything, even with my eyes closed, and I can hear him speak to me, and my heart overflows with the kind of joy I never thought possible. I feel I can survive anything, Aristobulus's treachery, this fortress, the cold, the dark, the lack of proper bedclothes or proper meals. I can experience joy even here."

Yannai did not want to contradict this newly found brother, whose mind, he saw, was so damaged by the prolonged isolation that it found a roundabout way to turn it into something good. Despite the misery of his imprisonment, Yannai never doubted his future as king, and the fact that Aristobulus found it necessary to lock him up only proved that he knew very well that the crown would fit Yannai's head better than his own.

Yannai did not wonder what motivated golden-haired Aristobulus to imprison Ramah, his mother, and Absalom, his brother, neither of whom was a likely contender for the crown, despite the rumors that John Hyrcanus had bequeathed it to Ramah before he left this world. All these thoughts passed through Yannai's mind as he sat on a bench next to Absalom, mourning the mother who had not been his. Neither of them knew how much time had passed—was it night or day—nor did they want to know, since such things stop mattering after confinement substitutes the flow of time with the flow of one's own thoughts. But at some point the same shaggy man who had brought Yannai here from his cell approached the brothers with an air of servility, the opposite of the hostile indifference with which he had treated them before, and this in itself was so startling that they could not wait for him to speak. Their impatience grew as the man's tongue struggled to enunciate a piece of news that obviously excited him very much, so much, in fact, that, as his excitement gave rise to fear, he started to shake, and this complicated the delivery of his message even more.

"Well, what is it?" Yannai shouted.

"Ah, ugh," struggled the shaggy one, "k...k...ing," he said.

"The king what? What does he want now?"

"D...d...dead."

"He wants us dead?"

"Ugh."

"So it wasn't enough for him to have us forget the beauty of the sky or the brightness of stars or a tree in bloom? It wasn't enough for him to lock up his own mother, who is now dead. None of it was enough for our king Aristobulus, our sweet brother. He wants us dead," Yannai said.

"I had long suspected that it would come to this," said Absalom softly.

The guard put his hands on his temples and rolled his eyes, expressing despair at being so misunderstood. He didn't mean *this*.

"N...no," he stumbled, "N...not you d...d...dead. The k...k...king d... dead," he said finally.

From that point on, events seemed to acquire a speed of their own. A delegation consisting of one member of the Great Sanhedrin and five soldiers was sent to the fortress with the purpose of freeing the prisoners and bringing them back to Jerusalem. Yannai declared that he could not wait for the delegation, which might take forever to arrive. He had wasted enough time in this fortress. He used the double authority of being a free man and a royal son to order the gates of the fortress unlocked immediately, so he and his servant, who had remained loyal to his master throughout their long imprisonment, could set out on their way to Jerusalem. Absalom, he said, should wait for the official delegation to take him back; it would be better for all concerned, and when Absalom looked at him doubtfully, he added, "Better for you, gentle Absalom."

When the members of the official delegation arrived and heard the news of Yannai's escape, they were ready to return to Jerusalem empty-handed, at which point one of the delegates remembered the other brother, the one who was still there, waiting to be freed. They requested that Absalom be brought to them, almost as an after-thought, which Absalom, when he found out about it, did not mind as much as the delegates feared he would, for this particular prince seemed to be immune to pride, and it became obvious very quickly that the workings of his own mind had a greater effect on him than whatever slights were rendered unto him by others.

It was Salome who had ordered that Yannai and Absalom be brought back to Jerusalem—not because she longed to see them, not because she was afraid of growing old as a lone widow, not because she wanted to marry one of them in a levirate marriage—but because Jerusalem needed a king, and no matter what private feelings she had about entering into a marriage with yet another Hasmonean, her duty as a Jerusalemite came first.

She was only doing her duty, Salome informed her brother Simeon ben Shetah when his face expressed less enthusiasm than she had expected when she told him that Yannai and Absalom were free. My duty as a citizen of Judea, she said solemnly, comes before my feelings as a woman. This was a point that Simon ben Shetah did not wish to contest, because he knew only too well that Salome's womanly feelings had been trampled on so many times in the past that he was surprised how she managed to look unaffected by it. Not only had all three Hasmonean brothers been feverishly in love with that orphan girl, Moriya, to the point where none of them would even consider his beautiful sister—the only marriage their parents, John Hyrcanus and Ramah, deemed right for a future king—but when Zachariah ben Gabba, a notorious busybody who should never have become a priest in the first place, had brought evidence, as he called it, of Moriya's Davidic origins, it seemed that Salome's claim to the throne was gone, totally and irredeemably.

The evidence was a soiled and tattered scroll with names of the girl's birth parents, and their parents and their parents' parents, generation upon generation, a well-established line of the House of David. The scroll described her parents' sumptuous life in Jerusalem before a mysterious misfortune robbed them of what was rightfully theirs and plunged them into a state of fear for their lives so complete that, to make their daughter's life more secure than their own, they looked for a home for their child with people who would never be suspected of any connection to them. No family in Jerusalem or in the villages outside the city seemed trustworthy enough for them to leave their daughter with. After traveling from village to village in a horse cart, they stopped in Anebta. Even when neighboring towns and villages struggled with drought or other seasonal mishaps, Anebta yielded such a rich harvest of grapes, figs, and almonds that no one starved there, and plenty of fruit was allowed to remain on trees past the point of ripeness. During their stay in Anebta, which lasted longer than they had planned since the rain had turned roads into streams of mud, they were told of Nethaniah and his wife Naomit, a Samaritan couple living in nearby Shechem, who were childless and faithful to God as well as to their fellow men and women. When the rain stopped and the roads dried, Simon ben Moriya's parents arrived in Shechem and knew at once that fate was looking after them, because the first house where they were offered shelter for the night belonged to the very couple they were seeking. After a fortnight spent in each other's company, they had no doubt that they had found the right home for their baby girl.

The soiled scroll that revealed the story of her origins was a surprise to many in Jerusalem, but most of all to Moriya. Now she could be free of her own little cult. She no longer had to recreate the words and gestures of Nethaniah and Naomit to keep them alive in spirit, because the good deed that the Samaritan couple committed when they took her in and gave her all the love they had in their hearts for a child had been repaid, she felt, by all those days and nights she had spent in silent prayer for them, throughout her years in the Hasmonean palace.

Now she was called Moriya bat Simon—daughter of Simon ben Zerubbabel—and instead of being a Samaritan girl turned Jew she was a bona fide Jew like everybody in Jerusalem, perhaps even more so, since her lineage compiled by a senior sage of the Great Sanhedrin, Josiah ben Yonathan, revealed without any doubt her birth parents' direct descent from the House of David. She was free to stay in her apartments in the Hasmonean palace and live in the shadow of the royal family as each prince's most secret object of desire, or she could choose one of them and let the Law join them as man and wife, in the eyes of God and men.

These were the words gentle Absalom said to Moriya after he returned from his imprisonment, with all his love for her intact, as he liked to say. He repeated again and again: in the eyes of God and men, in the eyes of the Law, the Hasmonean House and the House of David, joined by the Law, it was fate itself, it was more than fate; God's will had brought them together before her lofty origins became known. And now that they were known, nothing could stop them from standing under the wedding canopy.

She responded with pointed questions. "I wonder if Yannai—I mean, King Yannai—is happy being married to his dead brother's wife?" or, "Has anyone found out exactly what caused light-hearted Antigonus's death?"

It was a long time before Absalom made his dissatisfaction known to her. He could not go on admiring his dream bubbles, he said, if she was going to pop each one with a slender finger just when he was about to believe in it with all his heart.

"Why, you can continue to believe in them if you want to," she said reasonably. "I was simply trying to tell you that we can't go on with our daydreaming while essential matters of life and death in this palace remain unresolved."

"Such as?" he said, avoiding her eyes, as though he himself was guilty of light-hearted Antigonus's death.

"You don't have to look away," she said. "Nobody is suspecting *you* of masterminding your brother's murder."

"I know, but—" Absalom said shyly.

"For two reasons," said Moriya. "One, you were imprisoned in the fortress from which no one could escape. And two, you simply don't have a heart for murder, gentle Absalom."

"This sums it up," Absalom whispered sheepishly. Seeing Moriya's uncomprehending look, he added, "It sums up your image of me as a weakling, someone who can't accomplish anything. Not even a murder."

"That's a good thing, not a bad thing!" she exclaimed. "I could only marry a man who I would deem incapable of it the way I deem you incapable. Don't take me wrong, Absalom: to be incapable of murder is a compliment. In Moriya's eyes, to be gentle is more of an achievement than to be ruthless."

"If you say so…" He didn't raise his eyes at her and avoided her in palace hallways for the rest of the week.

Many years later, Moriya remembered those days with a frankness that continued to upset Absalom, despite his pride in having won a measure of mental and spiritual independence from his family over the years. She said, for example, that the murder of light-hearted Antigonus was not an exception and an accident, as Absalom liked to think, but the rule, and that had it not been for Antigonus's bad luck on that particular morning, he would have succumbed to the wiles of fate sooner or later—fate being exemplified by the fear with which his brother Aristobulus held on to the crown and the disregard of caution and the love of the good life that were light-hearted Antigonus's signature style.

"It was all Salome's fault," Absalom said, wanting to exonerate both Aristobulus and Antigonus and to blame only Salome, Alexandra Salome, Shlomtziyon. Her many names attested to her power and her all-pervasive influence in the Hasmonean kingdom. "Her fault," he repeated glumly, wishing that with every repetition he could wipe clean the slate on which the blood of one Hasmonean brother was spilled by the order of another.

"No," Moriya said, moving her right hand, with its raised index finger, from left to right, in front of Absalom's face. "You were locked up in the fortress when it happened, you have no idea how it was."

Then Moriya told him how Salome had filled her husband Aristobulus's mind with suspicions, telling him that his much-loved brother, his own Antigonus, was conspiring to steal the throne from him, and that if he didn't believe her and wanted proof, he should call Antigonus into his presence and specify that he should come completely unarmed. And what did she tell Antigonus as soon as she had Aristobulus's consent to call his brother into the throne room unarmed? Why, nothing short of "come in full armor," and Antigonus complied, to please his pretty sister-in-law and having no reason to suspect her, as no pretty woman could be suspected by him of having any brains at all. "Tell him that the King wishes to see him in his new armor right now," she said to a servant, and the servant went, and as soon as Antigonus appeared on the palace threshold in all his splendor, he was brutally cut down by the guards, and he fell, with his new armor and his flamboyant smile and rosy cheeks, naïve surprise spreading through all his features. He couldn't believe, he just couldn't believe that anyone would want to do this to him, the light-hearted Antigonus, of all people. "That's how it happened," Moriya said.

"Yes, that's how it was," Absalom said thoughtfully. "I was right when I said it was all Salome's fault. My brothers fell into her trap, both of them."

"And Yannai? What about Yannai?" said Moriya, letting the conversation drift into the same old channel that they had both unsuccessfully tried to avoid for years. She had her own theories about Yannai, or King Jonathan Alexander, the official name given to Yannai by scribes he had hired to write a complete history of his rule. She knew the first objection Absalom would raise every time she began talking about King Yannai was that Yannai and Absalom were only half-brothers, with an emphasis on "half," that they shared the father but not the mother—and isn't it true that the mother means more to a child than the father?

Yes, you're very different, Moriya would say. I couldn't love you if you were even a little bit like Yannai. But your father was John Hyrcanus, king and high priest, and while you inherited your father's gentleness, Yannai inherited everything else. All the military conquests, from the Galilee to the Northern Transjordan; his turning Judea's class system around to suit his whims; his elevating the Sadducees over the Pharisees; and his spilling the blood of ordinary Jerusalemites as though it were water—this was Yannai, this summed him up, she would say.

Just when Moriya's musings about Yannai were about to reach a point of no return, Absalom would remind her that this was the subject they had tried to avoid for years. Moriya would quickly agree with him. She would proudly comment on the apolitical direction their small family had taken. This, she said, was her idea of how she wanted to live her life. Outside of the palace. Outside of history books. Outside of the unending flow of calamities in which kings flounder like insects in poison that kills them all, with rare exception. Glory was short-lived, she liked to say, while life outside of the confines of power could be long and quiet. She wanted to raise her family in the anonymity of peace, but peace was no easier than anonymity, even though neither she nor Absalom lusted after the crown. Her Davidic lineage and his Hasmonean one were known to many influential people, and no matter how quietly they lived, the fact that in their veins flowed the blood of the two most powerful dynasties was bound to arouse someone's desire to do away with them and their only son, Avner. The fact that Avner survived long enough to reach adulthood was proof that Moriya's insistence on anonymity worked. Still, she often said that it would have been better for them to move far away from Jerusalem, to some obscure village where no one would know them.

But Absalom was attached to Jerusalem. This was his city, he couldn't leave it; this was where his roots were. "People are like plants," he liked to say, "and their roots matter: some thrive when transplanted, and some die." He belonged to the latter. It was enough that he had relinquished all claims to...not to the throne, he wasn't going to say that, but to the life of luxury, the palace, the splendor of baths. In his dreams he often saw himself bathing in gold water.

"Gold water?"

"Yes, gold water. Do you know why I dream of it?"

No, Moriya never heard him talk about the gold water of his dreams. Was it perhaps an omen of a misfortune that was going to befall them? Didn't they say treachery comes disguised as gold?

"I'm not talking about superstitions, Moriya. I'm talking about a dream, a longing I have. I spent many hours of my childhood soaking in a bath, watching the water reflect the gold of the ceiling. This is the gold water I still see in my dreams, ripples and all. I was raised in opulence, Moriya. I come from wealth. And even though I've renounced it, I still carry in my veins a desire for it. Sometimes it overcomes me, and you know what happens then."

Indeed, she knew, and she didn't want to revisit those days when Absalom lay spread-eagled on the floor, unable to get up or move his limbs, not even a bit, not even to let her know that he'd heard her begging him to wiggle his fingers or to lift his arm, no, he wouldn't do even that. He wasn't sick in a physical way; it was his spirit that ailed, and she was helpless when it came to healing his spirit. What could she give him except her love, which she'd been giving him all along—and he seemed happy enough with that, except for the times like these when he turned into an immovable heap of flesh without spirit.

Moriya had heard of sages who were said to have healing powers, and now that Yannai, the Slaughterer of Pharisees, the enemy of the sages, was dead, she knew it would be possible to contact them. In contrast to Yannai, the queen was so generous in restoring the Pharisees' privileges that in certain circles they called her "Shlomtzion, queen of the Pharisees." The way to the sages lay through the queen, but Moriya loathed taking this route. Didn't she structure her life just so she would stay out of Salome's, Alexandra's, Shlomtzion's way? Moriya thought of the queen's many names. She thought of historians of the future who would read one name in one chronicle and another in another chronicle and make the predictable mistake of piling up too many queens in the middle branch of the Hasmonean dynasty. There would be no one to set the poor historians straight as to the identity of the one and only regnant queen in Jewish history, whose many names were merely a reflection of her political skills. Who but a consummate politician could manage to please the Pharisee and the Saducee, the Jew and the Greek?

No, going through the queen was out of the question, Moriya thought. But there was Simeon ben Shetach, the queen's brother, a much better choice. Moriya wondered if he remembered her first visit to his house, many years ago, when Salome gazed at her in that room at the end of the long corridor and how she wept silently with her eyes on Moriya, because Moriya was loved by the three legal sons of John Hyrcanus, while Salome was scorned.

If Simeon ben Shetach, the first sage and the thinnest man she ever saw, remembered that long-ago visit, he never showed it or mentioned it in recent years. His ability to be both friendly and distant made it easy to think of it both ways: that he both remembered and didn't remember it. Moriya's feeling that she was *known* to him and that he could read her like a book was something she preferred to attribute to his wisdom rather than to that old memory.

She sent a messenger to Simeon ben Shetach but did not expect him to come so soon. When the sound of hoofs stopped near her house, she did not run out to greet him. That is why, after he came out of the carriage and knocked and there was no answer, he had time to look around and appreciate the choices these scions of two royal lines had made for themselves. The neighborhood was a humble one, and the sight of his splendid carriage attracted immediate attention. Boys of various ages surrounded it, and his servant had to shoo them away so Simeon ben Shetach could come out without overhearing their comments on his carriage or his rich attire.

"Humbling, truly humbling, to see you two living like outlaws," he said, when Moriya greeted him at the door.

She did not agree with Simeon ben Shetach's definition of their lives, but it was not to convince him that their life as ordinary citizens was happy that she had asked him to come. It was because on the floor lay her Absalom. He did not respond to his name, did not speak or move or recognize her. She was hoping there was a cure for his sickness, and if Simeon ben Shetach couldn't cure it, at least he could name it. Could he? Simeon ben Shetach walked around the spread-eagled man. In silence, his hands clasped behind his back, he circled and circled, and Moriya had to turn away so as not to become dizzy from watching him.

"An impossible disease needs an impossible cure," he said finally.

I want more than this, Moriya wanted to say. She wanted him to instruct her in the ways of healing Absalom's sickness, no matter how impossible, but Simeon ben Shetah knew her thoughts without her saying a word.

"Yes, indeed, there is a cure for this. But it is hidden."

"Can anything stay hidden from Simeon ben Shetach, the president of Sanhedrin?" Moriya asked.

"You'll be surprised, dear Moriya, how much stays hidden." After a moment's thought, he added, "For centuries."

"What sort of a cure is it, Simeon, that stays hidden for so long, and how can such a thing help Absalom who, even if he survives this and lives a long life, can hardly be expected to live for, as you say, centuries?"

Simeon ben Shetah said that he expected no one, not even Moriya who sent thought signals better than many sages, to understand his words about a cure that would take centuries. No, he expected no one, he repeated, no one, to realize the meaning of these two words put together, the cure and centuries. We have a tradition of prophets, he said. It is in our blood. And what are prophets? Merely people who know the future. Some know more, some less. He sighed and said modestly that he did not call himself a prophet; his knowledge lay somewhere in between. But from his in-between knowledge he could tell that Absalom's sickness was a sickness of the spirit, not of the flesh: a kind of spiritual un-ease. It required a spiritual cure, such as prayer. A familiar enough cure in our land, yes, but not a prayer by any so-called healer. The right man was needed, a man with a prayer in his hands.

Moriya wanted to know who the right man was and could Simeon, with his in-between knowledge, which was more than she herself could boast of, make the right man come?

"Your knowledge is no smaller than mine," Simeon corrected her gently, "but it travels in a different part of the world of the spirit, and even though you may know as much as I do, we do not know the same things. The man I'm talking about is familiar with both your part of the unseen world and mine and Absalom's, because the travels of his spirit encompass greater areas than any of us can imagine. He is a man of the spirit in a truer sense than anyone alive right now, and his knowledge is not constrained by the body, his own or anyone else's. And no, I cannot bring him to you, but you can bring him here yourself if you concentrate and send out a plea for help."

That night Moriya dreamt of baths. She dreamed of small houses built in a circle, and next to each house was a small pool—more like a well than a bath. She was looking at them as though from above and she could see everything. The baths were so close to the houses, they seemed like porches with water inside. In the middle of the circle of houses was a larger well, and it was this larger well was the center not only of the architectural design she was surveying but also of the spiritual life of the people who lived here. Someone emerged from the central bath, a man or a woman, she couldn't tell, as in this community long hair was an attribute of both men and women. Other than the long hair, she could see no gender differences, for the person was instantly robed. More people were emerging from smaller baths, one after another. The purified ones were hurrying toward a house of prayer, while a few others were bustling around a long table behind one of the huts. Time probably flowed faster in dreams, because soon enough the door of the little prayer hut opened to let out men and women lost in thought, walking silently one after another, toward the long table. Seats were taken; a short prayer was said by a man who half stood from his seat. He did not need to stand up completely or lift up his face for Moriya to realize that he was the one Simeon had told her about. Now all she had to do was wake up, compose a message, have it delivered to this man, and hope that the urgency of the message moved him enough to undertake a journey to Jerusalem.

She tried the words: "Scion of David, heal the husband of thy sister-in-spirit-and-in-blood." No, this won't do. She couldn't count on the importance of their common lineage, which was only a rumor for which she hadn't seen any proof in her dream. Besides, the first message was too wordy. She tried: "Absalom's fate lies in your hands." This was short and to the point. He would know what to do. But what was Absalom to this man? Was he important enough for him to leave the people of the village, whose leader he obviously was?

She was awake now. She didn't want to have another dream. She'd seen what she had seen; she had composed her message. Yet the need to lie down again was more powerful than her satisfaction in her message. So she lay down, and the dream that she dreamed this time was more real than Absalom's illness and more urgent than the need to cure him, and even as she dreamed it, she knew she would never forget it, which was something her grandchildren and great-grandchildren would testify to, because even in her decrepit old age she talked of the Man in Her Dream, as they called the Teacher.

In this new dream the noise of the crowd died down when the Teacher placed his hands on his heart, then lifted them toward the sky and spoke to it as one speaks to a friend, with quiet certitude. She could not make out his words, but she could see his moving lips. There was a moment of total darkness. It took her several moments to realize that he had entered the abode of the sick and that she was trying to see him from behind the film on the eyes of a blind person. She struggled to get out from that consciousness, but she was trapped in it. She felt the Teacher's hands on the head of the man in whom she was trapped, and the eyes through which a second ago she saw nothing were suddenly able to see. She saw the Teacher's hands. He was moving them in front of her eyes in uneven waves. He was raising his hands up and cupping them as though collecting the energy of the air and then spreading it in front of her eyes. With each wave of his hands she could see more. She did not like being stuck inside the mind of the blind person, and now that the crowd was celebrating the blind man's reentry into the world of the seeing, she liked it even less, because the first thing she saw with his newfound vision were gangrened arms and legs and stumps where limbs had been and festering wounds in place of noses and rotting scabs where ears had been. Seeing so much deformity and misfortune made her stomach fill with fluid that quickly rose up and filled her mouth with an ugly taste. She woke up, covered with her own filth. She had seen the Teacher in action; she had inhabited the mind of one healed by him; she had no need of any other proof. She walked over to Absalom, whose position on the floor had not changed.

"The Teacher will cure you," she said with certainty.

Absalom was not cured yet, therefore he did not respond.

GALIA

I haven't seen Alejandro for so long that I'm beginning to get used to a feeling that the world is not a good place for me. Something basic is wrong between me and the world, something that can't be fixed no matter how hard I try, and it can be set right only by his presence. I need to tell him how much his presence means to me, and even though he won't care to hear it, I need to tell him anyway.

I invent a plan to go to Manhattan after work just so I can call him from there and tell him that I'm just about a block away from his new job site. It takes a split second to scroll down to his name on my phone, but it takes forever to summon up the courage to hit the call button. When I finally press it, it's like plunging into deep water, head first.

He says hello in an indifferent voice, and this makes me speak too fast, even though I know that speaking fast to a person of limited English is the worst mistake I can make. The other mistake is speaking to him at all, but that can't be helped because I've already pressed the call button, and if I hadn't pressed it, I'd be torturing myself like Hamlet: to press or not to press. I tell him that I'm only a block away. I ask if I can stop by. I ask for a number of the building.

"But I finished work, I not in Manhattan now," he says in a warmer voice.

I ask him where he is and he says he is home, getting ready to do his laundry. With every word his voice is warming up, which fills me with surprise and suspicion.

"I want to talk to you," I say.

He says that he can come to me or I can come to him. His voice is so warm that I don't know what to think. I want to ask what happened, why is your voice suddenly so warm, I'm so used to your coldness that now I'm at a loss. But the conversation is over, the rush-hour crowd is jostling me, and I must decide what to do. Do I go back into the subway? There's nothing else for me to do in Manhattan, so I go down the same subway steps that I went up a few minutes ago. I take out my metro card and walk through a turnstile. I've made a decision: I will take the subway to his stop and call him from the street.

When I call him from outside his station, he sounds like he's forgotten that half an hour ago he said I could come to him or he could come to me. Now that I came to him, he doesn't even remember that we talked.

He asks, "Where are you?"

"I'm near Tutankhamen, the little Egyptian restaurant by the subway."

"Ah," he says tonelessly.

"I thought maybe we could meet in this restaurant and talk."

He responds with a silence that I could touch with my fingers. Then he says, "We go to my place?"

"Whatever."

By "Whatever" I mean "yes," only it's a slightly veiled, slightly less eager yes than a regular yes. By "Whatever" I mean I will go with you wherever you want to, it doesn't matter where. I say, "Whatever," meaning yes.

I wait by the restaurant, and I see crowds passing by and no sign of Alejandro. Maybe he forgot our conversation just like he forgot about my calling him from Manhattan. Maybe his work does this to him, handling wall paint all day long without a mask. He is proof that paint fumes kill brain cells. If this is what his job does to him, I will find him another line of work, where he won't inhale fumes that make him unable to remember simple things, such as meeting me near the Tutankhamen restaurant. When a woman agrees to go to a man's home, it shouldn't be taken for granted. Even if she herself thinks it's about nothing but talking. But talking at his place is not the same as talking in the street. It means something else.

When I'm almost sure he forgot about meeting me, I see him in the crowd. There's something more refined about his face than usual, as if he'd turned into a poet overnight. I follow him to his house, up a flight of stairs, into a spacious living room that he says he shares with three hard-working Muslim men. He fumbles with a key to his room and opens it wide for me. He stands aside with Eastern hospitality and says, "You arrre welcome!"

I didn't say, "Thank you," so why is he saying, "You arrre welcome!", or is it just another one of his mistakes? But soon I realize that his "welcome" is not a response to any kind of thank-you. That he is actually welcoming me to his house. He is welcoming a woman to his small room. And because his room is his bedroom, he is welcoming this woman to his bed.

But all of this comes to me much later. It comes in retrospect. Now all that registers is the happiness of being with him in the same place. His place, my place, the in-between place—it's a kind of togetherness, no matter where it is.

"Drink?" he says.

"Drink?"

"Water, juice, milk, coffee?"

"Thank you," I say. "No."

He gives me a glass of juice anyway and his hand briefly touches mine, and I know it's intentional, because a glass of juice can change hands without any touching. He puts on music that sounds like a mixture of a muezzin's call to prayer and some kind of pop. I ask him to please turn it off, I don't like it. He asks what kind of music I like, and I say, "Classical."

He says, "But this is classical Egyptian music."

"I mean something else by classical."

He turns it off and sits at the other end of a small table.

I look at a small bookshelf over his bed. There are ten or twelve books with Arabic letters on their spines. One of the books is big, and the letters on its spine are golden.

"Is that the Koran?" I ask innocently.

He is silent for a moment. It's not a good silence; it's the kind that breeds unfriendly thoughts, and I can feel them in the air, even before he opens his mouth.

"How you know Koran?" he says suspiciously.

"What?"

"You said Koran. How you know Koran?"

"How I know Koran?" I repeat stupidly as if Koran is a man I'm meeting secretly, while I shouldn't even know his name. Like Jake or Robert. How do you know Jake?

"I...well, I read parts of it."

"Why you read Koran? It's not your book."

"What do you mean, it's not my book?"

"What's the name of your book?"

"My book? You mean, the book I wrote? The book of my poems?"

"Not your poems, Galia. The book of Jews."

"You mean...the Torah?"

"Yes. That's your book. That's what you can say. The name of your book, you can say. The name of our book, you don't say. And that other one, the book of Christians, you don't say."

"Why can't I say the Koran or the New Testament? What will happen if I do?"

"You have your book. So talk about your book. Don't talk about our book."

"Look, Alejandro. I read many books. English, Russian, French, Spanish. I even have a collection of poems translated from Arabic. I can read any book I want. And I can say the name of any book I want. My tongue isn't going to wither away in my mouth and God isn't going to punish me."

He turns away from me. Something has changed in the room. The fog of feelings that enveloped us before the start of this conversation and made me so soft and pliable that he could have done with me anything he wanted is gone. But this man who works as a simple wall painter and goes by the name of Alejandro while at the same time not exactly hiding that his real name is Ammar has unusual ways of handling his desire. After the conversation about the book I'm supposed to read and the ban on naming the books that are not mine, I feel there isn't much left to say. I pull my jacket off the back of the chair and stand up.

"Going?" he says with regret.

"Yes," I say. I'm surprised to hear regret in his voice. What did he think I would do after his telling me that I can't say the name of his book?

I walk toward the door, and he opens it for me, almost as gallant as he was on the way in, when he said, "You arrre welcome!" in the most meaningful way, only now something else is mixed in with the gallantry. I'm not sure that I want to look at it too closely, because I'm out of the fog of feelings, and I have no intention of getting enveloped in them again.

When I walk to the subway station, the fog returns. It's as though he stopped being a physical person and his vapors are surrounding me and holding me and blending in with me. There is a simple word for it: attraction. I have heard of it, read about it, I know it happens to others, but it never happened to me quite this way. The fog makes me stumble. I almost fall down in the middle of a street and someone catches me. I can barely see him through the fog, but I don't need to see in order to know it's the fog maker himself. He says that I left too quickly—he wanted to walk me to the station, and do I mind if he walks with me?

"No," I say, "I don't mind at all."

He asks if I have heard of Khalil Gibran, the Arab poet who lived in America and who wrote a famous book of poems.

"But it's your book. I'm not supposed to read it or even say its name, right?"

"No, why?"

"Didn't you just tell me? When I was in your room? Didn't you tell me that I have my book, and you have your book, and Christians have their book, and that I shouldn't say the name of your book because I'm not a Muslim?"

"Galia," he says, with his hand on his heart. "I was talking about the books that came from God. Those books you can't say if it's not your religion. But these are poems, Galia. You said you like poems. You even write them."

"Yes, I like poems."

"Let's go back to my house, I'll show you poems from his book."

"You have a copy of Khalil Gibran's *The Prophet* at home?"

I didn't expect him to have any poems at home at all, and now that he tells me that he does, I'm glad. Maybe we'll have something to talk about, books to like and share, instead of those that can't be shared because he's a Muslim and I'm a Jew. I'm also glad that he ran out of his house and caught me when I almost fell.

This time, when he opens the door to his room, he doesn't say, "You arrre welcome," like he did the first time. I'm no longer a stranger here; I've taken root in this place, while the solemn words of welcome are meant for a first-timer, a total newbie. There's the bookshelf over the bed again, and I can't tell which spine with Arabic letters is Khalil Gibran, so I point at the shelf and ask, "Which one?"

"It's not here, it's on computer." He keys in some Arabic characters into a search window. I sit and wait while he is searching Arabic texts on the screen. It's taking so long that I want to encourage him to stop. I tell him I'll find it later in English. And anyway I can't read Arabic. He says it doesn't matter that I can't read Arabic, he wants to read it to me because of how it sounds, it's so beautiful. Arabic language is so beautiful, he says, you should learn it.

"Then teach it to me," I say.

"No," he says with humility so charming that the fog is now covering half the room and part of his face. "No. You're the teacher. I can't teach."

"If I loved a language as much as you love yours, I'd be able to teach it," I say.

I can see him thinking, going over the subjunctive. If I loved...as much as... I'd be able...I help him out by offering an easier sentence, "All I meant was...you love your language. That's all."

"I love my country," he says gravely. "I love my people. Everyone thinks we are terrorists, bad people. It is not true. We are not bad people. You don't love my people."

"But I didn't say anything bad about your people. I don't divide people into 'mine' and 'yours.'"

"Jews think they can kill everyone who is not Jew."

"Where did you get that?"

"It says in the book."

"What book did you read it in?"

"I didn't read it. I can't read your book."

"We're back to the old topic…your book, my book. It's the twenty-first century, Alejandro."

"In the twenty-first century important things will happen. Things that our book…how you say? Predicted?"

"And what was it that it predicted?"

He doesn't want to say it. He thinks I won't like it. Still, I coax it out of him, because if it's important to him, I want to know it. Finally he mumbles it.

"The struggle between Muslim and Jew."

All the time, while we are talking, there are changes in the room that I'm only half conscious of. Before he was sitting at the table, now he is sitting on the bed. He has drawn a curtain on the window and turned off the overhead light, but there is still dim light coming from somewhere. Our conversation makes me so uncomfortable that I jiggle a pack of cigarettes in my pocket. I jiggle it so vigorously that it falls out of my pocket. I bend down to pick it up. He misunderstands my movement. He thinks I'm kneeling in front of his bed. He pats the blanket and says, "You want to sit here?"

"No," I say. "It's just…my cigarettes fell out of my pocket."

"Cigarettes…" he says thoughtfully.

"So who will win?" I ask.

"What?"

"That struggle you were talking about. Who'll win?"

He is telling me how his people will kill my people, and his eyes are penetrating mine. I want to hide my eyes but can't. He falls silent and his eyes move to my lips, burning a hole in them, willing them to open. And my lips obey, but instead of receiving his lips, they form words and more words. It's a strange battle between love and repugnance: love on the personal level and repugnance on the collective.

He says, "Jews think Palestine is their land. It's not their land. It's our land." He says this almost lovingly. He says it with passion for his people and for my lips and my eyes and my arms and my shoulders.

My lips open to shoot out words. "There's a word, do you know it? It begins with an a. A modern word for the ancient hate. And now I hear it coming from you."

"We Arabs are Semites too. If we are anti-Semitic, then are we anti-ourselves?"

His English is so much better that I wonder how he managed to improve so fast.

"This is a specific word, it means only one thing, even though Arabs are Semites and Arabic is a Semitic language, this word means one thing only. It was coined in the nineteenth century and it means hatred of Jews."

"You Jews love playing the anti-Semitic card."

"You're just repeating other people's opinions. What does it all mean to you? You said you lived in Mexico and you even took a Spanish name and then you came here to earn money in construction. Why should it matter to you? You have your money problems, your painting jobs, your Venetian stucco jobs, your tools, all those rollers, brushes, plaster, and grout. These things are real. All that talk about your people, my people, your book, my book…it's abstract."

He looks into my eyes, and then he looks somewhere else. When he looks at me again, it's from far away, and it's almost impossible for me not to touch him, but it's also easy, because I'm used to doing the opposite of what I want. I take a few brisk steps to the door and stand still, glued to the floorboards. I put my hand on the doorknob, just to make it clear that I won't be reduced to this. I won't be controlled by attraction. Now the silence is over, and he stands up and walks over to where I'm standing. He swallows hard as though a pebble got stuck in his throat, opens his mouth and says shyly, "Galia," and then a pause, and again, "Galia, I want to kiss you."

I take a step, and although it's a small one, it gets me close enough, maybe an inch between us, maybe two. I put my arms around him and no inches are left. I'm expecting a kiss, therefore I'm surprised when he pushes me away and lifts up my shirt at the same time. He pushes and he lifts, and I understand what he wants to do with my shirt but I don't understand the pushing. Out of naïveté or perhaps stupidity I continue to resist until I find myself pressed close to the bed. He didn't even kiss me; he only said the words, and now the bed. I didn't expect this. But his place is only one room and the room is a bedroom, and I came here myself—what did I expect, coming to a man's bedroom like this. Like what? Unbidden. But he invited me; he wanted me to come, didn't he? No, that was later. I came here myself, yes, unbidden, because I wanted to…Wanted to what? I wanted to be with him, maybe not like this, but how? Ah, it must be my prudery speaking: I have too much baggage left from my Soviet Jewish upbringing. No, don't think Jewish, don't think Arab, because then it'll stop. But what is it that can stop, that I don't want to stop? What is happening? Nothing is happening. I'm half-lying on his bed, and he is taking my clothes off. He is speaking to me in sign language of his own invention, and I understand: this gesture says take it off, and this too—off, and this.

I cooperate. I take off my jeans, my undershirt, and finally I take all of it off. I gather my underwear in a little pile on my side of the bed, where he can't reach, although he is reaching all over me, his hands on my stomach on my breasts on my thighs he is ironing me with his hands unfolding me like a shirt until I'm open for him and he comes into me like into a room a house he moves from corner to corner from top to bottom this house just right for him he buries himself in it he moves again then he becomes still and now he is lying on his stomach next to me and I roll onto my side so I can look him in his eyes because they are exuding something I like so much what is it only a smile so deep dark tangible entering me through my eyes lips cheeks.

My Jew, he says softly.

ALEJANDRO/AMMAR

She calls and tells me to meet her near the subway stop. I meet her, and we go to my home. This is how Western women are: a man doesn't even have to ask. They go wherever they want, no supervision, no rules, it's a free country, for them too, and why not, maybe women need freedom too, not just men, but where I come from, there are rules for everyone, especially for them. That's why it burns so purely, my flame, and she likes it, but she doesn't know what it is that she likes so much about me; she doesn't know it's the flame. I carry it daily, hourly, burning inside my chest, a pure white flame that is my love for my land. I'm not in the habit of snuffing it out just so I can take it out and show it to strangers, see how safe, no danger here, see, this is how to light it, see how it burns, you like it, eh? She talks about things she doesn't understand, things that are sacred to me, as they are to every man of my faith. Then she goes even further. She quotes some

British politician quoting a Muslim sheikh who said that Islam would return to Europe as a conqueror, and in the same breath she says that if the Arabs didn't reject the UN partition plan in 1947, there'd be no conflict now. And as if that's not enough, she points at her chest and asks why are women not treated fairly in Islam, and she wants to know what I think about it.

What can I say? I'm a devout man, a faithful husband to my wife—just one wife. I don't know why she thinks I have two. It's a misconception these Westerners have about us, about all of us, as if we are all the same, as if each man has four wives and twelve or fifteen children total, three or five with each wife. I'm not like that. I love my wife. I fear my wife. Maybe fear isn't the right word, because it is not her that I fear. I fear offending her and making her sick and angry and jealous, and I have to be careful because she put her heart in my hands and I have to walk with her heart in my hands and not break it. When the Jew calls me, sometimes I pick up and sometimes I don't, but I never call her back when she leaves me messages and says that she misses me. Several times she asked me about my wife. I don't know where she got the idea that I have two. Maybe when I said that in our culture a man can have more than one wife, she took it as though I was speaking about myself, as though everything I say is about me, and it's not. I was speaking for all of our people. I was speaking traditionally and in general, and I didn't feel like setting her straight; if she wants to think I have two, let her think two.

But her mistake didn't stop there; it made her take more wrong turns, because somehow in her mind a man couldn't love two women—loving two meant loving none. This meant that I was free to be loved by yet a third woman, and that she would be the first to be truly loved. Where does she get these ideas? She is full of them. Every time I see her, she is full of new ideas, and she spits them out right away, and sometimes I think that's all she needs me for: to listen to her talk about her ideas. But whatever it is that she needs me for, she is a woman, and I'm a man, and I've been faithful to my wife. Abstaining from contact with women, sending money home, working long hours, twelve, thirteen hours a day, the longer the better, not only for the money, but to exhaust my body so it would not have the strength to torment me with desire. But she comes here for reasons of her own; she says she wants to talk, and I believe her, she talks and talks, and she says she has no interest in talking to anyone else, only to me, because I inspire her. She knows my religion, but that doesn't bother her, maybe that's just what inspires her, all this business about her being a Jew and me a Muslim, and how do I feel about this and what do I think about that, and when I tell her how I feel and what I think, she doesn't like it. She tries not to show it, but I can see that she doesn't like it. And she doesn't stop, she asks me more questions, drawing it out of me, to show me how stupid I am to believe in such things, teasing it out of me and then presenting it in such a way that makes me look like a racist or an anti-Semite or just a fool.

Why does she have to talk all the time? Why does she have to remind me all the time that she is a Jew? Doesn't she understand how I feel when she says things like that, because I have an automatic reaction to the word "Jew." I never thought I'd be friendly with a Jew, that I'd welcome a Jew to my room, and that I'd actually like her, that I'd even want her to stay. She is one of those women who feel they have to keep on talking so as not to feel trapped by silence, especially when they are alone with a man, something that could never happen to our women. But here anything goes, everyone's free, including them. Yet despite all their famous freedom, these women are afraid to sit still and hear desire throb in a man's veins, or perhaps in their own veins, because they're still not free enough to acknowledge it. Maybe some are free enough, but not the ones who keep on talking as if to ward off something. I concentrate on not answering her, so she'd notice the silence, but instead she jumps up and kneels by my bed and I can't help but wonder what she is doing—does she want to sit next to me on the bed? She says no; she just dropped her pack of cigarettes. She's breathless saying it, as if the silence is really doing its job. Good. The tension is becoming unbearable; something has to happen in the next five minutes. Our eyes must meet for it to happen, but she keeps on talking and not looking. The talk doesn't work anymore. She knows it. She is not a fool after all. That's when I know it's time to act. I was never in a situation like this before, with a so-called free Western woman, waiting for me to do it, knowing that I'll do it, and yet fearing it at the same time: not unlike a woman from my culture, the only difference is that our woman would not be caught dead in the room of a man she is not married to. There's respect and fear in our women, a good fear, not the kind mixed in with desire, which is

187

more desire than fear, while here the only fear part of it is about who will take the first step. This liberated Western woman, she still wants the man to take the first step. But there are no rules here, the lines are blurred, unlike in our world where you always know where you stand: men here, women there. Here, instead of relying on an age-old formula, you have to invent yourself every time—invent new thoughts, new words, even new gestures.

When I finally say it, she freezes. I can almost hear an echo of my voice in her head, repeating, "I want to kiss you, Galia." She puts her arms on my shoulders, lifts up her head so her lips are an inch away from my face, and I have to remind myself not to let my lips come in contact with hers, because even at this moment I can't forget her origins and that kissing a Jewish woman is forbidden. But she doesn't seem to understand that all I want is to use her the way a man uses a woman, without entanglement, without involvement, a burst of pleasure and good-bye. She sees that I want her and she thinks this is love; she is like a baby with me, her body compliant to my touch. I can do what I wish, without worrying that a touch would harm my soul. I tell myself that she came here herself—her desire made her come to my room, and if she wants me, she can have me. Was there ever a man who could resist a pretty woman so obviously wanting him? No, there was never such a man, and no need for me to be the first, and with these thoughts flitting through my mind, I place my hand above her breasts, and I exert gentle pressure until she understands and allows herself to be pushed. Just a couple feet back: the bed is right behind her. Good, we're there. She still doesn't understand. What a baby. I have to nudge her again, push her down, until she feels the edge of the mattress behind her. She finally understands. Still, she resists. She doesn't like being pushed, I can see that; and not just being pushed in general, but being pushed on the bed. It seems unromantic to her. They like being free, these Western women, but they want this romantic nonsense, too. I don't know how to be with a Western woman. I have no experience. I make mistakes. Why does she resist being pushed on the bed? Didn't she come here herself? Maybe she wasn't thinking of this when she came here; women never want to think of it, never want to be aware of the bed, even if they come into the man's bedroom, and it's his only room. She sees the bed, but she doesn't want to think that it has anything to do with her. Well, I'm sorry to disappoint her.

I didn't know she wanted to play the I-don't-know game. I thought if a woman comes to a man's room, she knows what she is doing. Maybe I don't understand this Western woman, why she does what she does. She is liberated, but where does her liberty take her? Same place as her unliberated sister: a man's bed. This so-called liberated woman is like a blind kitten, not knowing what to do. I have to lead her, like I did in the beginning with my wife. Thinking of my wife makes me feel guilty, and I don't want to feel guilty. I'm a good man, I send money home, I support my children, I work hard, always alone, living in fear, without papers, always at risk of being found out, the lock on my door broken, my body pushed down on the floor and dragged away, my hands twisted behind my back and cuffed. Better not to think of it, what's the use, especially now when the Jew is taking off her clothes for me. Everything I point at, she obediently takes off: shirt, undershirt, jeans, bra, panties. I don't understand why she fell for me; what does she see in me? Doesn't she know we're at war? But she doesn't seem to care. She wants me in every way, including this one. I want to say, Don't make me do what's forbidden. But I'm a man, and even as I'm thinking "forbidden," I can't resist a beautiful woman lying naked in front of me, waiting. I put my hand on her white stomach and caress her, forgetting her origins, the perfidy of her people, the arrogance with which they despised us, and the lies with which they accused us of having stolen their prophets and copied their sayings in our Book. I open her up, fold by fold. I bury myself deep into this woman, and the softness, the buttery softness, it lulls me, so I forget myself and I fall into deeper waters still, and I move in them with confidence unknown to me until now. I swim. At a moment of my greatest joy, Fatima appears. Her right hand makes a sign for "forbidden"; her left hand rests on our child's head. She implores me to stop. But I can't stop now; she has to understand this. She fades away, having seen the proof of my unfaithfulness. Another second and I burst through the buttery ocean, I float weightless, sheer joy holding me up, and Fatima appears again, this time with both children, the boy and the girl, and the word "forbidden" written in large letters on a paper in her raised hand. She looks just like the Mastermind and speaks in a shrill voice I don't recognize, accusing me of failing our people, our fate, and our future, of forgetting the task for which I had been selected and trained, of consorting with a despicable Jew, a cowardly, perfidious, feeble dhimmi...Stop! I cry. She shouts, "Those who forsake us in the final battle will burn in the fire of our fury forever..." No, I say, wait. Or better, go. Leave. Another final battle was raging here a moment ago, and a battle of sweetness and succor it was, and instead of coming out victorious, I brought peace: not victory for myself and defeat for her, but peace and joy and forgiveness...

My Jew, I say lovingly, my head resting on her shoulder, my right hand under her head, and my left hand on her white stomach.

GALIA

He lies next to me, his hand on my stomach. Suddenly he withdraws his hand, as though not trusting himself, then again he allows it to touch me, then again pulls it back. So indecisive, it's almost painful. But it's painful only when he withdraws his hand, because when he touches me, it fills me with sweetness, even though he caresses me hard, as though kneading dough. When he withdraws his hand again, I look at him and see that he is drenched in sweat. I say, "You're sick! You should take an aspirin!" He sits up in bed and says, "Yes, I'm sick," sounding like he's glad that I noticed. Now that I know he's sick, he can attribute everything that happened here to his sickness and not to his conscious will. He gets up, sweat falling off him like raindrops. He takes a towel, brings it to his face, dabs at his cheeks. He sits at the table, patting his face in gloomy silence.

I can't quite put my finger on what bothers me. What exactly is going on? I'm lying naked on a man's bed. The man is sitting at the table. It doesn't look like he's coming back to bed. This means I should get dressed and leave. But where are my clothes? Here they are, thank God. I should get dressed, and maybe I should go. What happened here is more than I expected. I expected a kiss. A light, airy kiss, that's all. Everything else happened but not a kiss. I look up and see a poster on the wall. I didn't notice it earlier. It says "Viva Palestina!" It has people with black socks on their faces...things that look like ski masks with holes for eyes and mouth, but I call them socks. I've seen posters like this in the outskirts of San Cristobal de Las Casas, a city in the Mexican state of Chiapas, in streets marked with poverty and neglect. What am I doing here, naked, in the bed of this Arab laborer, an illegal immigrant, with murky connections to Mexico and even murkier ones to his wife—or wives—in a village near Hebron, or who knows where. It's a bit of a problem, my not knowing if it's singular or plural: one wife or two or three. I watch him as he pats his face dry with the towel, lost in thought.

"What are you thinking about?"

He makes an indistinct sound.

"But I want to know," I say. He shrugs. He's not used to anyone being curious about his thoughts. He is a worker, a laborer, who cares about his thoughts? I care. As I put on my bra, the elastic gets stuck on top of my breasts, and I have to pull it down with force. It's a little funny, the way I force down my bra. Does he think it's funny? He's not looking. He's staring into the empty space in front of him. He's thinking. I fish out my underwear, my shirt, and my pants from the small pile on his bed. I stand up to put them on. He's still thinking, and I don't know what, and I need to know. I have the right. Now, after what happened here, I have the right.

"Tell me."

"Nothing," he says, almost humbly.

He has a chain around his neck; what is it? I reach for it and pull it out from under his half-buttoned shirt. I can do this now; I have the right. It's a round metal, about an inch and a half in diameter, with some Arabic letters.

"What does it say?" I ask.

He shrugs. "Just...some word."

"What word?"

"Why you need to know so much?"

"It's not so much. It's about you. I just want to know about you. What you think. What you like. What you wear around your neck." Without answering, he reaches for my hips and zips up my pants. I look down at his hand, zipping me up. I should value this gesture: it's the only sign of his caring after he got off the bed and walked over to his chair and assumed the posture of Rodin's Thinker. Alejandro aka Ammar the Thinker. Once his hand is done zipping me up, it flutters around and pats the zipped up part of my body. It's good to know he has fond memories of it.

"Well," I say, putting on my jacket. I'm ready to go, but hoping he'll say something, ask me to stay, offer me a seat at his table, anything. "We-e-ll," I say again. Obeying a sudden inspiration, I bend toward his lips and kiss him. A kiss so light, it's almost chaste. This is all I expected when I came here. Didn't he say, "I want to kiss you, Galia"? And then there was nothing, or rather everything, but not a kiss. His lips respond perfunctorily, kissing me back lightly, his mind still far away. Where is he traveling, what spell is he under? I wrap my scarf around my neck and look for my bag. "Where is it? Oh, it's right here, thanks."

"Keys?" he says in a caring voice. I told him that I used to forget my keys everywhere, that's why I carry this bag, to keep everything together. He opens the door for me. I walk toward the stairs and down. I stop on the bottom step. He walks after me. I turn. I give him another light kiss on the lips.

He holds the door for me like an old-fashioned gentleman but doesn't offer to walk me to the station. He's sick, after all. I tell him that I'll call him tomorrow, to ask if he's feeling better. If not, I'll bring him a thermometer, take him to a doctor, and give him my medical insurance card, so he wouldn't have to pay. Yes, I know it's illegal and he can't pass for me, but the details can wait. I walk away, and the pavement under my feet feels soft like cotton.

THE HASMONEAN CHRONICLE

MORIYA WAS ASLEEP WHEN THE Teacher arrived at their house.

He knocked and waited but no one rushed to open the door for him, so he pushed it and walked in. He stood in the dusk of the hallway, rubbing his feet on the floorboards. His feet, in their threadbare sandals, were themselves as hard as floorboards, and the rubbing emitted a distinct sound, which was his goal. He had come a long way to answer this call, and now someone had to be here. Once in a while he needed a direct proof that his understanding of his mission was correct and that the mission itself was real, and it was in answering calls like this one, which came through his internal hearing with a clarity of an unspoken request, that the proof was given him.

Moriya was asleep in the big bed she had shared with Absalom for so many years that his side of it still retained the warmth of his body just as the hollow in the pillow bore the shape of his head. At the entrance the Teacher was rubbing the soles of his sandals on the floor, considering that he might as well step inside and look for the one who needed his help. Yet even before he stepped inside the parlor he saw a man spread-eagled on the floor.

The best way to diagnose a patient was to watch the images flowing ceaselessly through every living creature's mind, and this man was still living and therefore no exception to the rule. Yet no matter how he strained to enter the man's mind, he encountered resistance, which was unusual because it felt like a material rather than a spiritual locked door. He could almost touch it. Hard, cold, closed. He raised his hands so his open palms were parallel with the ceiling. Words formed themselves into a spontaneous prayer and poured out of him as though they offered a solution to his own grief, yet all he asked was to be allowed inside the man's mind. He formed his requests with diamond-like precision, as he knew only too well that Father would grant exactly what he asked, no more and no less, which is why he did not ask for help in diagnosing or curing the man. That would come later or, depending on the flow, speed, and content of images, might not come at all. Now the images began moving instantly, rapidly, and he had to follow them at once. He peered into the flow but saw nothing, only a kind of continuous blur moving past him. He focused still more patiently and began to distinguish a procession of spears, helmets, arms holding shields, a battlefield covered with bodies, crowds of villagers following several men, and one in particular, a fiercely bearded one, surrounded by his brothers. The Teacher knew their names: Jonathan, Simon, John Gaddi, and Eleazar. Judah Maccabeus was instantly recognizable, not least by his one-toed gait, which was how the Teacher knew it was he and not one of his brothers. The line which had been started by their father, Mattathias Hasmon, and which had won decades of sovereignty for Judea, was about to expire in vapid enmity between two brothers, Hyrcanus II and Aristobulus II, sons of Queen Salome, aka Alexandra, aka Shlomzion, widow of King Aristobulus I and of King Yannai, her second husband, the most blood-thirsty of all Hasmonean kings and the one rumored to know the name of a man in possession of the Toe. It was said to have been preserved in special juice that some claimed was the spit of Ariel, who rules over the elements and who, despite his formidable lion's head, was often confused with Uriel—a grave mistake, because despite his many names such as "spirit of the air," "angel of waters of the Earth," and "wielder of fire," which emphasized his way with the elements, Ariel wished to be known solely as a healer.

Whether or not the first man known as Keeper of the Toe acquired it from Judah and passed it on to his successors was not essential, because the Toe lived on, floating in its pickle juice or Ariel's spit, while the legend of its healing powers grew to have a life of its own. All the many versions of the legend, though they differed in everything else, shared this conclusion—and though it was expressed differently in each version, it came to the same thing: a rightful Keeper of the

Toe hasn't been found yet; the three Keepers so far had been temporary keepers; the rightful Keeper would be a worthy descendant of Judah but, unlike Judah, he would be a seer, not a doer; his destiny as the Keeper would be concealed from him until he fell so ill that he would be unable to move and a healer known as the Teacher would heal him by letting him see with his inner eye, and only then would the Toe float into his vision, and he would acknowledge it as his own and would become its Keeper and would be cured and pass on the vision of the Toe to his descendants, so that in every Hasmonean generation there would be one rightful Keeper, and as the Toe is not only sacred but also beneficial and all its benefits are not yet known, it would be vital to keep the Keeper and his descendants alive and safe from generation to generation.

"Your husband is well, lady," said the Teacher.

Moriya was awake now. She was watching the Teacher help Absalom up from the floor, and she was watching Absalom, whose limbs had been weakened by a prolonged immobility, lean on the Teacher's arm, try to steady himself and remain standing without the Teacher's arm supporting him. Moriya knew she wasn't seeing the Teacher through someone else's consciousness, not this time, because not only was she wide awake and able to see what was happening, the intentions of each person were clear to her. It was as though a small part of the Teacher's power had entered her, and she was a miracle worker like the Teacher, and at the same time she knew that it was his generosity that made her feel as though she was his equal while she was not. She most certainly was not, she said to herself with humility. Yet she could see into the hearts of men, at least of the two men in the room, and what she saw was astounding.

Absalom was not only the stuff of which this miracle was made. He was also a witness to the miracle, and now that conscious life had been restored to him, he wanted to be the-witness-who-tells-the-world, the bringer of the good news, the one whose legacy would be a record of the Teacher's life and times. Words were forming in his mind, and those that were already formed needed to be written down as soon as possible, so that new and better words had a chance to be formed. Moriya could read the words in her husband's mind—*he came, he healed, he left*—as clearly as if they had already been written.

"No, no," said the Teacher. "This won't do at all. I don't want it written down."

But Absalom was willing to brush aside the Teacher's injunction as so much modesty, noble perhaps, and beautiful, but unhelpful to future generations for whom the knowledge of what happened today might be as essential as water.

"No," the Teacher said again, this time quite firmly. "If you write it down, it will inspire faith not only in those among whom I dwell but in those who live far from us and who don't know us, and your writings would be the only thing they would know of us. With the help of your writings they will make me their own god, and there'll be no one to stop them, all of you will be long dead, and I will be gone too, so I would not be able to stop them from turning the legend of me into a weapon against my people."

"What do you mean, 'a legend against my people'?" Absalom asked.

"I will be made into the most formidable weapon," the Teacher said, "against the very people from whose midst I have sprung. I will be made into a weapon that, in the name of love, will go on killing, century after century. It will definitely be so, if you write it down, which is why I tell you not to."

"I shall not write a single word if you say so," said Absalom, lowering his gaze.

"Indeed," said the Teacher with obvious relief, "I say so."

"But," Absalom persisted despite being forbidden to do so by the very man he wanted to immortalize in what he was thinking of as "the book," "Explain to me, what is the harm in letting others know that there indeed exists a miracle worker and that his power comes from God?"

The Teacher could not help but realize that no matter what answer he gave to Absalom, or to others whom he healed, sooner or later this very Absalom or those others would write about the experience that changed their lives, and the writing would go from hand to hand, the message would spring from lips to lips, the news would spread far beyond the borders of their little Judea.

He wanted to repeat what he had said earlier, about the idea of him becoming a weapon that will strike his people, but realized that the more he said, the more material he was giving to Absalom to write about.

"If you really have to write," he said to Absalom in a voice that was barely more than a whisper, "make sure you write that I belong to my people. That I never renounced them."

Moriya demanded to know what he was talking about. She wanted to understand him. She asked, "What people?"

"Jews," the Teacher said quietly.

"And what weapon?"

"What he will write about the healing, the words he will believe he heard me say, and the thoughts he will believe I had, and the thoughts I did not have, it will all be part of the book, and it will survive him and me, and the world will misinterpret it, and make a new religion out of it. I will be confused with another, the one who will come after me. They will call me by his name and they will not know that we were two different people, many years separating us. There will be stories about me, by people who had never seen me, and they will cast me as the Good, and my people as the enemy of the Good—and the scourges my people will endure for thousands of years as the result of your husband's desire to write it down are too horrible to contemplate. It was prophesied that one of those I heal will be the man who would write it, and if I had known it was your husband, I would not have come here, because, honestly, if I weigh my duty to my people and my duty to one patient, which do you think weighs heavier on me? And remember that it is not only my *duty* to my people; it is also love."

"I will see to it that he doesn't write a single word," said Moriya, "if this worries you so much."

The Teacher said yes, indeed, it worries him so much, and thank you for promising to keep your revived husband from writing. This is the only payment he wanted: the promise not to write about him.

"Speaking of payment," Moryia said, but the Teacher was already outside. The session was over. He had felt the force of a silent call, and like a bird that flies south without asking the way, he was walking to a town where his next patient was waiting for him.

———•———

The first few weeks after the Teacher's visit she was not so strict; she still allowed him to write, provided that he showed her everything, which he did not object to, since he always wanted to share his writing with her. But no matter what he started to write, it always ended up being about the healing and the Teacher's words and what the Teacher did or did not do while he, Absalom, was lying on the floor without a sign of intelligent life and how this life was returned to him, and what this return meant, and what kind of power it was that could heal a man so completely, it was not a simple human power, and at a certain point Absalom always stopped because he, too, remembered the Teacher's warning. But he didn't stop early enough. He stopped only after he had written so much about the healing that Moriya, reading it, would exclaim, "But you can't know this! This is not what he said at all! You couldn't have heard anything—you were lying unconscious on the floor." She would roll up the parchment, secure it on her lap with both hands resting on top of it, and say, "You have to stop this, Absalom. He asked you not to write about it, but no matter what you start writing about, you always end up writing about *this*."

There came a point when she started hiding fresh parchment from him, and he, in turn, started writing on linen which he hid from her so thoroughly that no matter how well she searched and how much she complained about his wasting all their linen on his forbidden pursuits, his writings remained intact, and the fact that her own home served as a hiding place for the thing that could inflict untold suffering on the entire people gave her grim determination to pursue her beloved Absalom in ways that she herself both despised and resented. The fact that he was writing at all was good, because it meant that he had completely recovered, and more than anything in the world she wanted him to be well. But the fact that he was writing about the healing was bad, because it meant not only that he was disobeying the Teacher but that he was committing the kind of sin for which there was no name yet and the consequences of which were too terrible to contemplate, not least because she could not imagine the "thousands of years" the Teacher said the effects of his writing will have on their people, and even though she spent her early youth believing herself to be a Samaritan, she was now so firmly ensconced in her identity as a Jew that nothing was more mortifying than to think that her Absalom, with his harmless habit of writing, the very thing that had made him so different from his brothers, who had wanted power even more than they wanted her, would be the ruin of her people, and that the ruination would go on and on, for millennia. She couldn't imagine what would happen, how could the entire people be persecuted for thousands of years, what shapes would such a long persecution take, and how could Absalom's writing about the Teacher cause it? But the Teacher said it would be so, and she trusted the Teacher more than anyone.

She hounded Absalom until he stopped writing about *that* completely. Now he wrote only lists. They were lists of clothes or furniture, things that he already possessed or wanted to acquire or that his wife possessed, and items of furniture that were as old as their house, as well as some new ones they planned to acquire or that he planned to surprise Moriya with. There were also lists of strange things that Moriya did not understand, and when she asked him about the meaning of the words in those lists, he only shrugged and said nothing, or he waited until they were in bed, half-asleep, to tell her that she had no right to rummage through his things, and because she was on the verge of sleep, she would say nothing, only murmur something about her relief that he wasn't writing about *that*, by which she meant the Teacher and the healing.

Her relief, such as it was, was short-lived, because soon after her discovery of his lists, she started noticing the absence of the listed items, so that his lists were now the only place where these things existed. Moriya's favorite copper mirror, delicate silver earrings that were her wedding present from Ramah, bottles of precious oils, bowls, jugs, even the old blanket in which they wrapped their infant son many years ago, all these and more were missing. Her handmaid Kefira suspected unknown thieves, but the triple lock on the front door made sure that thieves remained Kefira's fantasy and nothing else. As there was no other entrance into the house, the items' disappearance looked like the work of a very sick mind. It took her a while to admit to herself that the sick mind was Absalom's; that the items went missing in the exact order in which they appeared in his lists, and that, as much as she grieved over the loss of her treasured objects, it was not so much the loss of the things that was alarming as the fact that her Absalom was disposing of them for reasons he himself could not explain—and it was a good thing he wasn't writing *this* down, for his account of how his own unwell mind forced him to dispose of their things would not earn him much praise from their descendants.

The items were never recovered, even though she had Ezer, Kefira's husband, hire helpers who searched every imaginable hiding place, even going so far as tapping the ground following a mad clue given by one of the men who claimed to have heard a story of underground tunnels part of whose trajectory ran under their courtyard; treasures had been hidden there for years and men had been seen going in and out of these tunnels at night, carrying strange objects that looked like pottery or casks of wine.

"From which they drank as they left the tunnels, of course," Moriya said with a short laugh while Ezer tried to continue with his report, which he wove out of bits of old tales and rumors to conceal the fact that he had nothing to say, absolutely nothing, and that he had found nothing at all.

One day, when Absalom thought he was alone in his room, not knowing that Moriya was hiding behind a curtain and watching his every step, he pulled a chest from a secret place in a wall that she didn't even know existed, and as he began taking things out and stuffing them into a sackcloth, she watched his face and saw in it the expression that was strangely familiar to her even though it was not his usual one—and as she struggled to remember where she saw this expression, he tied up the sackcloth and was on his way out of the room. She called out to him, without bothering to come out from behind the curtain, and he dropped the sackcloth. Then, not seeing anyone and assuring himself that he had imagined her voice, he picked up the bag furtively, like a thief trying to escape with his loot. She felt that he left her no choice but to come out from behind the curtain and ask him what he intended to do with the things he had stuffed into the bag.

"Why, I'm looking for an important scroll," he said quickly, without meeting her eyes. "What scroll, my Absalom?"

"A scroll…of lists…," he said uncertainly.

They both knew that what had come out of his mouth was a lie, and even if it contained a grain of truth, it was clear that he said it only to ward off any further questions. Moriya knew him well enough to yield and not ask anything else, but they both knew that it was only a temporary yielding on her part, that she would not be satisfied with anything less than a complete and sincere truth, and that even though this truth was something he wasn't capable of at the moment, it would come. She had to wait for it to come in its own time, and since her love for him had grown from a naive admiration of his talent to a mature love that was three-fourths patience, she waited. The sackcloth remained in his room. She watched it closely, checking it every morning, coming into his room whether or not he was there, as though it was the room itself that she was paying a visit to, not Absalom. The sackcloth stayed open at the same place where he dropped it, and its contents welcomed her searching hands. She didn't know what she was searching for; she only knew that she had to search because the answer to the riddle of his throwing out their possessions lay here. Not in this particular bag; she wasn't stupid. The answer lay in a certain object, but because she didn't know what the object was, she had to track him endlessly, until she became his shadow, and as a shadow she no longer had thoughts of her own.

She was surprised when he told her the truth one day, in bed, his face half-buried in her shoulder. It sounded almost ridiculous. It sounded like something a much simpler man would say or do. A toe. He was looking for a toe, he said. Not just any toe, of course. It had to be a royal toe. Judah Maccabeus's toe! The toe that was chopped off his grand-uncle's foot when Nehora, Judah's wife, had administered that famous cut that saved Judah's foot at the same time as it left him toeless.

Moriya listened to him as a mother listens to a child, letting him go on. But he did not go on. Perhaps he didn't feel that an explanation was needed. Perhaps he was falling asleep, as he usually did at this time. Why were you searching for Judah's toe, she wanted to ask. She also wanted to know why he had thrown away so many other things if it was the Toe he was searching for. She did not know how to ask him without offending him how could he be foolish enough to believe that a body part could stay intact for such a long time. They were not Egyptians, after all; they did not preserve their kings' organs in clay jars in the hope that their owner would be able to make use of them in the afterlife. They were Jews, and they knew better. And he, Absalom, definitely knew better. If he didn't, he should. He was a parent, after all. What would their child think of his father searching for a toe of a long dead man?

"You don't understand me at all," he said into her shoulder.

She waited for him to continue, but he was asleep. When he woke up the next morning and she asked him about the toe, he made a face as though she was the one talking nonsense. "You're still dreaming," he said.

But the toe became a reality in their life. It was with them on long afternoons, and evenings when they stayed awake with mutual help, waiting for their son Avner, whose arrival was never a certainty due to contradictory messages he sent them. Avner was a young man of promise. He was also a young man of instinct, the kind that lets well-born young men forget appointments with their parents and releases them from parental bonds with a shrug and a lovable smile that attest more to the young man's charm than to his seriousness about remembering such appointments in the future. Nevertheless, they waited, as parents would. It was on those long afternoons and evenings of endless waiting, when Moriya and Absalom half-sat half-lay in their respective chairs in the parlor, which was growing darker despite two oil lamps, one in front of each of them, that Kefira insisted on keeping lit, as though it was her son and not theirs who was late to family reunions, when the Toe appeared. It circled in the air, first at the ceiling where its pirouettes were most impressive, and they admired its circling, without knowing about orbits or planets, which the circling resembled, as such things were not known in their time. Neither did they know that its ability to travel between past, present, and future, or rather, between eras of human knowledge, was exactly what propelled it into Moriya's and Absalom's parlor and filled Absalom's mind with fear and longing.

"Fear and longing!" he would exclaim.

Moriya thought that perhaps they could ask the Teacher to come and cure Absalom one more time but she didn't say it, because she wasn't sure that Absalom would like the idea of being cured now that he was walking and talking and sitting in their parlor and seemingly acting like everyone else. Besides, if it had been so hard to keep him from writing about the Teacher's first visit during which he was mostly unconscious, imagine how much harder it would be to restrain him from recording every detail of the Teacher's second visit, now that he was functioning like everyone else except for his foolish fixation on the Toe.

Only once Moriya heard him call out to the Toe. She was half-asleep in her chair, no longer hoping for their son's arrival that night. The oil lamps had burned out, and as she forbade Ezer and Kefira to bring new ones, they were sitting in the dark, and she wasn't worried about it until the total silence of the room was pierced by Absalom's voice.

"Hold it," he shouted, "Not so fast!"

She asked him who he was talking to and he replied with, "There! Don't you see it?"

She said no, she didn't see anything, it was a dark Jerusalem night, and she wondered if the thing he was seeing was something in his own mind, but he reached for her from his chair and took her hand in his, but not, as she thought at first, for the purpose of an amorous squeezing or kissing or telling her how much he treasured her. He shook it so violently that her wrist bones ached for a long time after and he said a vehement, "No!" This was as much as she was willing to take from him that night. She got up from her chair and didn't come back until Avner arrived the next day. He found his parents in a silence so total that it had no room for him anymore, and he didn't know what to do with it, as he wasn't used to this new feeling of not being able to fit into his parents' lives. No matter how hard he tried to start a conversation at dinner or in his parents' bedroom, sitting on the edge of their bed, awkwardly telling them about a vineyard in the Galilee where he wanted to cultivate bigger and tastier grapes as a present for his bride, Chasina, whose mother couldn't boast of a lineage as noble as Moriya's but whose father was said to be related to...to have come from...not the House of David as you, Mother, but...The silence in the bedroom was too awkward for Avner to go on.

"No matter what Chasina's parents' lineage may be, she will find love and acceptance in our home, provided she loves you and reminds you to visit us more often," Moriya said kindly.

Absalom was half-lying with his eyes closed and seemed to be asleep, but when his son rose to go, he lifted himself up on his elbow.

"Her mother comes from the House of David just as yours does. The female line is harder to trace, but we've traced the connection through her great-grandmother's aunt." He lowered himself back onto the cushion.

"Who are 'we,' abba?" Avner said. "And how do you know her family—"

"Your father receives messages from the Toe," Moriya said with a careful sigh. "That's why, from time to time, we must be ready for certain pronouncements about the past, present, and future, things no one can know by ordinary means."

Avner had never thought of his father as a prophet. His writing was the only thing that made Absalom stand out. In everything else, he was as ordinary a man as he had set out to be on a long ago day when he renounced the privileges he had been entitled to as John Hyrcanus's youngest son. Royal privileges and royal power, royal palace and gold—he had renounced them all for the sake of love and obscurity. He became the kind of ordinary citizen he had always wanted to be. And now this: a prophet.

"This is what it has come to," Moriyah sighed.

Whether covering scrolls with his meticulous writing or wandering from room to room with an absent look, Absalom was a man bewitched. His worry about the future of his people acquired such hopelessness and so desiccated his body that soon enough, instead of wandering from room to room, he could barely drag himself from bed to chair. Moriya's concerns about his health irritated him so much that he stopped telling her how the heritage of his people would be stolen from them and how the written Law itself would be used as evidence against them. When Moriya made it clear that she cared more about keeping him warm and well-fed than about keeping their people from becoming the oppressed minority they were destined to be in the future if he didn't do something about it, he grimly refused to accept whatever comfort she brought him, whether it was a bowl of chicken soup or a blanket made of special wool sold by Galilee shepherds at a Jerusalem market only on certain days every year—so rare was that wool that when Ezer finally bought a blanket for an extraordinary sum she had given him for this purpose, she rushed to show it to Absalom, who had been known as a connoisseur of rare kinds of wool. He had so little interest in it that he held out his arm—not to take it as she had supposed at first but to create a physical barrier between himself and whatever well-meaning distraction she wanted to foist on him.

There came a day when he seemed willing to listen to her, maybe because the Toe provided him with nicer visions of the future or because it had left him alone for a while. Moriya asked him if another visit by the Teacher might perhaps complete the healing that had not been entirely finished the first time. He answered her with a grunt, the meaning of which was not quite clear to her at first but after some thinking she interpreted it as, Yes, ask him to come again, but not because I need to be healed.

In the time that had elapsed since the Teacher's first visit, his fame had spread so far and wide that there was hardly a family in Judea that hadn't sought him out. This was why Moriya's messenger found it almost impossible to get the Teacher's followers to accept a scroll with Moriya's request. The Teacher was so busy curing the sick that his disciples had no time for sleep. Even though the Teacher himself was able to go without sleep for days, his followers were made of less durable stuff, and they often fell asleep while waiting for him to finish curing a child or an old man. "Sleepwalkers!" he chided them, and it was on one of those occasions that he had spotted a man standing behind him. From the way the man hastily hid a scroll in the folds of his cloak, it was clear what he was doing.

"You are sleepwalkers indeed! This man was writing, and you did not see him! Did I not tell you that he who records my words falsifies them? And even if this man had managed to record them correctly, they would be rendered false in the future when the original scroll is copied again and again, and no matter how much a copier may try to do his best, mistakes will be made, and every mistake will cause another generation of copiers to ponder the meaning of a changed line and offer its own interpretation. I never tire of telling you to exert care, for this is where the greatest danger lies. If the interpretations of these future copiers become the official record of my life and deeds, then men and women of the future will follow those words that have as little to do with my words as this man's denial of his deed has to do with the reality of it. Hand me your scroll, stranger, and be on your way."

It was clear that the man had no wish to part from his writing yet he handed the scroll to the Teacher, who ripped it up without bothering to read it. Now the man stood in front of the Teacher and his disciples ready for punishment, but the Teacher said that the man's knowledge of his ungodly act was enough punishment for him, and so they moved on. When the note with Moriya's request finally reached the Teacher, after having passed through so many hands that the writing on it was barely visible, he held it briefly to his eyes and said "Yes" to a disciple who had handed it to him. "Yes. I shall come to them," he said.

Moriya did not know whether the Teacher's answer was going to be yes or no, therefore she was surprised when Absalom woke up one morning with an announcement that the Teacher was on his way. Moriya didn't have to ask how he came by that knowledge, because his eyes were radiating light as they did every time the Toe conveyed an important piece of news to him. The Teacher did indeed knock on their door a day later, and when Kefira, who let him in, asked if all those other people with him had to come in too, he said those were his disciples and they were willing to wait outside because Absalom's case was the kind that required privacy. Kefira said she was glad to hear that. Very glad, she said, and in a moment they were in the parlor with Moriya offering her greetings and Absalom sitting with his radiant eyes, and the Teacher saying that the idea of privacy did not exist in their ancient homeland, and they all smiled at that because it was true that their homeland was ancient and it was also true that there was no privacy, because even when one was not in the presence of other people one was never completely alone.

The Teacher said, "Let's talk about why you called me this time."

Absalom said that he was not the one who had asked him to come; it was Moriya with her worries. "You know," he said, "how women are."

"Yes," the Teacher said gently, and then he said that a man who could see Judah's toe was indeed a prophet, and there was nothing he could do for Absalom because knowledge of the future was not an illness, even though sometimes it resembled it.

Moriya had wanted to ask him something but now that he was here she forgot what it was except that it kept floating in the darkness of her mind and reminding her that it was very important and that it had something to do with writing. Then she remembered.

"Absalom is still writing," she said. "You didn't want him to write, but he is still writing."

Absalom looked away from them all. First he looked at a wall next to him, then at the floor. At this moment he loved the Teacher much more than his writing. He wanted the Teacher to approve of him, and the thought that he might be scolded instead of praised was too painful for him to contemplate. The Teacher explained that it wasn't just any writing that he had warned him about. It was writing specifically about him, the Teacher, his words and deeds. "Once I'm no longer in the body," said the Teacher, "all that would be left of me would be this." He held up a piece of a torn scroll for everyone to see.

"What is written, that is all they'll know of me. And what is written can be stolen, because it is a thing." Again he held up the torn scroll. "A thing can be taken from the original owner, and once it's taken, a thief can say, 'It is mine now,' and everyone will believe him, because thieves who steal ideas are the most charismatic of thieves, and people tend to believe them passionately, since people have a great hunger for ideas. But in their hunger, most people cannot tell apart ideas that look almost the same to them. They will take a scroll stolen by the thief and they will read in it the words with which I scolded my people, and they will read them hundreds of times for hundreds of years, long after it is completely forgotten how and why those words were said, and instead of being seen for what those words really are, proof of my concern for my people, they will see them as proof of my people's sinfulness. Your descendants, who will live hundreds, even thousands of years from now, will pay for those stolen words with their lives. The words will pursue them; the words will stoke the hatred against them. Generation after generation will be accused of having killed me, and the vengeance exacted upon them will be terrible, and my stolen words will keep that hatred alive. Now," said the Teacher, "you understand why I asked you not to write it, my friend."

"But," Absalom began, "if I record your words so precisely that no one would be able to change or interpret them wrongly—"

"Once they're written down, they belong to the world, my friend. Neither I nor you will be asked to explain their original meaning. Oh, certainly they will want to talk to you about it and they will imagine that they do. Just as they will *think* that I talk to them...the way Judah's toe talks to you, Absalom. But it will not be me, it will be someone else. All I can say, my friend, is that innocent people will suffer for your writing. Ashes will fly into the sky."

"Ashes..." Absalom said quietly.

"Yes. That is why you must stop writing."

Absalom wanted to ask if he could write about something else, his daily life, for example, or the Toe, but he knew the answer, that no matter what he started writing about, it would end up being about the Teacher, and no, he didn't want any ashes to fly into the sky, even though he didn't quite know what that meant. He knew only that it had to do with death and destruction—and he was a peaceful man.

AMMAR

The Professor, aka the Mastermind, wants to know how it is going, and I have nothing to tell him. I don't tell him about Galia's offers of rides and sandwiches and how she wants to know about my childhood and how at first I resist and then succumb to her questions and tell her things I don't tell anyone else, even about my brother who lives in kibbutz Kiryat Anavim and calls himself Eleazar. I don't tell him about what happened when she came to my room and how she took off her clothes for me because he doesn't need to know that. The Mastermind wants one thing, and I don't have that one thing for him. He says that the target has bewitched me, and when I don't say yes or no, he asks me again, "Has she bewitched you? Have you become a slave of the Western woman with a pretty face? A pretty face she may have, but what's in her mind? Put the mind before the face and what will you have?" The Professor goes on and on, inflaming himself with his own rhetoric. I have to wait for him to say everything he has in him on the subject of Galia's face, because once he starts, there's no stopping him until he empties himself of all his words.

I have a bad feeling when he talks about her this way, because even though he's the Professor and the mastermind, he's a man, and I don't want another man to talk about her face this way. I notice that my right hand is beginning to rise as though it has a will of its own. I mustn't let it do it. I force it to lie back on my knee. When he's done talking, I say, "I need more proof of her wanting to be a queen of the Jews and all that, because what if she's innocent?"

He says, "Innocent?" with a smirk that is worse than his words. He walks over to his computer, opens a file, tells me to come closer and read it. It's the same file he showed me last time, the one with his cracking the hidden code in Galia's writing, but it's much longer now—he has added more points to the list. "Read it," he orders and pulls up a chair for me. "*The Hasmonean Chronicle, Chapter Three. 'The Shimmering Ones': code for the three players (participants) of the Road Map: the US, the UN, and the EU. The missing fourth is Russia."

I look up from the screen and see the Mastermind standing with his arms folded. I want to say, "So why did you choose these three? You might have as well included Russia and left out the EU, for example." But the way he looks, waiting for me to read more, I'd rather not say anything now.

"*The Hasmonean Chronicle, Chapter Four. 'Olympian gods' copulating with Jewish women = code for our demographic superiority. Olympian gods=non-Jewish seed. Our seed is the reason—"

I don't know how to tell him that I don't want to read it anymore. I say:

"So how does it connect to...you know? The throne and all that?"

"Her last name is Kozmin," he says significantly.

"Kozmin," I repeat thoughtfully.

"Yes," he says. "Kozmin. And what is the name of that dynasty of Jewish kings? The Hasmonean dynasty. And those folks, they know all about languages. K and H were interchangeable in Hebrew, they say. And even though some scholars disagree with this, these people insist that they're right. And s and z are also interchangeable. And the 'on' became 'in' to sound like a Russian surname: Putin, Lenin. So 'Kozmin' and 'Hasmon' is the same. Now you know why."

"But!" I say. I'm too stunned by the revelation of the significance of Galia's last name to say anything else. I brood on it in silence.

"Nice woman," he repeats with unbecoming sarcasm. "A generous, kind woman," he says.

"But she is," I say softly. "And she doesn't go to a synagogue or observe Jewish holidays, which means she is not really a Jew, she is okay."

"They point at the only remaining wall," the Mastermind raises his hand and points at the wall behind the computer, "of their temple and the ruins of the City of David and the ruins of the Masada and they say these are proof that the land was theirs before we came from the Arabian peninsula or from Syria and started growing our olive trees here. But the ruins are only one kind of proof, and they need other kinds, they need every possible proof on earth because the war between them and us--I consider myself part of you, therefore I say "us"--is conducted not only on the ground or the sky and not just in buses or pizzerias. The war is now conducted in the minds of journalists and diplomats and on pages of newspapers and on college campuses, and we're obviously on the winning side of this war. But sometimes they get to celebrate some small victories, and we don't want to give it to them, this particular victory, this little proof of what they think of as their right to the land just because there are still some people alive whose line can be traced back to the Hasmonean dynasty. So now you know what an honor I'm bestowing on you with this assignment. We are talking about centuries of history."

"History," I echo him, thinking there's no way I can protect this woman against centuries of history her own writing claims to represent.

He hits a computer key to reopen the file, reminding me that I didn't finish reading his points.

"*The Hasmonean Chronicle, Chapter Five: Ptolemy's killing Simon and Simon's two sons=code for our eventual victory over the Jews.

"*The Hasmonean Chronicle, Chapter Six: John Hyrcanus opening King David's sepulcher to pay off Antiochus VII Sidetes=code for America's attempts to pay us off, in the hope that money will make us give up our aspirations for statehood."

There are many more points; I can't read them all. Not while he is standing over me, commanding me to read. I could ask him to print out his points for me, so I could bring them to Galia and watch her face as she reads them and hear her say that this is no proof of anything at all and where did I get this nonsense. But if I ask him to print them out for me, he will look at me as though I'm an idiot or worse than an idiot—a traitor. So I move toward the door, hoping he will let me leave without making me read any more of his points and without forcing me once again to commit to a deadline for the completion of the task.

"It must be definite," he says.

"Yes."

"The mission must be accomplished."

He talks about deadlines, how I left them behind, one after another, and I want to say, You don't even know what you're saying, because if you could see Galia the way she really is, you'd know a thing or two about your points but you'd still not want to admit it. But that's the problem, isn't it, that you'd never get to know her the way she really is because you prefer to think of her as an evil that has to be wiped out, a Jew, a Hasmonean queen, whatever.

He blocks my escape. He says something about the guys. Do I remember the guys? And specifically, do I remember his promise to use his channels to get me a green card and to make it okay with the guys so they won't come after me to make me pay for the past? I remember both the green card and the guys and I know very well what he is talking about. It's a kind of game he's playing with me, pretending that he has the channels and the guys at his disposal, and that they carry out his wishes at a snap of his fingers. Yet he's so good at controlling my mind that even though in the depths of a part of my brain I know it's a game, I believe him anyway and my heart skips a beat when he mentions the guys. His promise to get me a green card and to keep the guys away from me was not a *present*, he says, meaning that it wasn't given for nothing but as an exchange for doing the deed. If I'm not going to do the deed, he wants to know what is going to hold him to his promise about the guys. He is sure that I'm aware of the exchange nature of the transaction: the guys--for the deed, and he would like to know if I have anything to say to this, he really would.

Nothing. I have nothing to say. I'm late for my evening painting job. Besides, the green card channels and the guys aren't even real. His pretending they're at his disposal, well, that's not real too. Only he's real, and I, his domesticated little terrorist, his brave militant, I'm real too, but not in the way he thinks. He will see it in a moment, the way in which I'm real. I step outside. I walk faster and faster.

CHAPTER 9
THE HASMONEAN CHRONICLE

———

MORIYA AND ABSALOM ENTERED THEIR old age with an unfulfilled hope for a grandchild, and every year, as they became older and their daughter-in-law's belly remained as beautifully flat as on the day she had married Avner, they suffered from their son's childlessness more than Avner himself did. They suffered so much, in fact, that at a certain point they realized they had to put a stop to it. Their watching their daughter-in-law's belly and mentally comparing its size to the size they remembered from two months before also had to stop, because it was not only making them unhappy, it was making them older and more prone to sicknesses. When they finally relinquished all hope and stopped watching Chasina's belly, it began to acquire a perceptible roundness.

The expected number of months later, the family gathered around Chasina's bed was more worried about baby Zohar not issuing his first cry than about the news, brought to them by a messenger at the very moment of Zohar's birth, about Pompey entering the Sanctuary, a sacrilege for which there was no equal in the memory of the living members of the family, although they were well aware that Pompey was not the first conqueror to do so: Antiochus Epiphanes, Judah's nemesis, committed this sacrilege a mere hundred years ago. This was the moment when Judah's Toe appeared to all the members of the family. It hung suspended over their heads, and before it floated away, Absalom, who didn't know yet that the Toe had left him forever, pointed at it and said, "There!" at the same time baby as Zohar finally issued the cry they had all been expecting. Since it had come simultaneously with the Toe, the future of this new family member was clear: he would follow in his great-grand-uncle's footsteps and liberate Judea from the Romans just as his great-grand-uncle had liberated it from the Greeks.

Yet Zohar was no Judah Maccabeus, even though he was the one now favored by Judah's Toe. He grew into a bookish young man whose primary interest, other than interviewing the Toe on its unique take on current events, was fine-quality parchment, which his parents ordered for him from a Jerusalem merchant with ties to a famous parchment maker in Pergamon. Young Zohar could put the most diligent students of the Torah to shame: if they could study the texts twenty hours a day, he was able to spend twenty-two hours studying his empty scrolls. The scrolls remained empty for the same reason his grandfather Absalom's scrolls did, and although no one told Zohar about the Teacher's request that his grandfather stop writing, he was so aware of the responsibility implicit in the act of recording events that he denied himself the pleasure of writing lest it inflict unimaginable suffering on the future generations of Jews.

While Zohar's struggles began, progressed, and ended inside his own mind, the world outside lived in wary anticipation of each new shudder of Herod's rage. No one knew what caused those bouts of mania—a torn spleen or a weak liver or a chronic kidney disease—and since no one could predict who Herod's next victims were going to be, a feeling of dread overtook Jerusalemites every time Herod was not seen in public longer than a few days.

Among the many stories of Herod's cruelty that circulated among Jerusalemites, the story of Mariamne was most instructive. Mariamne, Herod's wife and daughter of Alexandros, was a Hasmonean, and Zohar had met her several times on family occasions such as weddings and funerals but had never spoken to her because she was a demure teenager who followed her mother, mad-eyed Alexandra, like a lamb on a leash. On the last occasion, which was Mariamne's trial his grandmother Moriya had asked him to attend in her place because a sickness had confined her to the house, Mariamne was the same demure creature; only her eyes seemed to have changed. The trial was a farce and, listening to testimonies of witnesses, Zohar had no doubt that Mariamne's guilt was concocted by Herod's sister, the scheming Salome. He had to sit through the trial despite his disgust. Several times he wanted to stand up and say what everyone was afraid to say: that there was no truth to Salome's claim that a magic potion was the cause of Mariamne's passionate hold over Herod, that the claim risked sounding like an everyday metaphor for passion until Mariamne's eunuchs were subjected to prolonged torture and agreed to everything Salome wanted them to say at the trial. The eunuchs described in nauseating detail how they had seen Mariamne prepare the magic love-potion, how it had made Herod so obsessed with his Hasmonean wife that he let her get away with anything, including adultery, which they also claimed to have seen and heard. When asked to disclose the name of the lover, these fake witnesses broke down and between sobs and hiccups begged Mariamne's forgiveness. She sat through it all with an expressionless face like a statue: her anger at their lies made her abandon her usual shyness for pride. Her mother had always insisted on this pride because she wanted to teach her daughter to act like a queen, but Mariamne lived too deeply inside herself to display anything that wasn't a true feeling. At the moment when her death sentence was announced and the guards moved toward her with an unmistakable intent, it was this new pride that made her speak with the serenity of a sage.

"The charges are fake," she said slowly. "The only thing I'm guilty of is my Maccabean descent, the same thing my brother Jonathan had been guilty of: his body was found floating in Herod's pleasure pool when the Jerusalemites' obvious pride in him as their high priest filled my husband's heart with fear. But even if you try to hunt down every Maccabean, a few of us will survive, and history will be a fairer judge than this court."

It was at this moment that Zohar saw Judah's Toe. It floated above the heads of the judges, visible to no one but him, or at least he thought he was the only one who saw it, because no one pointed at it or shouted, "Toe in the air!" or, "Miracle!" or paid it any attention whatsoever. He watched it out of the corner of his left eye, trying not to let his face reveal his fascination. He looked at Mariamne and saw that her face had acquired the same faraway look his grandfather Absalom had when he conversed with an empty space underneath the ceiling, failing to remember, in his old age, that the Toe had left him forever on the day of Zohar's birth. Zohar worried briefly whether he, too, was giving himself away with his faraway look, and a thought occurred to him that had crossed his mind before, about the faraway look being the mark of a Hasmonean man or woman chosen as a contact by their illustrious ancestor who had set up this unusual mode of communication with the living generation, using the Toe as a go-between. In each generation, only one Hasmonean was chosen as a contact. Yet here was Mariamne, with her far-away look, clearly a contact. That made two in the same generation, Zohar and Mariamne, distant relatives brought together by their ancestor's choice. Zohar thought with regret that only now he was beginning to appreciate this sister in spirit whom he could have gotten to know years ago but who would remain unknown to him forever: she was being led away by the guards to pay with her life for Herod's jealousy and Salome's intrigues.

At some point during her progression toward the door, Mariamne lowered herself on a nearby bench, her legs proving weaker than her spirit, and everyone, including the guards who had not been known for compassion, waited patiently for this Hasmonean queen to regain enough strength to stand. Just as she was about to rise, her mother's voice pierced the stillness of the room. Mad-eyed Alexandra must not have been a true Hasmonean, nor a true mother, and she certainly had never seen the Toe, whether floating under the ceiling of her sumptuous quarters, or outside, between earth and sky.

Alexandra, who had been tired of being a mere mother of the queen, had always felt herself more suited for queendom than her daughter, whose hours were now numbered anyway and whose weakness was out there for all to see: Mariamne was a condemned woman, unable to walk because she knew that each step was taking her closer to her death. It was Alexandra's fatal mistake to make her piercing bid for power while her daughter was rising from the bench, falling down, slowly rising again and walking with uncertain steps, with two guards in front of her and two in the back. When the crowd heard the mother denounce the condemned daughter, it rose as one against the mother, and only the appearance of more armed guards kept the crowd's fury under control.

Alexandra suffered no bodily harm, but the crowd had booed her so thoroughly that she did not dare to show herself in public until the day of her own execution, which came without a trial and seemed more like an afterthought for Herod. He missed Mariamne so violently that the love potion for which she had been condemned and in the existence of which he believed even more strongly after her death, became, in this grieving tyrant's brain, proof of the highest love a man ever had for a woman and for which God would surely destroy him since his love for his dead wife was greater than his love of God. Although it was said that Mariamne died like a real Maccabee and that the courage with which she took those steps toward death transformed her from mere royalty into the stuff of legend, it was the gentle words with which she had forgiven her mother, her husband, and her sister-in-law that drove Herod so mad with grief that he had her dead body preserved in honey.

What Zohar didn't know but should have guessed from the pattern of events was that as one of the few remaining Hasmoneans he was next on Herod's list. Whether or not the physical list of Herod's enemies, or people Herod thought of as such, ever existed, no one knew, nor did it matter, because those who had any blood ties with the Hasmonean dynasty had been lured into an elaborate trap of intrigue set up by Herod's sister Salome or by Herod himself. No matter how loved they had been by him or her and how innocent they were of any dreams of power, they were murdered with cruelty that, despite being standard for tyrants of the time, never failed to surprise Zohar, as though he had expected better from this intelligent king.

The only son of Avner—who had died in early middle age on the same night and the same minute as Absalom, as though they had teamed up to spare Herod the effort of murdering them—Zohar was now an obvious target. Yet when his grandmother tried to talk him into hiding out in a village in the Galilee, far from Herod's reach, he walked out on her in a fury that was so unlike him and so unexpected that he himself, once he reflected on it in a calmer mood, could not understand it and attributed its cause to a poorly digested breakfast, despite the fact that he had never complained of digestive troubles before. Moriya was now so ancient that not even Herod with his swings of paranoia could imagine her as an enemy, which is why she was allowed to live out her days in peace.

Zohar defied danger, walking wherever he wished and at any time of night or day, for no purpose other than thinking. He said that walking helped his thinking and without thinking he could not live. One night Moriya had a dream in which she heard a voice she identified as her birth mother's, informing her that Zohar would survive not only Herod's attempts at his life but Herod himself, as long as the Toe remained on his side. The Toe must remain on his side, Moriya's birth mother said rather sternly in the dream, and when Moriya awoke and told the dream to Absalom's spirit, who stayed with her long after his body was gone, she admitted that she could not remember her birth mother's real voice because so many years separated her from her early childhood that it had long since become a blur. Nevertheless, she said, she recognized the voice in the dream as belonging to her birth mother, for nothing is as strong as worries passed on by generations of mothers, and no one senses danger as mothers do, be they living people or shadows in our dreams.

"So what do you want me to do?" Absalom's spirit said in exasperation. "When we asked him to hide out in the Galilee, he stormed out in a fury."

Moriya remarked that Absalom must be very old indeed to hear and speak so inaccurately, for her birth mother had been talking not about the Galilee but about the Toe, and not about hiding, which was useless anyway because Herod had the means to get him anywhere, but about their own family protector, and it was their grandson's life they were talking about, after all.

Whether or not Absalom agreed with Moriya, there was nothing more he could do to protect his grandson from Herod. Absalom was dead, and even if he hadn't been dead, the Toe had stopped appearing to him many years before. It was Zohar now to whom it appeared; therefore it was Zohar alone who could secure its protection.

When men came to the house to take Zohar away, Moriya was in her room, asleep. A guard who was in the process of putting Zohar's legs in shackles and whose clumsiness betrayed the fact that he was new at his job first yelled at Zohar for not keeping his legs in the position most propitious for his work, then suddenly stood up with a cry resembling a baby's. Other guards followed the direction of his gaze and gave out a similarly primitive cry. They crowded together like sheep in a herd, the shoulders of one touching the shoulders of another, and fled, leaving Zohar half in, half out of shackles. When he looked up expecting to see the Toe, all he saw was a strange glow that suffused the sky, and knowing that the guards who disobeyed Herod's order would be put to death immediately, he understood that they had fled because the glow of the Toe filled them with a fear much stronger than their fear of the king. Zohar offered thanks to God for their fear and went inside. The shackles were left lying on the ground, and the sky assumed its usual color.

GALIA

The next time he calls, his voice is different, both soft and hard, hushed and insistent. He says there is something…He stops, and then corrects himself: he needs to ask me something. I say, Go ahead, but all I hear are sighs and other unintelligible sounds, and while they are better than the indifferent grunts he used to emit during our phone conversations a few months ago, they leave me unenlightened as to the purpose of his call.

"Why don't we meet somewhere so you can tell me?" I say. "Because the way you're saying it now, it's not clear to me, and I really would like to understand."

After a few more grunts and sighs he says okay. We agree to meet at the corner of Steinway and Twenty-Eighth Street, and when I see him there, standing next to a closed storefront, I wave to him, but there's no change in his face, as though he is trying to prove to himself that resembling an inanimate object has certain benefits. We walk silently for a while. Then he says, "Convert, Galia."

I'm not sure I heard him right. "What?"

"Convert to Islam," he repeats clearly. "It'll save your life."

"Why are you so concerned with saving my soul?"

"Not your soul, Galia," he says impatiently. "I said life."

"I thought you said soul. That's what they usually mean when they say that faith will save you."

"This is not usually, Galia. You have three weeks. Two and a half, exactly."

I want to ask him what the hell he is talking about, but I have to be careful because it's not an everyday thing, this stroll with Alejandro and his speaking with me in such an urgent way as though there's nothing more important in the world than this. I shouldn't ruin this moment with impatience and crude words such as "hell," even if I don't mean anything by them, because who knows what it means or doesn't mean in his religion.

He stops walking and turns to me. He bends down to my eye level. He says he wants to know the truth.

"Truth about what?"

"About your last name," he says.

"About my last name? What do you mean?"

He straightens. He doesn't look at me when he says, "It's Kozmin, right?"

"Yeah," I say. "So what? What about it? You knew my last name back when you worked in my house. I didn't make a secret of it. It was on the mailbox."

"Yes," he says, "it was on the mailbox. But at that time I didn't know anything about you."

"And what do you know now?"

"Remember that time when I told you to stop writing about your Hasmoneans?"

"But why is this so important to you? What do you care about a dynasty of Jewish kings in the second and first centuries BC? Why make a fuss about it, again and again?"

"Oh," he says, "so you don't know? You don't know why make a fuss?"

"No, I don't. You call me and tell me you want to meet and then you say you want me to convert to Islam and you ask if I remember the time when you asked me not to write about a dynasty of ancient Jewish kings. So what am I supposed to do with this? Am I supposed to figure something out? To see a connection of some sort? Is it some kind of game? I really don't know."

"I want to know about those Hasmonean kings," he says. "How they are proof of Jews being there all the way back."

"What proof?"

"Hasmon," he says. "Just listen to the sound: Has-mo-n. And your last name, Koz-min. K and H are interchangeable in Hebrew. And a and o sound the same when they are...what is it called?"

"Unstressed?" I say helpfully.

"That's right. Unstressed. So talk."

"What should I talk about?"

"If you are their...ugh..." He searches for an English word, and I'm not helping him, even though I know that the word he is looking for is "descendant." "If you come from them, then what? What will you do?"

"Like, you mean, will I declare myself a queen of the Jews? Rule Israel? Establish monarchy? Perhaps even a matriarchy? Disband the Knesset, let the prime minister go, and make all decisions myself?"

"Yes," he says seriously. "What decisions would you make?"

"I don't know...I guess if I had absolute power in Israel, I'd make a change or two. Maybe I'd make renewable energy a requirement for every house. You know, solar panels would work so well there. Lots of sun."

"That's all? Nothing else?" he asks with an urgency I hadn't heard in his voice before.

If this is all because of a fantasy, I have to admit to myself that I misjudged this man, even though I consider myself an intuitive type who sees through surfaces into the dark corners of the soul. Yes, I definitely misjudged this man. I had no idea he was capable of such flights of fancy. Or that he would want to meet me for this: not to talk me into going with him to his room or some other secluded place for the satisfaction of his masculine urges but to make me tell him in detail what laws I would enact if I were Queen of the Jews.

"I don't know. Really, I haven't thought much about this," I say.

This is a date, I tell myself, and I want it to be peaceful and mutually enjoyable, and what better way to peace but asking him what *he* thinks I should do in an unlikely chance I become the queen of Israel.

"If I give you an answer, you won't like it," he says, "because I Arab. I care about our interests, not interests of you people."

"I don't like when you say 'you people.' It's a bit...you know, rude."

"I told you, Galia, you won't like what I say."

"But you haven't said anything yet, and you're already being rude. And this is right when I'm about to tell you that I don't have anything against converting to Islam, if only to please you, just because you asked—just because you said you wanted me to, and I was almost going to say okay. I'm irreligious, so it's not like I would change one belief for another—I'd do it for you. I wore the headscarf at the Muslim school where I worked years back, and I might agree to wear it all day, if that'll make you happy, and if that's what converting to Islam is all about—"

"It's not just about a headscarf!"

"But for me it would be just that—"

"Then you have no right to convert!"

"Don't you see that I'm just trying to be tolerant, and even though I don't know much about converting to Islam and have no interest in any conversion, I'm being sympathetic and...well, friendly to the idea, you know? I think you should value this instead of saying intolerant things, like you don't have the interests 'of you people' meaning 'Jews.' I don't divide people into 'mine' and 'yours.' Everybody is the same...that's my thinking."

"'Mine' and 'yours' will be outdated by the time we overcome you through our numbers," he says solemnly. "The enemy will be subsumed by our high reproduction rate."

"Oh yes," I say lightly, "oh yes, the demographic threat. 'Thanks to our demographic rate, we will dominate you.'"

"How you know that?"

"I read."

"So you *are* a coordinator of a Hasmonean group. You *are* a threat."

"Yes, I'm a threat to you because I love you and because it looks like you love me too."

"You're a different kind of threat. A bigger danger than love—a threat to our right to our land."

"Is that why you are suddenly so interested in this dynasty of ancient kings? And why you want to know what I would do if I were a Hasmonean queen ascending the throne of Israel?"

"Look, Galia. It's hard to talk about it." He makes a meaningful pause. "I'm not allowed to tell you *everything*, you understand?

"But I thought you didn't want to sound like Tom, ending your sentences with 'You understand?'"

"We're talking about important things, Galia."

"Are these important things the decisions I will make when I become the queen of Israel?"

"No, Galia. We're talking about your life. Your life."

When I tell him I don't see what my life has to do with any of it, and anyway, what does he mean by bringing my life into this, he says he's not at liberty to disclose any more than what he has already said, but he saw some of the chapters I posted online about the Hasmonean kings and he was puzzled. Yes, puzzled, he repeats. And he wants to know why. Why?

"I love etymology, Alejandro. Or is it Ammar? You know what etymology is? It's about the origin of words. I was interested in finding out where my surname comes from. One of the theories is that 'Kozmin' comes from 'Hasmon,' and I've been exploring it in my writing about the Hasmoneans. There are other theories, and I would like to explore them too. You wanted to know why. So this is why."

He says that if I'm exploring all those things, I should also explore how I could make the lives of my Arab neighbors better, and when I say I don't know what he's talking about, he says that I could give an order to tear down the separation fence, and I could eliminate checkpoints, and I could make the army remove the settlements and give the land over to...you know, he says, all those things you didn't want to do for years.

"Me?" I say. "*I* didn't want to do all these things?"

"Yes, you," he says.

"But I'm not the head of the Israeli government, Ammar. I don't even live there. I don't make any decisions."

"Tell it to the Professor," he says sullenly.

I want to ask him what professor he is talking about, because obviously he is not talking about his former years as a university student. Instead of deciding whether or not I should issue an order to tear down the separation fence, I want to ask him if he, too, can feel the electricity between us, and if he says yes, I want to ask him if he ever felt it this strongly and this clearly, and if he says yes to that too, I want to ask him what does he think we should do about it. But he doesn't give me a chance to ask any of my questions. He stops in a leafy part of a street that looks like a dead-end, takes my hand, and says, "Convert, Galia."

Now that he's holding my hand, the energy is even stronger, and again I want to ask him if he feels it.

I say, "Yes, Alejandro, I will convert," and he says, "It's not so simple, because you have to be ready," and I say, "Ready for what?"

"Wear the hijab all day, be a proper Muslim wife, take my last name."

I say that I would like to know more about the other woman, or women, whose ranks I join as his wife, and I wouldn't want to part with my last name, and not just because it may or may not connect me to the Hasmoneans that fill him with dread and suspicion. Other than that I say why not. He says, "Are you sure?"

"I'll do it."

"Inshallah," he says.

I repeat after him, "Inshallah, whatever," hoping he won't hear the doubt in my voice.

He says the word "deadline" in the same ominous voice he used when he told me about the three weeks I have left to enjoy this life. I tell him that I love reading, therefore I don't mind reading the Koran, and I love languages, therefore I don't mind learning Arabic, but I don't love threatening intonations and this nonsense about the three weeks I have left to live.

"I save your life," he says, "at the risk of my own, and not free to divulge more, that's why I tell you only in nutshell. You know what they say about nutshell—so much has to fit into so little. So maybe it seems unclear and maybe puzzling, but some things in my life that I cannot talk about and I can give you these things only in nutshell and you must take them from me without questions and if you want to know more, you can read the news."

"How is the news connected to the nutshell?" I ask.

He says that the nutshell gives a lot in a small way, and the world news gives little in a big way, but somewhere out there they come together, the nutshell and the world, but this is as much as he has a right to tell me. I tell him that he is trying to sound mysterious again, just like when he talked about the three weeks I had left to live.

He says, "That's only if you don't convert! If you convert, three weeks will be cancelled."

I want to know how long I'll have left then, instead of the three weeks, and he says happily, "The rest of your life!"

He calls me the next day and says he wants to meet me after work. When I see him waiting for me on Steinway, I tell myself that it's the first time *he's* waiting for *me*, instead of the other way around, and it's a good thing, much better than all those times when I waited for him. He says we are going to his place, and he doesn't ask me whether I agree to come. I've agreed to so much already that this is not something I'm going to argue about. He walks, and I follow him, like a good Muslim wife. He unlocks the door to his room without a word, and I remember his "You arrre welcome," but apparently today we have no time for sentimentalities.

"Sit down," he says, and I sit on the chair at his small table. "No, not here," he says and points at the floor.

I don't understand what he wants of me.

"The rug," he says. Now I see a threadbare rug between the table and a wall. He sits on it first, and I follow him, awkwardly.

He says, "It's called Shahada, and we say it like this: La ilah illa Allah…"

I look at him silently. I want to see if he understands my silent question.

"You don't know what I talking about?" he asks. "I asked people about how to convert, and they said she must say the Shahada. You have to say the Shahada. So, repeat: 'La ilah illa Allah, Muhammad rasoolu Allah.'"

"I can't repeat it without seeing it on paper. Can you write it down for me?"

He scribbles it on a piece of paper and hands it to me.

"What does it mean?" I ask.

"It means, 'I testify that there is no true god but Allah, and that Muhammad is a Messenger of God.' With these words, you enter the fold of Islam," he says solemnly.

"And what exactly am I going to do in that fold?"

"You will submit to His will, and all your sins will be forgiven. You will start a new life of piety and righteousness. What more can anyone want?"

"Sounds kind of boring."

He shouts, "Your record will be clean, you understand? How you say boring? What does boring have to do with it? All your past sins will be forgiven! What else can you want?"

I tell him that I've agreed only because he had asked me to. It has nothing to do with what I want. Repeating some syllables isn't going to change my life.

"Won't change your life? You're a Jew! And with that last name! Do you know what can happen to you if you stay as you are?"

"What can happen to me if I stay as I am?"

"You will be liquidated," he says quietly.

"By whom?"

"By me," he says.

"You won't kill me. You can't."

"Why not?"

"Because you won't do anything bad to me."

"I obey orders."

"You don't have to obey them."

"I don't have a choice."

"Of course you do. You're free to make your own decisions."

"No."

"You don't look like the kind that can kill."

"I don't look, that's right. Maybe I don't look. But an assignment is an assignment. It is…how you say? A duty."

"But why? Can you tell me why?"

He shrugs. He's already told me too much.

"Because I'm a Hasmonean descendant? A pretender to a throne that had stood empty for over two thousand years?"

"Yes," he says firmly. "Because you all these things. But if you become one of us, you free me of the need to kill you."

"So you're saying that I would die as relatives of kings and queens died for centuries. Eliminated because of someone's fear that I might usurp the throne that no one has claimed for more than two millennia, since who knows in what direction I will lead my people once I become queen of the Jews!"

"That's right," he says. "Nobody knows. Not even you. That's why the decision has been made to liquidate you."

"Who made the decision?"

"I can't tell you."

"You can. You must. "

"No."

"Who was it, Ammar? Tell me."

"I can't. No, I can't."

"If you won't tell me, I will--"

"What? You'll report me?"

"No, I won't report you, Ammar. But you must tell me who it is."

"I can't tell you. I can't disobey."

"Yes, you can. You're free."

"Not so free."

"But you are."

"The decision has been made. At first, I thought he wasn't so serious, but then I realized that he was. He really means it. He wants you out of the way."

"Ignore the decision."

"I've been ignoring long time. Don't you see? If I hadn't been ignoring, you and I wouldn't be talking now."

"His name. Give me his name, Ammar. Disobey him just this once."

"I can't. He decides. I obey."

"You can decide to disobey."

"I can't decide like that. He is the mastermind. He decides."

"If he wishes to be a mastermind, it's his business. But you don't have to carry out his orders."

"Whose orders will I carry out then?"

"No one's. You won't have any orders."

"And what will happen to *you?*"

"I'll stay alive."

"Not forever."

"We're all mortal."

"He send someone else to kill you."

"I doubt it."

"He won't...how you say? Cancel his decision because I decide not to carry it out."

"I can try to have a talk with him too."

"No!"

"Why not?"

"He won't talk to you."

"There's no harm in talking."

"You the enemy. You understand? If you come to him, he'll set one of his other guys on you."

"You talk about them as if they're dogs."

"Dogs? No!"

"When you say 'he'll set one of his other guys on me.'"

"That's my speech, Galia. My English is not very perfect."

"Anyway, he is in a law-abiding country and he's not a fool. He knows what will happen to him if he does that."

"There is...how you say it? Human justice, and there is God's justice. Human justice is nothing to a man who believes in God's justice."

"He can despise human justice all he wants, but I doubt he'd be willing to test it on his own self."

"Human justice is nothing to a man like him. Especially to one who wasn't born into our faith but converted to it because of his beliefs."

"Ah, so he converted! He's not one of you--"

"Faith makes man strong. You, an unbeliever, can't imagine how strong."

"Why, I believe in some things too. Thou shall not kill. The Ten Commandments. Human or divine. I believe that killing is wrong. Besides, I believe that a normal man doesn't kill a woman he likes, no matter what his religion tells him about possible dangers emanating from her surname."

"But I don't...I don't want to kill you!" he cries, pressing his hand to his heart. "Why you say that I want to kill you?! I want you to live, I want to save you, don't you see? All I ask is you say the Shahada! Is it too much to ask? Tell me, is it too much? I think no."

"I don't mind saying it, but I must tell you in advance that I don't believe in it. I have to say this, that I don't believe in it."

"Please! I beg you! Do it, for me, please!" He presses both hands to his heart and speaks with the ferocity I found so appealing when I first met him.

"All right, Alejandro, I'll say the Shahada, if this will make you happy. But what else will I have to do? If I have to go somewhere and do this in front of other people, I don't think I can go through with it."

"Just say. Right here. I tell them you said the Shahada and I heard you say it, maybe they say enough."

He writes down the Shahada for me and I say it, and nothing happens. Not that I expected anything to happen, since I'm not the one who believes in the power of magic syllables, but still, something could have happened, good or bad, no matter how small, but there was nothing, even though I repeated the whole thing two or three times, trying to get it right for the sake of Ammar, who turned into a perfectionist of the first class. He even said so himself, "I'm perfectionist of first class!" Therefore I obliged him by repeating the syllables until I got all of them right. Even Ammar was eventually pleased with my pronunciation, which he called "Syrian Arabic," unlike his own which was—I don't know what he called it—perhaps the Perfect Arabic.

But none of it was any use, not my repeating the Shahada until I learned it by heart, not my perfect pronunciation, and not my willingness to sit on his little rug for as long as he thought it was necessary to give the Shahada syllables time to grow, because some people believe, he said, that once they come out of a person's mouth, they are like newborn butterflies with untrained wings, and it's best for the one from whose mortal mouth they issue to stay in one place while they move their wings up and down, up and down, learning to fly. Or maybe the problem was not the butterflies or their untrained wings but a simple fact that I did not believe, and would not believe, no matter what syllables I was willing to mouth, no matter how much I wanted to please Ammar, no matter how strongly I loved him. My love made me say the Shahada, but it was not the Shahada that I believed in: it was my love.

CHAPTER 10

THE HASMONEAN CHRONICLE

———◆———

IN THE YEAR 698, THE last Moriya in the long line of Moriyas was asleep in the room she shared with her two sisters. This was her last night in the house where she had spent every night of her eighteen years, and although she had promised her sisters that she would stay awake the whole night talking to them because they would never sleep together again in this room, she fell asleep in spite of herself. The following day she was to wed Suleiman al-Nahib, thus breaking the long line of Moriyas who got married to men with names such as Absalom, Simeon, or Judah. Her groom did not request that she convert to the Muslim faith before marrying him—this was not mere good will on his part but simply following a Koranic Sura that stipulated a Muslim man was allowed to marry a Jewish or Christian woman without losing his own spiritual capital, while a Muslim woman was not allowed to marry a non-Muslim man.

The last Moriya slept in her childhood bed and dreamed of a Moriya who lived three centuries earlier and who, like her, was not the first Moriya in the long line of women with that name, yet who, unlike her, lived out her fate to the last drop, or the last straw, the precise expression was not what mattered, and that last drop, or the last straw, was what made the last Moriya experience the dream as a kind of revelation, which indeed it was.

She saw the other Moriya, a girl eighteen years of age like herself, handing out bowls of lentil pottage to exhausted fighters, and as the mind of that earlier Moriya was open to the dreamer, she saw the earlier Moriya trying to concentrate

229

in order to follow her mother's instructions on the correct way of handing bowls to war-weary men in a way that would neither lead them into temptation nor let her succumb to temptation herself. "Don't look up," her mother's voice said in her head, "look only at your own hands, so the bowl passes from your hand into his without a drop being spilled. We are very low on provisions here in Betar and every drop is precious."

The girl obeyed her mother, carefully ladling the pottage into bowl after bowl, gingerly placing the bowl into waiting hands and never looking up, until a man's hand brushed against hers and set her hand on fire. She disobeyed her mother's advice and looked up. Absalom, her distant cousin and childhood play-mate, was smiling at her. She lowered her eyes, but it was too late.

At this point the sleeping Moriya could see into the soul of the Moriya she was dreaming about, and she knew that the shimmerings had invaded her, just like they did her ancestor Judah on the day when he first saw Nehora, the woman of the jug. The Moriya in the dream felt so guilty about that one look that her hand shook and the precious pottage spilled and she uttered a cry without words, because she could not articulate her horror: here they were, on a small hill, surrounded by Roman troops who were clearly in the last stages of building a siege wall, and what was she doing? How was she helping her people? Staring into a man's eyes and spilling priceless pottage, that's what she was doing. She turned away in disgust at herself and left. Her place was quickly taken by another girl, whose hands were steady because she kept her eyes on her task.

The next thing the dreaming Moriya saw was Absalom searching and find-ing the girl in a dark corner of a makeshift kitchen, sitting on her haunches, her head in her lap, so she appeared almost headless. Somehow she knew that Absalom had known the girl since childhood, back when the adults used to say that although they were not the same Moriya and Absalom as their ancestors, the original Moriya and Absalom who lived some ten generations back, the family tradition was that every girl named Moriya would possess the original Moriya's beauty and her desire for a life away from the turmoil of power, and that every male infant named Absalom would grow into a contemplative man whose love of writing would mark him as a true descendant of the original Absalom, a dreamer, not a warrior. Yet whatever was said in their childhood, he was a warrior now, and she was in turmoil—for survival, not power.

"There's nothing shameful in this," Absalom said quietly.

His words made the girl realize that something had been blocking her tears, and now they flowed out freely and she did not attempt to wipe them.

"Even in the times such as these," he said, "people fall in love."

She seemed not to hear the end of his sentence about people falling in love, and she asked him what exactly did he mean by "times such as these," and even though he thought she knew very well what he meant and that she only pretended to miss the second half of his sentence, he answered her.

"War," he said. "Defeat. No matter what Simon bar Kokhba says, our revolt is over. This is our last stand, this fortress on the hill defended by two and a half thousand fighters. All we can do is wait and watch the enemy complete his siege wall, move the catapults and rock-throwers closer to the wall and then…No need to worry about Roman engineers forgetting how to make those things work. We, on the other hand—" He stopped, because Moriya was no longer crying but looking him straight in the eyes without fear or shame.

"Yes," she whispered, "We, on the other hand? What did you want to say?"

"Nothing," he said. He walked away from the makeshift kitchen and from his bride, for that's what Moriya was for him, only he didn't know it yet, his spirit being so uncertain in these days before the final defeat and dispersal of the Jews that his heart failed to convey messages to his mind.

The last Moriya—not the Moriya in the dream but the one dreaming—was still inside the world that had ended in the year 135 AD, only now it was a dream without any images. The absence of images was compensated for by a voice that was narrating the story of her people, or what she understood to be her people. She had known fragments of this narrative, bits and pieces passed from generation to generation, from parent to child, by a long succession of earlier Moriyas and Salomes and Absaloms. She knew that she was the last in the long line of Moriyas, because her future children would follow the faith of their father and would not care to know about their mother's ancestors with names such as Judah or Simon or Absalom, who had rebelled against the Greeks and the Romans in varying circumstances and with varying success. The voice, which appeared to be reading from a book she could not see, said that the last rebellion against Rome ended in total defeat. It said these words—total defeat—three times, and one time it said "dispersal." The voice said that the struggle, known as the Bar Kokhba revolt, lasted three years and that Hadrian sent his XXII Deiotariana and Legio IX Hispana to Judea and that both were disbanded after heavy losses. The dreamer did not know who Hadrian was, nor did she know anything about XXII Deiotariana or Legio IX Hispana, and the voice patiently explained, again as though reading from a book, that Hadrian was the emperor of Rome, and that he had sent almost half of the entire Roman army to reconquer Judea. The voice continued with the story of Bar Kokhba's supporters, who took refuge in the fortress of Betar, and it said that when Betar was finally captured after a prolonged Roman siege, "the Romans went on killing until their horses were submerged in blood to their nostrils." The voice said that these were facts, they were written in a book, and at this point the sleeper's impression that the voice had been reading from a book was confirmed. The voice went on enumerating the dead. It said that half a million Judeans were killed, fifty towns and 985 villages ruined. It said that the Romans executed Bar Kokhba in a way too horrible to describe, and this was followed by executions of other leaders of the rebellion, such as Rabbi Akiba" whose flesh was torn off with a carding-implement," and Rabbi Ishmail, who was flayed slowly, and Rabbi Hanania ben Teradion, "who was wrapped in a scroll of the Law and placed on a pyre of green brushwood; to prolong his agony wet wool was placed on his chest."

Why are you telling me this, the dreamer wanted to scream, I don't want to hear any more, but evidently the voice did not consider her girlish squeamishness worthy of attention, for it went on reading from the book about how Hadrian prohibited the Torah law and the Hebrew calendar, how he had the sacred scroll burned on the Temple Mount in a ceremony he called sacred, how he installed a statue of Jupiter and one of himself at what was left of the Temple sanctuary, and how, in order to erase all memory of Judea, he renamed the area Syria Palestina, and out of Jerusalem he made a pagan city and renamed it Aelia Capitolina, Aelius being his own second name and Capitolinus being Jupiter's, and how Tisha B'Av was the only day of the year when Jews who had still remained in the land were allowed to enter what was once their sacred city, so that by mourning their losses they would learn the lesson of submission.

The voice stopped abruptly, although it seemed there were many more pages left in the book from which it was reading, and the end of the narration was not made clear to the dreaming girl. As soon as the narration stopped, the images started again, exactly where they were cut off earlier, and she saw Absalom coming out of the makeshift kitchen at Betar, saying "Nothing" in response to Moriya's question, "We, on the other hand? What did you want to say?" There were many more images of Absalom, and the dreamer saw him repeating this word "Nothing" many times in his mind during the final days of Betar. Then the voice returned, and it was the same voice as before but lower, almost a whisper, and it said that everything grew out of that nothing, and it didn't need Absalom repeating it or even understanding what it was, for it was, among other things, a child in Moriya's belly. This particular everything didn't grow out of their first meeting, which was, like his last word to her that day, "nothing," nor out of the second one, nor the third, but the fourth and the fifth ones were the most fertile nothings, because not only did they bring Absalom and Moriya together in ways that consecrated that particular nothing as marriage and gave legitimacy to their offspring, even though it was a marriage without a canopy and a birth without a midwife; as soon as the offspring was engendered, the two were separated, and it was this separation that resulted, nineteen centuries later, in two nationalities thoroughly unaware of their common roots.

Now the voice was back, narrating the story of Moriya and Absalom. Moriya, with a child in her belly, was among those Jews fortunate to stay in their land, which she was careful not to call "Judea" for fear of Roman punishment. Absalom was captured by Hadrian's soldiers, tortured like other Betar defenders, but unlike them, instead of being killed, he was put on a slave ship destined for Spain. The voice did not seem interested in continuing the story of Absalom, saying only that in Spain he was sold to a man who owned farmland near Juliobriga, a Roman city in the north of Spain, that he was put to work at his master's winepress, that he married a Jewish slave woman, had two sons and a daughter by her, and that eleven years later, following the master's death, his new master, the son of his original owner, an enlightened man who read Seneca and Epictetus to his slaves, freed the whole family, and subsequently offered Absalom a job as a teacher of Hebrew and Aramaic to his children. There was nothing more to tell about Absalom, said the voice, adding that while in far-away Spain Absalom taught Hebrew letters to the sons of his former master, in the land now called Palestina the child whom Moriya had conceived from Absalom in the last days of Betar grew into a woman. Her name was Yemina, and just like in the story of creation Abraham begat Isaak and Isaak begat Jacob and on and on through generations of sons and fathers, so Yemina's daughter Elisheva gave birth to Mariamne, and Mariamne gave birth to Moriya, and Moriya gave birth to Salome, and Salome gave birth to Yemina, and Yemina gave birth to another Moriya and on and on, down the female line of dreamers, while the land passed from one conqueror to another, until in the fourth decade of the seventh century the region became one of the many Muslim conquests under the leadership of Umar ibn al-Khatab, whose armies had swept through Persia, Mesopotamia, parts of the Byzantine Empire, and Syria.

The last Moriya had the dream that so many generations of Moriyas and Yeminas and Salomes spoke of without experiencing it themselves. She saw what appeared to be a man's foot, perhaps a toe, and this was the last and most vivid image of her long dream.

At sunrise her two younger sisters shook her awake, filling the room with shrieks and giggles, severing her connection with the images, and removing her from the knowledge imparted to her in the dream. Chattering with her sisters about her forthcoming wedding, she only vaguely remembered the toe and the word "Hasmonean," which were both quite meaningless to her, for she no longer remembered the long line of ancestors who ascribed great importance to the vision that had come to her unaccompanied by an explanation as there was no one left to elucidate its meaning and describe its long history—and she had utterly blotted out the memory of the voice that narrated the story in the dream. That day she had the honor of becoming the first wife of Suleiman al-Nahib, with whom she went on to have eight children: five boys and three girls. She never told them about her dream of the toe, just as she didn't tell them about the many Moriyas who preceded her, for she belonged to her new family and the new faith completely, and the vague memory of the old dream and the long line of kings and dreamers from whom she sprung was an embarrassment that she made every effort to eradicate. She succeeded in this perfectly, because she understood that to be safe in her new life she had to cut off the part of her that did not belong. This last Moriya did not know of the existence of distant relatives in far-away Spain, descendants of Absalom the freed Jewish slave, and even if, through some unlikely miracle, she could have learned of their existence, she would have had no interest in knowing that they had continued the family tradition of naming their male offspring Absalom, Judah, Zohar, and Simon, and their girls Moriya and Salome, just as they had kept alive the memory of Judah Maccabeus and his campaign against the superior army of Antiochus the Third, and of the first Absalom, the one who had been cured by the Teacher and forbidden to write about him, as well as the later one who had participated in the siege of Betar and been captured and taken on a slave ship to Spain. These memories were passed on from generation to generation, along with the legend of Judah's Toe and the prediction that out of their line would come another keeper of the Toe, but they did not know, nor could they guess, that thirteen centuries and countless generations would pass until the Toe would manifest once again to their distant descendant.

AMMAR

She talks to me about her thoughts. I listen to her, and I don't know what to say. Should I tell her what I really think about her writing? And that I don't know why a toe floating in the air has to appear to every successive generation of Hasmoneans, and what exactly does it mean? "It doesn't have to have a literal meaning," she says.

What's a literal meaning? I want to ask, but I don't, because I don't want her to think me a fool. She indicated more than once that this is what she thinks I am: a fool. A kind of bumpkin who doesn't have any idea of what *real* literature, *real* thinking, and *real* understanding of history is all about. She also made it clear that she loved me despite my being a fool about these things. And she also made it clear that I have to value it even more, her loving me despite her thinking that I'm a fool, as if her thinking of me as a fool has as much value as her love. If a woman tells a man she loves that she has a low opinion of his intelligence, the man has a right to fight back. In fact, he must fight back. And the most efficient way to fight her back is to use her tactics in reverse: she thinks my intelligence is not up to her standards, I think her looks are not up to mine. But as much as I would like to beat her at her own game, I can't, because I would be lying if I said her looks are not up to my standards. She has the kind of face I thought only a dream woman could have. And no matter what I think of our differences, the fact that this woman with the dream face loves me *is* valuable enough not to argue with her about things she holds so dear that she wouldn't even discuss them with me. Not only because in her opinion I'm not up to her standard of intelligence, but also because she thinks that I shouldn't have even been reading her novel about the ancient kings. I have a wrong purpose for reading it, she says. I read it only to find proof of my crazy theories, and this is not what her writing is about.

"Okay, then what is it about?"

"It's about a deeper truth than your side/my side."

"It's still not clear to me," I say. "What is it really about?"

"It's about patterns of events and things that happen without people noticing, because they're too busy with their daily lives and with passionately siding with one of the two warring parties."

"But I don't see you siding with both parties. Your writing is all about your people. Your side of the conflict, that's what you care about, like everyone else."

"No," she says quickly, "this just shows that you don't understand, and if it hadn't been for your Mastermind with his crazy ideas about the threat that my writing poses to your side's claims to Jerusalem, you wouldn't have even read it. And you *shouldn't* have read it. That's not what I wrote it for—your claims or our claims."

I ask her again what she wrote it for, and she says, "To get in touch with things that are deeper than our claims/your claims, and higher."

"Deeper and higher at the same time?" My voice is so heavy with sarcasm that I can't recognize it myself. "How can it be, both deeper and higher? Isn't there a contradiction here?"

She says there's no contradiction, and that I just want to show off my intelligence, such as it is, by saying that these two things are contradictory, and that "deeper" and "higher" are two sides of the same coin, and that only things that come from the depths of a person's soul can rise as high as—

She stops, looking for a word, and I help her out, "As high as the Toe?"

Yes, she says, looking past me. Although I supplied her with the right word, I'm still not up to her standards of intelligence when it comes to things that matter the most to her. Like her thoughts about literature. Or like her idea of "Judah's Toe" as some kind of symbol that gets passed from generation to generation of the Hasmonean family.

"No, not a symbol," she says. "But I'm glad you know the word." She stares into space and repeats that it's not a symbol. "It's meaning is perfectly clear."

"Then what is it?"

"It's what is given," she says.

"You mean that it's given to one person in every Hasmonean generation. But what is it, other than that?"

"It's what's given to *me*," she says. "What I mean by *given* is really simple. A voice dictates to me; I write it down. I'm not sure I believe in God, but to me that voice is like God. Whatever it gives me, I take. That's the meaning of the Toe. Every time it was given, I had to write it. It was an order that I couldn't disobey."

"So what will you say if I tell you that I saw it myself?"

I look away from her when I say this, because I know she will have a reaction to these words. When she has a strong feeling about something, her face gets a glow making her more desirable than usual, and if I show her that I want her at a time like this, she'll think less of me.

"So tell me, what did you see?"

"I saw it."

"But what is this 'it,' Ammar? I was talking about the—"

"I'm talking about the same thing."

"*You* couldn't have seen Judah's Toe," she says with conviction.

"But," I say modestly, "I did."

"Why would it appear to *you*? You're not a…"

"Yes, I'm not one of the few to whom it appears in your book. And yet I saw it."

"How?" she asks suspiciously. "In a dream?"

"I was working on a wall of a house. It was a contract Tom had before he got yours. I was standing on a scaffold, putting stucco on the wall. Regular stucco, not like your Venetian door. And then there was thunder and lightning, and a moment later a terrible rain. The scaffold shook; I grabbed a beam next to me but couldn't hold on. I fell down, and when I opened my eyes it wasn't raining anymore. I was lying on the grass and above me there was someone's foot or part of a foot. I thought it was one of our guys coming to help me, but there was just this part of a foot. I thought maybe something happened to my head when I fell down, maybe I was seeing things that weren't real, so I reached and touched it with my hand."

"You touched the Toe," she says slowly.

"Yes."

"You're a Hasmonean," she says even more slowly.

"I don't know if that's what it—"

"And you're a Jew."

"No! My whole family, for generations, we're all Muslim."

"Yes, but before these generations there were other generations, and if your ancestors hadn't come from somewhere else but had lived in that area for two thousand years or more, then they were Jews. They were the ones who didn't go into the diaspora. When the region was conquered by Muslims in the seventh century, they converted to Islam. That's what people did when they were conquered. It's part of known history. I'm not making it up."

She says that I, Ammar Agbaria aka Alejandro, should take a DNA test, so I can have proof that I'm a Jew. And not only am I a Jew, she says, I may be a Hasmonean descendant too. She says isn't it funny that my Mastermind wanted to liquidate her just because he read parts of her novel-in-progress and became convinced that she was Queen of the Jews, and now...who will he want to liquidate now? Now that she is a Muslim, and I, Ammar, am King of the Jews.

"He'll have to liquidate you now," she says. She laughs so hard that she has to put her head on the table to let the laughter out.

I can't allow this. I can't let a woman laugh at me. "Stop laughing!" I shout. But she laughs even harder.

"You must agree, Ammar, this is funny! Our roles have reversed! People identify with a religious or ethnic group and suddenly find that they are not from that group at all! You thought you were part of your group, and all the while you belonged to the group of your enemy. So what are you now? Are you the enemy of yourself?"

I say enough. I'm tired. I've had a long day. She stops laughing, says that I'm right that it's been a long day, and it's time to go. Before she leaves, she brings her face close to mine. I'm not sure that I want a kiss now, considering the kinds of things she said to me and all this laughter and this business about me being a Jew. But kissing me is not what she intends to do. She brings her lips to my ear and whispers: "Now you're a Jew and I'm a Muslim, so everything's alright, yes? Nothing stands in our way anymore."

When she leaves, I go to bed without changing into my night clothes and fall asleep at once and sleep all night without any dreams.

AMMAR

I call her the next day and say, "Look, Galia."

"What happened?"

"I'm married. I love my wife. I love my children. You understand?"

She says, "What are you trying to say?"

"I'm trying to say...It's hard, but I have to. I want to be a faithful husband, a loving father, and a good man."

"You're a hired killer," she says. "Is that also a part of being a good man?"

I ignore this last remark, because it's only a simple insult, a jilted woman's desire to hurt a man.

"Try to understand," I say to her almost sternly. "Try to see the situation I'm in. I love my wife. What happened between us must never happen again."

"What do you mean, 'between us'? Do you mean between you and your wife?"

"Don't play dumb!" I shout into the phone. "Between you and me, in my room. We have energy, yes. But I'm a married man. We have no right. We must not do it."

"I knew it," she says.

"So, let's be friends," I say, "instead of—"

"Yes, of course," she says quickly. "I would like to be just friends. I would even prefer it. I would never ever want to take you away from your wife and children!"

I thought she wanted me very much, so I'm a little disappointed at how easily she gives me up. She always called me herself. During the construction in her house she followed me around like a puppy. When the construction was over, she came to my room. When I worked at another site for a week, she searched for me all over the city. And now she says so easily, "Let's be just friends."

If there's one thing I don't understand, it's a Western woman who agrees to be "just friends" with a man and then begins calling even more often than before. She finds silly pretexts, like when she calls me to ask what I think about the situation in Egypt. "I'm not Egyptian, why should I care?" I say in an indifferent voice and hang up. A week goes by and there is another call. I don't want to answer the phone. Didn't I tell her that I'm married? She should respect it, shouldn't she? When I don't pick up the phone two or three times, I get an email from her. It's full of her usual big words, and I don't even care to read the whole thing. I skip to the last lines: "You wanted to be friends, but how can we be friends if you don't come to the phone?" I don't answer the email, because what can I say to her? I thought we were through; the part that mattered is over. I can't believe this woman is so naïve as to take the "friends" part seriously. She emails me again with a link about an art show that she thinks I might be interested in seeing with her. I feel like saying to her, "Lady, you got some heavy illusions about me. I have no interest in that kind of thing."

I ignore her emails. I don't answer her phone calls. I want to be true to my wife and faithful to my culture, that's why I will not go to any art shows with her. Even though she said the Shahada. Even though she thinks that I may be a Jew and a Hasmonean descendant, because I told her about my seeing the toe. I didn't lie about it. I did see a toe in the air when I fell down from the scaffold, but at that time I had no idea it was a vision of a relic that had been appearing to Hasmonean descendants for twenty-two centuries and that my seeing it meant that I was a Hasmonean too. I want to tell her she is a temptation. She made me betray my wife and my people. As for my people, I've already betrayed them by not carrying out the task I had been expected to carry out. I can't talk to her about that. I can't tell her what I felt when the Mastermind said, "You refuse?" He didn't have to say the word "traitor." I knew I was a traitor to our cause. I knew I could no longer depend on the Mastermind to help me with a green card which, he told me, his channels had been busy working on for me. She has no idea how much I sacrificed for her, and she won't believe me if I tell her. She thinks that her saying the Shahada was enough to put her out of danger. When I told the Mastermind that she had said the Shahada, he said,

"So you think it's enough to say a few syllables to become one of us?"

"But what can I do?" I said to him.

"You know what you have to do. You're past all deadlines."

"She is not a danger to us. She is just...a woman."

The Mastermind said that I was deeply deluded. He said that a task was a task and it was not up to me to decide who was a danger to us and who was not. By making these decisions on my own, I was defying his authority. He wanted to know if I realized what I risked by insubordination. I said, yes, I realize, but I can't do anything about it. I will not terminate the woman. She is just one of those young women who have ideas about things, but they are just ideas, not actions that can make any difference in the world.

"Ah," he said, "you know nothing about how these things work, my fine wall painter! Sometimes it's the ideas of dreamy-eyed young women that decide the fate of a nation! If the time is right for an idea, it doesn't matter who dreamed it up—an innocent-looking young woman or a tough politician!"

"I'm truly sorry," I said, "that I cannot accomplish the mission you've entrusted me with."

I knew what to expect by refusing, and when he said that he would send someone else to complete the job, I was not surprised.

Now I think that maybe I shouldn't have been so blunt with him. That maybe I shouldn't have refused so openly. I haven't achieved anything good by refusing, because now she is in danger from someone else I cannot control. I've also endangered Fatima and our two children, and the threat to my own life has never been as great as it is now. I always thought that his guys were amateurs like me, but now that I'm in danger of being terminated by them because I refused to terminate her, I begin to think they might be more skillful than I at the tasks he assigns them.

I should have continued pretending that I'm still trying to find the right moment to terminate the woman. I don't know why I told him the truth, and why I felt so proud telling it, as though I was accomplishing a mission—as though I had to substitute the mission he had forced upon me with a mission of my own, and what was mine but saying no to his.

———————

It's been more than a month without Galia's phone calls. It finally got through to her that I don't want to be "friends." I'm a man and she is a woman—there's only one way I can be with her, but that way is closed to me because I tell myself a hundred times a day that I love my wife, I love my wife. When I speak with Fatima on the phone, I think about the sacrifice I've made for her, and although she knows nothing about it, I tell myself that she appreciates it—or she would, if she knew. But Fatima's voice doesn't stir me, and her talk about the village and the people I left far behind bores me. The more I repeat "I love my wife," the less I believe in it. I would like to believe in it more, just as I would like to believe in Galia being a danger to my people, but I can't believe in it, and my love formula sounds tired and shallow, and I'm ashamed to admit to myself that I don't love my wife, and I want to be free, I want to be free.

I call Galia. "Everything is different now. I want to see you again."

She wants to know what's different now, and I say, "Everything," and by "Everything" I mean that I no longer feel bound by my faithfulness to my wife, and I can be with Galia without feeling like a traitor to my people.

"You said that you loved your wife," she says, "and now you say 'everything is different,' and I don't know what it means."

"In my thoughts it is different now."

She wants to know why I don't answer the phone when she calls me, and I have nothing to say to that. I didn't answer because I didn't want her voice to stir my feelings when I had resolved to have nothing with her, to be "just friends" as she calls it.

"It's different now," I repeat. "Visit me and you'll see."

She says that she is not going to visit me because I hurt her feelings when I said that what happened between us must never happen again. So if this is what I wanted, I can have it. It will never happen again. I can love my Fatima, and it's good that I'm faithful to her, she says, because she feels respect for a man who is faithful to his wife in a little village near Hebron. She doesn't need to be a marriage-breaker, she says, it's enough for her to just talk with me on the phone once in a while.

She calls me in a week, and again I decide not to answer the phone.

Sometimes I still believe in my love for my wife, and sometimes I don't. When she calls me in a belief moment, I don't pick up the phone because I want to believe I'm still faithful to Fatima and my people. This woman writes about the ancient world when belief was everywhere, yet she knows nothing about belief, the kind of pure belief that I have, that I was taught to have. That's why I don't come to the phone because she *always* calls in those moments, never in those when my love for my wife and my land seems tired and shallow, or when I want to see this woman from the enemy camp so much that I almost forget how to breathe.

Finally I call her myself. I say, "Hi, Galia," and there's no response, only silence.

I say, "How are you?" And again, nothing.

After a long silence, she says, "Why are you calling me?"

"Because I…" Her silence makes me feel so unsure of myself, I forget English words and say it in Arabic.

"What?"

"I want…"

I don't want to say it in a language she knows. She doesn't know Arabic, but she should have understood me anyway, because a woman who loves a man must understand everything he says, in whatever language he says it. Every time she says "What?" she makes it clear that she doesn't understand me.

Suddenly she says brightly, "To see me?"

"Yes!"

"But," she says. "What about your wife?"

"I…divorced her!" I say suddenly. Now that it flew out of my mouth, unexpectedly to myself, it becomes something I can't deny. It becomes almost a fact.

"You divorced your wife Fatima?" She emphasizes every word as if she never heard more unusual news. And the way she says "your wife Fatima," as though she still believes I have more than one.

"Yes," I say, in a strange belief that I'm telling the truth.

"Remember, when you said to me, 'I love my wife! I love my wife!' I never thought you would want to divorce her."

"Galia," I say quickly and quietly, "now I'm free man, you want to visit me?"

She says that this is a very big question, and she can't answer it right away, and do I mind if she takes a few days to think it over? Think it over, I say with more feeling than I knew I had in me for simple words such as "think" and "about" and "it."

AMMAR

She always talks. I don't talk. I just walk. This walking and talking is strange, because it feels as though it has always been like this, as though this is how it should be—the two of us walking and talking together, even though she is the one doing all the talking and I'm just listening, but by listening to her talk, I become a kind of silent talker myself, the one enabling her to talk, the one without whose silent participation she would not be able to say a single word. She acknowledges her need of my silent companionship; she says that without me by her side she wouldn't have any thoughts; it's my presence that gives her ideas. I would like to say, Lady, I don't care about your ideas, but I don't want to disappoint her, so I let her go on talking. And she goes on, as if this is what life is all about. I'm a man of action, not of words. She talks and talks, as though words are an end in themselves, something that can make a person happy without any action growing out of them. But what action do I want to grow out of words? I must have changed, because I, too, am perfectly content just walking and listening to her go on and on about her thoughts. She has so many thoughts, I don't know how they all fit into her head, which is so small and cute—it makes me think it should contain only woman thoughts, not the stuff about *meanings* of things that she talks about all the time. We walk and walk, and she doesn't seem to care that it was light when we started walking and that it has grown dark, and that some of the streets we walk on are poorly lit. She doesn't seem to notice that the further we walk the darker and *less safe*, as they say, are the streets; she is completely oblivious to danger, as though New York was the safest place in the world. She doesn't sense the danger because she hasn't been through what I have been. I can sense danger with my eyes closed but, all whims and thoughts, she doesn't let me steer her into safer streets.

"You care too much about what people think."

"What people think?" I say like an echo.

She brushes this aside, as though she expected more from me, something to equal the intensity of what she calls her love for me.

"But we must think about safety, yours and mine," I insist, knowing that she's going to look down at me for not paying attention to her profound thoughts.

By the time we learn that the danger I was thinking about is not imaginary, it's too late. The guys who bump into us in the dark street come out of nowhere at a moment when, softened by her nearness, I no longer was expecting any harm. She keeps on talking, but then I hear her cry out in surprise, as though she'd never known that there was such a thing as physical pain in the world, never known that the kind of pain I gave her by not returning her phone calls is nothing in comparison. It happened so fast. My hands are twisted behind my back, and I can't reach for my knife.

When I hear a pitiful moan that barely resembles her voice, I know it: in order to humiliate me they are to going to dishonor her. I know that she is to suffer because of me, because I allowed myself to be lulled into a serenity I should not ever have believed possible when near the enemy. The shame of it snaps something in me and I become stronger than the two holding me down. I am more experienced, and I break free. Now I would reach for my knife, but one of them is coming at me with his own knife. I hear it as well as feel it when my boot breaks his ribs under the right arm. His soft flesh squirms under my blows. The more I hit, the softer it feels. Its softness is a kind of justification for my blows, as though by becoming soft, the flesh is telling me that I am right, that I should hit it again, that it deserves to be beaten, because the person to whom this flesh belongs is wrong and I am right. The other one may not have expected to get stabbed. There are still two guys, one holding the woman down and another one between her legs, but they didn't expect me to get clear so quickly and I maim both of them.

Now I am carrying her away in my arms like a baby, her head banging against my chest and her legs hanging like lifeless sticks. I must take us out of this dark street into the safety of some lit-up avenue or boulevard...I should bring her to a hospital, but I can't do that, I have no papers. I will bring her to my room.

Or should I bring her to her house? A better choice than my room, because I have roommates, and my roommates have eyes and ears, and their eyes might see the limp body in my arms and their ears might hear her moans of pain and their brains will come up with explanations that have nothing to do with the truth—no, I can't afford this, becoming a perpetrator of a crime I did not commit. I will take her to her own house. I will avoid lit-up avenues because I must remember my situation and what can happen to me if I'm seen half-carrying, half-dragging a bleeding, limp, half-naked woman in my arms.

By the time I reach her house I'm so exhausted that I can't make another step. She is a small woman, but now that I've carried her for ten or twelve blocks she seems to weigh a ton. When I reach her house and put her down on the porch, which I helped build a year ago, I realize that I have no way of getting in. "A key," I say to her, "You have a key?" But she is so numb and silent lying there in the heap of her limbs that it may be too late to save her. I remember what she said about her habit of always forgetting her keys, which was why she carried her purse with her everywhere, but where's that purse now? The guys must have taken it or else it just fell, unnoticed, on the street where they jumped on us. I rummage in her pockets, hoping that just this once she put her key in one of her pockets instead of that stupid purse. No such luck. I know her house well enough. After all, wasn't I part of the team that built it? I know all the ins and outs.

Think, I say to myself. Think fast. Wasn't one of the basement windows the kind that could be pushed open from the outside? Yes, I say to myself, it was, but that side of the basement can be reached only through the backyard and how do

I get into the backyard if I don't have a key to the gate? When I worked here, the gate was always open, because our guys had to go in and out. I leave her lying on the porch and go to check the gate. It's locked, of course, but there's a gap between the gate and the ground that a slim man slithering like a snake could get through. I'm not very slim, but I can try. When my head and shoulders are inside, there's a shout from outside. I can't see who it is and when I'm almost completely through, I feel someone grabbing my left leg and then my arm. When I finally manage to turn and look, I see Brad, Galia's neighbor, the one who always hung around during the construction and ordered us around like he was our boss, and when we complained about him to Tom, Tom said, "It's better to have a neighbor coming over and bossing you around and criticizing every step of the construction than have him threaten us with filing violations, you understand?" I'm now completely inside of the gate, but Brad is holding my leg and I can't stand up. I must have kicked him a little too hard, because he makes a small gurgling noise that reminds me of something I heard this very night, the pitiful sound that came out of Galia when the guys were having their way with her. But I have no time for Brad, and I tell myself it was his fault: why did he have to grab my leg, did he think I was a thief trying to get into their communal backyard and steal a couple of bushes? The thought of her lying there on the porch, with her limbs pointing every which way, makes me run through the communal driveway, which is so overgrown with grass you'd think I was the first man to walk here in ages. I crouch by her basement windows, try each one and then break the glass of one of them, and I don't care that my hand is bleeding. I break some more, to make the hole large enough for my entire body to get through, and as soon as my feet touch the basement floor I make a huge leap toward the stairs. It's a good thing I know the house so well, because in less than a second I'm by the front door, holding it open and dragging her in. I'm so relieved that she's still there, that no one noticed her lying in a heap of her limbs, that wetness is streaming down my cheeks. I'm not one of those Western men who are so touchy-feely about nonsense that they tear at the slightest provocation. These tears, I tell myself, are tears of strength, and I will not be ashamed of them.

I drag her in through the doorway and put her down on her couch, and for a split second I stand there, not knowing what to do next. Should I remove what's left of her clothes and inspect her injuries? Should I prepare cold compresses by immersing paper towels in a bowl of icy water in her kitchen sink? When I hold the first cold compress to her face, she half opens her left eye and I'm so relieved that I run to the kitchen to prepare more cold compresses. I'm on the right track, I tell myself; she'll be better by morning. I check the wet paper towels every few minutes, and if they are too warm, I change them quickly, by wrapping ice cubes in them and removing the ice cubes so they are cold enough when they touch her skin, and around the twentieth time, she opens both eyes and half-smiles at me with a crooked kind of smile because part of her face is still numb from what the guys did to her. She moves her legs and arms a little, and I tell myself she doesn't need cold anymore, she needs warmth, so I make a cup of hot tea in her kitchen, and I hold her head as she drinks in small gulps like a baby. I go into her bedroom and pull a blanket off her bed and cover her with it completely so that not a single part is left uncovered, and she lets me tuck her in as though she's a child and I'm a parent. She opens her lips a little and tries to say something but I can't understand it through the wheezing, and I say, "Shh! Don't talk, you'll be better by morning." She tries again, and this time I recognize a few words. "Doctor Fish…Remember…you said Doctor Fish? Now you're my doctor…Fish." I pat the blanket and whisper, "I'm your doctor, yes, doctor fish. Try to sleep now" and her eyes smile at me through the tears and I smile back.

I close my eyes and rest in a chair next to her couch, and the next thing I'm aware of is someone banging on the door. I wake up with a start, surprised that I've fallen asleep when I should have been vigilant, guarding her, curing her, in this living room that I turned into a kind of makeshift emergency room, and she herself called me her doctor, and what kind of doctor falls asleep by his patient's bedside in an emergency room? The banging is so loud that she too is awake now. She stares at the door with a kind of terror in her eyes that I remember seeing in the faces of people in the videos the Mastermind showed me, people running away from soldiers, in the days when I trusted the Mastermind more than my own self, and now that I've come to trust my own self more than the Mastermind, I don't ever want to see this terror in anyone's eyes. I walk over to the door, but I don't open it. The banging stops for a second and I hear a voice saying the words I dread the most, the words that hounded me in my sleep and in my wakefulness throughout all my years in this country: "Police! Open up!"

Galia half-raises herself on her elbow and whispers that we have no choice but to open the door. "You have nothing to be afraid of," she whispers. "You've saved me." She is good and kind, but she didn't live my life. She doesn't know what it's like to be an illegal in this country, without papers, without protection, and now the police are here, and her saying that I have nothing to be afraid of is the kind of well-wishing nonsense that someone who hasn't been through what I've been through knows nothing about.

But she is right about one thing. I have to open the door.

I open it just enough to show my willingness to comply because I have no desire to be charged with resisting authorities in addition to whatever else they're going to charge me with. Four men in uniform and one without the uniform burst into the room. The ones in the uniform shout at me to stand still and raise my arms and because they're aiming their guns at me, I have nothing to do but obey. The one without the uniform is Galia's neighbor Brad, the one who made that pitiable noise when I kicked him earlier this evening. He stands in a corner, grinning, very pleased with himself. It's a good thing I don't have my knife on me, maybe I left it lying on Galia's countertop, I don't remember anymore, the night is a blur in my mind. They push me down on the floor, just as in my worst fears: my body on the floor, my wrists in handcuffs, and I don't resist because I don't want that extra charge added to my illegal status and whatever else they're going to cook up for me. I hear them talking to Galia, and I want to tell them that she is too fragile for this, she is barely conscious, what can they want with her, she doesn't know what happened, who were those guys that attacked us, she knows nothing at all. But they're not questioning her about the guys. They're questioning her about me. What did I do to her? She says I saved her life. How could he have saved your life? He trespassed on your and neighbor's property, he kicked your neighbor so hard that he almost crippled him.

"He had to get into the house," she says so quietly I can barely hear her. "Some guys attacked us, I was unconscious. He's been taking care of me all night. Don't hold him down like that. He's a gentle man. He's a doctor."

They laugh. "A doctor, eh? And if we ask to see his papers, what will the doctor say to that?" They find it so funny that they forget to hold me down, but I stay with my face down anyway—no need to make things worse than they already are.

"He's *my* doctor, he healed me," she whispers, but they're not paying attention to her whispers. One of them is calling 911, and a team of paramedics arrives a few minutes later. They wheel in a stretcher, and I can't see when and how they put her on the stretcher because just when the paramedics arrive the cops get an order to take me away. They pull me up roughly and push me toward the door. I hear her scream, "Let him go! He didn't do anything wrong! He helped me! He's my friend!" I don't know how she got the strength to shriek like that, but it has no effect on them whatsoever, and in the intervals when they're busy with their walkie-talkies, they joke about me being her friend or her doctor, and they say "doctor" with the scorn they reserve for the mentally ill or for illegal immigrants. They take me to a police van. I have no choice but to climb in and two of them climb in with me. They take out a form and ask my name, date of birth, place of birth. When I say "Hebron," they have no reaction. When I say "Hebron, Palestine," they exchange looks. They ask, "US citizen? Resident?" Although this is the question I've been waiting for all along, when they actually ask it, I'm surprised. Do they really have to ask this question to fill out the preliminary form? I tell them I want to see a lawyer before I answer any more of their questions, but they repeat the question, insisting that I answer it right away.

"US citizen? Resident?"

"No," I say finally.

The door of the van shuts. I'd rather be dead than go where they are taking me.

GALIA

I was too weak when they took him away. If they had asked me what he was doing here, I would have said, he helped me, he healed me, he did everything he could, but they don't ask me, and when I gather what little strength I have in me and shout, "Let him go! He didn't do anything wrong! He's my friend!", they don't react because I'm just a body to be tied to the stretcher and taken to a hospital where real doctors will know what to do with me. Maybe then I'll stop shouting nonsense like "He didn't do anything wrong!" about a guy who is obviously an illegal immigrant and not only that, maybe something much worse than a simple illegal, maybe someone plotting murder and destruction: a Muslim, a terrorist, an enemy of our United States.

I must have been out of it for days in the hospital, because the next thing I remember is a man's voice saying I'm being treated for pneumonia, which I developed while being treated for injuries caused by the violent assault, but that with the right treatment I will get well. I want to open my mouth and say something, but I can't move my lips because something is stuck in my mouth and it goes deep into my throat. A realization dawns on me, slowly, that I'm in a hospital, I'm intubated, which means that a machine is doing the breathing for me, and I want them to take it out, and I want to shout, "Stop! I'm alright! I don't need this thing in my mouth! Take it out right now!" But I can't say a thing. I'm intubated, after all. I have to prove to them that I can breathe on my own before they take it out, but how can I prove it while this thing is breathing for me, and there was nothing wrong with my breathing to begin with?

I want to tell them that it was a simple rape—not that any rape is simple, but the injuries they have to treat are not in my throat, so there's absolutely no need for the good doctors to torment me with this terrible machine that doesn't let me do my own breathing and makes me suffer the kind of agony that is even worse than what happened in that dark street because, no matter how violent, that was quick, while this thing has been in my throat for a whole day, maybe two, and no one is here to rescue me, because Ammar is far away, and I can't even use my mouth to ask where they've taken him.

At the end of the second day, or maybe the beginning of the third day, they take it out. My relief is so huge that I don't want to waste my recovered speech on cursing them. I just want to know about Ammar.

"Where is he?"

I have a right to know where he's been taken, but the nurse at my bedside just shushes me. She says, Take it easy, you'll be alright if you don't talk too much, and she says that she's a nurse, the man next to her is a doctor, and I'm a patient. I have nothing to do but be patient, because I can't get out of this bed and this hospital until they deem me worthy of being discharged, and my discharge depends on my good behavior, and they have a certain understanding of what comprises good behavior, and until I shut up with my question of a certain illegal immigrant's whereabouts and stop demanding that he be freed from wherever he's been taken, I won't be seen by these nurses and doctors as a person in full control of her so-called faculties and perhaps worthy of being discharged.

They bring me dinner, or is it lunch, on a tray. It's mashed potatoes and mashed chicken and mashed something else, and I figure that I'm being served soft food because they think I can't chew or swallow normal food, and they're wrong about that, but again, there's no quarreling with the doctors. Despite being mashed, the food tastes good, much better than anything I ever cooked myself or ordered in a restaurant, and it's not the food, it's the sensation of eating real food instead of lying there with a breathing tube stuck in my throat.

When I'm finally deemed well enough to stand up and even walk a little in the hallway, they send me a psychologist. He wants me to tell him about the trauma of being raped. I don't want to talk about the trauma. I want to talk about my friend; I want to know where he's been taken; I want to be able to call him on the phone and talk to him and make sure he's okay. The psychologist insists on asking about my trauma, and when I say the only trauma I'm conscious of is not knowing where my friend is, he dutifully writes it down in my chart, and says that the inability to talk about it is a common symptom of rape aftershock. I tell him he's talking nonsense, and he records that in my chart too, and tells me that my belligerence is directly proportional to my suppressed rage, a phase every rape victim goes through, which is perfectly understandable, he adds.

A lawyer visits me, too. It's what happens in cases of rape, he says, we need to find the bad guys. He asks for descriptions of the men who assaulted me, and when I say I can't describe them because I didn't look at their faces, he says, "Yes, that's how it is, a victim never looks." I ask him about my friend, who was with me that night and who carried me away and who brought me into my house and took care of me, until the police came and took him away—where did they take him? The lawyer shrugs. He came here for a specific reason: to get descriptions of the criminals. He did not come to talk about my friend. His time is expensive. I don't have to pay for his time, but his agency must file accounts to the city, and he came to my bedside to get descriptions of the criminals. If I want to talk about my feelings for my friend, he'll inform the hospital that I need to be seen by a psychologist.

The day comes when a nurse brings me my own clothes and tells me they're ready to discharge me. I haven't seen her before, which is something I've grown used to—there are new nurses here every day. When she tries to help me put on my clothes, I say thanks, I don't need help, I've been getting dressed on my own since I was five years old. But she insists on helping me, and once I'm dressed and ready to go, she says, You can't go just like that, you must have someone to take you home, and I say, What kind of nonsense is this? I'm perfectly capable of going home on my own. She says, Hospital regulations, and brings me a pile of papers to sign, which I do without reading. I just sign paper after paper, because I know that if I start reading them, I might start questioning the meaningless statements which I, a patient, am not allowed to question unless I want to be seen as noncompliant, and after all the days and nights I've spent here, I know what that may lead to. When I'm done, she hands me one more paper, and just as I'm opening my mouth to say haven't I done enough signing, she says, If you want to go home by yourself, sign this disclaimer. I sign it without looking and wait for a taxi. When it finally arrives, I'm escorted to the entrance, or the exit, of the hospital, by two nurses as though I can't be trusted to get there on my own. Thank you, I say. Please, I say, as I get into the taxi, please, don't help me, I'm fine. But while I'm still on hospital grounds, I'm not fine, I'm a patient, and I must behave like a patient.

When the taxi stops in front of my house, I see Brad waiting in the street. He's watching as I climb out of the car and walk past him to my house. I have a thing or two to say to him, but now that I've learned what a vengeful man he is, I don't want him to think I have anything against him. I remind myself not to speak to him ever again, but when I'm home I realize that not speaking to my neighbor might be a problem, that he might read who knows what into my silence, and I tell myself that the next time I pass him, I'll say a strategic hello.

I have no idea how to find out where Ammar was taken, so I spend three days calling police stations, until finally I'm given the name of the detention facility where he is kept. I don't like this word, "kept." He is not something that can be kept and forgotten, and he's certainly not forgotten by me. I have to think what to say to his keepers, and the only thing that comes to my mind is "He helped me, he's my friend." If I'm to find a way to get him out of there, I have to think of something better. If his being an illegal immigrant is the only reason they're keeping him, there's something I can do about his illegality—something no one else can do, only I. But in the same breath I tell myself that he is already married, his wife's name is Fatima, she has two kids by him in a village near Hebron…

When I call the detention facility, I'm told there's no person by that name, and when I insist that he must be there, I'm told that just this morning he was transferred to a hospital.

"Why?" I ask.

"He was depressed. He refused to eat."

"Which hospital?"

In forty minutes I'm inside a large hospital building. I poke my nose into the general ER, and a nurse at a small desk tells me to wait, don't I see there are people waiting? I stand in a crowded waiting room until I lose patience. Once again I poke my head in the ER. There's a different nurse at the small desk, and when I ask her for Ammar's whereabouts, she tells me to wait, she's busy. A long time passes until I ask her again, and before she tells me to hold on, I remind her that she already told me to wait and that I obeyed, while all I want to know is what happened to Ammar Agbaria, and can't she please check it for me, it won't take much of her time. Spell his name for me, she says without looking up, and when I do, she peers into the computer screen for a long time, and says finally, Psych ER.

I ask, "Where's Psych ER?" But she's done with me, she's given me more attention than I'm worth, so I'm forced to ask others who work here, attendants, nurses, doctors, and some of them don't hear me, some hear me but don't answer, and one—a paramedic who is bringing in an unshaven man on a stretcher—gives me friendly and detailed directions. I find myself in a narrow corridor that dead-ends into a door. Three bins overflowing with hospital waste stand on one side of the corridor.

"Is this Psych ER?" I ask a passing man in a white coat. He nods and shrugs at the same time, without stopping. The door is locked. I knock. No answer. I knock again. A large man with an earring opens it halfway and positions his heavy body between the door and the wall, so I wouldn't even dream of passing.

"My friend is there," I say.

"His name?"

"Ammar Agbaria."

"No such person here."

"He is there. They told me in the medical ER. They looked him up in the database and said he was here."

"Hey!" He turns his head and shouts into the space behind him. "Is...uh..."

"Ammar Agbaria"

"Is Ammar Agbaria here?"

A shout from the depths of the room is unintelligible to me, but it apparently informs the guard that Ammar is indeed there.

"So can...I see him?"

"Visiting hours eleven to twelve," he says and shuts the door.

I look at my watch. It's five minutes to eleven. I wait till five minutes are up, and I knock again. This time he takes even longer to open.

"Ye-es?" he says in a voice that shames me for disturbing his rest or doing something equally important.

"It's eleven," I say. "You said visiting hours—"

He moves his head imperceptibly in the direction of the room behind him.

But no sooner do I make a few steps in before he says, "Bag!" and hits his desk with his knuckles.

"Am I supposed to put my bag on the table?" I say.

He hits the table again, this time with the palm of his hand.

As I place my bag on the table for him to search, I think: if everyone here is like the people I've encountered this morning, then I must rescue Ammar from this terrible place. The man with the earring searches my bag without any demure respect for its owner's privacy. He pours the contents out onto the table and shamelessly picks up things that I don't show to anyone.

"What's this?" He holds up a medium-size medicine bottle. "Pills?"

"Vitamins."

"Pills are not allowed."

"But these are...I told you, these are vitamins! I'm just using an old medicine bottle to keep them in!"

"Vitamins or medicines, they're pills," he says. "And pills are not allowed. Rules are rules."

"These are stupid rules!" I say loudly.

"If you raise your voice here, I'll call the police."

"So call the police! I don't care!"

My fury at the guard and his ridiculous rules is exhausted as soon as I express it by inviting him to call the police, and I agree to leave the medicine bottle with the vitamins in his possession until I pick it up on my way back.

As soon as I enter the Psych ER, which is a much smaller space than the general ER, and without as many patients and doctors and nurses crowding in, I see him sitting in the posture of Rodin's Thinker, his elbows on his knees, his chin on his hands.

I say, "Ammar."

He's grown a beard, which makes him look a bit like a nineteenth-century Russian writer. I tell him that I want him to sign a marriage certificate with me just so he can apply for citizenship and get out of this place and that other place, the detention facility. He winces, as though I said something improper.

He's silent for such a long time that, like in the old days of construction when I was trying to make him talk to me, I wonder if I said something wrong. Of course I did: I just proposed that he make me his second wife.

There's nothing else I can say to him at this moment, even though so much needs to be said. There's nothing as authentic as the silence that he has worn for so long it has become his skin.

Without looking up, he asks if I can lend him a quarter, and I say of course, here, take two or three. One is enough, he says calmly.

He walks to a public phone, inserts a quarter and dials a number.

Apparently, no one answers at the other end and he hangs up.

"Who were you trying to call?" I ask.

"A lawyer."

"What about my proposal? It's the best way to set you free."

He says, "Thank you very much, Galia, but I have wife."

"I know you have a wife. I'm just trying to think of a way to get you out of this place. To make you legal in this country."

"And how are you, Galia? You okay?"

"I'm fine. I spent a week in a hospital, which was completely unnecessary, because you took such good care of me that night with your cold compresses. You're a much better doctor than those licensed doctors at the hospital. Doctor Fish, that's you."

"Doctor Fish," he says quietly. "I remember that."

"So what's your answer," I say, "to my marriage proposal?"

"I don't know," he says. "What you think?"

"I think we should go through with it, and when you get your citizenship, you can divorce me if you like."

"If I like," he repeats even more thoughtfully. "Or if I don't like."

"All I mean is it's going to be up to you. I'm not forcing myself on you. I just want you to be free."

"Yes. Free. That's good, to be free. I want it."

"Is it a yes?"

"Yes," he says hesitantly. And a second later, he repeats firmly, "Yes."

He resumes his posture of Rodin's Thinker, and I sit on a chair next to him, trying not to impinge on his brooding privacy.

The visiting hours are over. When I leave, the guard at the entrance gives me back my bottle of pills. "Your pills," he says, and even though they are just vitamins, I don't care to set him straight.

On the day of our marriage I walk to the large reception desk in the lobby of the hospital and when the man behind the counter looks at me questioningly, I say, "Agbaria." It's not my first time here; I'm familiar with the procedure; I know that the man needs to hear the last name of the patient and I don't go into explanations that today the patient by the name Agbaria will sign a marriage certificate that will make him a free man. The fewer words the better. After searching in a file of differently colored plastic signs, the man hands me a purple one that says 5A and next to it, on a transparent tape, in smaller letters, his name. I walk past the long lobby to a set of six elevators. When the elevator comes, I push a lit-up button with number five, step out of the elevator on fifth floor and look for an arrow with the letter A and the word "Psychiatric." I walk through a corridor with rooms on both sides, and try not to look inside, but I can't help seeing patients, lying, half-lying, sitting in their beds, and I know these are medical patients, not psychiatric ones, because they can walk in and out of this ward and press the elevator button if they so desire and leave the hospital for good. When I stand in front of a locked door with a complicated system of bells and alarms, I know I've arrived. This is 5A, even though there is no sign that says so. I look for a visitor's bell, but when I push a button, nothing happens. I'm not a novice at entering locked wards; I know that I must be patient until I'm buzzed in. When I've almost given up hope, the door is opened by an attendant, a stout woman with large earrings that cover half of her cheek and neck. She asks who I am here to see, and I say the patient's name. She says, Wait here, and leaves me standing between the two doors, the solid one behind me and a bullet-proof glass one in front. Among the few patients pacing the corridor in front of the glass door I can see Ammar, the lost expression of his back. I can't wave to him—not only because his back is to me, but also because I haven't yet been authorized as a visitor. When the woman with large earrings returns, I'm sure she will open the glass door for me, but instead she sits down at a desk near the glass door and chats with another attendant. I knock lightly on the glass door to remind them of my existence. The second attendant looks up and rises slowly from her seat, her body language eloquently expressing one thought only: what a bothersome creature I am. I must agree with her assessment of me, and when she finally lets me in, I apologize for my polite knocking. I know very well what happens when I do not act contrite about the very fact of my existence when I enter a locked ward. Show me what you brought, she says, and I take out a volume of Khalil Gibran's poems in English translation and a box of pastries. The attendant is not interested in the book and the pastries; she only wants to know if I have hidden something sharp, a razor blade or a knife, among the pages. I give her my plastic bag and when she says I can have it on my way out, I say I don't need it, I'll have nothing to put in it because I'm giving the book and the pastries to my friend who wouldn't try to kill himself with the plastic bag over his face anyway. She tells me I can't wait for my friend in the hallway and points toward the guest room where I'm supposed to wait for him, but she is too lazy to stand up and walk across the hall to unlock the door, so I have to wait for another attendant, a young man with a friendly face, to get the keys, to unlock the door, and to call the patient.

I'm sitting at a table in the guest room when I see Ammar waiting for the attendant to unlock the glass door. His beard has grown so long that it covers his neck. When he sits down next to me, I say, "Look at what I brought you," and move the book and the box of pastries over to him. He nods slightly but doesn't change his position or look at the things I brought.

"We're getting married today," I say in a cheerful voice. "Remember?" He nods slightly again, and after almost a minute he says a barely audible, "Yes."

The signing of the marriage certificate takes place in a conference room in the hospital. Many legal papers must have been signed here over the years, but I suspect this is the first for a marriage license. After we sign it in front of two witnesses, a social worker and a director of the hospital, our courageous marriage officiant, an old lady recommended to me by the Society for Ethical Culture, says gently, "You can kiss the bride now," and I know that these words add one more embarrassment to a whole series of embarrassments and insults my new husband has had to endure for helping me on the night of the attack. I ask the officiant if she could please refrain from telling us when to kiss, because these things are private, even if we did sign the paper in the hospital, which robs us of privacy and respect. She nods her understanding and wishes us good luck.

I fill out an application for Ammar's green card the same day. All he has to do is sign it like he did the marriage certificate, and he does it silently, without objections, as though by letting me make all the decisions for him he is letting an unknown fate take over his life. I send a copy of his completed citizenship application to the detention facility, and when I call a few days later to ask if the copy has been received, I'm told to call another number. I call number after number, until someone at the other end says that he will be released *eventually*. His marriage to a US citizen changes his status and sets him on a path to citizenship, or at least resident status.

"The guys attacked us that night," I say to cheer him up, "Now that the bad stuff is almost over, what did they accomplish? US citizenship for you and an official marriage for us, neither of which would have happened without their help. You should write them a thank-you note."

He smiles at the suggestion of a thank-you note to the guys. It's a ridiculous idea, he wants to say, but he's beginning to know when I'm joking and when I'm speaking earnestly, and he allows himself to be silently entertained by it.

We are both so sure that he is on his way to becoming a US citizen that we have a set of jokes about it.

"I don't know what it like to be a citizen. I was never a citizen before. No country, no citizen."

"What it's like, not what it like."

"What it's like."

"I think being a citizen won't feel any different from being a noncitizen. The only difference is that you won't live in fear of being deported anymore. Otherwise, it will feel pretty much the same. You remain yourself, but with papers that make you legal here."

"Not the same. No. My whole life I lived without citizen."

"Without citizenship."

"Yes, citizenship."

"So you'll have your citizenship and then—what? How will it change you other than removing the fear of deportation from your life?"

"You don't understand! Because you never lived like I lived. Whole life without citizenship. Whole life with fear, whole life waiting, waiting for them to come take you away. When you live whole life like this, the fear makes you like monster. Like I was. I was like monster."

"I know. You even wanted to kill me, but you weren't very good at it. You're much better at cold compresses than at killing. "

"I had orders, mission, Mastermind."

"So that's another thing that having a US citizenship will change. You won't have to obey that man anymore. You might even…get *him* deported. If you let the authorities know about his activities."

"No, no. I can't do that. I will cut ties, but I will not harm."

Apparently, the man he called the Professor wasn't as honorable, because when Ammar's application for a legal status was rejected and I tried to find out why, all I got for an answer was that new information about his past made him unfit for citizenship, and I was advised to stop getting more deeply involved in the situation. I don't know what they meant by "involved" since I was already married to the guy. I was visiting him every day in that terrible detention facility he had to go back to upon his discharge from the hospital. His treatment team found that his depression had been cured by the proper use of medication, while I knew that it had nothing to do with medication, which was making him so groggy that he could barely stay awake during the day. It had to do with hope, and with me, and with a dream of a life free of the Professor and the guys and of the hospital and of the detention facility and of the fear in which he had lived all these years. I couldn't say for certain that it was the Professor who had informed the authorities, but I doubt that any of the so-called lesser "guys" would have taken this step without the Professor's permission. When I told Ammar it must have been his Professor who reported on him, he said no, it can't be him, he's not a traitor.

"How well do you know your Professor?"

"I know him."

"But how well?"

It was no use. Although he cut "the ties," as he said, with his Professor, he wouldn't let me go on with my suspicions of the man. It didn't matter who had informed on him, he said, nothing could be changed now. He would be held in the detention facility until the day of his deportation, which was being postponed for reasons too intricate to understand, even though they were explained to us by our lawyer, and every time yet another postponement was announced we were ready to believe he'd be cleared of all charges, get his temporary residency, and be released. But each postponement simply led to a lengthier stay in the detention facility, and even though Ammar said that it was better to be deported than to stay in that place, I was still hoping for a happy end. To keep my spirits up, I wrote down several versions of our future life together. Here's one of them.

SEVERAL YEARS LATER

After Ammar's green card came through, we had to go through another legal battle, this time for his divorce from Fatima. It took longer than usual because Ammar insisted on paying higher alimony than Fatima and the law demanded.

When it was over, Ammar said he wanted a real wedding, and I said, okay, so I bought salads from the Russian store—Olivier, beet, and the rest of them—and we cleaned our living room for a "wedding dinner," to which we invited some of his construction friends, Tom the contractor, my parents, as well as a few of my friends, male and female. We live in my house, despite the memories, both good and bad, of everything that transpired here. We have twin girls, Nehora and Moriya, ten months old and already, according to Ammar, real Hasmonean princesses. I smile when he says that they look Hasmonean, because they look like ten-month-old babies usually look, and also because no one knows what any of the Hasmoneans looked like, except for pictures in encyclopedias and history books that Ammar and I peruse in search of more information about our common ancestors. Those pictures, made by artists who lived many centuries after their subjects, cannot be trusted with verisimilitude, and therefore it is safe to say that no one knows what Judah or Simon or John Hyrcanus looked like. As for the female Hasmoneans, except for Queen Shlomtzion, aka Aleksandra Salome, their existence went completely unrecorded, so that even their names are a matter of conjecture.

Last year I had Ammar's toe cast in bronze, and now it sits on top of our bookcase, in a see-through box with a small plaque that reads "Judah's Toe." My *Hasmonean Chronicle* was published a day after we were married; a sequel, set in the tenth century CE, is progressing slowly as the twins don't give me much time for anything but themselves. The Professor, aka Ammar's mastermind, has disappeared, and we no longer live in fear of "the guys" coming after Ammar to avenge him for his refusal to murder me. Tom has more contracts than he can handle, and the last we heard he was working on a twenty-two story building in Manhattan…good for him. As for Ammar, I insisted that he put his construction jobs on hold and return to marine biology. His degree had been issued so many years ago that he needed to take additional coursework to reactivate it, as it were, here. I look at my husband studying at his desk and think of the disheveled wall painter emerging from a corner, a palette knife in one hand and a brush in another. He looks up from his textbook, smiles, and takes an envelope out of a top drawer. "Come here, Queen of the Jews," he says. He shows me a typed note he received from "a well-wisher." He points at the words "forgotten yet not forgiven."

"These old quarrels never die, do they?" I say. "Vengeance is too powerful an emotion to leave behind."

"If *we* left it behind, then maybe they can too." He puts the note back in the envelope and the envelope in the drawer. "Forgotten yet not forgiven," he muses. "C'mon, guys, it's been years. Mission accomplished." He shuts the drawer with more force than necessary, in my opinion.

———◆———